Tidings of Victory
Jonathan Kinkaid in Europe

By Michael Winston

Copyright 2011

An adventure in the continuing saga of Jonathan Kinkaid of the American Navy

For The Hooligan

Preface

The year 1777 brought one defeat after another for colonial forces. Fort Ticonderoga had fallen, General Schuyler had evacuated Fort Edward, and British armies threatened to split the colonies. General Washington had lost battles at Brandywine and then again at Germantown. Finally, the British marched into Philadelphia. Things looked dark indeed for the American cause.

But then something amazing happened at Saratoga, New York. While the American General Gates sat brooding in his tent, a disgusted General Benedict Arnold took charge at the front and led colonial forces to a magnificent victory, helped by the sharpshooters of Morgan's riflemen. The result was that "Gentleman Johnny" Burgoyne was forced to surrender his army of 5,700 men on the 17th of October. From near disaster had emerged triumph.

Benjamin Franklin was in Paris as the events at Saratoga were unfolding, applying all his charm and diplomatic skills trying to convince the cautious French Court to not only keep sending war materials to sustain American armies in the field, but to enter the war on the side of the colonies. He was also always concerned about the plight of American seamen confined in British jails and constantly pressed for prisoner exchanges which England constantly refused. Franklin was one of three commissioners in Paris, where spies and intrigue abounded. His colleagues, Arthur Lee and Silas Deane, caused him no end of headaches with their jealousies and conniving. And John Paul Jones and other captains were pestering Franklin for ships of war.

The news of the American victory at Saratoga reached Franklin on the 7th of December, 1777, and was exactly the kind of event Franklin was hoping for. Realizing that the Colonies might just win their war against England after all, the French signed a Franco-American Treaty of Commerce and Alliance that became the turning point of the American Revolution. France then declared war on Great Britain and sent warships, blocking Cornwallis in Yorktown, bringing an end to the war and independence for America.

Sickness was rampant aboard ships in the eighteen century when a doctor's most popular treatment was bleeding and it was thought that disease and infection was caused by bad vapors. Long voyages meant rotten food and bad water, and men weakened by such conditions were more susceptible to diseases such as typhus, called "ship's fever," spread by lice and fleas carried on rats.

In this installment of the Jonathan Kinkaid series, Kinkaid's marital bliss is interrupted when the diplomat, Mr. Simpson, insists that it be Captain Kinkaid and the *Active* that will take him and the news of the great victory at Saratoga to Benjamin Franklin in Paris.

Contents

I Bliss Interrupted
II An Easy Sailor, I'm Told
III Of Shipmates, Old and New
IV Strange Men, Strange Sails
V An Old Trick
VI Ship of Rags
VII Saved by the Bell
VIII Post-Chaise to Hay Wagon
IX Frivolities and Flatteries
X Three Birds with One Stone
XI Only with Audacity, Pure and Simple
XII Newfound Men and Lost Keys
XIII Give Us Liberty or Death
XIV Triumph and Tribulation
XV Wise Choices

I
Bliss Interrupted

Kinkaid sat in the coach, a happy but nervous man. Impeccably dressed in his best uniform and with his hat on his lap, he allowed the breeze coming in through the window to dry his freshly-washed hair. Having tried on more than a few wigs and finding none that suited him, he had foresworn wearing one altogether. The sight of O'Toole, seated across from him, grabbing onto his wig as they bumped along the rutted road, only confirmed his opinion that wigs should be outlawed as fashion foppery. Even so, Kinkaid had to admit that the hardened Boatswain's Mate looked the gentleman of refinement and taste in his new gray suit and neatly trimmed beard.

"Why, you could be King Lear," Kinkaid teased him.

"Ah, but there's still a self-respectin' boatswain under all this prettiness, Captain," O'Toole assured him, recognizing, "Yep, shiny as new doubloons we be…'cept' for your footwear, if you'll pardon me, sir."

In order to keep from scuffing his new black shoes, Kinkaid still wore his everyday brogans. But with the Boatswain's reminder he looked about and then asked, "Now, where are my new shoes?"

"They're not here?" asked O'Toole, searching under their feet. "I'm sure I…" Only now did he remember placing them on the luggage rack while stowing the Captain's valise. "Driver, stop this instant!"

O'Toole leaped out as the coach came to a dusty halt, disturbing some crows that had been breakfasting on the carcass of a careless woodchuck. He checked the luggage rack and found that the shoes had bounced out. Hanging his head in embarrassment as the crows cawed in mockery, O'Toole could only admit, "They're gone, sir. Harebrained of me, Captain. Don't know what I was thinking."

Kinkaid checked his watch. "We've just time to go back. Turn us around, driver!"

"Very good, sir!"

"I'll ride up top, Captain," suggested O'Toole, "keep my eyes peeled."

Relieved at first not to have to think of things to assuage the old man's guilt, Kinkaid soon had to admit that the misplacement of his shoes was no one's fault but his own; he should have put them in his valise, not handed them to O'Toole. But then, one did not get married every day, and with Cato in charge of the wedding party and O'Toole wound up like a corkscrew, it was no wonder they'd misplaced his shoes.

And he began to reflect on his present circumstances, a luxury he had not had the time to enjoy for the last few weeks, rushing here and there with last minute preparations, and he could only conclude that it all seemed like a miracle to him now, his joy matched only by his disbelief. Of course he had often thought of asking for Elizabeth's hand in marriage, the chief impediment always his relative poverty, but then fortune had smiled when those prizes taken by the *Randolph* had finally been adjudicated, with more to come when Blackstone's treasure trove would finally be tallied, and with promises of more from the last northern cruise he would have more than enough to ensure a comfortable start in life. Finally, the jovial comment from Elizabeth's father: "Well, not only a hero, but a man of means as well," had been enough to confirm that nothing more stood in his way.

On inactive status for over two months now, he knew that he should have enjoyed his time off more than he had. But newspaper accounts of "Gentleman Johnny" Burgoyne's invasion of Lake Champlain and the subsequent fall of Fort Ticonderoga were difficult to ignore and had everyone scared. And when Mr. Whipple had told him that British privateers were enjoying success in attacking American merchant shipping all along the coast, he felt almost ashamed, knowing that other men were dying in defense of their country while he remained idle in a paradise of frivolous parties and lover's delights. And so it was with almost relief when he received the Marine Committee's message to report to Commander Nathanson's office in three weeks.

That's when he knew what he had to do.

They had taken a picnic along the river. It was late September and the weather was perfect. He could see her so clearly now, kneeling on the bank, washing away the stickiness of the honey she'd spread on those biscuits. He had crept up behind her and held her.

"My hands, they're all wet..." she began, turning around, but his ardent kiss silenced her protest and she returned it with equal ardor.

Dizzy, and almost drowning in wanting, he had said the words, "Elizabeth, you will marry me...won't you?"

She had gasped at first, and almost laughed, surprised by the sudden proposal. But when she saw the seriousness on his face and perhaps even detected the trace of fear that he might be rejected, she had held him tight, tenderly stroked his hair with her wet hands and whispered, "Of course I will, my Jonathan."

Backtracking was a futile waste of time, and now here he was, about to become married to the woman of his dreams, late for his wedding, family, and guests already seated in the church, and his marriage shoes were lost in the tall grass somewhere along the roadside. His grandfather, a reader of signs and almanacs, would have said it was a bad omen, a man losing his shoes on his wedding day, but Kinkaid resolved that nothing would interfere with his rapture on this day, not the loss of a pair of shoes, and certainly not a superstitious thought.

"What size do you wear, Boats?" he asked as they drew up to the newly whitewashed church, framed in a cluster of maples ablaze in brilliant autumn hues.

"Ah, of course, Captain!" O'Toole's face lit up at the chance to amend his mistake. He plopped down on the lawn, quickly removed his shiny black brogans, and handed them to Kinkaid. They were too large, but better too large than too small.

"Perfect!" exclaimed Kinkaid when he finished tying the laces. Then he handed O'Toole his scuffed brown shoes.

O'Toole struggled in vain to pull Kinkaid's shoes on over his stockings. He tugged his stockings off and tried again; again in vain. Finally he stood up, wiped the sweat from his forehead, and concluded, "I doubt anyone will notice, Captain; what with all eyes upon your lovely bride this day…uh, what I meant to say, sir, is…"

"I won't argue that, Boats," said Kinkaid, glancing toward the church, "even had we the time."

"After you, Captain," insisted O'Toole with dramatic sweep of his arm.

He could see through the open doors that the church was

filled to capacity; Boston society, family and friends of the Whipples, all dressed in their finery, hushed and awaiting the ceremony. Taking the blue ribbon from his pocket, he tied his hair back while deciding that the best course of action would be to sneak along the outer aisle, unnoticed, toward the altar. Except that he immediately tripped and stumbled loudly over the doorsill, causing those at the back to turn in time to see a barefoot O'Toole catch him by his jacket. The low sighs of disgust were enough to tell him that some of the guests had mistaken the two for a couple of drunks. Recovering his balance if not his composure, there was little Kinkaid could do but throw back his shoulders and walk squarely up the middle aisle, ignoring the stares as the big black shoes clopped loudly on the plank floor. Boatswain O'Toole brought up the rear, tiptoeing along in his bare feet, a sheepish look on his face.

Reverend Spencer hid his relief with a benevolent smile, and then motioned toward Kinkaid's place at the altar where Elizabeth waited patiently, her parents standing stoically beside her.

He had to catch his breath, so radiantly beautiful was she, so elegant in her Wedgwood blue dress. She seemed to float before him like an angel with Forget-me-nots in her hair, her face framed in auburn ringlets. Her cheeks were dusted with freckles from the summer sun. Her eyes were only for him.

"You were almost late," came the whispered chide.

He scarcely noticed the bridesmaid cousins, Sophronia, 22, and Dorothea, 13, standing nervously beside her in shades of blue as Reverend Spencer began to recite the marriage vows.

"Wilt thou have this man to thy wedded husband, to live together after God's ordinance, in the holy estate of Matrimony; wilt thou obey him, and serve him, love, honor, and keep him in sickness and in health; and forsaking all others, keep thee only unto him, so long as you both shall live?"

"I shall," she answered.

The husband's words were identical, except that in place of obey and serve, he was to love and comfort her.

"I shall," he pronounced.

They exchanged simple gold rings and then drank a toast of sweet wine to conclude the ceremony. Afterwards, the crowd was ushered outside where they watched from the steps of the church, the bridesmaids giggling nervously, expectantly, as the couple walked out, arm in arm under an arch of crossed swords.

There stood Lieutenant William "Billy" Weatherby, blonde and handsome, first one on the right of the six-man honor guard. On the left was a dark and equally handsome Mister Midshipman Briggs. Two additional midshipmen and a young lieutenant, all unknown to Kinkaid, had been cajoled to volunteer their services. And there, at the end, was an officer who Kinkaid was most pleased to see…in spite of his terrible transformation; Lieutenant Hill, a crooked smile lighting his disfigured face, the left side of which was scarred; pink and melted from the awful burns he had received aboard the burning *Randolph*.

It was under the arch of steel and a shower of flowers, then down the stairs to the waiting coach where O'Toole stood, acting as footman, a wry and happy smile on his craggy face. Meaning to take Elizabeth's hand to help her into the coach, O'Toole accidentally bumped her arm as she tossed the bouquet, sending it flying straight up and landing in the arms of a surprised and embarrassed Lieutenant Hill. A disappointed sigh from the bridesmaids was followed by a murmur of shock as the wedding party noticed for the first time the horrid burns disfiguring Mr. Hill's face. Saving what might have been an ugly moment, Elizabeth ran up and planted a joyous kiss upon Hill's pink and wrinkled cheek, drawing a cheer of approval from the crowd and a crooked smile from Mr. Hill.

He followed his beautiful bride into the carriage that took them to the Beacon Hotel in the center of the city where the wedding party soon followed; the barefoot O'Toole, Hill, young Weatherby and Briggs, and almost another hundred guests who drank and toasted, danced and laughed the evening away in the great common room of the hotel.

It was late when Kinkaid finally gave his speech. First he thanked all of the guests for their wonderful gifts, inadequately, he knew, for he was embarrassed when he failed to remember all their names. But he fumbled through, nonetheless, with the help of forgiving and comical comments from the relaxed gathering. Finally, turning to his four comrades in arms, seated together at the end of the long table, (Hill was actually slightly inebriated, a first in Kinkaid's recollection) he raised his glass and ended with, "And if it weren't for the loan of my Boatswain's shoes—and it's a good thing he has captain's gigs for feet—I would have had to appear before all of you and my beautiful and long-suffering bride, barefoot, on this, the happiest day of my life."

But of course it was that evening, after the couple had retired to their room, that Kinkaid remembered best, Elizabeth lovingly forgiving all his social sins.

"What time did you say the coach was to fetch us?" asked Elizabeth, seated before the mirrored chiffonier in her morning gown, bathed in warm sunshine, slowly drawing a tortoiseshell comb through her lustrous hair.

"You needn't worry, my dear, we've plenty of time," answered Kinkaid, watching her in adoration, for once unconcerned with time as he reclined on the bed against a stack of down pillows, the cluttered breakfast tray still beside him. The night had been one of infinite pleasure and mystery; simply being alone now with Elizabeth was a delightful experience, and with the prospect of many hours over the next days and nights spent entirely alone in a world of their own making before him, Kinkaid took guilty pleasure in the knowledge that at that very moment he was an entirely fulfilled and contented man.

"Plenty of time for you, perhaps," answered Elizabeth with a look of mock indignation in the mirror. Then, smiling, she asked, "Are you pleased with your new robe?"

Kinkaid regarded the dark blue velvet material with the gold trim, and admitted, "I'm not sure."

"Well, I think it makes you look as dignified as any ship's captain ever looked in the morning."

"Which only proves that Mr. Africanus is a man of exquisite taste."

"Who will be most pleased to see you wearing it," she advanced.

Kinkaid paused before venturing, "I'm afraid he shall remain disappointed in that respect," knowing as he said the words that he had said them much too seriously.

"Not even when you are relaxing?" She knew he was unaccustomed to wearing a robe, that he only wore one now for practical reasons and would never consider wearing such a thing aboard ship.

"A ship's captain, relax?" he asked. Mustering a stern look, Kinkaid announced importantly, "A ship's captain, especially a captain who wishes to remain free of accusations of foppish style, must in no way have a look, no, not even the hint of a look, of relaxation about him."

She laughed, which brought him to laughter as well, the smug and delirious laughter of a newly-married man. And then suddenly, inexplicably, he found himself comparing his life at the moment with his life aboard ship, a hard, and uncomfortable life at best, even for a captain, perversely recognizing that no person aboard ship would dare to speak so familiarly with his captain as Elizabeth had spoken to him just now, for a ship was a place where rank and rule commanded respect, a place where other men might live or die by his decisions; right or wrong, his word was law, and a feeling of grace overcame him as he realized the balance this brought him in his new life with this woman that he had been so fortunate to have found and now married, betrothing years of faith and fidelity, in a state of equality, friendship and love that was more natural than shipboard life, where he was the follower, and following gladly, finding pleasure in pleasing her, gladly bending his will in obedience to her unspoken and sometimes mysterious rules, one of them being that a woman always required and deserved more time to prepare for an excursion than a man would.

His mirthful yet distracted look did not escape Elizabeth's vigilance. Guessing that the sea was in some way responsible, she brought him back from his capricious pondering, asking, "Jonathan, are you laughing at me?"

"Of course not, my dear. I was simply laughing for the sake of hearing my own laughter," he said, the full and correct answer requiring so much thought and explanation, which Elizabeth would patiently hear and appreciate, no doubt, but Kinkaid was not always wanting to analyze or willing to speak about his innermost feeling. Unaccustomed as he was to sharing them, he tended to regard feelings as so many ocean breezes, coming and going, lingering for a moment but eventually changing, always fickle, never amounting to much of any consequence. In contrast, he could see that Elizabeth's world was full of emotions and that in many ways it gave her strength; her inner world seemed always in tune with the relationship of things in ways that he could not understand, and that in some ways gave her a resilience that he could only admire but never completely understand, just as he suspected that there was much that he could tell her that she would not understand in the way that he understood it, even if he were inclined to attempt to explain it. No, sometimes it was better to simply tender the simplest response, he judged, without taking the chance on spoiling the moment with a difference of opinion resulting from the simple fact that men and women might sometimes view the world differently.

Elizabeth, of course knew that there was more to Kinkaid's laughter and far-away look than his answer provided as she sat in front of the mirror, gathering and pinning her hair back, but she too was learning the ways of her man and would let the matter rest, feeling pleasure in the fact that they were happy together, in fact, cherishing the time all the more, knowing she would soon have to release him to his duty upon the sea. The thought made her turn and come to him, her silky chemise flowing behind, her eyes meeting his, when there came an almost imperceptible knock upon the door.

"Was that someone knocking?" Elizabeth asked. There, again, a bit louder this time, still barely audible.

"I'll get it," said Kinkaid, rising, and trying to keep the annoyance out of his voice.

It was the shy and diminutive chambermaid, Eleanor. Upon their arrival at the hotel on the previous evening, Kinkaid had innocently warned the young girl to be careful of Elizabeth's train as the young chambermaid followed them too closely up the stairs to their room. With her arms full of linen, she had been unable to see the steps in front of her and stepping on the gown may have resulted in an unfortunate accident. But the girl had reacted to Kinkaid's words of warning as if he had sharply rebuked her, which Kinkaid had not meant to do. Accustomed as he was to ordering sailors about, perhaps he might have warned her with a bit more tact, he allowed, while Elizabeth had explained that her new husband was "a rough and tumble sailor with the manners of a pirate." Now here she was, wide-eyed and apprehensive, and it occurred to Elizabeth that she had only added to the poor child's fright with her carefree remarks about her new husband.

Kinkaid made the wise decision to back away from the door, whereupon the girl managed to blurt out, "Excuse me ma'am, but there is a gentleman downstairs in the dining room who wishes to inform you…well, that he is terribly sorry to interrupt your morning, but he has most urgent business with your…husband."

"Did this gentleman, perchance, mention his name?" asked Elizabeth.

Young Eleanor's face flushed crimson as she bowed her head in shame and answered, "I'm terribly sorry, ma'am. He did tell me his name, but…Oh, I forgot it coming up the stairs. I shall go back and…"

"Now, don't be silly. That won't be necessary. It isn't important," said Elizabeth, sorry she had asked. When the girl remained standing in the doorway, Elizabeth asked, "Is there anything else you would like to tell us?"

"Is there anything I can do for you, ma'am? Perhaps draw your bath? Take your laundry? I'd be most happy to take care of some shopping."

Elizabeth had just finished her bath, all of her clothes were clean, she needed nothing from the stores, and they would soon be leaving. Casting her gaze about the room, she said brightly, "You could take the breakfast tray."

"Yes, ma'am. Thank you, ma'am," answered Eleanor as she quickly retrieved the tray.

"Why, thank *you* so much, Eleanor...and please inform the gentleman that my husband shall be down presently."

"Yes, ma'am," answered Eleanor with a curtsy, "I shall tell the gentleman, ma'am."

Kinkaid felt equally puzzled and annoyed. He would have to wear his uniform. He had intended to wear his new tweed suit today, but if it were naval business...

"Such a sweet thing," mused Elizabeth, seemingly unconcerned by the interruption.

"Too sweet for this world," agreed Kinkaid offhandedly, wondering who it might be downstairs that would have urgent business with him, and on the day after his wedding, no less. He could think of no bills that were overdue, nor did he believe he was in trouble with anyone. It could only be some matter from the Marine Committee and so it was with some urgency that he finished buttoning his collar and then, standing before the door, hesitated as he thought to say something of comfort to his new bride.

But Elizabeth, always sensible, said first, "The sooner may you return, my love."

"Kinkaid," came the familiar silky voice from the dining room.

"Mr. Simpson. Why, we thought you were in Philadelphia...there were rumors that you were captured. And how did you know to find me here?"

"Too many questions for so early in the morning,"

answered Simpson with a ready smile, asking instead, "Who is your tailor? That uniform fits you perfectly."

"You don't have to tell me how you found me, if that suits you, but I must draw the line at your flattering me. I was married only yesterday, as if you didn't know, and..."

"Of course I knew...and allow me offer my sincerest congratulations. You've made quite a catch, I understand. Here, sit down," said Simpson, pulling out a chair for him, promising, "I won't keep you but a moment." A small gift-wrapped package sat on the table next to the sugar bowl.

Kinkaid's previous assignment had been to convey Mr. Simpson to the Caribbean Island of St. Eustatius earlier that summer, the knowledgeable and capable diplomat providing many hours of interesting and thought-provoking conversation during their voyage aboard the brig-of-war, *Swift*, their mutual admiration leading to a fast friendship. However, they had no sooner returned to Boston than Simpson was off on some mysterious assignment.

Mr. Simpson had already ordered coffee and filled a cup for Kinkaid, saying, "You must wonder what I'm doing here...so soon after your wedding."

"We would have invited you if..."

"Of course. Actually, I only just arrived from Philadelphia."

"We heard the British had taken the city."

"Escaped by a hair, I'll tell you. Close call. Had to leave some things behind, at that. Shame. Congress has shifted its offices to Lancaster and..."

It was good to see Mr. Simpson again, yet at the moment Kinkaid had little interest in hearing of his adventures or where Congress might have shifted their offices to this time, concerned more with getting back to Elizabeth so they could meet the coach that would take them to the Whipple farm where they planned to set up housekeeping and enjoy whatever time was left before the war interrupted his domestic bliss.

"Well, I suppose Congress can take care of itself, though I'm glad to see the British didn't get you," he had to admit, reminding himself that enjoying a cup of coffee with an old acquaintance should not take very long and couldn't be avoided, regardless. Recalling that Mr. Simpson had always appreciated his honesty, Kinkaid took a sip, smiled, and said affably, "It was kind of you to stop by with your regards, Mr. Simpson, but we were about to take a coach back. I have a meeting with the Commander in a week and..."

"Actually," interrupted Simpson, "that is what I came to talk to you about. Your meeting has been moved up, I'm afraid."

"And it won't wait until tomorrow?" asked Kinkaid, making little effort to hide his annoyance.

"Oh, it can certainly wait until tomorrow," said Simpson agreeably, then added more gravely, "but not a day later."

"If you can't tell me the reason, can you at least tell me what I am to say to Elizabeth? That is my wife's name, you know."

"Elizabeth Constance Whipple," answered Simpson too cheerfully. "Now Mrs. Kinkaid." Even seeing the gloom that fell over Kinkaid's face, Simpson made no effort to allay Kinkaid's disappointment in having his marital bliss come to naught, brightening instead with the news, "Burgoyne has surrendered!"

"His entire army?" asked Kinkaid in surprise in spite of himself.

"Five thousand, seven hundred men. At Saratoga, just three days ago!" exclaimed Simpson. A well-dressed couple in the corner glanced over with a mixture of disdain and interest, causing Simpson to continue his explanation in a quieter tone. "Cut off from his supply lines…out of food and ammunition…word is that General Clinton ignored his plea for help; Burgoyne had little choice."

"That is, indeed, good news," Kinkaid had to admit, observing, "especially for American prisoners." As a prisoner of the British only a year earlier, his first thought was that the capture of almost six thousand British soldiers would mean the probable release of as many Americans from British compounds and jails.

"Actually, there are to be no prisoners," answered Simpson. "The terms of the surrender specified that Burgoyne's army be disarmed and sent back to England under an agreement that those men will never again serve against the colonies."

Kinkaid was incredulous. "And they expect the British to abide by a gentleman's agreement?" It seemed preposterous.

"What matters is that it establishes our side as humane and honorable," answered Simpson with his consummate rationality. But, detecting how maddening his statement might appear to Kinkaid, added, "I know how you must feel about the prisoner situation and the possibilities of exchange for our men, but you must understand that this is something that will show the nations of the world that we are better than the mightiest country on earth. There are other battlefields, Kinkaid."

"The power of words," gave Kinkaid reluctantly, recalling one of Simpson's speeches. It was an important and almost unbelievable piece of news, a great and unexpected victory after months of military setbacks and so he could at least allow that perhaps Simpson had a point about the message such surrender terms would tell the world. "Well, that will certainly take the pressure off of Washington."

"But don't you see what this means? When the French hear of this, they may well decide to come in on our side."

"I suppose..." began Kinkaid, unconvinced that anyone could predict what the fickle French might or might not do.

"Oh, of course they'd be responding more as poor losers to the British and only see us as helping them get their revenge," observed Simpson. "Let's face it, I can't think of a single nation that takes too eagerly to the concept of men being free. It's a new and threatening idea, and..."

"I take your meaning, Mr. Simpson," interrupted Kinkaid, not in the mood to consider Simpson's philosophy at the moment, thinking of Elizabeth waiting upstairs and that their coach was soon expected. "But what has this to do with me?"

"Commander Nathanson will inform you of all the details...tomorrow at noon."

"As if I couldn't very well guess," lamented Kinkaid.

"Oh, I almost forgot," said Simpson, picking up the small gift-wrapped package and handing it to Kinkaid. "Something for you."

Kinkaid opened it and found inside a book, 'Chambaud's Grammar of the French Tongue.' Kinkaid thumbed through it and said uncertainly, "Well, thank you, Mr. Simpson. I see you wish to make a linguist out of me."

Simpson merely smiled and said, "Well, I will take no more of your precious time, Captain. I know you think I'm needlessly interfering with the happiest moment of your life, but let me assure you that these are momentous times for our country. The news of this victory, brought to Paris, is exactly the kind of news that Franklin has been anxiously awaiting." Simpson, having said too much already and noting the impatient look of his reluctant audience, concluded, "Captain, I look forward to our continuing association, but for the moment I bid you good day and wish you and your new bride much happiness." He stood up from the table, strode toward the lobby, hesitated, turned, and added, "By the way, Kinkaid, I have been granted the privilege of informing you that your promotion to full Captain has been approved."

Elizabeth knew something was amiss the moment he returned to their room, for his grin had vanished as if carried away by an errant gust of wind. It was not easy telling Elizabeth that their plans would be cut short, notwithstanding the news of his promotion.

"I suppose I'll have to become accustomed to this if I'm to be a sailor's wife," she said philosophically as she picked up the small book he had dropped on the nightstand. Then, putting on a brave smile, she suggested, "We should cancel the coach, Jonathan," drawing near to him.

"What do you mean?"

"Well, it only makes sense," she explained in her practical way. "That way you won't have to come all the way back for your meeting with Commander Nathanson. Besides, I understand there is a tavern not far from here famous for its seafood."

With but a few well-chosen words, she had brought back his lost grin and he could only love her more, if that were possible. He brightened, answering, "You know, I do suddenly I have a terrible longing for fresh halibut."

"Well, I'm glad that's settled," she said, drawing him to her, "and I have a terrible longing for a certain brave and handsome Captain."

Their kiss was maddeningly interrupted by a faint and uncertain tapping upon the door. Both sighed, now recognizing the hesitant taps as that of the chambermaid.

Elizabeth answered the door this time. "Why Eleanor, so

nice to see you again."

"Your coach is waiting, ma'am," she announced shyly.

Kinkaid dug two coins from his purse and handed them to Elizabeth who pressed them into Eleanor's hand, explaining patiently, "Would you be so kind as to give one of these to the driver and inform him that we regret that we shan't be needing his services after all. The other is for you, Eleanor, for being so sweet and helpful."

"Anything for you, ma'am," she said with a curtsy. "Thank you very much, ma'am."

Closing the door, Elizabeth turned to him and they kissed again, sweetly and tenderly at first, and then rapturously, and then fiercely...

Later, with Kinkaid wearing his new gray tweed suit and Elizabeth her blue crinoline, the couple stepped out onto the sidewalk. The air was cool and the first stars of the evening were twinkling above.

"Now, what were you saying about Paris?" she asked, taking his arm in hers.

II
An Easy Sailor, I'm Told

The office looked the same. Dark bookshelves along the walls, the gold-fringed carpet under the oak desk; the heavy drapes that shut out the light of day. Commander Nathanson hadn't changed much either. Seated behind his desk, his bushy sideburns appeared even bushier, as if in compensation for the ever-thinning hair, but he still retained that look of staunch resolve. The bifocals were new, suddenly the rage, popularized by the scientist, Franklin.

"A fine piece of work down there in the Islands, Kinkaid," began Nathanson, thrusting out his bare chin. "Set the Brits back a bit, not to mention the blow you dealt those pirates. And Mr. Simpson's fine commercial agreements should keep us in shot and powder...that is, as long as our ships can continue to evade English patrols. I suppose he told you about Burgoyne's surrender."

"Very good news, Commander," admitted Kinkaid with a glance of recognition Simpson's way.

"Exactly what Franklin has been waiting for," noted Simpson.

"And none too soon," added Nathanson, peering over the rim of his spectacles. "By the way, congratulation on your wedding, Captain...and we deeply regret interrupting your plans, but this is something that simply cannot wait. And you'll have to bear with us today. Things are rather in a rush, what with the recent news and the need to act quickly." He picked up a parchment. "And now I have received this memo from Congress, brought only this morning, outlining a few things...for our consideration as possible undertakings...looking forward, that is." Taking off the spectacles, he placed them on the desk and said gruffly, "Which all means that the sooner we can get you on your way, the better for everyone concerned."

Kinkaid was not happy to hear this, more for Elizabeth's sake than his own, being resigned to the fact, expecting as much.

"Of course, your primary and foremost consideration, Kinkaid, will be to transport, with all due haste, Mr. Simpson to France, specifically, to the port of...."

"The port of Nantes, Thomas," provided Simpson.

"From there to Paris. Mr. Simpson shall be carrying dispatches from General Washington to be delivered in person to Franklin, describing the events and outcome of Burgoyne's surrender. You'll be given the *Active*, an easy sailor, I'm told, at least that is before her sail plan was expanded. Of course there won't be time for sea trials; you'll simply have to work out any adjustments enroute. Her bottom was just careened," he added for good measure.

Of course it was good to know that the ships bottom had been stripped of barnacles and algae that could slow her speed considerably, but having seen *Active* down at the docks, a lightly armed corvette of twelve guns, Kinkaid was well aware that she would be no match for even the smallest British man-of-war that he was likely to meet on the open ocean. Yet a speedy ship need not be powerful and an expanded sail plan was meant to increase her speed, but an untried plan could mean tricky handling characteristics requiring major adjustments, some perhaps impossible to correct while at sea.

"I'm sure she will be adequate, Commander," allowed Kinkaid.

His previous command, *Swift*, was still in the Boston yards, as were the two prizes they had brought in from the Caribbean, the pirate vessel, *Moondog*, and the British ship-of-the-line, *Isle of Wight*, which he had renamed *Cutler*, after the young midshipman killed during the chase of the British sloop-of-war, *Reprisal*. *Swift* and *Moondog* were both still under repair, and with sailcloth and hardware, materials and labor difficult to come by, would remain unready for some time hence. The heavyweight British double-decker would have been the ideal warship with which to meet the enemy, a ship-of-the-line of 44 guns, but Kinkaid knew that a more senior captain would take command of her, the ship having been renamed *American Eagle,* Congress unwilling to name such a powerful vessel after a young midshipman of little distinction.

"I'm afraid she's all we have at the moment, under such short notice," admitted Nathanson. "She has a minimum crew already aboard her and they have been taking on stores for the last two days. As usual, you'll have to scrounge the city to fill out your crew, but since we have so few ships, you'll have no shortage of officers."

"That is at least something, sir."

"Yes, well, that's not all, Captain," grumbled Nathanson. He replaced the glasses over his long nose and peered once again at the parchment before him before wincing in irritation. "This list…given me by…certain members of Congress."

"The Board of War, Commander," explained Simpson. "A new committee, formed, actually, on the same day as the surrender."

"Well, I don't know how one keeps up with all their boards and committees…it seems Congress comes up with a new one every week," complained the Commander peevishly, "but I assume that this is tendered in the spirit of…suggestions." Gazing over the rim of his spectacles he added, "Not to appear negative, Mr. Simpson, but…"

"Of course not, Thomas. It's just that some of the members thought as long as Captain Kinkaid was over there…"

"Yes, and I can well imagine who those members might be…it amazes me how a taste of victory can turn the staunchest naysayer into a master of grand strategy overnight. Of course, I'm all for taking the war to the enemy, and the taking of prizes that might offer themselves afterwards is all very well and good, but I had hoped that we would have been provided with more resources and less suggestions." Not expecting an answer to his complaint, Nathanson continued, "In my opinion, commerce raiding should be left to privateers, but knowing that crew moral always benefits with a bit of prize money, if any easy pickings should come your way, Kinkaid, naturally, you may act at your own discretion. But I believe, and I'm glad to see that Congress is inclined to agree with me, that a better strategy, given our situation, would be to make attacks upon the enemy in defenseless places."

"Preferably upon their mainland," said Simpson. "Somewhere remote and easily approached, of course, but to do enough damage to cause a stir, something to make the enemy realize that their shores are inadequately protected from American marauders."

"We don't expect you to make war on civilians, Kinkaid," Nathanson assured him. "We want only property damage here; in spite of the fact that the British have burned, bombed and pillaged our towns, we cannot stoop to emulate such barbarity. You are to avoid any civilian loss of life, let us be clear on that."

"Very clear, Commander," answered Kinkaid with some relief.

"The idea is to create uncertainty and unrest," said Nathanson, "make their people clamor for better protection against such attacks in the future...make them tie up their ships closer to home, keeping them spread thin and with less to blockade our own shores."

"The international press must see such an action as a daring raid, not a cowardly slaughter of civilians," added Simpson.

"Of course," allowed Kinkaid.

The Commander once more glowered at the parchment. "Simpson, this thing about the Baltic. Certainly, it's a good idea, disrupting the Baltic trade, but I don't believe this...War Committee is aware of how well protected the Baltic is...and where would an American ship take her prizes? Hell, we're lucky enough to be able to sneak a few ships into French ports...and, in spite of Saratoga, there's no telling about the French...how long this state of affairs will last. The Baltic makes little sense to me and I can't in good conscience order a vessel under my command to undertake such a useless venture. If I had a dozen ships of the line I might..."

"Granted," said Simpson, knowing when to yield the point. "The Baltic is out. But once the French learn of Saratoga, I'm certain they will open their ports to us in an official capacity. No more need for lies and deceit, which by now is becoming so obvious anyway."

"Well, if Franklin is able to manage that, it will make Kinkaid's time there much easier...and more profitable."

Nathanson gave Kinkaid a comradely wink.

"Thomas, if I may," came in Simpson. "Captain Kinkaid, how long would you estimate our passage?"

"Depending upon *Active*'s speed, and if the winds remain favorable, and autumn storms are not severe, I would estimate our making the port of Nantes in, say, a month," provided Kinkaid.

"By which time the situation may have changed," judged Nathanson astutely.

"So you believe we should allow some time for our news to, hopefully, precipitate some change in attitude of the French?" asked Simpson.

"Certainly before attempting any secondary mission," judged Nathanson.

"Therefore, you are proposing…" Simpson smiled at the prospect.

"That Kinkaid join you in Paris, naturally." Nathanson turned to Kinkaid. "Captain, I'm sure you can see the need for you to better ascertain the situation over there before we send you running off on some half-cocked adventure. I propose you talk to Doctor Franklin; he's been over there for some time now and will have a better idea as to what we might accomplish. Keep your eyes and ears open and I'm sure the three of you will come up with something more sensible than anything we can only conjecture about at this point in time."

"Of course, sir," Kinkaid answered stoically, his fate decided by a superior whose practicality and good sense he could only admire and respect.

"Good, then. And let me assure you that whatever you come up with will have the full backing and approval of this office."

"Thank you, sir," gave Kinkaid, grateful for the

confidence shown.

"So there we have it," stated Nathanson with finality. "Your foremost objective will be to safely deliver Mr. Simpson to France with all possible speed. You will then accompany him to Paris for recent intelligence, and afterwards, if circumstances are favorable, you will make an attack upon some British harbor or shore installation. The question of prize-taking will be left to your discretion as will the area of cruising and the period of time you deem necessary to accomplish as much damage to the enemy as possible. Your orders will be drawn up forthwith," concluded Nathanson, "and please keep Mr. Simpson and myself informed as to your state of readiness so that we may avoid any unnecessary delays."

"I shall, Commander."

"Oh, and if I may recommend an advance for Captain Kinkaid," said Simpson, giving Kinkaid a wink. "If he is to accompany me to the French court…"

"By all means," agreed Nathanson, "we must present an impeccable impression upon our hoped-for allies, mustn't we?"

In spite of the gracious request for money with which to purchase new suits, uniforms, and silk stocking for Kinkaid so that he would not embarrass Mr. Simpson at the French court, Simpson remained somewhat cool toward Kinkaid after the meeting, merely providing him the address of a house on the hill where he could be reached when the ship would be ready for departure. It was not the best start, but they would soon have plenty of time in which to renew their friendship.

It was the second of November before *Active* was ready for sea, the lack of a crew being the primary impediment.

Kinkaid was pleased to find that Active's twelve original guns, six-pounders, had been replaced with nine-pounders. With her expanded sail plan, the increase in firepower would not appreciably slow her, and the added weight would ensure better stability in heavy winds. And of course, there was some comfort in the fact that a few of the faces he saw on the deck were familiar ones, having served under him aboard *Swift,* for those men had proven their worth and loyalty, having been forged in fire and steel in the Caribbean, providing a small but toughened core of veterans.

As for the rest, and even with Mr. Whipple's help, finding able seamen to round out his crew proved daunting. In the port of Boston, where so many sailors might be found, possible able seamen, enticed by profit-hungry privateers who promised untold wealth from a single cruise in local waters, showed little interest, while others were off to join General Arnold's Lake Champlain fleet. As it was, a scrounging of Boston jails produced, if not the best hands, at least enough bodies somewhat glad to gain a limited freedom, with a chance to redeem themselves as the handbills proclaimed, "in a glorious endeavor," yet only time would tell if a crew rounded out with criminals and misfits would be worth the risk. Already there were fights in the 'tween decks and reports of petty thievery, and two men's names had been mentioned as possible troublemakers, Nicholas Sterling and John Cole, loudmouthed ruffians both, but so far Kinkaid had allowed the men to police themselves. The petty thief, Cole, was made to run a gauntlet of fellow crewmen, appearing on deck the next morning with a black eye and numerous cuts and bruises to show for his trouble.

As for officers, Nathanson had been right, there was a

plethora; eleven in all, counting the three midshipmen. Too many, in fact, there being not enough separate berths for them all in the diminutive ship, her belowdecks already stuffed to the overhead with stores, the carpenters busy installing additional partitions.

One of those officers was the gruff and stooped Mr. Sykes, whose first duty each and every morning was to make a complete inspection of the ship, taking note of any and all irregularities, whether with the maintenance of the decks, the rigging, the trim of the ship, the sails, the stores, or the men themselves, ensuring that the respective division officers were apprised of any concerns and passing his observations on to his captain, and now he was reporting that another dozen men had "volunteered" themselves, dregs from a certain disreputable quarter of the city, a few straight from the jails, probably signed on with the promise of a steady ration of rum.

"That last lot looked worse than the ones before, Captain," growled First Officer Sykes out of the side of his mouth. "Nothin' but skin and bones, most of 'em, and more'n a few that appear sickly, but I've got 'em squared away and put to work, Captain."

Kinkaid had preferred to make Lieutenant Charles Hill his First Officer, but since the scowling Isaac Ebenezer Sykes had loudly and vociferously claimed seniority, there was little to be done except post him to the position instead, a fact which Kinkaid found himself already regretting, for everything about the man Kinkaid found repugnant, from his foul breath to his dirty hat to his waddling feet. He had bushy black eyebrows that met in a tuft over his bulbous nose, his eyes were deep-set and bloodshot, and under a pinched mouth protruded a scruffy iron-gray beard that defied direction. Not that one saw much of his face since he suffered from lumbago and was therefore always stooped over, which gave him the strange habit of standing sideways to whomever he happened to be speaking, a blessing given the man's offensive breath. Yet it was not enough that the man's overall appearance gave an impression of filth, disorder and chaos, for what was worse was his equally repugnant character, contrary and belligerent and Kinkaid soon came to the realization that it would take all of his patience to tolerate the man's contentiousness. But for now, Kinkaid tried his best to focus on the practical, concerning himself with the ship's business, reminding himself that he would have to abide the shortcomings of his associates.

"I hope you will ensure that those recruited are examined by the surgeon, Mr. Sykes," Kinkaid advised him. He had read only yesterday of outbreaks of disease in the city.

"I doubt there's anything serious amongst 'em, Captain." Sykes conjectured. "Shirkers, I suspect."

"You just informed me that a few appeared sickly, Mr. Sykes," Kinkaid reminded him.

"So's I did, Captain," came the ready retort. "But any shirker worth his hide can 'appear' sickly when there's work to be done."

"We'll get little enough work out of any of them if they're stricken with something," said Kinkaid, little hiding his irritation.

Yet the man seemed oblivious. "Well, we'll get no disease as long as the men stay fit, Captain. Drill and condition, condition and drill," proposed Sykes bombastically. "To hell with loyalty, sir. You want to drill and condition 'em till they jump to your tune out of sheer habit. That way…"

"Mr. Sykes," snapped Kinkaid, "you will ensure that every man that comes aboard my ship is thoroughly examined by the surgeon. Do you understand?"

Sykes gave Kinkaid a sideways haughty look, half saluted and said, "I'll take care of that right away, Captain."

Damn the man, thought Kinkaid, for he abhorred losing his temper even more than he detested this abhorrent man telling him how to train his crew and Sykes seemed bound to test him. He would have to remain on his guard to keep his temper, knowing it might prove difficult, when, in fact, merely thinking along these lines made him furious.

"Captain?"

"What is it, Mr. Rosetti?"

Lieutenant Tomas Rosetti was a stalwart officer and Kinkaid felt fortunate to have him. Powerfully built and with an erect military bearing, Rosetti seemed everything that Mr. Sykes was not; intelligent and capable, and with an agreeable and cheerful disposition. Of Italian descent, he had sailed the Mediterranean for 6 years before coming to the colonies. Possessed of a firm and confident manner, Kinkaid had made him his overall deck officer.

"Two things, Captain. Mr. Hill asked me to inform you that he has gone ashore to pay a visit to the munitions depot. Something about damp powder."

"Very well, then. And the second thing?"

"Peterson was asking me how we might apportion our supply of canvas, sir. We've not enough for decking, flags, signal flags and extra sails."

"Decking?" asked Kinkaid.

"Peterson thought you might like your cabin deck canvassed, sir."

"If we are short of canvas I certainly do not need my cabin canvassed," answered Kinkaid abruptly, the conversation with Sykes still with him. The captain's cabins on British warships were likely to have the luxury of canvas decking, but with little canvas to spare, Kinkaid could do with a bare wooden deck. Besides, it would be Mr. Simpson who would have to be careful of splinters since he would relinquish his cabin to him.

"Of course not, sir," gave Rosetti.

"Do we need more flags?" asked Kinkaid.

"We're sorely short signal flags, sir."

"I don't believe we'll be needing signal flags, Mr. Rosetti."

"Very well, sir. I'll tell Peterson to keep all our extra canvas in storage for sail replacement, then."

"Mr. Rosetti, have you noticed any sick men aboard?"

"Nothing out of the ordinary, Captain. The usual run of colds and upset stomachs. The young Shaw was complaining this morning about how his feet hurt and Hayes took that chop to his wrist yesterday when his knife slipped, but Dr. Morrow stitched him up pretty good, sir."

Dr. Kendrick Morrow was thin and balding, with a nervous disposition. When Kinkaid asked him why a married man with four children would volunteer for sea duty, Dr. Morrow had laughed and said it was the one place where he hoped "to find a bit of peace and quiet." It was fortunate enough to have found a medical officer even if his reasons were to escape a hectic family life.

Instead of a sailing master they had received a middle-aged and seemingly inexperienced master's mate by the name of Mr. Harold Grimes who had arrived with little more than a small suitcase and without a single chart of his own. Having previously served aboard a privateer that had caught itself upon some rocks off Martha's Vineyard, he was one of the fortunate few to have been rescued by a passing fishing shallop; at least that is the story he told and the reason for his lack of charts. Yet, in spite of the fact that he claimed to have had twelve years at sea, the man seemed to know next to nothing about his duties, but Kinkaid had little choice but to accept him, having had no other's apply for the position and detecting little or no skills which might qualify him for some other position, and in truth, Kinkaid was somewhat relieved. Having confidence in his own navigational abilities and taking into account his overbearing First Lieutenant; at least his sailing master would not be constantly second-guessing him as well.

Then there was the dawdling Mr. Robert Wells, the purser, who, with Mr. Grimes assisting, seemed to take forever to oversee the last of the stores aboard and ensure that the ship was properly trimmed, in spite of Weatherby's constant exhortations. Finally making his report, Kinkaid followed both men to the dock and all agreed that the ship seemed properly trimmed and ready for sailing.

Since Lieutenant Hill would happily take over his previous duties as Gunnery Officer, Kinkaid had made Lieutenant William Weatherby their Quartermaster, with special instructions to oversee Mr. Grimes's navigational duties as well as Mr. Wells's cargo responsibilities, in addition to his own quarterdeck and signals obligations, with confidence that all these tasks were easily within Mr. Weatherby's superior abilities.

Mr. Simpson finally arrived late in the evening and Kinkaid was not surprised when Simpson brought along his usual prodigious chest of clothes, which had to be manhandled into the orlop, but he was somewhat surprised to see that accompanying him was a gangly middle-aged man by the name of Mr. William Palfrey, a very tall man who appeared even taller than he actually was due his long gray coat, long face, long eagle nose, and stiff salt and pepper hair that rose straight up from his head like the bristles of a broom.

Mr. Simpson introduced the man as a newly-appointed Congressional Agent assigned to transact maritime business, namely procuring arms and military supplies for Washington's army. The man gave an impression of unmitigated gray, his hair, his cold gray eyes, even his skin had a gray unhealthy patina, and although he seemed pleasant enough, with quarters already so cramped aboard the tiny ship, Kinkaid was less than pleased to be taking on another "important" guest, especially since the man had almost as much baggage as Mr. Simpson, with four boxes that looked like they might hold dueling pistols, and a couple of longer boxes a little over sword-length. Aside from this, most of Kinkaid's irritation came from the fact that it meant moving his own things out of the master's berth. By all rights Kinkaid should have moved into Mr. Hill's space, but instead he moved himself to the very end of the officer's berths, closest to the crew's quarters, a tiny space not much larger than a closet. Irritated as he was to be evicted from his second choice of a cabin, Kinkaid determined that he would not cause all his officers to change berths as well. After all, the space was meant for sleeping and, as captain, he would in all likelihood do less of that than anyone else aboard. He would take most of his meals in the wardroom when not invited by Mr. Simpson, and would write his reports there as well as study the French grammar book Simpson had given him.

Most of his nights were spent ashore with Elizabeth. Of course it was difficult, especially for Elizabeth, for rarely was he on time to have dinner with her, and often arrived exhausted and distracted after a long day aboard where every task for making ready for sea was, ultimately, his responsibility. But Elizabeth never once complained or let on that there were times when she was becoming exasperated, knowing that his ship would always come first.

November came in with a touch of morning frost and a present from his bride. A miniature of her, painted in secrecy during the day by an itinerant artist named Ogden Oglethorpe. His name being a long one, he had taken to signing his tiny works with double O's which looked like a couple of staring mouse eyes where Elizabeth's right arm ended. The back of the miniature held a lock of her auburn hair, set behind a glass crystal and meticulously spread into the shape of a fan. She had waited until their last morning to give it to him and when he arrived aboard ship he hung it over his bed from a peg in the bulkhead next to his tiny mirror. It was a very good likeness, he had to admit, for it caught her expressive eyes and the tilt of her chin, though the artist had taken the liberty of rendering her nose somewhat straighter than it actually was, the fact pointed out by Elizabeth when she gave it to him. She told him that the artist had been accustomed to having his clients request that they "doctor" certain blemishes or imperfections and so he had taken it upon himself to give her a "perfect" nose. Kinkaid may not have even noticed it at first if Elizabeth hadn't brought it to his attention, but he would have in time, and soon, for he enjoyed the habit of running his finger over her nose at times, a habit which she pretended to object to.

And now here he was, at sea, the miniature swinging back and forth from the peg, sometimes taping against the pewter frame of the mirror as if reminding him of her presence. He found that when he looked at the portrait he wanted to run his finger along her nose and now regretted that it had been rendered so perfectly, unlike her real nose, and that it would perhaps make him forget how her nose actually looked. But, in fact, he had little time for such personal thoughts, for there were soon distractions enough to keep him from worrying about how he might remember his wife's nose.

The first of which was the noise and clamor of the crew. Having taken his berth at the far end of the officer's partitioned spaces, he was immediately subjected to the raucous and profane substantiality of men who enjoyed riotous living, gaming and gambling, singing, drinking and carousing, activities in which most had indulged themselves ashore and meant to continue aboard ship as much as was possible. Of course, each and every man was allotted his fair ration of rum, mixed with water and limited in amount at any one time to keep a man from becoming overly intoxicated, and the gambling was of little concern to Kinkaid, for a man had every right to pass his free time as he wished and if he wished to try to take the money of his peers and give them a chance to take his in turn, well, good luck to him was how he thought of it, as long as the activity was kept from his sight and did not cause fights. But the noise. It was the loud and boisterous behavior of blustery men that bothered him and disturbed his peace that first night at sea. At first he tried to ignore it, recalling how in his midshipman days he had been tossed into the very midst of loud and raucous young men and how he had soon learned to sleep through anything, but now the more he tried to ignore it, the more it bothered him, certainly a sharp contrast to married bliss.

One man kept telling jokes, one joke after another, some the men laughed at, some the men did not laugh at, but the joke teller himself, Able Seaman Sweeny, had the habit of laughing at every one of his own jokes, a cackling, ridiculous laugh. Kinkaid lay there, listening to the mad laughter, thinking it would soon cease, but of course as soon as he thought the man must have surely told his last joke, the lunatic would begin anew, the gist of which could not be heard, only the inevitable and remorselessly insane laughter at the end, until finally Kinkaid yanked back the curtain of his cubicle and shouted, "Sentry!"

A young and wide-eyed marine stepped up, gave a crisp salute and said, "Private Steven Miles reporting, Captain."

"Have Boatswain O'Toole report to me immediately."

"Right away, Captain."

O'Toole soon arrived, bleary-eyed and yawning, evidence that he had been sound asleep. Noisy men made no impression upon the old man, apparently, or he'd found a quiet corner somewhere in the forecastle.

Holding the rough curtain aside, Kinkaid said, "O'Toole, can you do anything to keep those men quiet?"

"I'll see to it right away, Captain." Whereupon he strode into the midst of the crowded 'tween decks and bellowed, "Silence!"

Every man had stopped whatever he had been doing, the man telling jokes, the men laughing at his jokes, the men against the starboard bulkhead throwing dice, a few men reading by candlelight, a few more roused out of their much-needed and much-earned sleep, all now gave the Boatswain their undivided attention.

"From henceforth, no man will make any unnecessary noise anywheres about this ship, especially in the presence of officers," he announced loudly, and giving Sweeney a scowling look, added, "or by God you'll have a taste of the cat for breakfast."

Silence.

"Do I make myself clear?" he said more quietly.

"Yes, Mr. O'Toole," came a few timid voices.

O'Toole returned to Kinkaid's curtained doorway, informing him, "They should be mild as kittens now, Captain."

Other than a few murmurs, O'Toole was as good as his word, for the deck became almost inordinately quiet and a moment later Kinkaid was fast asleep.

III
Of Shipmates, Old and New

It was a clear and chilly November morning, with a stiff and steady breeze out of the northwest. A long line of clouds was leaving by the southeast, having passed during the night, and the ship was on a course of north by east, heading toward the rising sun only a few degrees above the horizon.

Kinkaid stood on the quarterdeck, watching as the crew began to turn out on the deck forward and form into their respective divisions. He had his collar turned up against the wind and was swinging his arms to aid the circulation, his body still stiff and achy from the hard chaff mattress and the cold air that had crept in under his blankets during the night. He had not slept soundly and had even come up on deck sometime during the midwatch, feeling that something was not quite right about the way the ship was pitching on the moderate sea. Going forward he soon determined that she was overly heavy at the bow, a fact that dwelt on his mind for the rest of the night. They were probably losing at least a knot of speed and for this reason he was somewhat perturbed with his master's mate, Mr. Grimes, for not seeming to notice. It was not so much because the ship had been incorrectly trimmed, after all, from the dock she looked as balanced as she could be, but every ship had her individual idiosyncrasies under weigh and with an expanded and untried sail plan it was now evident that her taller masts and greater spread of canvas was forcing her bow down from the added pressure. Some men could tell blindfolded if a ship were handling her best while others would never gain the feel for it. Mr. Grimes, it seemed, fell into the latter category.

Mr. Simpson had become seasick soon after the ship made the open Atlantic on the evening before and now he was out on the deck amidships, attempting to gain some control over his ailment by coming out into the fresh air, having learned through experience that remaining below would only prolong his bout of illness.

Mr. Weatherby too, was on the quarterdeck, having the four-to-eight watch, and was also looking a bit pale. He noticed Mr. Simpson slouching pitifully at the rail, a line of drool hanging from his mouth, but then turned away, afraid the sight would trigger an unwelcome response from his own queasy stomach. He put on a weak smile and looking up at the billowing sails, bravely offered, "Good to be at sea again, sir. Away from the odors and filth of the city."

Kinkaid, recognizing that Weatherby was struggling with his nausea, took a deep breath of the cold and bracing wind and gave back, "Nothing as clean and refreshing as good sea air, Mr. Weatherby."

Of course it was good to be at sea again, especially with the knowledge that there were other officers with more seniority still ashore, do doubt jealous of the faith and trust placed in him by the Marine Committee, but more than this was the satisfaction in knowing that he was participating in great events. He also knew that he had Mr. Simpson to thank for this, for Mr. Simpson had insisted upon Kinkaid as the captain who would deliver himself and the news of the great victory at Saratoga to Benjamin Franklin and the French. Yet, he was also responsible for taking him away from Elizabeth. Duty was duty, but to interfere with a man's honeymoon was asking for almost more than a man should have to bear, but now all he could do was accept the fact that he would not see his new bride for some months, the duration of his cruise left in doubt, indeed any secondary mission, other than delivering Mr. Simpson to his destination left in doubt, to be determined by events and circumstances not yet realized. At least he would be busy with his ship and his duties; it would be more difficult for her, he reminded himself, awaiting his return.

The groups of men on deck made way for Mr. Sykes to pass through them in his shuffling, ponderous fashion.

"Morning, Captain." He mumbled, barely perceptibly.

"Good morning, Mr. Sykes," returned Kinkaid. He wondered for a moment if Sykes may still be smarting from their last encounter but refused to consider the matter further, more concerned with the hard pounding of the sea against the bow of the ship, and with each shudder there came a great splash high over the forecastle, wetting the lower half of the flying jib.

"Mr. Weatherby. Your assessment of the handling of the ship, if you please."

Weatherby, without hesitation, offered, "Seems more sluggish than she should in this sea, Captain; pressure on the bow, I'd say."

To which Mr. Sykes said, "Something to which I expect you will attend, Mr. Weatherby, directly following inspection?"

"Of course, Mr. Sykes," gave Weatherby, cheerfully. "I'll arrange a working party and have the trim corrected before they take their breakfast."

Kinkaid could only nod in approval while he was irked that Mr. Sykes had given the order before he had the chance to. There would of course be grumbling among those men chosen for the working party for they would be moving heavy shot and sweating in spite of the cold while their mates enjoyed their breakfast. But any unreadiness, any unwieldiness in the ship, no matter how marginal, could mean the difference in life or death aboard a warship in a sea full of enemies and any captain worthy of his command would take immediate measures to correct such imperfections.

Here came Mr. Grimes from below and Kinkaid found himself wishing that his master's mate could have overheard the brief conversation he had just had with Weatherby concerning the trim of the ship.

"Good morning, Captain," tendered Grimes affably enough, though he was rubbing his temples.

Kinkaid returned a curt nod, and then turned to his First Lieutenant, saying, "Mr. Sykes, you have the quarterdeck."

"Aye, Captain. I have the deck," answered Sykes, stepping forward to emphasize the fact.

"Mr. Hill, you will accompany me, please." Kinkaid had to repress a smile at the invitation, for it was a distinct pleasure to have the quiet and efficient Hill once more aboard. A stickler for perfection, Hill was a man who paid attention to the smallest details, and though he might not be a natural leader, Kinkaid was certain that his manner and way with the men would stand him in good stead as Second Officer and Gunner.

"My pleasure, Captain," answered Hill, tipping his hat in salute to his captain. Then, turning to the rows of men, he called out, "Attention on the deck!"

"Mr. Grimes, you should join us as well." It could only be hoped that the man would absorb what he needed to know as he went along.

If Grimes was aware of any negative feelings about him

by his captain, he did not show it; in fact, he seemed uncomprehending, staring into space. Then he came out of it and answered, "Of course. Thank you, sir."

Kinkaid strode forward, keeping his knees bent to the roll of the pitching deck, steadying himself with the rail as soon as he reached it. It would take a few days to get used to the rhythm once more, get his 'sea legs', but, knowing this, he would be extra careful as he made his way about the decks, especially when in view of the crew, a captain always having to look as if strolling the deck was second nature in spite of having been ashore for some months. He stepped gracefully down to the gun deck, timing his descent with the dip of the ship, and turned to starboard, making his way forward, toward the line of men swaying at their positions at the guns, Mr. Hill and Mr. Grimes following behind him.

"Guns and crews ready for inspection, sir," offered the dark-skinned Mr. Midshipman Briggs with a crisp salute, Hill's assistant and in charge of the powder rooms and passing of shot and charges to the gun deck and, since Hill was to accompany Kinkaid on his inspection of the ship, to present the gun crews for inspection.

Kinkaid passed by the double line of men, a rough and rowdy-looking lot, he found himself thinking, though he had to consider the fact that half of them had come aboard with little more than the clothes on their backs, fresh from civilian life on shore or recently released from jail and the fact that many were unshaven may have added to the undisciplined look, though there were no rules that enforced shaving, many sailors giving up the habit at sea, finding it too time-consuming and a torture besides, what with the lack of hot water available to melt the hard soap to soften the beard. The officers and few able seamen would have to show many of these men the most rudimentary skills, ensuring they knew their stations and duties in quick time.

Hill was inspecting the tubs, quoins, flexible rope sponges and rammers, the tools of the gunnery business, occasionally peering down a gun barrel, looking for signs of rust and pitting, and checking the blocks and heavy cables running through them for signs of wear to make sure they would hold the recoil of a discharged cannon, keeping them from tearing loose and damaging both ship or crewmen in the event. There were five cannons on each side of the main deck, also serving as her gun deck, her firepower quite modest compared to almost any British ship she might encounter, save for the occasional message-running packet, which she resembled, making up in speed and maneuverability what she lacked in offensive firepower. Yet her cannons were nine-pounders, quite large and heavy for a ship of her size. Also mounted were four long-barreled small-bore swivel guns, two mounted on the forecastle, the others aft behind the quarterdeck, the two pounders giving at least some capability to inflict minimal damage while giving chase or being chased, their purpose more to inflict personnel casualties with buckshot or tear up rigging rather than to damage the hull of an enemy ship. Overall, *Active*'s scanty armament made a poor command for a gunnery officer of Mr. Hill's seniority and experience.

Next was the main division of sail handlers where stood the tall and confident Midshipman James Sutherland at stiff attention. Kinkaid had made his way halfway down the line of men when he came to a short and squat seaman with a scar running alongside his cheek and a large bent and crooked nose, obviously having been broken several times, a decidedly ugly man, his features unforgettable.

"I see we are fortunate to have the best ship's carpenter in New England," said Kinkaid appreciatively to the short man, bringing a gap-toothed grin, taking not a whit of ugliness from the man's countenance.

"Thank you, Captain," answered the man, bringing a stubby hand up in salute, openly pleased at having his captain single him out. "And thank you for, uh, rescuing me, as it were, Captain." He brought his stubby hand down with a quick jerk.

"A man with your skill left ashore would be the bigger crime, Grubb."

Grubb had gotten drunk and started a fight with a town constable that resulted in the destruction of much of the Land's End Pub, even breaking a rather large and valuable antique mirror behind the bar. Having no money to pay for the damages meant that Grubb had sentenced to three months in jail, something which Kinkaid would not mention either, nor would he mention paying a portion of his fine to bail him out before his sentence was complete.

"Well, I'm glad you could join us this time, Grubb."

"The pleasure is all mine, Captain," returned the carpenter, still grinning.

The pale and slight Mr. Midshipman Norman Phillips was in charge of the after division. Phillips saluted and then stood aside as Kinkaid stepped before a young Negro gun captain with a serious face who kept his gaze fixed on the distant horizon, mouth set in proud determination, his chest puffed out as if ready to burst. Kinkaid glanced down at the number six gun, where the name "Bertha" was painted in white letters on the black barrel.

"Is Bertha your girl, Smith?"

"That she be, Cap' m, suh," answered Venture Smith, his mouth breaking into a broad grin.

"Is she pretty?" he asked.

"Looks like a bullfrog, Cap'm," admitted Smith, "But she

can sing like an angel, suh."

"I suppose that is fair compensation," said Kinkaid, returning the grin. "And how's that foot, Smith? Are you still the fastest man in Rhode Island?"

"Foot be good, Cap'm, but don't live in Rhode Island no mo'. Fastest man in the Navy now, suh."

"Well, I'm glad you found a new home, Smith, and we'll see what we can do to keep you busy."

"Thank you, Cap'm, suh."

"Mr. Sutherland," said Kinkaid, "your division seems to be short-handed. Where are the others?"

Midshipman Sutherland stepped forward and reported, "Four men reported as sick, sir."

"Anything serious?"

"Dr. Morrow says it's the usual colds, sir."

Kinkaid completed his inspection of the line of men at their guns, taking particular pleasure in the fact that he had recognized two former seamen from his last command, and that he was able to sincerely praise these valuable and skillful men in front of the rest of the crew. Though it was no great feat in recognizing the distinctive features of the men, it was fortuitous that he had remembered both men's names, knowing the incident would go a long way toward impressing those new men who had little idea of the qualities of their captain other than some overblown newspaper accounts that had made of him somewhat of a local hero, hopefully causing them to be grateful of their luck in having such a captain in command of their vessel, and a captain who appreciated, knew and recognized his hands by name. Now he came to the end of the line where Midshipman Briggs said something to Mr. Hill and handed him a length of slow wick.

"Guns are in top condition, Captain," gave Lieutenant Hill

in his quiet way, handling the ten-inch length of slow wick. "Though we might check the magazine for damp, sir. This wick feels wet to the touch and Mr. Briggs tells me it just came up not ten minutes ago." Hill had mentioned his concern over damp powder as early as last week while in port, so the comment seemed of no immediate concern. Besides, the bulkheads of the magazine were lined with felt and when they were made wet they might remain wet for some time, eventually becoming moldy and mildewed, which could explain the damp wick.

"Very good, Mr. Hill. I should expect Mr. Briggs, with your assistance, to see to it forthwith and make some tests of the powder."

"I'll have a report to you this afternoon, Captain," said Hill.

He next turned to the marine contingent, twelve men in green tunics and white crossbelts, standing in two rows behind the foremast with their muskets on their shoulders, fixed bayonets gleaming in the hazy sunshine.

"Marines standing by for inspection, Captain," announced their pugnacious commander, Lieutenant Harlan McDowd. His pockmarked face was never cleanly shaven, but he was known to be a strict disciplinarian and had a reputation as a fierce Indian fighter.

Kinkaid strode along the line of stern-faced men with Lt. McDowd at his side. Reaching the end, he turned to salute him and asked, "I assume your equipment and weapons are satisfactory?"

"Quite, Captain. However, if I might tender a suggestion, sir."

"By all means, Lieutenant."

"With your permission, sir, I'd like to install that extra swivel gun in the tops. Right above the fore mains'l would be the place."

Kinkaid was not aware of any extra swivel gun, but if there were one, it would do little good being 'extra'. "By all means, Lieutenant. And you might see the boatswain and the carpenter for any tools or assistance."

"Right after inspection, sir."

"Very good, Lieutenant…and your men look very smart, very smart indeed."

"For your pleasure, Captain."

Kinkaid then made his way to the forecastle, where awaited his Boatswain, Patrick Michael O'Toole. Standing beside him were sixteen men of the deck crew.

"Five on watch, two sick, Captain," reported the elderly white-haired boatswain. Mr. Grimes still tagged along, offering no comments but appearing to pay attention to the proceedings.

Behind O'Toole was the chain locker, where was housed the heavy hawser connected to the anchor chain, it's strong links connected directly to the anchor, the long coils of the heavy rope warped neatly many times upon itself. Boatswain O'Toole was in charge of the main deck, and all the tools and machinery of a working ship, including the brightwork, handling and care of the ship's boats, painting and caulking, and his hands having the responsibility of holystoning the entire deck from fore to aft each and every morning before the rest of the crew took their breakfast, most of them also forming the bulk of the gun crews, others having sail handling duties, either in the tops or hauling on the sheets from the deck, depending on their age, vigor and skills. O'Toole had also been responsible for the many ingenious and skillful renderings of 'fancywork', twists and turns of painted rope work, decorative as well as protective, festooning the rails, stanchions and brightwork found throughout the ship. Beside O'Toole was the bust of a figure that he was in the process of carving, the face still indistinct but a recognizable rendering of wings on either side. Noting Kinkaid's interest in the figure, almost three feet high, O'Toole explained, "It's to be Mercury, Captain."

"And whose idea might that have been?" asked Kinkaid, suspecting he already knew.

"Mr. Weatherby thought Mercury would help us move more quickly to… wherever we're heading, sir."

"Most appropriate." Kinkaid was not surprised by the choice of the figurehead or by the fact that Weatherby had made the suggestion to the crusty Boatswain, the experienced seadog and the brilliant young officer forming a mutual admiration society. Nor would he have been surprised to hear that the two of them had fairly quickly determined what their mission was and, therefore, where they were heading, though Kinkaid had not even informed his First Officer of their destination. "I can think of no figure more active than Mercury. I shall look forward to its completion."

"A couple more days should do it, sir," beamed O'Toole.

At the end of the line was seaman Cole, the man caught stealing a shaving kit from one of his mates, his eye still bruised and swollen, half closed from the beating he'd endured. Behind him lay the extra swivel gun, a stubby cannon that would spray a deadly hail of pellets like a shotgun.

"Lieutenant McDowd mentioned he'd like to mount that thing in the tops, O'Toole."

"Aye, Captain. Said as much to me when he saw it."

"Well, it's a good idea and I'll expect you and the carpenter's mate to lend any assistance in the endeavor."

"Grubb and I will be glad to be of help, Captain."

Borrowing a cabin lantern from the boatswain's locker, Kinkaid then led the way to the 'tween decks', where the crew called home, the space now almost empty of men, their hammocks, seabags and ditty boxes stowed neatly along the bulkheads, the air somewhat musty from the odors of stale tobacco, breakfast fires and aromas of the food being cooked and various and not-so-pleasant smells of rotting timbers, rotting food and musty, moldy scents coming up from the hold, where sloshed at least a few inches of putrid water and more than a few rats, living heartily on the leftovers and what they could steal from the stores lockers, now brimming full, the ship at the beginning of a long cruise. A long and marred table was nailed to the center, with sundry names and initials carved into its stained surface, in and between overlapping rings where had sat many pitchers of rum and ale.

Kinkaid passed through the crew's sleeping quarters, a deck of cards strewn here, a frayed and much-read book stuffed into a crack there, but mostly looking shipshape; he would not quibble over a few personal items mislaid in the scramble to get to quarters so early and before breakfast. Six hammocks were occupied by awake and quiet, supposedly sick men. Kinkaid ignored them, noting only that one of them was the usually loud joke-telling Sweeney.

Then through the midshipmen's berthing space and their cramped mess area, their own well-used planked table taking up the whole of the floor space, a long bench fastened permanently to either side. Kinkaid looked only briefly into the galley where the bald head cook, Jason Pinkney, mumbled a warning to two others, one busy stirring a pot, another inspecting a basket of eggs, causing them to stand at attention.

"As you were," said Kinkaid.

"Thank you, Captain," answered Pinkney as the pale man beside him continued to stir his pot with exaggerated deliberation.

The other man, short and dark, with black greasy hair and a straggly mustache, began juggling three eggs and whisper-whistling a tune as he did so. He glanced at Kinkaid, a sharp, intense look.

"Who was the juggler?" Kinkaid wanted to know after leaving the galley.

"Nicholas Sterling, sir," Mr. Hill informed him. "An odd one."

"Likes to be called 'Nicky'," offered Mr. Grimes. "An odd one is right. Always consulting a deck of cards. Nice cards, though, beautifully painted, but 'not the kind you can play games with' was the way he described them."

"I thought he was in Mr. Sutherland's division."

"He was, sir," explained Grimes, "but Mr. Sutherland asked if he could place him in the galley. Said he had cooked in some capacity ashore."

"I see," said Kinkaid, letting it go for now. He then made his way along the narrow passageway between the officer's cabins, Mr. Hill and Mr. Grimes still following in single file behind him. As he reached the master's cabin, he heard a loud snoring. Mr. Palfrey seemed to take quite easily to a life aboard ship, thought Kinkaid. Kinkaid decided to poke his head, partly out of curiosity, part shamefully, into Cato's closet-like kitchen between the master's and captain's cabins. His thin, elderly black steward was just now removing a pan of freshly baked rolls from his tiny oven. He looked up, smiled, and said, "Your breakfast is served, sir."

It was only now that Kinkaid realized that although he had mentioned to his steward that up to six officers would join him this morning, he had neglected to inform the man that his breakfast, indeed breakfast for the entire ship, would be delayed because of his inspection. Mr. Africanus took immense pride in his profession, which meant that he took all too seriously the culinary happiness of his captain, in fact, never disappointing. This fact was enough to place Kinkaid in a reciprocal stance insofar as he felt somewhat obligated to not displease, in return, his proud and efficient steward. Kinkaid's logical side knew quite well the unfounded, even ridiculous nature of the relationship, but felt helpless in the face of the man's charm and dignity. The situation was bound to cause disappointment for his steward and Kinkaid was only too aware of his feelings of guilt as he informed him, "I'm sorry, Cato, but breakfast will have to wait as my inspection of the ship is not yet complete." Cato would not be able to serve his buns freshly made from the oven as he had planned; he would have to keep them warm until the men were ready for them and they would be crusty and dry because of the delay. In spite of the fact that Mr. Hill and Mr. Grimes were right behind him, Kinkaid felt obliged to add, "I should say no longer than a quarter hour."

Hill and Grimes now had to press themselves against the narrow passageway so that Kinkaid could take the lead and head them back the way they had come, but now the door to the master's cabin opened and a large head protruded, forcing the cramped party to a halt.

Mr. Palfrey looked up with a silly smile, his unruly hair sticking up in patches as if haphazardly pasted on. "Good morning, Captain."

"Good morning, Mr. Palfrey," gave Kinkaid diplomatically, waiting for the man to move his head back into his cabin.

"Ah, excuse me, sir, but would it be possible to obtain a bite to eat this morning?"

"An officer's breakfast will be served in the wardroom following the completion of my inspection of the ship, Mr. Palfrey," he patiently informed the man. "You are, of course, invited."

Mr. Palfrey grinned, and then said through a yawn, "Why, thank you so much, Captain."

But Kinkaid was already down the passageway, holding back a sigh.

With the lantern held before him, he made a cursory check of the orlop, where the surgeon, Dr. Morrow had his instruments laid out on a small plank table and his four assistants stood at attention behind another plank on two barrels, serving as operating table.

After exchanging polite greetings with the Dr. and his loblolly boys, Kinkaid made his way down a narrow ladder into the lowermost hold. He had to duck his head to enter the dark and low space belowdecks and did not go far before the sour reek from the murmuring bilge determined for him that he'd gone far enough...until he heard something; a low whimpering sound, coming from forward. Holding high the cabin lantern, Kinkaid had to crawl awkwardly on his knees in black muck before finding the source of the plaintive whimpering; a tiny puppy, white with brown and black spots scattered indiscriminately round its plump torso, a beagle, a braided leash about its neck, the end secured to a nail in a rib of the ship. The poor animal's mouth had been tied shut to keep it from barking. Picking up the furry ball and removing its muzzle, Kinkaid was rewarded by having his face happily and fiercely licked.

Backing out of the low, foul space, and turning to find Grimes right behind him, Kinkaid pressed the puppy into the man's hands. Kinkaid waited for the surprised Grimes to turn around and go back up the ladder, but he simply stood there, seemingly dazed and oblivious as the puppy licked his face as happily as he had licked Kinkaid's.

Only now did Kinkaid notice the perspiration on the man's forehead. "Are you ill, Mr. Grimes?"

"Just a headache, Captain," answered Grimes as the puppy squirmed in his arms. "And what about…this, sir?"

"Well, see it's properly cared for…and you might make an effort to find out who brought it aboard."

"Of course, Captain."

The three returned to the open deck, whereupon Kinkaid decided to address the crew who by now had been turned in his direction by their respective division heads. Since the quarterdeck was flush with the rest of the main deck, Kinkaid stood on the after hatch cover, giving him a view of the men standing in their divisions. There, behind all of them, leaning unsteadily against the base of the jib boom, was a very pale Mr. Simpson.

"At ease, men," he began, placing his hands behind his back as the men relaxed and gave him their full attention. "I am pleased by the look of the ship. I am just as pleased to find men aboard who have previously served under my command. Most of you I do not know, but I can tell you that we shall have plenty of time to become acquainted." A few men laughed dutifully at the comment before Kinkaid continued, "I can also tell you that we are on a very special mission; that is, we have the honor of delivering the news of our great victory at Saratoga to the King of France."

The men broke out in a spontaneous cheer at the news. After the hubbub died down, Kinkaid continued in a more serious tone. "Crossing the Atlantic necessarily means that we shall remain in enemy waters for the duration of our passage. Therefore, we will hold training exercises on a daily basis until we have honed our skills to my satisfaction.

Those of you who are new aboard ship will benefit from the instructions of your officers and veteran fellow seamen. Much will be expected of you and I know every man will do his duty to the best of his ability." Determining that his speech had reached its conclusion he felt at once relieved that it was over as well as pleased with his performance. "Secure from inspection, Mr. Sykes."

"Aye, Captain," said Sykes before giving the orders that sent the off-watch below and the bulk of the crew to breakfast. Sykes then spoke briefly to Mr. Grimes and Grimes handed him the puppy.

Mr. Weatherby was already rounding up his working party.

"Mr. Grimes, you might find it beneficial to accompany Mr. Weatherby with his duties this morning." Kinkaid decided that in lieu of asking Mr. Grimes about his assessment of the handling of the ship he would instead provide the man with a working appreciation for what he and Mr. Weatherby were hoping to correct.

Grimes looked about in a bewildered way for a moment before he realized that Weatherby was leading a group of a dozen men below, then blurted out, "Of course, Captain. Right away, sir."

Having taken the proper pause after sending the crew to their breakfast, the sight of those fresh rolls coming out of Cato's oven was too much to resist.

"Mr. Sykes, you have the deck. Keep her on our present course. Call me if there is a change in the wind or weather or if a sail is spotted."

"Aye, Captain," came the dry growl.

"And pass the word that officer's breakfast shall commence immediately in the wardroom. Mr. Simpson and Mr. Palfrey will be our special guests."

"Right away, sir."

"Shall we, Mr. Hill?"

Midshipman Briggs was already waiting when Kinkaid and his Second Officer arrived and entered the tiny wardroom. Then the dark-haired and muscular Mr. Rosetti; behind him, Mr. Palfrey, stooping low, his hair brushing the overhead.

Kinkaid greeted them, "Please come in, sit down, gentlemen. No formalities, please."

"Most gracious of you, Captain," said Rosetti, taking his place.

"Mr. Simpson regrets to inform you that he is not at the moment disposed to partake of your kind invitation, Captain," said Mr. Palfrey as he sat down, leaving a space between himself and Mr. Rosetti.

"Ah, that is unfortunate," replied Kinkaid, suspecting as much.

"Mr. Simpson tells me you have a French chef," intoned Mr. Palfrey with a sniff.

"Yes, Cato does wonders with ship's food."

Cato stepped into the cabin just then, a pot of coffee in one hand, a basket of rolls in the other. He wore an immaculate white shirt and gave a slight bow as he placed the basket on the table next to the butter dish.

"Your Captain was just complementing you, Cato," said Mr. Palfrey.

Cato eyed the man with studious appraisal before saying, "It is my pleasure to serve him."

"Mr. Africanus is not a slave," Kinkaid made clear.

Palfrey gave another sniff. "I see."

Kinkaid reached for a roll and asked, "Cato, you must have heard that we are to pay a visit to your home country."

Cato smiled. "Of course, I am delighted, sir. And since

our bread, cheese and vegetables will be depleted by the time of our arrival, I look forward to surprising you with some very special fare, Captain."

"Well, let's try to keep things simple, shall we? Snails and frog legs are not my idea of dinner," Kinkaid warned him in jest.

Cato raised a finger in the air and remarked, "Only because you have not had the pleasure of their experience, Captain."

"And I'm not certain I have that much courage, Cato," he admitted. "How about you, Mr. Rosetti? Are you an aficionado of unusual cuisine?"

"If calamari is unusual, then I am guilty, Captain."

"Italy?" asked Mr. Palfrey.

"Naples, sir. On the beautiful Mediterranean," answered Rosetti, spreading his arms as if presenting a panorama of that warm and blue sea.

"I was in Naples in '64; a colorful, enchanting port. And the restaurants…most excellent," noted the lanky Palfrey, handing the butter tray to Mr. Hill.

"Mama Mia!" exclaimed Rosetti, recalling his home and happy to know that another remembered her as well. "The food, the wine, the clear skies and calm blue sea…"

"Mostly calm," observed Palfrey. "But when she's not…"

"Ah, how true," agreed Rosetti. "The Mediterranean; she's like a woman. When she's a' happy, she will feeda you and lova you like only an Italian woman can, but when she's a angry, you better watch out!" he explained, slipping into a strong accent and shaking his finger, bringing lighthearted laughter from around the table.

"An apt analogy, Mr. Rosetti," observed Mr. Palfrey. "What about you, Captain? Have you sailed the Mediterranean?"

"I've not had the pleasure," Kinkaid admitted. "Mr. Hill has, however," he added, hoping to bring his taciturn colleague into the conversation.

Hill buttered a crusty roll as he answered, "An overgrown lake, actually. No tides to speak of."

Hill was wont to stick to the practical of any subject and Kinkaid, knowing he took little pleasure from culinary delights, could not resist asking him, "But what about the food, Mr. Hill? Surely you must have sampled the Mediterranean fare."

Hill turned slightly toward his captain, his scarred face adding gravity to his words. "Can't say as I recall, sir; remained aboard most of the time. But I'd rather face a broadside than eat a slimy snail."

There came a knock at the door. It was the tall, redheaded Midshipman Sutherland. "Good morning, Captain," he said as he ducked through the doorway.

The frail Mr. Midshipman Phillips followed behind, nodding shyly and mumbling, "S-Sorry we're late, Captain." The young Phillips had torn a stocking on the ladder and had been offered a new pair by Mr. Sutherland and was the reason the two were late in arriving at the captain's breakfast.

"Please be seated, gentlemen." said Kinkaid congenially, ignoring the fact that they were late.

Sutherland took the seat at the end of the table opposite Kinkaid; looking around him all the while, more with curiosity than awe, appearing to enjoy the cramped social event, open for anything.

Phillips had to take the only place available, uncomfortably wedged between Mr. Rosetti and Mr. Palfrey. He kept his eyes down, his hands folded in his lap.

"So, from where do you hail, Mr. Phillips?" asked

Kinkaid in an effort to ease the lad's apparent anxiety. "And please don't neglect the rolls or my steward shall be disappointed."

Phillips glanced up and answered, "P-Portland, sir." He deftly lifted a roll from the basket and set it upon his plate.

"You must know something of ships, then," guessed Kinkaid.

"F-Father is a whaler, Captain," gave Phillips quietly, appearing much too gentle to take easily to the rigors of shipboard life. Had he joined the Navy more to please his father; perhaps to prove himself, wondered Kinkaid? And was the stuttering speech an ingrained habit or was the boy simply anxious in the presence of his superiors?

"Did you enjoy chasing whales, Mr. Phillips?" asked Mr. Briggs.

Before Phillips could answer, Mr. Palfrey stated, "I've heard it's a hard and dangerous life, but quite lucrative."

"It is h-hard and dangerous, sir," he admitted earnestly, looking up and squirming slightly. "B-But honorable."

"I should say so," answered Palfrey defensively. "All hard and honest work is honorable."

"Some butter, Mr. Phillips?" offered Hill.

Phillips took the dish and diligently smeared some of the soft butter over his roll.

Mr. Sutherland had already finished one and was reaching for another.

"And your home, Mr. Sutherland?"

"Boston, Captain."

"I understand your father is a newspaperman."

"Yes, sir. He thought it would do me good to know about real work," answered Sutherland gaily.

"I was not aware that there was any other kind," observed Mr. Palfrey provocatively, bringing silence to the table.

"You may assure your father, Mr. Sutherland, that we shall keep you quite busy," Kinkaid told him.

"Most honored, Captain."

"And what is your reason for joining our ship and company, Mr. Sutherland?"

"Well, there's less chance of me getting into trouble out here, for one thing."

"Are you inclined to cause trouble, Mr. Sutherland?" Kinkaid asked him with a sly smile.

"Oh, no Captain," he insisted, then, catching Kinkaid's jest, grinned and admitted, "Well, aside from a few pranks."

"Speaking of trouble, Mr. Sutherland," said Kinkaid more seriously, "I understand you had a man in your division transferred to the galley."

Mr. Sutherland nodded, answering, "Seaman Nicholas Sterling, sir."

Detecting that Sutherland seemed reluctant to discuss the matter further, Kinkaid felt obliged to ask directly, "And why did you find it necessary to remove Seaman Sterling from your division?"

Sutherland hesitated, and then answered, "The man seemed bored with gunnery exercises, sir, and…well, to be honest, the other men…don't like him, sir."

"H-Harris likes him," interjected Mr. Phillips.

"That is true," agreed Sutherland. "Seaman Harris does seem to take to Sterling, both odd ducks."

"Is there any particular reason why the other men, excluding Harris, don't like him?"

"Well, he's generally…different…and, well, they call him a witch…because he tells fortunes with that deck of cards he carries."

"Sounds like the Tarot," guessed Weatherby, having read about such things in a book about the occult.

"And what makes Harris an odd duck?" Kinkaid wanted to know.

"He c-calls himself a poet, sir," offered Phillips.

"A sensitive poet, at that," said Sutherland.

"What other kind are there?" said Hill.

Kinkaid had heard men about the deck refer to Sterling as "Crazy Nicky", and he wanted to know why the other men didn't like the man other than the fact that he played with a strange deck of cards and claimed a poet for a friend, but could see that his questioning was making Mr. Sutherland uncomfortable. As he was deciding whether the answer to his questions were more important than Mr. Sutherland's comfort, Mr. Palfrey spoke.

"I take it university life began to bore *you*, Mr. Sutherland," guessed Mr. Palfrey with some cynicism.

"At least there are no dusty books or classrooms out here, sir," answered Sutherland testily.

"So you have joined us for a different sort of education, Mr. Sutherland," observed Kinkaid, coming to Sutherland's defense, feeling some responsibility for the unsettling turn of conversation.

"Absolutely, Captain."

"Well, I believe a man should go for what he wants," proclaimed Mr. Palfrey.

Mr. Phillips raised his head and surprised everyone by saying, "Experience is the b-best teacher…my father always says, sir." Phillips seemed to have surprised himself by his statement for he glanced nervously at the faces looking back at him.

"Quite right, Mr. Phillips," gave Kinkaid, "and I hope both of your experiences aboard *Active* profit your education."

"Thank you, sir," intoned Sutherland while Phillips

merely nodded, eyes darting back and forth and then down again.

Cato brought in a platter of potatoes, onions and eggs, the steaming mixture surrounded by crisp slabs of bacon, which he set in the center of the table. As the men took their share, Cato went around filling their mugs with coffee and Phillips noticeably sniffed the air as Cato poured his cup.

"Are you fond of coffee, Mr. Phillips?" asked Mr. Palfrey.

"S-sometimes…on my father's ship," said Phillips, then added, "I like it very m-much, sir."

"Compared with the affairs of men and nations, I find coffee to be one of life's reliable pleasures," said Mr. Palfrey, taking a sip from his mug, "especially if it is made correctly…as this coffee most certainly is."

"You are too kind, sir," acknowledged Cato as he filled Mr. Rosetti's mug.

Mr. Palfrey seemed to leap from rudeness to pompous cordiality and back again. Of course changeability was no crime, Kinkaid reminded himself as forks tinkled against plates, but as a landsman coming aboard a strange and tiny ship he seemed quite adaptable.

"I hope you have found your accommodations acceptable, Mr. Palfrey?" asked Kinkaid.

"I shouldn't complain, Captain."

"Well, you seem to take most agreeably to the seafaring life."

Mr. Palfrey smiled and provided, "I've spent some time on ships, Captain."

"In what capacity, sir?"

"Not as an officer, and certainly not as crew either…though there is no shame in that."

"Of course not." Kinkaid waited for Mr. Palfrey to chew his bacon, but instead of adding clarity to his comment Mr.

Palfrey asked Sutherland to pass the tray of rolls, now cold and hard.

"So you took a cruise or two, then," ventured Kinkaid.

Mr. Palfrey forced a smile. "I find ships a handy way to get from here to there; my line of work provides no end to travels."

"And what would your line of work be?" asked Kinkaid, aware that Mr. Palfrey's affability might be reaching its limits.

Palfrey held his head high and looked down his long nose directly at Kinkaid, his gray eyes cold as ice. "I began as a lawyer. But now my main line of endeavor is in arms procurement, protection my second."

"Protection?"

"I protect people from those who would wish to harm them. I am an expert marksman," he said proudly. "And I'm not bad with a rapier or foil."

"I see," was all Kinkaid could manage, not wishing to appear rude by further grilling the man. Yet, there was much more that Kinkaid wanted to ask of Mr. Palfrey. Where and with who had he traded in arms? What seas had he traveled upon, where might "here to there" have been? Had he been hired to protect Mr. Simpson? And how often and against who had he used his skills with pistol or rapier, dueling weapons all? Weatherby gave his captain a quick raise of eyebrows.

But Mr. Palfrey had not finished, and asked, "In order to keep my skills sharp, I would ask a favor of you, Captain; to allow me to practice my shooting somewhere on the deck, where it would be safe, of course."

Kinkaid hesitated. "I suppose, if you must."

"I assure you, Captain, it is more than a question of diversion or recreation. As you must know, martial skills are quickly eroded if not constantly honed."

"Of course, sir, practice makes perfect. Very well, then, I see no reason why not. The bow would be the best place, as long as the proper safety precautions are taken."

"Thank you, and I would welcome any who might care to join me. Captain?"

"Uh, no thank you, sir," answered Kinkaid instinctively. "Unfortunately, I have little time for such activities."

"Of course, Captain. You have a ship to run."

"I would be pleased to join you, Mr. Palfrey," said Weatherby. "If my captain has no objections."

"By all means, Mr. Weatherby."

The breakfast proceeded from that point somewhat subdued, almost with a chill in the air, Kinkaid's guests wary of deviating from safe topics such as the food or the weather.

Mr. Simpson never did make it to that breakfast, preferring to remain out on deck where the cold spray stung his face as he stood facing the rolling sea, determined to keep his eyes on the horizon, fighting to keep his stomach on an even keel, his nose still running. He had learned that remaining below would not help to abate his attacks of seasickness, that the fresh air of the open deck and the passing of time was the best remedy. Though his stomach was empty, food was the farthest thing from his mind, and while he was inordinately thirsty, drinking water only had the result of bringing on another bout of nausea and so he would take only small sips at a time, accepting his thirst as the price one must pay to feel at least half alive.

After breakfast Kinkaid brought his log up to date and then paid a visit to the hold where Mr. Weatherby was still supervising the working party as they moved almost a ton of shot farther aft. It seemed the right weight to try at first. But

Mr. Grimes was not there and Kinkaid had hoped he might learn something about the way a ship handled.

"Where is Mr. Grimes?" he asked.

"He didn't seem to be quite here, Captain," answered Weatherby. "I sent him to sick call."

"Yes, very well, Mr. Weatherby." He would not begrudge a sick man proper attention.

But Mr. Sykes was there, unable to pass up a chance to tell other men to work harder, no doubt, surmised Kinkaid, and the probable reason that he had been missed at breakfast. And under his coat was the little puppy, only its tiny head poking out from his collar, its bright eyes looking curiously about, relaxed and happy.

Mr. Palfrey was there as well, talking with Weatherby. Questioning Weatherby about it later, the young Lieutenant merely informed him that Mr. Palfrey seemed interested in many facets of the ships workings and that Weatherby was glad to answer his questions, "…if there are no objections, Captain."

"Why, no, of course not," Kinkaid had to answer again. After all, why should he harbor any objections to Mr. Weatherby answering the questions of a curious passenger? Yet Kinkaid could not help but feel somewhat uneasy, and he did not know exactly why. Of one thing he *was* certain; it had to do with Mr. Palfrey.

IV
Strange Men, Strange Sails

The shifting of ballast did much to improve the ship's seaworthiness and now *Active* was bounding over the rollers with a delightful swagger. It seemed that her new sail plan suited her admirably. The marines, with the carpenter's help, had the extra swivel gun mounted at the fore crosstree, just above the mainsail spar, and afterwards the marine commander kept his men busy with weapons exercises and running up and down the ratlines to man the newly-installed scatter cannon. And in spite of his misgivings about the quality of his crew and the fact that more than a few seemed to be unavailable for duty due to fevers and intestinal disorders, Kinkaid had to be pleased with their overall progress as they jumped to the various drills and sail evolutions he called at all hours of the night and day, endlessly variable and challenging enough to make the crew gripe and complain but not enough to inordinately fatigue. Any number of unexpected emergencies might ensue and a well-drilled and disciplined crew would cope far better than one untried. It was also a comfort to know that if they were going to meet British warships, they would have likely met them in the first few days, the enemy watch along the shore fairly well coordinated; now the open sea would provide the best hiding place in the world.

Mr. Palfrey made good on his request to take target practice with his assortment of expensive pistols, and he had Grubb the carpenter make half a dozen wooden placards to attach his paper targets to, and almost every day, after the noon meal, the sound of pistol shots could be heard from the quarterdeck. It was annoying, at best, but became almost maddening when he noticed Mr. Weatherby and Mr. Phillips joining Mr. Palfrey in the pugilistic activities, first shooting for half an hour, then another hour of swordsmanship. Yet Kinkaid had given permission and it would appear petty to change his mind. Besides, he told himself, it would only add to his officers' confidence and competence by gaining proficiency in arms.

It was a cloudy morning. The fifth day at sea. Lieutenant Weatherby and Midshipman Phillips had the watch. Kinkaid stood on the windward side, just behind the mast. The crew was just finishing their breakfast and a few hands were skylarking on the forecastle, talking and joking, out of the wind on the leeward side. Kinkaid appeared disinterested in their shenanigans by gazing up at the sails or taking in the state of the weather or the sea.

"C'mon, Osborne. Let's see it again," he heard John Cole say.

Thus cajoled, the lanky Seaman Osborne rolled up his sleeve to reveal a tattoo on his bicep, which he commenced to flex. Kinkaid could not see the work of art under scrutiny from where he stood, but he did hear the delightful laughter of the audience gathered there and Venture Smith blurt out, "Dat girl sho' can dance!"

"Aye, she can dance with me any time!" shouted Cole.

"Can I borrow her, Ozzie? Just for tonight?" asked the round faced and pudgy Knox, whereupon the three began to scuffle before realizing they were under the scrutiny of their captain. They quickly composed themselves, but not without a bit of nervous laughter.

The incident might have passed, except that Mr. Sykes was just now coming up on deck, and only now did it occur to Kinkaid that Mr. Sykes had failed to make his report from the morning before, and that he was attempting to avoid him now by pretending to be interested in the play scuffling.

Sykes stopped beside the men and gave his attention to a coil of halyard on the deck that the men had accidentally disturbed from its perfectly symmetrical snakelike coil, and, incapable of passing up a chance to indulge in his favorite pastime of berating sailors, he asked, "Is this how you coil a line, Osborne?"

The three sailors merely stood there, awaiting the inevitable. Kinkaid stepped behind the main mast to keep himself hidden, not wishing to influence the outcome of the scene.

"And you men rate Seaman status?" Sykes then began kicking furiously at the coiled line while holding the lapels of his coat together, as if clutching something dear and valuable to his chest. Having turned the coiled line into a tangled heap, he pointed to it and said, "Would you care to show me how to coil a line, Osborne?"

Osborne, a head taller than Mr. Sykes, immediately acquiesced to the command by bending to the task.

Sykes stood over Osborne and watched only distractedly until the line was perfectly recoiled, seemingly more interested in the object under his coat.

"That's better," announced Sykes at last. "Now I won't have to worry about tripping and falling overboard, will I, Osborne?"

"No, Mr. Sykes."

It wasn't until Sykes turned in his direction that Kinkaid could see that the object that Mr. Sykes clutched so protectively to his chest was the puppy, only it's tiny spotted head showing between the lapels of his big ragged coat, bobbing happily up and down as Sykes approached the ship's boat, its little ears flopping cutely as it looked curiously about the deck.

Sykes noticed Kinkaid standing behind the mast and then made an abrupt turn across the deck toward the ships boat, where four cages of chickens and a half-dozen pigs were corralled, where he happened upon Pinkney, the ship's cook, and his helper, Nicky Sterling. Sterling had a struggling pig trapped between his legs and the two were engaged in a shouting match.

"That's no way to kill it!" yelled Sterling over the screams of the terrified pig. "Just hit it over the head with a hammer!"

Pinkney stood over a cooking pot, with a cleaver in one hand and a stout line in the other and yelled, "Dammit, man, I told you how I wanted to do it! Now here, tie this line about his back legs!"

"How would you like me to string YOU up? Cut YOUR throat?" threatened Sterling.

"You contrary sonofabitch," returned Pinkney, his face turning red. "Get out of my way! I'll do it myself!"

"Oh no, you won't!" shouted Sterling as he lifted the squirming pig in his arms and staggered toward the rail with it.

Other seamen about the deck had been attracted by the shouting and commotion and had formed a circle around the two. The poet, Harris, was one of them, Sterling's only professed friend, a frail-looking man, his long curly hair blowing out from beneath a red knit cap.

"What in God's name is going on here?" growled Mr. Sykes.

"Pinky likes to see them suffer," explained Sterling breathlessly.

"Yeah," added Harris. "Likes to hear 'em scream, don't ya, Pinky?"

"You crazy bastards," said Pinkney. "I need to catch the blood for sausage, Mr. Sykes," he explained.

"Oh, no you don't," Sterling kept on. "You're not gonna get this one. Not if I can help it"

"A plague on you, Sterling," cursed Pinkney.

"Fighting over how to kill a pig," said Sykes, baffled, the sound of the yipping puppy adding to the din. "I never heard of such a thing."

"Let me do it, Mr. Sykes," insisted Sterling. "I'll do it quick, and then Pinky can hang it up and bleed it."

"Pinkney is in charge of the galley," Sykes reminded him, "which means he'll decide how it's done."

"I'll throw him over the side before I hand this animal over to him!" threatened Sterling as he lifted the squealing pig over the rail.

"Very well," said Pinkney, giving in. "Let him do it his way, but I'll no longer have this man in my galley!"

"You heard what he said, Sterling," gave Sykes. "Kill the damned pig and then I'm turning you over to Boatswain O'Toole; he knows how to keep a troublemaker like you busy...and mark my words, if you keep to your stubborn ways, I'm going to enjoy seeing you flogged within an inch of your life before you leave this ship. Damned fool," said an angry Sykes as he slouched along the deck, heading toward the after hatch, the agitated puppy trying to squirm loose from under his coat.

Young Mr. Phillips had witnessed the incident and made

the comment to Weatherby, "F-father says that all cooks tend toward lunacy."

To which Weatherby asked, "Now, upon what facts had your father made this determination?"

"Oh, he said it was the p-price they pay for so much attention on the culinary arts...and women's work, in general."

Chief O'Toole could not help but overhear the conversation and offered, "If I might make a suggestion, good sirs. I've always found it prudent policy to make friends with cooks, even those who might appear daft, in case you need to dry your socks or mittens or want to light your pipe. And never to argue with one, or you'd never be able to eat without wondering if he'd spit in your food, or worse."

Kinkaid chuckled at the banter, but could not resist calling out to Mr. Sykes, "Mr. Sykes, I'll have a word with you, if you please!"

Mr. Sykes took two more steps before he decided to halt and turn. "Of course, Captain," he answered.

Kinkaid approached him so as not to have their words heard by the quarterdeck watch. "It has come to my attention that you may have forgotten to apprise me of your report of yesterday's morning inspection."

"Aye, Captain," agreed Sykes, "You were in conference with Mr. Weatherby, Captain."

"Then you should have seen me directly afterward," said Kinkaid, aware that he was thoroughly enjoying finding fault with the disheveled perfectionist.

"An oversight that won't happen again, Captain," said Sykes, appearing eager to be dismissed.

"Your report, Mr. Sykes," said Kinkaid impatiently, but as Sykes gave his report, Kinkaid found himself distracted by the activity in the waist.

Sterling asked his friend, Harris, to hold the pig, but Harris refused, so he had Venture Smith to hold onto the pig so that its head was pressed flat upon the deck. Sterling then took up a marlinspike, placed it carefully between the pig's eyes and then slammed it hard with a hammer, driving the spike through the pig's skull, killing it instantly. Harris had turned away from the sight and noticeably shuddered at the sound of the hammer striking. Then Sterling tossed the dead animal at Pinckney's feet. "There. You can bleed it now," he said and walked off.

A most unusual man, thought Kinkaid, and wishing he had not witnessed the gruesome business.

Returning his attention to Mr. Sykes as he finished his report, Kinkaid reminded him, "I suppose you are aware that I asked Mr. Grimes to find out who brought that…stowaway aboard."

"Uh, yes, Captain, so he said," admitted Sykes. "He also told me he had been unable to ascertain the facts of the matter, so I relieved him of the animal, and said I would make the proper inquiries."

"So you have taken the matter into your own hands."

"That's right, Captain. I've been making inquiries, sir."

"And have you been able to ascertain who the animal might belong to?"

"Couldn't guess about something like that, sir. And it seems no matter how much I threaten, not a man jack of 'em has the courage to come forward to claim 'im. But the investigation continues, Captain, and I intend to get to the bottom of this matter if it's the last thing I do, sir," Sykes assured him, clutching protectively at the furry bundle.

"So there *is* a continuing investigation?" asked Kinkaid, playing the play out.

"Why, of course, sir. Bringing contraband aboard ship is a serious breach of misconduct and the man responsible should be severely punished...that is, if we ever find him, Captain."

A morning of surprises, thought Kinkaid. First Sterling with his preferred method of killing pigs, and now Mr. Sykes. Having made little effort to appease his captain before, Mr. Sykes now appeared to be trying too hard, which gave him away; Mr. Sykes had no intention of finding out who brought the dog aboard; to do so would mean relinquishing it to its owner.

"Which seems in the meantime to leave you its master," observed Kinkaid, softened to the gruff, outspoken man.

"Aye, t'would seem so, Captain," answered Sykes, rubbing the puppy's head and not at all distressed by the prospect.

"What name have you given him?" asked Kinkaid, spontaneously reaching up and touching the cold nose and having his fingers licked in return.

"Why, Jonah, sir."

"Caught in the belly of the whale."

"Thought it appropriate, sir."

"Quite, Mr. Sykes," answered Kinkaid, still stroking the puppy's soft ears. When he realized that Mr. Weatherby and Mr. Phillips were watching him pet the animal he stood back and said, "Carry on, Mr. Sykes."

"Aye, Captain."

"Mr. Weatherby, I'll be taking my breakfast with Mr. Simpson this morning. He seems to think he can teach me French before our arrival. You have the deck."

"*Bon appetite, mon Capitaine*," answered Weatherby with a sly mile.

Kinkaid had finished his breakfast a half hour later, but at

Mr. Simpson's insistence still struggled with his French lesson when he was saved by the shout from the lookout, "Sail ho, just off the larboard quarter!"

Weatherby was already standing on the stern rail with his telescope braced against the mizzen backstays, scanning the horizon. There it was, a blur of faded topsails. "Lookout, can you tell her course?" hollered Weatherby.

"Looks to be following, sir!" came the ready reply from the ungainly Seaman Knox, the man stooping low to see under the main course.

"Mr. Phillips, take this telescope up the main…as high as you deem necessary." Weatherby was careful not to turn the order into a challenge for the shy and diffident Phillips, but added the reminder, "A full report for the Captain, mind you!"

"Aye aye, Mr. Weatherby," answered Phillips as he looped the strap over his neck and headed for the main shrouds. Then he bounded up the ratlines like a monkey, and climbed straight up, all the way up to the main spar, then stood upon it and leaned back against the topgallant sail as if with no care in the world, to the surprise of all. He even returned Boatswain O'Toole's jaunty wave before swinging the heavy telescope up to his eye and with two hands trained it in the direction of the ship. A moment later he called out, "Small bark, two points off the starboard quarter, ten miles distance, under easy sail! Can't make out any colors as yet, but she's following, all right!"

Kinkaid heard the shouting from above as he reached the quarterdeck. Weatherby pointed aft and Kinkaid brought his own telescope up and immediately confirmed the lookout's report. She seemed to be tailing *Active* at a discreet distance, under easy sail.

Now sang out Phillips from on high, "Sun reflecting from

her deck! Could be guns, Captain!"

Here was Mr. Grimes, making his appearance on the quarterdeck. "Shall I call out the hands, sir?" he asked.

Kinkaid thought to ask Mr. Grimes where he had been keeping himself, for he had made it quite clear that he expected the man to be on the quarterdeck while he took his breakfast, but instead he ignored him, instead asking, "Mr. Weatherby, who is the lookout?" Who would guess about guns at such a distance?

"Why, that's Phillips, sir," answered Weatherby.

Surprised, Kinkaid craned his neck to see for himself. "Well, so it is." And nary a stutter.

Kinkaid once again found the faded white sails through the telescope. She could have been a merchant vessel that had taken notice of *Active* leaving port and had decided to join her for the sake of safety. Or just as likely, she may be an enemy vessel, bristling with guns, her crew out for blood. But if so, why didn't she put on all sail and approach nearer…at least find out for certain what ship she was following…unless she already knew. At first he was of a mind to increase canvas, but then, judging her to be ten miles distant, decided he would not allow her to disturb his breakfast. "Keep a close eye on her, Weatherby; try to identify exactly what she might be. Call me if she looks to be closing."

"Aye aye, sir."

A simple rebuke to Mr. Grimes might do. "I'll trouble you to remain on deck while I finish my breakfast, Mr. Grimes."

"Of course, sir."

Kinkaid returned to the captain's cabin where Simpson had taken the liberty of pouring him a fresh cup of coffee. Simpson must have heard the shout from the mizzen top, for he asked, "A ship?"

Kinkaid offered the noncommittal, "Not much of one."

But Simpson was not so easily put off. "Not important?"

"Too far off to tell."

"Shall we continue with our French lesson?"

"Not now." .

After a moment, Simpson lent the neutral observation, "No need to let those eggs go to waste."

"No," answered Kinkaid, then commenced to pick at his eggs self-consciously.

Mr. Simpson, in sympathy, looked away and chewed on his bacon for a while before his curiosity got the better of him. "British?"

"Can't tell as yet."

"Is she following?"

"Yes, under reduced sail."

Finally, the inevitable, "What are you going to do?"

"Nothing, for now," said Kinkaid, appearing unconcerned.

"They know," surmised Simpson gravely.

"Perhaps," agreed Kinkaid. Of course the British might be on to them, to their mission of bringing news to the French, important news that could turn the tide of the war, yet, "She may simply be a merchant, looking for an escort." A foolish conjecture, and Kinkaid knew it.

"Can we lose her?" asked Simpson, unconvinced.

Kinkaid hated the conversation, yet it was Simpson's mission and he had every right to be concerned. It was imperative that he be delivered to France. No other outcome was acceptable.

"We'll see."

Kinkaid was acutely aware of the minutes ticking by, of the fact that the strange ship was following them as Simpson thoughtfully sipped his coffee. He wanted more than anything to return to the quarterdeck but he forced himself to finish his cold eggs and toast, then finish his coffee, slowly, bearing Mr. Simpson's silent presence. Finally, he dabbed his mouth with the napkin that Cato always provided and rose from his chair.

"Would you care to join me on deck, Mr. Simpson?"

Kinkaid opened the door to find Mr. Palfrey standing right outside.

"Do excuse me, Captain," he said. "Am I too late for breakfast?"

Annoyed, Kinkaid replied, "I'm sure Cato will accommodate you, Mr. Palfrey," before striding down the corridor to the ladder, Mr. Simpson following behind.

Mr. Sykes met Kinkaid at the top of the ladder and quickly gave his morning report, his eyes bloodshot and sleepy, and now he had Mr. Sykes and Mr. Simpson following him to the quarterdeck where Mr. Weatherby had the watch. Boatswain O'Toole stood beside the binnacle, intent on the distant ship.

"She's maintaining her distance, Captain," Weatherby informed him, "still under reduced canvas."

"Very well. Have Phillips come down...I'll have a word with him. Mr. Sykes, call out the hands; we're going to quarters. Full drill, guns loaded and run out, if you please," he said quietly, belying the anxiety he felt.

"Aye, Captain. Pipe the hands to battle stations!"

Weatherby cupped his hands over his mouth and shouted into the mizzen top, "Mr. Phillips, the Captain requests your presence on deck!"

"Aye, sir!" came the return shout from above.

O'Toole was piping the hands out as Phillips suddenly appeared from above, sliding down the mizzen halyard instead of climbing down the shrouds; so graceful that it appeared as if he were floating down like an angel, a feat that only a top hand would attempt. Kinkaid had not expected the impressive stunt from the seemingly timid young man and had to hide his astonishment as the young midshipman stood at attention before him.

"At ease, Mr. Phillips," began Kinkaid as seamen flooded up from below. "You seem quite comfortable aloft."

"S-started main lookout on my f-father's ship, sir," returned the youth, taking off the leather palm protectors.

"I see. But if I may ask…how can you tell that there might be guns on her deck?"

"W-well, sir, a telescope's reflection is usually just a p-pinpoint," said Phillips without hesitation, "but a r-row of reflections like that…well, c-could only be guns on her main deck, Captain."

Kinkaid had to give the boy credit, for under the right conditions, under the right angle to the sun, a row of cannons could very well show their presence to a good eye in the top.

"If you were to take a guess, Mr. Phillips, what would you say she is?"

"L-looks like your standard British p-packet, sir. Small and lightly armed, but fast."

"Seems you learned well under your father."

"F-father is a h-hard man to p-please, sir," said Phillips with a forced smile. The crew was forming into their respective battle stations now.

"You may take your station, Mr. Phillips."

"Aye aye, sir."

"Let's back the tops," Kinkaid ordered. "And have us prepared to tack on my order, Mr. Grimes."

"Aye, Captain," answered Grimes before giving the orders that would slow the ship.

Mr. Palfrey was standing by the mainmast, a thick bacon

sandwich in his hand, chewing a mouthful and looking interestedly at the activity taking place on deck. Kinkaid wanted to ask both Mr. Simpson and Mr. Palfrey to leave the quarterdeck, but then realized that they would only be in the way of the crew if they retreated into the waist and so changed his mind. And he could not, in good conscience, drive them below. They were both honored guests, though dead weight when it came to running the ship.

"You intend to let her come to us, then, Captain?" asked Mr. Simpson.

Kinkaid ignored the question, training his telescope upon her as the readiness reports reached the quarterdeck, "Crew at their stations, pumps are manned, decks sanded, guns loaded and run out…and tops are backed and we are ready to tack, sir!"

"Very good time, Mr. Sykes. Compliments to the crew." And now as he watched the ship, her own tops narrowed from oblong rectangles to squares and then narrowed further until they were unseen. She had immediately backed her tops as well, showing a state of alertness that few merchant vessels would maintain. And if she were indeed a merchant seeking an escort, she should have come up and identified herself.

For some reason, Mr. Grimes had to put his words to the obvious. "Why, she's backed her tops too, sir."

"Bring us about. Larboard tack, close hauled…as close as you can bring her, Mr. Grimes."

"You've a mind to chase her, Captain?" asked Simpson, unconstrained.

"Just a test," said Kinkaid, intent on the ship. The fresh breeze blew in his face from the larboard quarter where the ship was. Therefore, to head straight for her was out of the question, but coming about on a larboard tack would suffice and be immediately construed as a sign of pursuit. Bowlines were already lined up on the starboard side so all that was required was to release the halyards, come about on the new course, and brace the yards on the opposite side.

Active was halfway through her turn when Mr. Grimes observed, "There she goes, sir," as the distant ship mimicked *Active's* maneuver, making her own turn to larboard. "Wants nothin' to do with us, now, Captain."

"So it would seem, Mr. Grimes. Let's keep an eye on the jibs, now. When I say close-hauled, I mean it."

Kinkaid waited until *Active* was running as close to the wind as was possible. Grimes kept an obsessive watch on the fore jib as it alternately luffed and caught the breeze, constantly giving orders to the helmsman, Osborne, who seemed incapable of following them. Grimes was certainly trying to do his best and it didn't help that Mr. Sykes was standing beside him, watching him over his shoulder, as it were. But personal feelings could not be considered at the moment; only the handling of the ship.

"I want the helm relieved, Mr. Sykes."

Nicolas Sterling, yet to be assigned to any permanent action station since his argument with the head cook over the killing of a pig, stood idly in the waist next to his friend, Harris, assigned to Venture Smith's gun crew to swab out the bore. "Sterling, relieve Seaman Osborne at the wheel."

"Aye, sir."

"Let's see if you can keep her close-hauled without luffing," said Kinkaid as Sterling relieved a flustered Osborne at the helm.

"I'll try my best, sir."

The following ship was now the pursued, and the first thing Kinkaid noticed was Seaman Sterling's remarkable ability at the ship's wheel, anticipating every twist and turn of the hull, watching intently for every errant shift of breeze, keeping the sails taut and full of wind, never losing an inch of headway, and never requiring a word of instruction from Mr. Grimes. It was a skill few acquired overnight, yet Nicky Sterling possessed it as an innate trait.

As for the strange ship, only superior speed and weathering could catch her, but Kinkaid was of no mind to continue the pursuit. He had ascertained all that he needed to know. The ship was interested but not interested enough to close with *Active,* at least not alone. If she were the typical British packet, which she appeared to be, she would carry few guns and those of light caliber; four or six-pounders usually.

"Mr. Grimes, bring us back on the same course, northeast by east. Secure from quarters."

As *Active* settled back on her original course the small brig turned as well, quickly finding her position relative to them the same as before. Relieved at the wheel by Osborne, Sterling returned below, but not before exchanging a knowing glance with Harris standing beside 'Bertha," Smith's gun.

Kinkaid said to Mr. Sykes, "I want that man Sterling assigned to the helm whenever we go to quarters."

"As you wish, Captain."

"She seems content to keep us in sight, sir," observed Grimes unnecessarily.

"Can we outrun her?" asked a concerned Mr. Simpson.

"Not today," answered Kinkaid.

"She's no real threat to us by herself," judged Sykes.

Mr. Weatherby provided the crucial information. "She is fast, though, and could alert passing warships to our presence."

Simpson stood at the rail, looking to where the assumed

enemy ship bounded over the Atlantic swells. "Damn her," he said.

"Perhaps tonight," gave Kinkaid with some reassurance. "There's very little moon, and if we've some cloud cover... Until then I suggest you enjoy the scenery, Mr. Simpson. She's a beautifully crafted vessel, and a sight to behold."

"She is at that, Captain," agreed Weatherby. "Why, just look at her."

"Like a racehorse going through her paces," observed Sykes, catching the spirit.

All during that morning the little ship followed, neither gaining nor losing distance, her captain and crew ever vigilant, ever alert to the smallest change of *Active's* course or speed. The afternoon passed in the same fashion, only the clouds increased, leading to a dull and somber end of the day. Except that the crew was noticeably keyed up, curious men taking their turns on deck, craning their necks sternward, unable to ignore or forget the strange ship that dogged them. Finally Kinkaid could stand it no longer, rasping, "Mr. Sykes, can you find nothing for those men to do?" Of course, Mr. Sykes was more than happy to find plenty for the men to do.

The sun was setting astern under dark red-tinged clouds as Kinkaid paced his quarterdeck in solitude, refusing to acknowledge the quarterdeck watch and especially a nervous Mr. Simpson, refusing even to look at the ship, refusing as well to look at any crewman who dared to steal glances her way, acting as if nothing out of the ordinary were occurring. But the fact that a small but fast vessel was following and that there was little if nothing Kinkaid could do about it, played on his nerves. How long had she been following them and how long had they been in ignorance of her, possibly lurking just beneath the horizon, showing herself only now. And why now? She could very well have had lookouts high in her tops and, without setting topsails, could have easily kept herself from view. And now, after assessing *Active's* potential as a sailing vessel, she might have concluded that she was more than a match for *Active*'s sailing qualities. The fact that evening was bringing with it a heavy cloud cover was at least something to take into consideration.

"She's putting out her t'gallants!" came the shout from the evening watch lookout.

It was not surprising that the stranger should want to close the distance with the approach of nightfall.

"We'll put out ours as well, then. In fact, make all sail, Mr. Grimes."

"Aye aye, sir."

The men went to their task with alacrity and purpose, the results lending considerable speed to the ship. Kinkaid could not help but feel a rush of excitement as *Active* heeled and surged forward, the brisk quartering wind driving the ship, the spray from her bow splashing up onto the deck, sending a few sailors on the forecastle out of its range. Kinkaid once more had the ship in the sights of his telescope and watched her as she quickly sent her hands aloft as well.

"Twelve knots, sir!" came the report from the waist.

A smiling Lieutenant Weatherby strode hatless up to the stern rail, his blond locks blowing free in the wind. "At least we'll make her work, Captain!" he shouted over the wind. Simpson was not far behind and took his place beside Weatherby, only looking askance at Weatherby's apparent delight in the situation.

The three men stood there, watching as the ship gained sail, then as she heeled precipitously when her sails caught the breeze, almost touching the water before her hull could get a grip on the sea. Now she was pitching fast and regularly, bounding over the waves, a glorious and impressive sight in spite of the fact that she was probably an enemy vessel, and it soon became apparent that the small ship was closing the distance, their efforts to outrun her for naught.

It was an hour into the first dogwatch that the sky grew suddenly dark. The distant ship had closed to within half a mile astern and maintained that distance while the thin slice of a moon alternately ducked behind low, dark clouds, lending eerie shadows to the sea as the night fell fast. And with it went the breeze. Now *Active* lazed along with all sail set, making all of three knots. There would be no losing her on this night.

Kinkaid pondered calling the crew to quarters, to make a quick turn into her, but deeming she would not be taken by surprise, decided against it. "I'm going below," he announced to the watch, trying to keep the peevishness out of his voice. "Wake me if she closes or if the weather should change."

"Sir… Captain…" It was Mr. Hill knocking on the partition of his closet, holding a cabin lantern.

"What time is it?' His head was heavy with sleep, his eyes were dry and crusty, eyelids stuck together.

"Just past four, sir."

Kinkaid sat up and rubbed the sleepiness out of his eyes. Then he stood up, hunching low, and looked at his image in the tiny mirror that hung over the washbasin. The red-eyed face that greeted him looked ghastly with the candle throwing its feeble yellow light from below. He splashed his face and then dried it with the towel. He would shave later. "What is it, Mr. Hill?"

"Someone's been trying to wet our powder down, sir."

"We went to quarters this afternoon," Kinkaid reminded him.

"No sir, it's not the powder room this time, but those extra barrels in the hold. Somebody has been trying to ruin it, make it unusable or unreliable by wetting down the kegs. Some of the kegs are wet on top and I found this just now." Hill bent down and showed Kinkaid a wooden bucket, explaining, "Insides are still wet, too. Believe I might have scared whoever it was as he was in the act."

"How many have keys to the powder room?"

"Just myself, Miller and Mr. Briggs, sir. But whoever is doing this doesn't have a key."

"How do you know, Mr. Hill?"

"Well, sir, the bulkheads and overhead to the powder room are always wet too…in spite of all my efforts to keep them dry."

"This is serious, Mr. Hill." .

"Yes sir."

"Who else knows about this?"

"Mr. Briggs and the powder boys have been aware of the problem since we was in port, sir. Couldn't figure where the moisture was comin' from."

"Do they know what you just found?"

"No sir. I came direct to you as soon as I discovered this bucket."

"How wet is the powder?"

"A couple of rolls of slowmatch is ruined sure, and there's a few barrels I wouldn't trust, Captain. I can dry it out and test it later, but if there's somebody about with a mind for mischief…"

"We'll move as much as we can into the powder room," he determined, suddenly feeling vulnerable.

"Won't be much room to move about in there, sir, but I know it's got to be done," answered the practical Hill. "You want me to canvas the deck above, sir?"

"That's a good idea, Boats, but better yet let's post a double guard, both outside the powder room and above. Make it a regular watch from now on."

"Yes sir."

"And let's keep this information to ourselves; tell the watch it's to protect against thievery."

"Aye, Captain."

An enemy aboard ship was a dangerous thing. There was no telling what mischief a man might attempt, to ruin their mission, to keep the ship from crossing the Atlantic, no telling what lengths a man would go to, what sacrifice a saboteur might make in the name of patriotism. First the following ship and now this. The two could very well be connected.

V
An Old Trick

The dim light of early morning filtered its way down the ladder and, knowing he would be unable to sleep anyway, Kinkaid decided to shave. When he was finished he stepped out into the corridor. Only two of the officers' compartments had doors; one was the captain's cabin where Simpson slept and the other the master's cabin where Mr. Palfrey was quartered. The other officer's berths had only canvas curtains. Kinkaid briefly parted each curtain as he made his way toward the ladder. There was Mr. Rosetti, sleeping peacefully. Then Mr. Grimes, also asleep, and though his blanket was pulled up around his neck, he looked to be shivering. Mr. Weatherby was lying in a fetal position, face to the bulkhead. Kinkaid wanted to knock on Mr. Palfrey's door, check on the man, but dared not.

It was a bright clear morning, though cold. Mr. Briggs was on the quarterdeck, as was Midshipman Sutherland. The two were looking toward the west where the familiar sails of the ship still bobbed two miles astern. The helmsman was one of the waisters, a portly young man by the name of Grossman. He murmured something under his breath when he noticed Kinkaid, whereupon Sutherland and Briggs both turned and offered their greetings in unison, "Good morning, Captain."

"Morning, gentlemen," returned Kinkaid, blinking his red and sleepy eyes against the sunshine. "Anything new?"

Briggs indicated the following vessel and provided,

"She's backed off a bit since it turned light and seems to be backing off still, sir, quite slowly. Clouds passed during the night and the wind hasn't picked up much at all yet. Course remains…"

"Have you noticed anything unusual, Mr. Briggs…anything at all?"

Briggs pondered the question a moment, not quite sure what his captain expected.

"Well sir, she took in her top sheets at around…"

"Very well, Mr. Briggs."

"Yes sir," answered Briggs, confused and a bit stung by the curt reply.

Kinkaid was more concerned at the moment about the danger aboard their ship than from the one that followed, so he scarcely noticed Briggs' discomfort. It was with an uneasy feeling that he decided to go forward, take a stroll along the deck as Briggs had the morning watch roused out and soon the boatswain's mates were coming out with their holystones, buckets and sand. Able Seaman Miller was in charge of the party and was standing by with the group of seven men, apparently waiting for their captain to approach for whatever reason.

"Carry on, Miller," said Kinkaid, realizing his idea of strolling the deck would have to be put aside to give these men room to do their work, the morning ritual that took place before anybody had their breakfast. They would begin at the bowsprit and work their way aft, scrubbing and hosing down the main deck before turning their attention to recoiling the lines and then attending to the brightwork. Kinkaid was about to turn around when he caught sight of a man's head protruding just over the crossbeam of the belfry where the ship's bell hung, where the bowsprit met the main deck, a man with an unruly mane of salt and pepper hair.

"Mr. Palfrey, I'm surprised to see you up and about so early this morning."

If Palfrey was surprised he hid the fact with his consummate charm. "And a good morning to you, Captain, and a fine morning it is. Nothing like a morning at sea...nothing to stop one's view of the sunrise. And nothing like seeing the sun come up to remind one that one is alive."

A long and foolish explanation was Kinkaid's first impression, and he wanted to ask Mr. Palfrey what he was doing up on deck so early in the morning besides looking at the sunrise, for he knew the man to be late riser. Yet the man had already given an answer to that question and for a moment Kinkaid was at odds how to respond. "Do you need reminding that you are alive, Mr. Palfrey?" he asked, unconcerned how his question might be taken, hoping even to rouse the man's ire.

But Palfrey took the question in stride. "The thought that one's life may be in danger is reminder enough, good Captain," whereupon he cast a glance aft toward the ship on the horizon.

"Oh, she's not interested in a fight; only to keep us in sight."

"A poet," gave Palfrey, twisting away once again with the offbeat comment. The man was slippery as an eel. Kinkaid had not liked the man from the moment he met him and attributed the reason to the simple fact that one could not possibly like every person one met in life. Only time would tell if there was more of a reason than that. As if reading Kinkaid's mind, Palfrey added, "But I'd imagine every sailor must acquire a spot of the poet in him, wouldn't you say, Captain? The sea possesses more moods than a woman."

"I suppose. Perhaps we'll see you at breakfast, Mr.

Palfrey."

"I believe I shall wait before I break my fast. Make sure the sun gets a good start this morning."

"Suit yourself, sir." But Kinkaid didn't notice the sun burning away the morning mist, didn't notice even the men on the deck as he passed, so engrossed was he in turning the conversation over in his mind, a curious conversation to say the least, and arriving at no satisfactory conclusion, and left with a feeling...almost as if someone had stolen something from him. It was all very tiresome.

Kinkaid considered talking with Mr. Simpson about Mr. Palfrey, but immediately discarded the idea as too tactless. It would be considered invasive by Simpson, who would no doubt conclude that Kinkaid held the man in some suspicion for no good reason. The next decision came close upon the heels of the first and meant that he was now compelled to avoid Mr. Simpson altogether, for the temptation to discuss Mr. Palfrey over breakfast was too great. Simpson's French lessons were difficult enough to concentrate on and the act of avoiding the confidential conversation would only lead to Mr. Simpson wondering what was bothering him.

So breakfast proved a desultory affair, taken in his tiny closet-like space, with Cato having to duck low and back out after he had set the plates down. Kinkaid was only thankful that Cato did not question why he was not having breakfast with Mr. Simpson in the captain's cabin, accepting that it was not his place to do so, but nonetheless Kinkaid found himself looking for excuses as if he owed some explanation, and so he sat there with a plate on his lap and a chart of the Bay of Biscay spread out on his cot which he pretended to be interested in, when in fact his thoughts were distracted and he ate little.

When Cato finally cleared away the remains of the meal,

Kinkaid remained lying on his cot instead of making his way to the quarterdeck where he normally would be early in the morning. He was aware that the ship was rolling gently and making very little speed in the light air and so he sent word to the quarterdeck to set studding sails. Then he must have drifted off for some moments, for the next thing he heard was the marine sentry greeting Mr. Weatherby.

Kinkaid rose at once and met Weatherby coming out of his compartment, his hat in his hand.

"Good morning, sir."

"Are you busy at the moment, Mr. Weatherby?"

"I have the forenoon watch, sir. I was about to relieve Mr. Briggs."

"I'll accompany you to the quarterdeck, then."

"After you, sir."

Kinkaid waited for Weatherby at the top of the ladder and then took him aside, saying, "I'd like a word with you, Mr. Weatherby, if you have a moment."

"Of course, sir."

Unsure how to begin, Kinkaid ventured, "You have made the acquaintance of Mr. Palfrey, have you not?"

"Of course, sir," stated Weatherby factually. "He seems quite interested in how the ship is run. As I explained to you, sir…" Weatherby apparently saw little to be suspicious about from a man who sought information about the environment around him, for, in fact, Weatherby would have acted in much the same way, questioning, seeking knowledge, ever curious.

"Yes, I know, Weatherby. What I mean to ask is…well, have you come to know the man…I mean, closely, that is?"

Weatherby looked questioningly at his captain, answering, "Not exactly, sir. I am learning a great deal about marksmanship, however. Why, the man is a brilliant shot;

hardly ever misses, even on a rolling deck, quite remarkable, sir. I never knew there was so much to shooting. From the correct stance, to breathing, to barrel alignment, sight picture, why it's an art and a science both. And his swordsmanship is…"

"I'm glad you are able to apprise yourself of the man's great knowledge, Mr. Weatherby," answered Kinkaid with some irritation. "Damn it, Weatherby, I want you to…to take him into your confidence, so to speak. Let him find in you a trusted…ah…"

"Confidant, sir?" completed Weatherby.

The comment exasperated Kinkaid to the point that he blurted out, "I want you to find out what he is about. In a subtle way, of course," he added, trying to keep his voice low.

Weatherby looked at his captain and whispered back, "Why didn't you say so, sir? Do you suspect the man of something?"

"I don't know, Weatherby," he had to admit. "Just talk to him…about things…other than marksmanship."

"Well, now that you ask, I can tell you some things about the man just from our conversations about marksmanship."

"Such as?"

"Well, sir, as for having a conversation with him, it is always one-sided. Unless he is asking questions he is totally uninterested in anything anybody else has to say. Everything he thinks and says has to do with him and him alone, a subject upon which he can go on and on about yet reveal absolutely nothing about his person, in fact the more he talks about himself the more elusive he becomes. Quite remarkable, yet he seems to be unaware that this is the impression he makes upon others. Reminds me of a certain mad doctor we once met in the Caribbean. Yes, Captain, in spite of the man's knowledge and skill, I have to admit that I think he is a complete snob and an utter bore. Oh, and he has no sense of humor."

Kinkaid was a little stunned by Weatherby's sudden diatribe. "Good God, Weatherby, I thought you didn't know anything about the man?"

"I don't. That is only my opinion of him, sir."

"Well, if you find out anything, or reach any more…opinions about him, please let me know."

"Of course, Captain," answered Weatherby in that confident tone. Kinkaid suddenly had the strange thought that Weatherby would have answered in the same way if Kinkaid had asked him to hold back the wind or drain the ocean, for it often seemed as if there was nothing the young man was not or could not be master of, a bastion of resourcefulness and reliance, a maddening observation if it were not for the fact that Weatherby took his character and exceptional abilities quite for granted.

Midshipman Briggs had been expecting Weatherby and now he was providing all the information that he was required to pass to his relief; remarks about the weather, direction of the wind, course of the ship, the obvious fact that an unknown ship was still tailing them at a discreet distance, that the log had just been heaved, showing a speed of 4 knots, and that studding sails had just been ordered and set and to make sure they were watched for possible adjustments. Weatherby nodded dutifully after each of Briggs' remarks, then said, "You are relieved, Mr. Briggs."

Kinkaid took his place on the windward side of the quarterdeck, his legs slightly apart, feeling the ship roll gently with the swell, facing the bow. And though the following ship was not far from his thoughts, he found himself thinking of Mr. Weatherby's unvarnished opinion of

Mr. Palfrey, in fact, taking great pleasure in it. He had watched the two taking target practice together and practicing their swordsmanship and he had felt a twinge of jealousy, believing that Weatherby was becoming enamored of the man. Yet he had been wrong and the realization brought a smile. While Mr. Weatherby could be charming and allow himself to be charmed, he could never be the fool, and Kinkaid had to berate himself for forgetting that simple fact.

Daybreak brought a light cloud cover, making for a bright but dismal sky. The strange ship remained at about three miles distance, matching *Active*'s sail plan and keeping pace for the rest of the day as the wind continued light into evening, then tapered off even more as the sun dipped below the horizon and the sky darkened fast, the ship barely making headway. And once again the distant ship made all sail and scurried nearer to lessen any chance that *Active* might lose her in the night.

Sometime during the midwatch the wind picked up to the point where the Captain was informed and at almost three in the morning Kinkaid ordered the hands called out to take in studding sails before returning to his cot.

A stiff and chilly breeze blew the next morning, giving steamy breath to the watch who all had their collars turned up. The lookouts were wrapped in blankets. Mr. Rosetti was the morning watch officer and he was stamping his feet on the quarterdeck to keep the circulation going. Mr. Phillips was his assistant and had taken Grubb's place at the wheel as the carpenter stood to one side. As part of Midshipman Phillips' overall training, he would be assigned to each division in turn so that he would become familiar with each and every job aboard ship. Mr. Grimes was standing by the binnacle, holding down the flapping pages of a seamanship manual, and quizzing Phillips.

Kinkaid came up on deck in his oilskin coat that Cato insisted he wear, turning up its collar against the bitter blow. Grubb made room for him while Grimes closed the book and Mr. Rosetti informed him, "Glass has been falling all during the night, Captain."

"I suppose we're due for something," allowed Kinkaid, glancing at the hard edges of dark clouds to the northwest. So far the weather had been dreary and cold, but kind, so it was not surprising that a storm was in the offing, especially this late in the year in the North Atlantic. The distant ship was clawing its way closer but Kinkaid did not mention the fact nor did anyone on the deck. As if to reinforce that *Active* would not have her routine changed because of a pursuing ship, Kinkaid said, "I believe Mr. Phillips is prepared for the next question, Mr. Grimes."

"Aye, Captain," answered Grimes, shivering violently and struggling to find his place once more.

Mr. Sykes strode ponderously up to the quarterdeck in his heavy coat, his frayed hat pulled tightly down over his ears. He turned stiffly and looked back from where he had walked, where sailors were busy upon the deck. He simply stood there, watching for a moment, before he said out of the side of his mouth, "I've just passed the word to stow all loose gear, Captain."

The comment from Mr. Sykes was a reminder that he had not given much thought to preparing for the blow that was coming and did nothing to improve his mood, reflected by the dark line of clouds coming their way. "Very well, Mr. Sykes."

As if in punctuation, a strong gust tore across the deck, heeling the ship sharply to starboard, causing the men on the quarterdeck to lean in unison, while giving little thought to the exercise. A born seaman like Mr. Hill or Mr. Sykes welcomed a change in the weather. Rough seas were no stranger to the breed and were accepted as a matter of course, as entertainment of sorts, accepted as a challenge, a test of man and ship.

Grimes was only momentarily distracted by the shift of the deck, and, grasping hold of the binnacle, slowly read the question, "Mr. Phillips, what is the rule describing relative motion?"

Phillips cocked his head at an angle, answering, "R-relative motion is present, uh, only when the actual movements of t-two or more objects are not the s-same."

"Very good, Mr. Phillips. Now let's add relative bearings to a situation. When determining the relative motion of another ship, if one does not maintain a steady course, what should one do?"

"Convert r-relative bearings to t-true bearings."

Another gust hit the ship and shivered the mainsails, bringing the question and answer session to a halt. "Mr. Grimes, let's take in fore and mains'ls," Kinkaid decided. They may have to reef tops and jibs later if it picked up, which seemed likely, but Kinkaid would take advantage of the wind for now. The regular rollers were not so regular any more, interfered with by choppy seas from the north, from where the gusts were coming and the ship began pitching erratically.

"Hands to the braces!" shouted Grimes, whereupon Miller, the duty boatswain's mate, piped the men out.

"Bring us nor' by nor' east, Mr. Phillips." Coming into and putting the ship closer to the wind would take pressure off the sails, giving the handlers an easier time, and heading eventually north was necessary regardless and would put the bow at an angle to the waves that were forming with the increased wind.

"Aye, Captain."

Men were quickly climbing the shrouds, making their way up masts that swung wide arcs across the swirling sky. Halyards were loosed and the big mainsails were gathered up, furled, and made fast to their respective spars. As the ship settled on her new course, her bow fairly slammed into the waves on the port side, sending heavy spray flying over her forecastle, wetting the deck forward and even a quarter way up the flying jib as the ship heeled sharply to starboard. Now *Active* plunged over the ocean with the following ship racing after her, both ships on the same course, both beating to windward under reduced sail.

Kinkaid had to watch her now as everyone's attention was on the pursuing ship, to see if she would weather her way ahead of *Active*. She was a speedy ship, no doubt, and she heeled in *Active's* direction, her billowing sails almost touching the crests, her bow crashing into the oncoming waves, sending up plumes of white spray that formed rainbows over her bow every time the sun peeked out from behind increasingly dark and swirling clouds. Mr. Grimes kept taking periodic readings at the binnacle as she gained on them, and finally he looked up, spray dripping from his nose, and confirmed, "She's abeam of us now, Captain."

She was less than a mile directly off *Active's* port beam, maintaining her upwind advantage and still moving ahead and slowly closing as well. By the time Phillips rang six bells the ship had closed to within a half mile as the first rainsquall covered her with a ghostlike veil. Five minutes later the squall hit *Active,* with strong and erratic gusts bowling her on her side. The sun was obliterated now behind heavy and fast-moving clouds and the sea turned lead gray.

"Double reef tops and t'gallants, Mr. Grimes," ordered

Kinkaid.

The men had been awaiting such an order and turned out in good time to shorten sail, leaving only thin rectangles to catch the gale now. A heavy squall turned into a steady drumbeat of water as the pellets struck the sheets and beat on the deck and men alike. At eight bells Mr. Hill and the forenoon watch relieved the thoroughly soaked morning watch, coming up on deck better prepared against the cold and wet, allowing the shivering morning watch to retire below to warm and dry hammocks and a few hours furtive sleep. Mr. Sykes also took his place on the leeward side, to a spot that he habitually claimed, hulking silently and morose as ever, watching everything with a disapproving eye, the small bulge on his chest evidence that his faithful companion took refuge under his coat, protected from the blow.

Kinkaid remained on the quarterdeck, for once keeping his eye on the pitching ship, less than a half mile off the port bow now with her reefed tops, and he found himself recalling a similar scene, albeit in the West Indies, when a speedy sloop suddenly turned to attack, and tragically killed a vibrant young man, Weatherby's best friend, Mr. Henry Cutler.

Visibility had deteriorated steadily since the morning and the day had grown ever darker toward noon with the steady downpour. The seas had built as well, with six-foot swells pushing the ship to leeward, their tops blown by the wind into frothy spray, sliding down their troughs in jagged patterns of foam, with *Active*'s bow fairly slamming into the choppy waves. Chief O'Toole and Mr. Briggs had a party out on deck, snuggling up the train tackles to ensure that the guns would remain in their places.

Mr. Grimes had likewise remained on deck through the

watch change. "A lot of wet chickens up here, sir," he morosely observed through chattering teeth.

It was almost noon now, with the watch about to change again, and Kinkaid forced a smile at the comment from Mr. Grimes. It crossed his mind that the man was making an attempt to impress him with his sense of duty, but mostly Kinkaid's attention was on the shadowy outline of the ship ahead of them now, his thoughts on hopes that the storm might continue into the night. And, if her captain were tired and her lookouts lax, perhaps...

Suddenly, Mr. Grimes swooned and stumbled, falling into Mr. Hill, who caught him and knelt beside him on the deck. Chief O'Toole was there and bent over to touch the back of his hand to the dazed man's forehead.

"Seems a touch of fever, Captain," said O'Toole, looking up.

"Better have Dr. Morrow have a look at him," said Kinkaid.

"Aye, sir," answered O'Toole before calling on two hands to help him carry Mr. Grimes below.

Cato poked his head out of the after hatch, squinting into the maelstrom towards the quarterdeck, by his action inquiring if his captain would come below for dinner, but Kinkaid waved him off and the gray head quickly ducked back down again. Yet, cold and hungry, the thought of a hot meal made him realize that he was accomplishing little by remaining on deck. He could just as easily ponder relative position problems while taking his dinner in dry clothes. "I'm going below. I invite you to do the same, Mr. Hill; get some rest."

Hill was onto something of Kinkaid's intentions, for he answered, "Might be a busy night, Captain?"

"It just might be, Mr. Hill," gave Kinkaid, water running

off the end of his nose. Turning to Mr. Sykes, his collar up and shoulders hunched against the rain and wind, Kinkaid informed him, "Keep her on the same course. If the wind changes or if she does anything different," Kinkaid jerked his head in the direction of the mysterious ship, "anything at all, call me at once."

Sykes did not look at his Captain, only mumbling, "As ordered, Captain."

But their unwelcome escort did nothing different, keeping her place upwind of *Active* all that afternoon and after a hearty dinner Kinkaid took a fitful nap during which time his thoughts were never off the following ship, knowing she would have to draw quite near to them during the night. He thought of turning and raking her rigging with a broadside of double-shotted canister and grape; guaranteed to slow her and make it easier to elude her in the storm. Yet, there were other considerations, the first of which was that he had no proof that she was an enemy and to fire at a friendly or neutral vessel would cause an incident that could very well cost him his career. Attempting to board her was likewise out of the question. She would have every right to fire upon them in the process and so he could only return to the same conclusion, that he could not jeopardize his ship and therefore his mission by either course.

Kinkaid was back on deck by the first dog watch at four, the watch from four to eight in the evening divided into two dog watches to ensure that a man would not serve the same watches on the following day. The wind had steadied, blowing hard from almost directly north, though the rains had let up, but now sending a light stinging sleet across the deck at a sharp angle and it was with visible relief that a shivering Mr. Hill was relieved by Mr. Weatherby who kept his eye stubbornly on the shadowy form to the north, slipping ever so slowly closer as the light faded ever more. Still, pondered Weatherby, she was out of long gun range, and even had she closed, the jumbled seas took away any chance of accurate cannon fire. Weatherby had an active mind and it was only natural that he entertained his own plans for losing or hurting the ship that clung so tenaciously within their sight. He would not voice those plans unless asked, but could not help but say as Kinkaid stood nearby, "It's certain to be quite dark tonight, sir."

"Dark as pitch, Mr. Weatherby," gave Kinkaid.

"She'll have to come quite close if she doesn't wish to lose us tonight," he observed.

"Perhaps we should help her," he answered.

"Sir?"

It was a rare and satisfying moment to have the keen Lieutenant Weatherby momentarily puzzled. "A lantern on our stern rail should suffice, don't you think?"

Now Weatherby realized the implication as he smiled and said, "Of course, sir. I'll see to it right away, Captain."

Weatherby summoned the messenger and had him fetch a lantern from the forecastle. It was then lit and attached to the stern rail, to the puzzlement of the watch.

"A proper beacon, Mr. Weatherby," observed Kinkaid.

"She can't miss that, Captain," agreed an amused Weatherby.

Mr. Rosetti and the second dog watch at six was likewise puzzled and so did the word spread among the crew, bringing Mr. Grimes, Mr. Simpson and Chief O'Toole out onto the windswept deck, and that is when Kinkaid relented. "Her captain will be wondering as well, no doubt, but he cannot ignore the signal and may think we believe she is a friendly ship seeking an escort. But regardless of what he believes, we'll give him time enough to associate that light with us. Chief, do we have an empty barrel to spare?"

O'Toole gave a crafty grin. "With a bucket or two of sand on the bottom and a stout spar on top. An old trick but a good one, sir, and as likely to work as a new trick."

"Which is why old tricks become old tricks," added Mr. Rosetti, giving Mr. Simpson a conspiratorial wink.

The empty barrel was soon brought to the quarterdeck by Miller and the latest member of the deck crew, Sterling. The barrel was properly weighted and a three foot spar had been nailed to the side to support the lantern on top. They looped stout lines around the barrel and then secured it between the binnacle and the wheel.

"We'll need as much line as you can find, Chief," said Kinkaid.

"I'll round up every spare yard, Captain," came the ready answer.

There was nothing to do now but wait and, Mr. Simpson, astute enough to know that Kinkaid would be loath to entertain speculations from the officer's mess, invited him to take dinner with him in the captain's cabin. The had agreed that French lessons were to be confined only to the breakfast meal and so it was a leisurely dinner, with Simpson, as usual, bringing up a host of interesting topics.

"Yes, I do believe this idea of bloodletting is a useless medicinal treatment," Simpson theorized. "In fact, it seems to me that God would have provided an outlet for our blood if we were meant to release excess quantities to keep us healthy. What do you think, Kinkaid?"

"Seems reasonable enough," gave Kinkaid noncommittally, his mind on other matters but glad that Mr. Simpson was trying to distract him from them.

"I mean, let's take a practical view of this, Kinkaid," Simpson went on. "The result of an unabated loss of blood leads inevitably to one and only indisputable conclusion…death."

"That has been my observation," agreed Kinkaid, aware of the state of the sea outside. The unsteady winds that the rains had brought seemed to have steadied and calmed, though there still fell a light drizzle of rain as night approached.

"Proving at the least that blood is a vital fluid," Simpson continued, "and as such, I fail to see how the loss of any percentage of blood cannot make a man weaker."

"You may be right, Mr. Simpson. I can't say that I've ever witnessed a good loss of blood result in a man gaining in strength."

"Exactly my point."

"Perhaps you should take this matter up with our surgeon."

"I already have," Simpson informed him. "It seems our esteemed Dr. Morrow has no valid proof that such a practice has any benefit whatsoever. He admitted as much to me, yet then I find him bleeding Mr. Grimes."

"Well, he is, after all, a doctor," offered Kinkaid in Dr. Morrow's defense, wishing to move on to a different topic, one in which he might participate with more knowledge and opinion.

"That's the trouble with Doctors in general," complained Simpson. "Once a man pins the title of doctor before his name he suddenly thinks himself an infallible expert. I once attended a conference of doctors in New York and never met a group so enamored of themselves. Never saw such a sight…a room full of men with their noses in the air. I at first thought that there must be something of immense interest on the ceiling until I realized they were having a pomposity contest."

Kinkaid laughed and seeing his chance, said, "Why don't you tell me more about your visit to New York?"

"Ah, the city. Well, it grows daily and is sure to become a center of commerce, someday rivaling London, I should think," said Simpson, off on a new tangent. "Yes, a country becomes great from her land and her people, but it isn't until she grows great cities that commerce and culture unite to give her character and depth. There's a certain energy to New York, Kinkaid, an energy that I for one could become addicted to."

"I can see how it would attract you, Mr. Simpson."

"Yes, I suppose I'm a city boy by nature," he admitted.

"Well, I can do without the noise and smells of the city," said Kinkaid.

"Ah, but wait till you see Paris," said Simpson. "A city unrivaled by any in the world. Why, the refined culture and civilization of France will astound you. I'll show you around. You'll dazzle your bride when you return with your new knowledge of culture, art and science, not to mention your facility with the language."

"Ha!" Kinkaid had to laugh for both knew that Simpson's French lessons were forced upon him. He found them akin to torture sessions and rarely remembered without a great struggle what Simpson had taught him only the day before.

Aware that he might have embarrassed Kinkaid, Simpson said, "Getting back to my visit to New York. I met a man there who had found evidence that the land there, even many miles inland, had once been covered by an ocean. He showed me slabs of rock and shale that he had found hundreds of miles from the coast, full of seashells and strange plants and animals encrusted in the rock. One such rock held the remains of a gigantic insect-like creature that probably once lived at the bottom of the sea, a trilobite, I believe he called it. Frightening thing! I'd hate to have a creature like that grab hold of my leg while I was wading in the surf. Of course such creatures roamed the world long before our kind came here, according to the experts. Anyway, this man's theory was that the world was much older than any of us could imagine and he intended to set up a museum of such curiosities."

After Cato cleared away their dishes they played Backgammon as the evening turned to night. Simpson was an accomplished player and so Kinkaid found playing him a challenge, but the longer they played the more games Kinkaid won. After a dozen games, Kinkaid won three games straight and Simpson, tired of losing, relented with the observation, "My energies are quickly spent, Captain, unlike yourself, who seems to tend them more judiciously than I."

Five bells of the night watch rang out and Kinkaid stretched and said, "Just as well, for my duties require me back on deck."

Simpson seemed to revive with the reminder. "A bit of fresh air seems in order, Captain, therefore I believe I shall keep you company a while longer, if you don't mind."

In addition to the quarterdeck watch, consisting of Mr. Rosetti, Midshipman Phillips and the boatswain, Miller, at the wheel, the quarterdeck was crowded with all the ship's officers even as a light rain continued to fall. O'Toole was busy splicing medium-sized line from a huge pile as Nicky Sterling neatly coiled the finished line into neat circular piles on the deck. Mr. Rosetti stood at the stern rail where the lantern still hung and was the first to notice as Kinkaid's head appeared at the main hatchway and he immediately gave Mr. Sykes a nudge, the stooped figure calling out gruffly, "Captain on deck!"

"At your ease, men," answered Kinkaid as they made room for him on the windward side. His eyes had yet to adjust as he peered out into a black misty night.

"She's drifted abaft of us, sir," provided Mr. Rosetti, pointing in her direction.

There she was, just a smudge of main and topsails visible against the drizzly, moonless night, almost half a mile astern.

"The wind has abated considerably, Captain," added Rosetti.

Kinkaid had almost constantly thought about the ruse as he had sat with Mr. Simpson and now he asked O'Toole, "How many yards have we, Chief?"

"A little over three hundred, Captain," answered O'Toole. "Should suffice, sir."

"Good work, Chief."

He waited until O'Toole had made his last splice, then said, "Let's ready our beacon."

O'Toole signaled for Sterling to help him with the barrel. First they untied the line that secured the barrel, then moved it against the stern rail and finally fastened the lantern to the top of the spar. O'Toole made three loops of the cable around the barrel, tied it off, then stood back and said, "She's ready, Captain."

Kinkaid's eyes had adjusted to the night by now and he was worried that they might be still too visible to their escort to cast off the barrel yet. "We'll wait a bit longer," he said, looking up at the sky to the northwest where black clouds hung heavy. The ship had slowed and was barely making two knots, wallowing in the gentle swell.

And so they waited and waited some more, for the sky to darken further, for the dark clouds to approach nearer, all the while hoping for the rain to fall harder, which it finally did, partly obscuring the sight of the ship, which looked to be setting studding sails in order to draw nearer to them in the light air.

The night would not grow much darker, reasoned Kinkaid, and with the passing of those heavy clouds overhead, the rains would also probably taper off. "All right, let's put it over the side," he said. "A hundred yards, at first."

O'Toole, Sterling and Grubb hoisted the barrel over the stern rail and lowered it into the sea and it quickly drifted aft. O'Toole then looped the rope once around a cleat and let it out a fathom at a time as Grubb and Sterling neatly paid out the line to keep it from kinking or snarling. All watched as the makeshift buoy trailed behind them, bobbing up over the swells, then dipping down into the troughs, up and down, up and down, it's motion unlike the stern of the ship, which was more steady, and Kinkaid could only hope the difference in its movement would not be detected from a distance. Most of the crew, curious to watch the experiment, was already turned out in spite of the rain, and so all Kinkaid had to say was, "Set all sail, and let's do it quietly, Mr. Rosetti."

"Aye, Captain."

"Steer us south by east."

"Steering south by east, it is, Captain," replied Miller.

The men were already climbing the ratlines and others took up the halyards as Miller turned the wheel and the ship steadied on her new course.

A slow change of course as the barrel trailed behind would further confuse, but what helped more was the rain, falling in sheets and heavy at times, blotting out the sight of the ship completely. She would be scrambling to move closer, yet would still be careful not to come within long gun range, her lookouts intent to keep the lantern in sight, hopefully comforted by the light.

Mr. Sykes was moving about the deck in his ponderous way, giving orders and actively directing the hands in the tops to brace the spars just right as *Active* steadied on her new course. Even with all sail set, the ship made no more than four knots in the light breeze. Mr. Rosetti stood on the stern rail, squinting aft, trying to locate the ghostly shape of the following ship. "I don't see her, sir," he announced, smiling.

But Kinkaid knew they were not clear yet. Ten minutes passed and O'Toole deftly tossed a reverse loop on the cleat, reporting, "One hundred yards, Captain."

"We'll trail it for a while," said Kinkaid. The barrel needed to have some weigh on to resemble a ship's movement. He waited another ten minutes before giving the order, "Fifty more yards."

O'Toole once more went to work loosening and then holding back, loosening and holding back, allowing enough line to slip out while slowly keeping the buoy dragging through the water.

O'Toole's arm was tiring, but dauntless, he refused to relinquish the task. "At least allow Sterling to give you a hand," suggested Weatherby, which he reluctantly did. And now the two of them were playing out the line together, side by side, the tension much stronger now, the pull much harder. It took all of ten more minutes for O'Toole and Sterling to let out the last coil. O'Toole made his last reverse loop, securing the line, before reporting, "That's it, Captain."

"Very well," answered Kinkaid. "We'll trail it for a while." If the captain of the other ship suspected the trick, they might appear through the mist at any moment, abreast of the buoy, the ruse ended. The buoy trailed astern by three hundred yards now and if the following ship was still unaware of the trick, then they were three hundred yards farther away than she knew, a fair advantage on this dark and rainy night. Kinkaid forced himself to allowed another tense and silent fifteen minutes to pass before ordering, "All right, let it go."

The bitter end hit the water with a splash and every man on the quarterdeck watched it as it drifted astern in their wake.

"Helmsman, bring us on a course of north by east by east."

"Aye, Captain. Coming to nor' by east by east," repeated Miller as he spun the wheel to port.

More minutes passed as all intently peered aft, watching for any sign of a sail or foamy bow wave.

Finally Mr. Sykes cleared his throat and growled, "It just might work, Captain."

"At least for some time," Nicky Sterling could be heard to say.

Kinkaid ignored the comment, forcing himself to look up at the sails, around the deck, out to sea, anywhere but behind them, as Mr. Sykes once again turned his vociferous attention to the resetting of the braces as the ship steadied on her new course.

Silence then returned to the deck as Mr. Rosetti and Weatherby kept their eyes in the direction of the bobbing lantern until it was but a speck on the dark and bleak horizon. For some time after, it looked to be winking off and on and then, finally, it was lost from sight, far behind. The following ship would have noticed the light dead in the water by now, might have closed the distance and realized they had been tricked, but hopefully, *Active* would be well away into the night, on a different course before they would catch sight of her again. It was almost eleven and there was nothing to do now but put as much distance between them as possible before morning light.

"Have the off-watch turn in," said Kinkaid. Yet he remained on the quarterdeck. An hour later the midnight watch came up.

Mr. Simpson had been leaning heavily against the binnacle and gave Kinkaid a knowing wink before he went below. Others soon began drifting away from the quarterdeck to snatch a couple hours of sleep before the watch changed again, Mr. Sutherland sniggering smugly at their apparent success. Mr. Briggs could not contain himself, saying, "Looks like you did it, sir."

"Now that's exactly why an old trick becomes an old trick, Mr. Briggs," observed O'Toole wryly.

But Kinkaid knew there was still room for doubt. The captain of that ship would have discovered the ruse by now and would no doubt be cursing himself at this very moment for falling for it, left with only his best guess as to which course Kinkaid had taken. Uncertain, he would even now be doing everything in his power to gain every iota of speed out of his ship and crew, determined to right his mistake. And so Kinkaid remained on the deck even as his officers retired, one by one.

He was there still when the mid-watch was over and by four bells the dark clouds had passed overhead and the rains finally abated. Mr. Midshipman Sutherland made an attempt to engage his captain in conversation during the morning watch, but finding Kinkaid sleepy and unresponsive, soon gave up. By five a.m. a thin sliver of light had spread across the eastern sky. Behind them was only open sea. It appeared they had lost her. The wind freshened and Kinkaid turned in with orders not to awaken him unless sails were spotted.

VI
Ship of Rags

"Captain?"

Kinkaid awoke to the sweaty face of Dr. Morrow standing in the doorway, a cabin lantern in his hand. "What is it, Dr.?"

"It's Grimes, sir. He's...well, he's quite sick, Captain."

"You woke me to tell me that?" asked Kinkaid, feeling groggy. "What time is it?"

"Almost six."

"Which means I've had less than an hours sleep," he related irritably.

"Sorry, sir, but I've been up most of the night myself, waiting to confirm what I've suspected for some days now, that we have some cases of disease aboard."

Kinkaid rose on an elbow at the news. "What kind of disease?"

"I can't be certain. Mr. Grimes and...four more have had recurrent headaches for the last three days; fever and chills and now Grimes is in a delirium and has broken out in a rash. I've seen it before. Ship's fever for lack of a better term."

"I see," said Kinkaid. Then, giving the Dr. a concerned look, he asked, "Can you tell me exactly what this means, Doc?"

Dr. Morrow took a breath and related, "Well, most likely we can expect it to spread among the crew. Some might die from it, Captain."

"How many?" he asked. "I mean what percentage are we talking about?"

"Hard to predict, sir. Depends on what it is and on each man's overall health, age, strength..."

"What can we do about it?"

"Other than bleeding, my Lititz Pharmacopoeia suggests Peruvian bark for the fever."

"That's something, at least," he said hopefully.

"Except we don't have any Peruvian bark, Captain," answered Morrow, shaking his head wearily.

Kinkaid had to fight to keep his feelings of dread under control. "What does your book say causes it?"

"It doesn't, and I doubt anyone knows for certain, Captain...but some think it's from excessive fatigue or bad diet or unclean conditions."

"Likely conditions on any ship," observed Kinkaid.

"Which is why it's called Ship Fever," noted Dr. Morrow. "I can't say as the men are overworked, Captain, and seeing as we're just out of port with full stores, I doubt poor diet is a factor."

"So that leaves unclean conditions."

"Could be. These men are a hard and slovenly lot, Captain," deemed the Doctor, "which is why I believe that frequent washing of bedding and clothing might help to keep it from spreading, sir."

"Very well, then. I'll declare today a wash and air bedding day," said Kinkaid, his mind seeking comfort in the practical solution.

"Yes, sir. We could scrub down the ship as well, Captain. With hot vinegar water."

Kinkaid sat there a moment, digesting the news, news that seemed like a bad dream, before asking, "Who are the other two?"

"Pardon, sir?"

"You mentioned there were four others afflicted," Kinkaid reminded him.

"So I did. The gunner's mate, Knox, and Riley, O'Brian, and Rupert in the second division…and then there's myself, sir."

Kinkaid looked at the Doctor and only now noticed him leaning heavily against the doorframe, beads of perspiration on his forehead. "You're not supposed to become ill, Doctor," said Kinkaid, and immediately regretted the poor joke.

"Sorry, sir," he answered with a weak smile.

"Well, inform your assistants of the problem and what we need to be doing about it. And then get yourself to bed. That's an order, Doctor."

"Yes, Captain."

Kinkaid lay there for some moments after the Doctor left. He had felt some success by evading the following ship only to find that he had little enough time to enjoy it before this news, this nightmare, came intruding. He did not look forward to the coming days or the reaction among the crew. But they would have to be told, and better to do it himself and immediately rather than let the rumors fly and so he resolved that he would tell them after breakfast. Kinkaid sighed and murmured to himself, "What next?" He lay back on his cot and met her gaze in the miniature, swinging gaily from the peg above his head while absentmindedly turning his wedding ring on his finger, the one Elizabeth had inscribed on the inside, "Remember Me."

Kinkaid took his breakfast in his tiny cubicle that morning, reluctant to share the dire news with Mr. Simpson, thinking of and hoping to find the right words that he would employ to tell the crew that the ship they were riding in the middle of the vast Atlantic was plagued with some pestilence that would spread until it ran its course, that no man might escape it's effects, that their very lives might as well be wagered on a throw of the dice.

Cato found him glum and uncommunicative but attributed the fact to his lack of sleep, even congratulating him on the fact that they were no longer being followed.

"Why, even Mr. Sykes said it was a miracle," Cato told him, well aware that Mr. Sykes had no end of criticisms of the ship, its crew and its captain, and had early on made it well known among the officers that he was senior to Kinkaid.

"Well, that is a miracle in itself," said Kinkaid, a man searching for miracles, and making Mr. Sykes's approval the last of his concerns, while somewhat aware that Mr. Sykes reminded Kinkaid of his first captain, Jules Davenport, a hard man who showed no mercies to tender midshipman.

Cato returned to find that Kinkaid had barely touched his food, but he said nothing, believing his captain, a newly married man, entitled to some melancholy, while the crew, unaware of the impending crisis, carried on as usual, oblivious of the dark cloud which hung over them. The sudden sound of raucous laughter reached him and might have annoyed him as he lay there on his cot at any other time, but now he welcomed the sound of it, knowing that the ship would know little enough of laughter in the coming days. He also knew he should be up on deck by now but could not quite bring himself to the effort of heaving out as yet.

Mr. Briggs was making his way down the passageway and was chuckling to himself.

"I wonder if you might share with me what you find so

amusing, Mr. Briggs?" he asked.

If Briggs was surprised to find Kinkaid still reclining on his cot so late in the morning, he kept his opinion to himself, answering, "The crew, sir, having a bit of fun at our Boatswain's expense. Seems O'Toole tired of seeing the crews quarters littered with garbage and dirty clothes, so he instituted a policy of fining the men for every infraction of litter and filth, all proceeds to go into a 'Liberty Pool'."

"Sounds like a good idea," said Kinkaid, knowing what he knew.

"Except that O'Toole ended up having to fine himself twelve pence, Captain," answered Briggs with a laugh. "They're saying if this keeps up, Boats will end up paying for the crews' liberty."

It was good to see the usually nervous Mr. Briggs speak so easily to his captain, but Kinkaid's apparent inability to share in the mirthful mood brought the young midshipman's laughter to a quick halt, and now he was back to his nervous self.

"Mr. Briggs, have the officers gathered in the wardroom. I shall be there forthwith."

"Right away, Captain."

After apprising his officers of the threat and deciding on a course of action, the crew was gathered together at noon for the announcement. A chill wind blew and he pulled his collar up as he stood before the men. Looking out at the motley and unshaven faces before him, he plainly told them, "We have an outbreak of ship's fever." After allowing a moment for the groans and murmurs to subside, he continued, "It starts with chills, rash and fever and so any man who suspects he is afflicted should report to Dr. Morrow. The sick will be kept separated from the healthy in an effort to halt its spread, but have no fear; all afflicted will be properly cared for, and there are some measures that we can take to stop it. Keeping a clean ship is important and so we will immediately commence to boiling all clothing and bed linen, and every square inch of this ship will be scrubbed from stem to stern. Every man will see his division head to comply and any man who tries to hide his illness or a piece of clothing or in any way shirks his duty will be severely dealt with. That is all."

There were no cheers after this speech, only low murmuring and some nervous laughter as the division heads quietly passed out their instructions. The cooks were already waiting, and all that day came the smell of boiling vinegar water as pile after pile of clothing and bed linen was cooked and then hung out to dry on the spars and rails.

"A ship of rags," observed Mr. Sykes, frowning his disapproval.

Ten-man working parties were soon busy scrubbing the overheads, bulkheads and decks with more buckets of boiling vinegar water. Rat details roamed the ship, searching out and killing as many of the loathsome rodents as they could find and catch. Three more men reported sick and joined Dr. Morrow, Mr. Grimes and the gunner's mate, Knox, in the forecastle, now the sickroom, the first area to be scrubbed down and displacing Boatswain O'Toole, to his consternation and dread. The only place to escape the smell and commotion was at the bowsprit where the wind blew clean and fresh and this is where Mr. Palfrey stood, staring out at the great expanse of ocean before him, his thoughts and ideas his own. The afternoon at least kept the crew busy with their scrubbing and boiling but as the activity ceased and the dreary day wore into evening a somber mood engulfed the ship. O'Toole tried to rouse the men to singing after their supper meal but they remained sullen and he soon gave up. Even the midshipmen's quarters were quiet. As he was drifting off to a fitful sleep Kinkaid could hear from somewhere forward the plaintive notes of a penny whistle playing a sad tune, which ended abruptly.

The first thing Kinkaid did the following morning was to pay a visit to the forecastle. Shut tight, the air was foul and stuffy with now nine men lying on cots. With little room to move about, Kinkaid knelt between Dr. Morrow and Mr. Grimes, both semi-conscious and shivering under piles of blankets. Samuel Carver, one of the loblolly boys, was trying to persuade the obese Knox, normally a heavy eater, to sip a bit of gruel.

"How are things, Carver?" asked Kinkaid.

"Well, Knox here seems to have made it through the worse, Captain. If I could just get some soup into him." Carver's forehead held tiny beads of sweat, apparently not from sickness but from the heat and humidity in the confined space. "Dr. Morrow and Mr. Grimes are in the fever and the others, well, chills and the rash."

"I can barely breath in here," said Kinkaid.

"I know, sir."

"Wouldn't a bit of fresh air help?" he asked.

"Well, Dr. Morrow said not to," answered Carver.

"What's got them is not in the air," said a gruff voice behind them. It was Boatswain O'Toole. "Excuse me, Captain. Didn't know you was in here."

"You were saying?" asked Kinkaid.

"The sickness, Captain. It's not in the air, it's in them, sir," he answered, "and these men need fresh air, just like healthy men."

"But Dr. Morrow said I was to keep out the draft..." Carver began.

"That doesn't mean suffocating them," growled O'Toole.

"Suffocating them? Now see here…"

"What do you know of this sickness, O'Toole?" asked Kinkaid.

"Seen it enough up in Maine, Captain. Among the Indians. Probably Typhus."

"And what did they do about it?"

"Died, mostly, sir." Noting Kinkaid's frustrated look, O'Toole explained further, "The Indians believe sickness is caused by bad spirits. And bein' warriors, they want to fight the spirits that cause them trouble. Certain herbs and poultices are their weapons against some spirits; others they try to drive away by dressing up real scary like; sometimes they believe the body needs to be roused and activated against the spirits that are tryin' to wear them down. Why, sometimes they'll throw a sick man out in the snow naked."

"Well, of all the foolish notions," said Carver.

"No, I've seen it cure men at the edge of death," claimed O'Toole. "Somehow it shocks the body into fighting for itself."

"Are you saying we ought to shock these sick men, these weak men?" asked Carver, incredulous.

"No," answered O'Toole, shaking his head, "that treatment don't work against this. Only makes a man weaker…like cutting off their supply of fresh air."

"Are you offering your services, O'Toole?" asked Kinkaid.

"I'd like to do what I can, sir."

Already insecure with Dr. Morrow unavailable, and now feeling cornered by the opinions of the venerable O'Toole come to take over his sick room, a confused Carver complained, "Sir, I don't believe I can in good conscience…"

"I'll take full responsibility," Kinkaid assured him.

"Well, sir..."

"Giving them soup is a good idea, Sam."

With the realization that the full weight of responsibility was being taken from his shoulders and then the welcome compliment from O'Toole, Carver seemed to relent. "Thanks, Boats."

"I've got some Joe Pye weed that'll make a nice tea to keep the fevers down," said O'Toole. "That's the most dangerous part about it...the fever cooks a man's brains. Best to give 'em the tea early on, before they get into the delirium. I'll go have the cooks brew some up and be right back. I'd leave this hatch open a bit, Sam. Let a bit of fresh air in here," suggested O'Toole.

"If you think it's best," agreed Carver.

"Just enough to let new air in and used air out. When you feel yourself breathing free and easy, Sam, then you'll know it's right for them."

The open doorway allowed a draft of chilly but refreshing air to enter the room, seeming to confirm that O'Toole might know what he was talking about.

But that didn't prevent six more men coming down with chills and fever that afternoon, one of them Venture Smith, a reluctant patient, intuitively afraid of being sequestered in a room full of sick men. Another was the strong and confident Mr. Midshipman Sutherland.

"Shakin' like a leaf in a hurricane," observed O'Toole, holding a cup of his herb tea up to Sutherlands trembling lips, half the bitter brew spilling down the young man's chin.

When Kinkaid again frequented the sick room after dinner, he found that two more men had been admitted, bringing the total sick to sixteen, too many bodies to cram into the forecastle, therefore he ordered that the sick room be extended to the midshipman's berthing area as well, forcing Mr. Briggs and Mr. Phillips to take up residence with the bulk of the crew.

The weather over the next two days remained dark and dismal as more men came down with the fever. And with the ship still flying clothing and bedding from the rigging and with more and more men shivering in their hammocks down below, it became impossible to escape notions of ill luck, of dread and depression, as fear and foreboding took its grip upon the ship. Lines and halyards, once neatly coiled upon the deck were now scattered heaps of rope. The brass ship's bell showed signs of tarnish. And a tie holding a bundle of spare spars along the larboard bulwarks had worked loose and every time the ship rolled the spars banged against the side. All evidence of neglect. Singing after dinner had come to an end. So had the normal joking and skylarking out on deck, and the crew appeared sullen and morose as they stood their watch or went about their duties in silence and with a lassitude and dullness that Kinkaid found disturbing.

Here came Carver now with the dreaded evening report. The man looked disheveled and distraught as he told Kinkaid, "Nineteen in all, now, Captain. I was about to take Sterling off the sick list, though. He must have had a mild case or perhaps just a cold, for he seems to have bypassed the worst of it. Knox continues to improve and is taking solid food now—could be back on duty tomorrow. Miller and Dr. Morrow seem the worse cases…and Mr. Sutherland, well he…"

"Carver, I'm relieving you of your duties for a while," Kinkaid told him. The man was obviously exhausted. "Get some sleep."

"But sir…"

"And that's an order, Carver."

"Yes, Captain."

"Where is Boatswain O'Toole?"

"I just saw him in the galley, sir. Making another batch of tea. It seems to be effective if we get it to the men before they…"

"Yes, I know, Carver," said Kinkaid. "Now get below, into your hammock. And I don't want to learn of you going back on duty for the next eight hours."

"Aye, Captain."

"Louis, go find Boatswain O'Toole and have him report to me."

"Aye, Captain," answered the messenger boy who hurried toward the after ladder only to have to wait and slowly follow Carver down below.

Boatswain O'Toole reported to the quarterdeck a few minutes later with little Louis in tow.

"You wanted to see me, Captain?"

"Boats, the brightwork is tarnished, the lines are a mess, that bundle of spars is not secured and is making a hell of a racket, and it seems that the general state of the ship is less than our usual standards," complained Kinkaid.

O'Toole looked as weary as Carver as he rubbed his forehead and answered, "I'm sorry, Captain. No excuse, sir. I'll roust out some hands right away and get this deck…"

"I know you've been busy," allowed Kinkaid. "And with Miller and half your hands down with the fever…"

"I'm worried about Miller, sir. Seems out of it for too long now," said O'Toole morosely.

"Carver tells me your tea has been a Godsend in keeping down the fever."

"Hasn't helped Miller, Captain."

Kinkaid suddenly felt guilty now for worrying about the condition of the deck. The ship was certainly not in chaos, nowhere near it, and he realized that he was seeking some kind of normalcy and the easiest way to achieve that was to do something visible, something tangible, to keep things as normal as possible. He hoped that O'Toole would understand that. "Boats, I've just ordered Carver to get some sleep."

"He could do with it, sir."

"And so could you," said Kinkaid.

"Yes, sir. After I've seen to the deck and then I need to…'

"O'Toole," said Kinkaid. He felt ashamed and thought for a moment about what he should say before explaining, "These are unusual times, Boats. I know you want to take your tea around and check on the sick…and I want to thank you personally for all you've done for the men…but I need to ensure that the ship is run in its usual manner, regardless."

"I understand, Captain. I'll get some people up here on deck right away, sir, and…"

"And then I want you to find somebody else to take your tea around and watch over the sick. You need to get some sleep, too."

"Yes, Captain, I do," agreed O'Toole. "Thank you, sir."

Some men, Davis, Harris and Nicky Sterling among them, did come up on deck and very quickly attended to the brightwork, the lines, and the banging spars. Meanwhile, both Carver and Boatswain O'Toole got some much-needed sleep. And Kinkaid remained on the quarterdeck, trying not to give in to his feelings of depression and the fatigue it seemed to bring.

He skipped his breakfast with Mr. Simpson the next morning, knowing his concentration would not be on Simpson's French lesson, and was on the quarterdeck by seven where he remained throughout the cold and dreary day. He was still on the quarterdeck that afternoon when Carver came up with his daily report.

"I thought Knox was over it, sir," he related uncertainly. "But I guess I was wrong."

"So he remains quite sick, then," surmised Kinkaid.

"What I mean to say, sir, is that he died…just now." Carver stood there as if confused, scratching his beard.

"Very well, Mr. Carver," was all Kinkaid could think to say, and knew immediately that he'd not said the right thing as Carver slunk away. He could have at least told Carver not to blame himself, that he'd done all he could to prevent it and thank him for his efforts. Angered, he had an impulse to curse God, but refrained. "God's will be done," was what his Grandfather would have said and this is the inadequate thought he consoled himself with as he gazed out to sea at the reflection of a crescent moon dancing upon the water. The clouds were breaking up, promising a cold and clear night.

Morning dawned clear and bright as well, while bringing the news from a very tired Carver, "Dr. Morrow is still quite sick. So is Mr. Grimes. Miller seems to be holding steady. Sutherland's got a bad case of the rash and won't shut up. Oh, and that Indian tea O'Toole keeps brewing does seem to help keep the fever down in some cases; helped Venture Smith and he's out of the woods." Carver sounded weary, his voice a low monotone as he continued, "Private Miles is our newest patient. The other marines tried to keep him among themselves but finally turned him over to us when Sergeant Lutz came down with it too."

"Carver, I don't want you wearing yourself out, getting sick yourself. You're getting enough help, aren't you?" asked Kinkaid.

"Yes sir," he admitted. "As you know, Boatswain O'Toole is tireless. And Mr. Phillips and Mr. Briggs volunteered; both tend to Mr. Sutherland like brothers. And Mr. Simpson, too."

Of course Mr. Simpson had wanted to pitch in, his energy always seeking an outlet, always wanting to be useful and having little enough opportunity aboard ship to be so. Yet he was the most valuable man aboard, the very reason for the voyage. To risk his life with men at death's door seem imprudent and Kinkaid's first impulse was to have a talk with the man, yet just as quickly concluded that there would be little he could say that would keep Mr. Simpson from doing what he pleased.

Two more joined the list of sick that afternoon, but it wasn't until O'Toole came and sadly told him that Miller had died, that the horror and helplessness of their circumstances hit him like a punch to the stomach.

He scarcely touched his food that evening. The dark Mr. Briggs had been invited to dinner and Kinkaid tried to make conversation with the young midshipman but found the young man's mood as dark as his complexion.

"How are your men faring, Mr. Briggs?"

"Well enough, sir, except for Seaman Harris."

"The sensitive poet?"

"Aye, Captain."

"Well, any poet is prone to moods, I should think."

"It's because of Sterling, sir. Seems Harris had him do one of those readings, you know, with those cards he carries. Sterling didn't want to show him the last card but Harris insisted and turned it over. Well, it turned out to be the 'death' card, and, well, Harris hasn't been the same since."

"What do you know of these cards, Briggs?"

"Not much, sir, although my mother could have told you all about them."

The dinner passed mostly in silence after that, each man

left with his own thoughts. Then Mr. Briggs left for his watch and Kinkaid resolved that he would have that talk with Mr. Simpson. He had to make an attempt, at least.

"Miller died today," he began awkwardly.

"I know," answered Simpson, his mouth full. "I was there."

"Of course."

He would have to take a different approach.

But before he could say anything else, Simpson made the observation, "You seem inordinately tired, Captain."

"Yes," he had to admit, "Can't seem to sleep through the night." He could have told Simpson about his worries. The obvious fears concerning men dying of the fever, that others might follow, and that he felt responsible in the way that captains are always responsible for anything that takes place on their ship. There was also his concern that a saboteur was aboard and might do almost anything to ensure that the ship never reached their destination. He might even have confided that Mr. Palfrey, who seemed to spend all his time forward, out on the open deck, wrapped in his thick coat, conveniently avoiding all contact with men, was at the top of his list of suspects. But to what purpose would telling Mr. Simpson any of these things serve?

Of course Mr. Simpson had his own ideas and made the suggestion, "Seems quiet enough this evening, Captain. Perhaps you might turn in early; catch up on some of that lost sleep."

At any other time, Kinkaid might have rejected the suggestion outright, but now he entertained the idea. The combination of illness aboard and the bad weather were depressing him and he felt for once as if he could put his worries aside. In fact, he could have easily fallen asleep right there at the table, helped by the second glass of wine that he normally would have refused. He could do little about his worries regardless, and so if he could only forget about them for a few hours, follow his own advice and get some sleep, he might be the better for it. "I believe I may do just that, Mr. Simpson."

The damp and chilly air seemed to penetrate to Kinkaid's bones as he lay on his cot that night and the extra blanket seemed of little help in keeping him warm as he tossed and turned, with dreams of monsters lurking just out of sight, hiding in dark corners on either side of him or behind him, tormenting him in strange and twisted nightmares. By morning he was shivering uncontrollably, in a cold sweat. His head felt as if it was squeezed between a vise, so badly did it ache. He opened his pained eyes and there was Cato, tucking another blanket about him. O'Toole hovered behind him.

"How do you feel, Captain?" asked Cato.

"Cold," was all he would admit. "Think I'll pay a visit to the galley…get warmed…"

"With all respect, sir, I think you'd better stay where you are," insisted O'Toole.

Kinkaid raised himself on an elbow. A big mistake, for the pain shot through his head like a lance. "Aaaah!" The slightest movement brought pain and agony, his thoughts unclear, his brain on fire. Simply turning his head to one side was almost more than he could bear. "This is the worst hangover I've ever had."

"Here, I've a cup of tea for you, Captain," said O'Toole.

Kinkaid could only slump back down on his cot as he took the cup that O'Toole held to his lips. He shivered violently as the warm, bitter liquid trickled down his dry throat.

"Have Mr. Weatherby report to me immediately, will you,

Boats?"

"Of course, captain," said O'Toole.

Kinkaid was already sleeping a tormented sleep when Weatherby reached the cubicle, with Cato still bent over him, wringing his hands nervously. With a dejected look, Weatherby said, "I believe I'll let him sleep, Cato."

"Yes," agreed Cato. "Let him sleep."

Kinkaid semi-awoke to blackness, and all he wanted was for the creaking to stop, the maddening sounds of hinges opening and closing so loudly in his ears, the hinges of coffins, opening and closing incessantly. All else seemed in doubt. Was he aboard ship? Was he the captain of a ship? There seemed nowhere to go except further into the black hell where he found himself, surrounded by coffins, hundreds of coffins floating in a fog-covered sea, their lids opening and closing endlessly, creaking and groaning like a Chinese torture, his soul tormented by a great and heavy feeling of sadness like the weight of an anvil around his neck, with his mind suspended in the grip of a giant hand that squeezed it without pity.

"Captain," he heard someone say. "Captain."

He opened his eyes and there, under a faint light, was revealed the black, red-lipped, scowling face of evil itself. "Ah!" he cried out in fear.

"It's me, Captain. Cato," came the gentle voice

Kinkaid allowed the face to become that of his familiar steward again and felt a deep shame for thinking that Cato was the devil, a shame and guilt out of all proportion to reality.

"Cato," was all he managed to say, knowing somewhere in his tormented brain that he had the sickness, that he was stricken with something terrible and powerful. He gazed past Cato at the miniature of Elizabeth swinging back and forth on the peg over his head. He could not see her clearly and the effort to focus his eyes proved futile, only making his head hurt worse. He closed them again, thinking the same thought over and over again in his burning brain, "I must live…for her…for her…I must…I will."

Kinkaid moved back and forth from tortured dreams to painful delirium, never knowing which was real, having no thoughts except that of escape from the cold darkness and the crushing, mind-numbing pain, his mind empty of light and life, left only in confusion and agony. At times French phrases ran incessantly through his brain, nonsensically, not understood and unremitting, the same phrase repeating over and over again as if containing some secret knowledge that he would eventually penetrate the meaning of. At other times he seemed to return to life and there would be Cato or Mr. Weatherby or Mr. Simpson attending him, wiping his perspiring forehead or pulling his blankets around his neck, making sure he was warm enough, sometimes coaxing him to take a few sips of O'Toole's bitter tea or a beef broth before the fever once again laid claim to him.

At one point, Kinkaid seemed to come out of it. At least he thought he did. Somehow, inexplicably, he had made his way topside. But he was high over the quarterdeck. Strangely, he could see the vague outline of the ship beneath him, far, far below, as if he were standing at the top of the mainmast. All around the ship was a vast and dense fog. He tried to look up, above the heavy clouds that seemed to bear down upon him, but could not move his head for some reason. Now there were sounds. Strange sounds all around him. Seagulls, perhaps? No. It was a sad and lonely sound. Human. The sad and pitiful cries of people, crying out for help, the sound of lost souls, the cries of the dead. There now, out in the water, someone was struggling. A hand reached out to him. He bent down to take it and could see that the person in the water had long auburn hair. But the hand was hard and bony. It's... "Oh my God... "No!"

"It's quite alright, Captain. I'm right here with you," came a soothing voice. "Nothing to be afraid of."

Kinkaid imagined seeing Mr. Sykes hovering over him, dabbing his forehead with a damp cloth, a look of infinite love on the rough man's face. No, it couldn't be. Mr. Sykes never looked like that, or acted even remotely solicitous. Kinkaid could not help but laugh at the image. At least he thought he laughed. And for many hours afterwards he lapsed back and forth from deep sleep to fitful dreams, from the ridiculous to the sublime, all reason distorted, all sense of time lost, his head throbbing violently, his body itching, sweating, cold and clammy at first, and then hot and clammy.

The light of day penetrated to his tiny chamber, it's feeble rays hurting his eyes as he opened them. He still had a headache, but at least he could think. At least he could tell for certain the difference between dream and reality.

"Cato!" he called out.

Something fell with a clatter onto the deck and a moment later there was Mr. Simpson, bending over him.

"Captain," he exclaimed. "Welcome back."

"Welcome back? How long have I been gone?"

"Three days, Captain."

The realization came as a shock. Three days lost. Three days of having forfeited the command of his ship.

There was Cato now. "We are much relieved to see you well, Captain," he said as he tucked a pillow behind his head. "And just in time for a bit of breakfast, if you're feeling up to it, sir."

"My clothes," said Kinkaid.

"But sir…"

"My uniform, if you please," he insisted.

"Of course, Captain."

Kinkaid stood up on wobbly legs, and then, feeling faint, fell back, leaning against the bulkhead.

"Perhaps you should take it easy, Captain," came Mr. Simpson's suggestion.

"I've taken it easy for three days," Kinkaid answered grumpily. Then he simply stood there a moment, feeling the roll of the ship, somewhat nauseous and light-headed, but when Cato returned with his uniform and tried to help him on with his pants, he said stubbornly, "I'll dress myself. If it's not too much trouble, you can fetch Mr. Weatherby."

"Right away, sir," said Cato, happily accepting the rebuke as the apparent sign of recovery that it was.

Mr. Simpson had remained to help him on with his uniform but even so, the effort had practically worn him out. And the fact that Simpson was treating him like an invalid irritated him.

"Mr. Simpson, I would be much obliged if you left me alone now." Instantly regretting his rudeness, he said, "Forgive me, but I must apprise myself of the condition of my ship and crew…attend to my duties."

"Of course, sir," said Simpson. And with that he was gone.

Kinkaid stood away from the cot, picked up his hat, and opened the curtain to his cubicle. He took a deep breath of the cool air wafting down the corridor, but then slumped against his cot as wave of nausea overcame him. Here came Weatherby now.

"Thank God, Captain," said Weatherby, happy at finding his captain out of danger. "So glad to see you up, sir."

"Your report, Mr. Weatherby," answered Kinkaid, trying to focus his thoughts on present business.

"Well, sir, there's good news and…"

"The state of the crew, Mr. Weatherby," Kinkaid wanted to know. "How many died and who were they?"

Weatherby sighed and with a grimace told him directly, "In addition to Seaman Knox and Boatswain Miller, five others died, sir. First Dr. Morrow. Then Mr. Grimes. Able Seaman Osborne never reported to sick bay…O'Toole found his body down in the hold. He'd been hiding himself down there, afraid of catching the fever from the others. Then the marine, private Miles, and rather quickly at that." Then Weatherby provided the good news that, "Smith pulled through, though he's still on the sick list. And Sterling seems to be recovering. Neither had a bad case. The good news is that the fever seems to have abated, sir."

Kinkaid remained slumped back against his cot as he listened to the depressing news. He was vaguely aware of his empty stomach and his head was spinning. But realizing that Weatherby had neglected to tell him who the fifth man was, Kinkaid had to ask, "The last man, Weatherby. Was it Harris?"

"Harris is fine, sir; never became sick. I'm afraid it was Mr. Sutherland, sir," admitted Weatherby, hanging his head. "Just yesterday. Mr. Phillips and Mr. Briggs are taking it hard, I'm afraid."

It was difficult, having to hear of so many deaths all at once like this. And not through battle, but from a silent enemy that no man, no matter how skilled a sailor or proficient a gunner could very well fight, and that no medical knowledge to date could adequately combat. At first Knox and then Miller. The old and frail Dr. Morrow. Then Mr. Grimes, incompetent as a sailing master, yet no less a man who valued his own life. The marine, Miles, whose face Kinkaid could not recall. At least he had gone quickly. And Osborne, too afraid to report to sick bay, yet hiding in the hold had not protected him and probably added to his agony, as he died alone. He could easily picture Osborne, the seaman with the dancing tattoo on his forearm, the man he had witnessed be rebuked by Sykes. And, as Weatherby had expected, the loss of the young and promising Mr. Sutherland was especially hard to accept. A bright and vigorous young man, enthusiastic and determined to make his own way in the world, looking for excitement and choosing to become an officer in training, away from dusty books and an over-protective father who would no doubt be devastated when he learned that his fine, strong son had met his end so ignominiously, so uselessly. Kinkaid stood there, stunned and only half alive himself. Yet Harris was alive, hadn't even come down with the sickness. Perhaps Seaman Sterling's cards were not infallible.

"As I said, Captain, the others have all recovered," reiterated Weatherby, in his attempt to bring something positive to his report, "some better than others. Boatswain O'Toole and Mr. Simpson were magnificent, tending to the ill. And Mr. Sykes too, none of them in the least concerned for their own lives. And the sickness seems to have left us, sir."

Kinkaid looked up and grimaced before saying, "Very well, Mr. Weatherby. That is at least something to be thankful for. And the ship?"

"On the same course as before, Captain, north by east by east. We just sighted Belle Ile off the larboard bow. If winds and currents remain favorable, we should soon make out the coast of France and the mouth of the Loire."

"My God, that means landfall in two or three days."

"I should think so, Captain."

"That is good news, Mr. Weatherby," gave Kinkaid. In fact, the news had so energized him that he stood up straight now, and in spite of his feelings of weakness and remorse, resolutely placed his hat on his head.

"Uh, there is one thing, Captain," said Weatherby with some reluctance.

"One thing?"

"That packet we lost last week. She's found us again."

The news was not unexpected and certainly having less impact than learning that six of his crew were no longer with them, three of them ship's officers. Yet it was not good news and another thing to worry his already frayed nerves.

"Spotted by none other than Mr. Phillips, just this morning," continued Weatherby, "Off our larboard beam, about two miles behind us now, following as before, Captain."

"Thank you Mr. Weatherby. I believe it's time I showed myself on deck."

Mr. Sykes was on the quarterdeck. The little beagle, Jonah, stared happily from beneath his coat and he tipped his greasy hat to Kinkaid as he approached. He even condescended to greet him with the words, "Good morning, Captain," and it struck Kinkaid that perhaps his dream of Mr. Sykes bending over him with the uncharacteristic caring countenance might not have been a dream after all and the thought made him uncomfortable.

"Good morning, Mr. Sykes," returned Kinkaid. With all greetings from the quarterdeck watch returned, Kinkaid turned and stood at the after rail and quickly found her as he gazed to the southwest where the familiar and somewhat faded white sails of their old partner stood out against the gray horizon.

Concluding there was little to be done about her, Kinkaid decided to pay a visit to the sick bay, where he found Sterling lying in a hammock.

"How are you faring Seaman Sterling?"

"I'm feeling fine, Sir, and ready for duty."

"Yes, but Mr. Carver wants you to rest easy until tomorrow," said Kinkaid. "Just to make sure. Does that suit you?"

"Aye, it does, Captain."

Bereft of what he might say to the strange man, Kinkaid found himself admitting, "I too had the sickness."

"Did you have visions, Sir?"

Taken off guard, Kinkaid stammered, "Well, I had nightmares. I don't know that they meant anything, but they were certainly frightening and seemed real at the time. Why, are you haunted by them?"

"I've had visions since I was a child, Sir. My mother said it was a blessing, a thing of grace, but I'm beginning to think of it as a curse."

"Why do you say that?"

"It tends to separate me from the world, from other men."

"I've noticed that."

"It's because they are frightened by things they do not understand. Why, I hardly understand myself."

Increasingly feeling the need to extricate from the conversation, Kinkaid merely gave a noncommittal, "I'm sorry."

"I had a vision about you, Captain."

"Did you?"

"I saw a man that you know. This man will try to trick you to your death, but will be tricked himself."

"Well, that is most interesting. Now I want you to take Mr. Carver's advice and get some rest, and tomorrow you may resume your duties if he is agreeable."

"Aye, Captain. And thank you for coming down."

Even with the packet that followed stubbornly in their wake as they crossed the vast Bay of Biscay, the next day passed uneventfully, monotonously without incident. And a good thing too, for not only did Kinkaid need the respite to further recuperate from his bout with ship's fever but the time was also welcomed by a tired and depressed, though relieved, crew. The officers watch roster was also reorganized and Kinkaid allowed the men easy duties, much needed rest from battle exercises and ship's routine. Even the weather cooperated with steady though moderate winds, pushing the ship ever closer toward their eventual landfall. And in spite of all of Kinkaid's protests, Mr. Simpson was eager to begin once again his infernal French lessons at breakfast.

"Shall we continue with our restaurant conversations?"

"If you insist," Kinkaid said with a sigh of exasperation. At least it would distract him, at least for an hour or so. "But start easy, would you? It's too early for such torture."

"I promise. Now then, let's see. How would you say you are hungry," asked Simpson.

"*J'ai faim*," said Kinkaid, adding the protest, "Now that is *too* easy. I have learned something, you know."

"Point taken," gave Simpson. "Try this, then. What would you say to the waiter if you found a fly in your soup?"

"Nothing. I'd simply remove the fly and finish the soup."

"And apologize to the poor hungry fly, no doubt. Come now, Captain, quit your stalling." Simpson was by now on to all of his tricks.

Kinkaid had to take a moment to gather his thoughts. It seems that all he could remember of the tricky French language had been washed away by the fever. But with Cato coming in with their coffee now, and not wishing to disappoint, Kinkaid took a deep breath and gave, "Uh...*J'ai une...grenouille...dans mon dejeuner.*"

"Ha ha, ha ha," Simpson had to laugh.

Cato could not hide a smile as he explained, "You just said there was a frog in your lunch, Captain."

Simpson was still laughing as he observed, "And nothing to complain about as far as your average Frenchman is concerned!"

"As I keep telling both of you, I'll never make a linguist."

"Ah, but it is only a matter of time, mon Capitaine," observed his steward. "Practice makes perfect."

"Cato is right," Simpson agreed. "Mark my words, Kinkaid, you'll be asking for frogs for lunch before we leave France. Delicious creatures, I assure you."

But Kinkaid's thoughts were not on his French lessons, nor on French cuisine, and he said, "Mr. Simpson, what do make of a man who has visions?"

"You're referring to Seaman Sterling, I presume."

"Yes, in a way, but more broadly. What is your opinion of fortune telling and such things?"

"Well, my father served in China for some time, and I recall this book he brought back with him that he would consult on occasion. He said it was a book that gave answers to all questions. One only had to ask a question while throwing three coins six times, and then consulting the book, filled with sixty-four variations."

"Sounds complicated."

"Oh, it's more complicated than that, for then there are moving lines and static lines which narrow even further one's answer."

"But do you believe in such nonsense?"

"I remember asking my father that very same question. You know what he told me? That belief itself had a large part in divining the correct answer. He also told me that we all know the answers to our questions at some deeper level, and that the Chinese system only reminded the asker of this fact."

"Hmm, have you made use of this book?"

"Yes, I must admit that I have."

"And it gave you a satisfactory answer?"

"Always."

"Then all ship captains should be issued one when they are commissioned," said Kinkaid with a grin.

"Indeed, Captain. But such things are more acceptable by the Chinese. They've developed a rather high state of culture over many centuries and such knowledge is not considered out of the ordinary, is not feared like it is in the west."

"Well, it does sound a bit…heretical."

"I believe there are many things that man does not yet understand, many things that we shall accept in the future that seem heretical today."

"I admire your confidence in the future, Mr. Simpson."

"Well, I've had a few strange experiences; experiences that tell me that all is not as it appears."

"Such as?"

"Well, I would not wish it to get around to my colleagues or those who employ me, but I've concluded through these experiences that my spirit shall indeed carry on after my body dies. And I must say it's given me some comfort to know this."

"But how can you be certain?"

"I've found myself out of my body."

"Out of your body? Isn't that the same as dreaming?"

"No, it is quite different than dreaming, although it has

happened while I am asleep, or about to fall asleep. You see, in dreaming, you are experiencing strange and unrelated events, more a kaleidoscope, a hodgepodge of images that rarely makes sense. But when I leave my body, all of my thoughts come with me. I know when it is happening, and I see the world as it is. I've seen my body lying there, and I've been able to move about wherever I wish to go simply by thinking about where I'd like to go."

"Mr. Simpson, you can't be serious."

"Oh, I'm quite serious. The first time it happened, I found myself hovering over my body, which frightened so much that I was immediately pulled back in."

"The first time it happened?"

"It's happened five or six times, mostly when I was a younger man. It hasn't happened for some years now."

"And you're certain it is your spirit and not a dream.'"

"Quite certain. The second time it happened, I was falling asleep in a chair when suddenly I could see everything around me; the furniture in the room, the patterns of the rug at my feet, the clock and candlesticks on the mantel behind me. I even saw myself sitting there, with my eyes shut. It fascinated me so much that I was able to overcome my fear and so it lasted a few seconds longer. The time after that I was so excited that I wanted to tell my friend about it and I passed through a door without opening it. Oh, did that surprise me. That, my friend, is spirit."

"Mr. Simpson, you continue to surprise and baffle me."

"As I do myself," said Simpson with a laugh, causing Kinkaid to laugh as well.

Both were still laughing when there came an urgent rapping at the door.

VII
Saved by the Bell

It was Mr. Weatherby who gave the shout, "She's making signals, Captain!"

Kinkaid was on the quarterdeck an instant later, followed by Mr. Simpson. Mr. Phillips was officer of the watch. Boatswain O'Toole and Mr. Rosetti were there as well.

"That is the th-third set of flags she's hoisted, Captain," Mr. Phillips informed him.

"Who is she signaling?" Simpson wanted to know.

"Sail ho!" came the answer from the lookout. "Two points off the starboard quarter!"

"What is she?" Kinkaid shouted as Mr. Sykes joined them on the quarterdeck.

"Can't tell as yet, Captain!" came the uncertain reply from the masthead. "All's I can see are tops'ls!"

"Mr. Weatherby..."

"Aye, Captain!" Weatherby was already climbing the shrouds with the telescope draped round his neck.

"They've found us, haven't they?" asked Mr. Simpson.

"It would appear so," he had to admit.

A moment later came Weatherby's report, confirming their fears. "A frigate, Captain! Setting studding sails!" A moment's pause brought the further information, "She's heading our way!"

"Can we outrun it?" asked Simpson.

"We'll see," said Kinkaid.

And while wishing Mr. Simpson would keep his questions to himself, Mr. Sykes offered, "Perhaps she is French."

Simpson gave Sykes a disgusted look, recognizing the statement as wishful thinking and, being Mr. Simpson, he was bound to be insistent. "We *can* outrun a British frigate, can we not, Captain?"

Kinkaid glared at Simpson with some annoyance, knowing the answer depended upon many variables. There was no need to call the men to quarters. The ship was already under full sail. And the wind was moderate off the starboard quarter, so there would be no apparent advantage in changing course at this point. The log showed they were making six knots. All they could do now was wait and watch. If the frigate could make better than six knots they would all soon see her topsails from the deck. In the event, he would have to think of something else.

"The packet is hoisting her flying jib, Captain!" came Weatherby's shout.

"Emboldened, it would seem, sir," observed Mr. Sykes.

Kinkaid, feeling faint, ignored the statement, indeed, ignored everyone on deck. It irritated him that the entire ship's company was aware of the development and had come out to see what all the shouting was about.

"Mr. Sykes, see to it that those men not on watch have something to occupy them."

"Aye, Captain. I'll keep 'em busy, sir." With that Mr. Sykes stormed toward the waist and began shouting orders to the idlers. By the time he had employed half of them with things to do, the other half had scurried below.

Kinkaid felt terribly weak and wanted to go below himself, and lie down. He was not fully recovered from the fever, not completely, yet he knew he had to remain on deck, not only to show to the crew that he was still in command, but he needed to ascertain if the frigate might prove to be gaining on them, what her intentions might be, indeed, whether she was British or not, clutching at the unlikely. In this light air and with all sails set, he could only hope that they would have the advantage if she proved to be enemy. And his hopes were rewarded, for, even an hour later they still could not see her sails from the main deck. The packet, however, had closed considerably, but was careful enough to remain well beyond the range of their guns.

Mr. Weatherby relieved Mr. Phillips for the noon watch as Kinkaid remained stubbornly at the stern rail, still looking to the west for any sign of the frigate's topsails. But as he watched he saw only a front of clouds moving down from the northwest and noticed that the wind was picking up, with sporadic gusts that occasionally swept over the sea and heeled the ship. He felt weak and empty, tired and hungry, his mind dull, the leaden sea a reflection of his mood.

Kinkaid stood there still almost an hour later, his knees locked as he leaned against the stern bulwark, gripping the rail with wet and cold hands, his knuckles white, his eyes closed, only half aware of the ship rising and falling under him, mesmerized by the sound of the waves under the stern, and it came as a surprise when he heard Weatherby's voice right beside him.

"Looks like a bit of weather coming our way, sir," said Weatherby.

"Yes," came his forced reply.

"It's almost one o'clock, sir," Weatherby informed him.

The statement angered him. "Is there some point in reminding me of the time, Mr. Weatherby?" he asked, refusing to look in Mr. Weatherby's direction.

Weatherby only smiled at the rebuke and explained, "It's only that Cato had expected you for dinner, Captain."

Kinkaid only now realized that his stomach felt like a bottomless pit, that his legs were almost too weak to stand, that his hands had stiffened rigidly around the rail and it was only with some effort that he released his grip. Yet, the opportunity to speak with Weatherby was here, and with the wind picking up their words would be carried away from prying ears.

"About Mr. Palfrey, Weatherby."

"Well, I'm not sure I have anything worth reporting, sir. He doesn't divulge much, and seems suspicious of inquiry."

"That in itself tells me something," Kinkaid assured him.

Encouraged, Weatherby went on. "He speaks of killing as if it comes easily to him, sir. Oh, and he keeps a razor-sharp dagger in a special sheath in the small of his back, just under the flap of his coat."

"How do you know this?"

"During one of our practice sessions, sir. I managed to knock his sword from his hands and wrestled him to the deck. Took me a week to get the better of him, and I thought I had him when the tricky devil poked that dagger in my ribs. Leaves nothing to chance, that one."

Kinkaid staggered from his fatigue and Weatherby steadied him. "Easy, sir."

"Yes, well, perhaps a bite to eat would be agreeable," he had to admit.

"And perhaps a bit of rest," suggested Weatherby, assuring him, "I'll be sure to inform you of any developments, Captain."

The information about Mr. Palfrey, though scanty, was more than he had before and took its place in his mind as Cato brought him an excellent onion soup, limiting Kinkaid to a small bowl of it, along with two slices of stale bread that he dipped into the soup, his appetite ravenous, warning him that, "Too much into an empty stomach is not good, Captain." He was thankful that Mr. Simpson had already eaten, for he wanted only to be left in peace. Afterwards, Kinkaid passed the word to the quarterdeck to inform him if the sails of the frigate or any other appeared on the horizon or if there was any change in the weather, then returned to his cot, his bedding clean and fresh-smelling. His intention was to take Weatherby's advice and simply rest for a few minutes, but he soon fell asleep, much to the relief of his devoted steward, who covered him with a blanket and ensured that he was not disturbed with any unnecessary commotion or noise.

It was almost four in the afternoon when Kinkaid awoke, jarred out of a deep and dream-free sleep by the pitch and roll of the ship. He immediately sprang out of his cot and made his way to the quarterdeck where the wind was whistling in the rigging.

"You were to have informed me of any change in the weather," he said forcefully to Mr. Weatherby as he jammed his hat tightly onto his head.

"I was just about to wake you, Captain," said Weatherby.

"We're making all of ten knots, sir!" It was Boatswain O'Toole in the waist with the log dripping in his hands.

The formerly calm sea was now showing whitecaps, the ship was pitching and the bow began a regular crashing into the swells.

"The frigate?"

"I can just make out her topsails now and again, Captain, right about there," explained Weatherby, indicating a point to starboard of directly aft.

"So she's gained a bit," said Kinkaid, squinting in the direction but unable to detect any sign of a ship.

"A bit, sir."

An hour passed and the wind increased with the coming of the storm front. And with the wind, there came into view the topsails of the frigate. Now Weatherby stepped beside him and said, "She's British for certain, Captain."

"Of course she is," said Kinkaid.

A half hour later her courses were showing, while *Active* began to heel dangerously under the sudden gusts, her decks awash. Seaman Cole was at the wheel. The swelling over his black eye had gone down but there remained still a dark ring under his cheek.

"We'd better take in studding sails, Captain," came the unsolicited advice from Mr. Sykes.

But Mr. Sykes was right. The pressure on the rigging and spars was too great. They were risking catastrophe unless sails were shortened.

"Very good, Mr. Sykes. Have tops and courses reefed as well."

Kinkaid gloomily considered the circumstances as the crew was called out to the dangerous business of shortening sail. The storm couldn't have come at a worse time. A larger ship, with her stronger rigging, greater mass of sails, and driving power to push through the chop, would gain a speed advantage, while the *Active* would be slowed by the heavy seas and reduced canvas. By five o'clock, Kinkaid could see not only the topsails of the pursuing frigate, but her main sails. If conditions remained the same, the results were predictable; the enemy frigate would overtake them.

"Land ho!" came the shout from the mainmast lookout. "Land ho, dead ahead!"

All turned to look forward, where the lookout indicated. There, beyond the bounding bow and flying spray was a dark blue-gray undulating line; the coast of France, some twelve miles distance.

"Mr. Weatherby!" shouted Kinkaid. "Where is Mr. Weatherby?"

"Up here, Captain!" Weatherby, as usual, had anticipated his captain's concerns and was already in the main shrouds, trying to determine where on the French coast they were pointing, and it was not long before he came down and gave his report.

"As near as I can make out, we're heading straight for the mouth of the Loire."

It was something, at least, to know that his navigation had been correct, given the chancy tides and currents of the Bay of Biscay.

But nothing could take away the fact that the frigate was closing, and inexorably so, and by six bells into the evening watch, she was hull up and within two miles. The wind had increased and Kinkaid was considering if he should call for another reef in the sails when he heard a loud cracking sound from forward, followed an instant later by the loud and violent snapping of canvas.

"It's the jibs, Captain!" shouted O'Toole as he rushed forward on the wildly bounding deck, calling for hands to follow him. The jib and flying jib was trailing out to starboard, flapping free in the wind and crackling like thunder in the stiff breeze.

"I'm going forward, Weatherby," said Kinkaid.

O'Toole was already at the bowsprit, taking charge. Nicky Sterling was there, as well, lending a hand. Also standing at the bow, to Kinkaid's surprise, was Mr. Palfrey. He was thoroughly drenched.

"Mr. Kinkaid, there's mischief been done here," said a shivering Mr. Palfrey.

"Loose the jib sheets!" yelled O'Toole. Then to Mr. Palfrey he politely said, "You're going to have to move aside, sir."

"I saw this man cut the halyard to the jib," said Mr. Palfrey, pointing at Sterling.

"You, sir, are a liar," came the retort from Sterling.

Palfrey stiffened and gave back, "If you were a gentleman, I would take that as an insult to my honor."

Kinkaid, gazing in horror at the stump of the snapped jib boom, had no time for accusations or honor at the moment. "Get yourself below, Mr. Palfrey!" he shouted over the sound of the rippling canvas.

Nicky Sterling was already crawling out over the bowsprit. In spite of being tossed up and down and being splashed by wave after cold wave, Sterling clung desperately to the spar, then reached down and held up one of the severed lines that had connected the end of the jib boom to the spanker, a line that supported the stressed spar from below. When that line had parted, the pressure from the jibs was enough to snap the spar. Even worse, the foretopmast had lost three of its supporting cables that had been attached to the end of the jib boom; they were hanging loose from the top of the foremast and the three-foot stub of boom at the end was flailing back and forth like a dangerous mace. One blow from that flying spar and Sterling might be killed or knocked off the mast, a dead man either way.

"Take in the foretops'l and t'gallant!" shouted Kinkaid frantically.

Sterling began backing away from the broken spar as the stub continued to whip threatening around him. When he was close enough, Kinkaid reached down and grabbed Sterling by his belt and with O'Toole's help, the two hauled the soaked Sterling back on deck.

"Take a look at that line, Captain. That spanker line was cut," said Sterling through chattering teeth as he stood up.

"Get below," said Kinkaid, in no mood to consider how or who might have cut the spanker line. But he did take a moment to inspect the line. Sure enough it was not a frayed part, but neatly sliced, certainly cut with a sharp blade.

Somebody picked up a grappling hook and managed to snag the flailing piece of boom and bring it back aboard. A driving rain began in earnest now and, with much shouting and frantic activity, the jibs were finally hauled on deck in a heap of crumpled canvas and secured from the clutches of the wind, even as the topsails of the foremast were released and taken in. But *Active* had lost half her canvas.

O'Toole and the deck hands now had to quickly replace the jib boom. First, the stump of the old spar had to be removed, which required men to go out and hang over the bow of the ship and subject themselves to regular and frequent dunkings into a cold and furious sea. Then the new spar had to be slid into its place and the standing rigging re-attached, a hazardous job that took even the expert efforts of Grubb the carpenter's mate almost an hour to accomplish.

"We won't lose her on this night," observed Mr. Sykes as a soaked and exhausted O'Toole reported to the quarterdeck that the deck crew had replaced the bowsprit, attached the standing rigging, had hauled up double-reefed jibs and reset reefed foretopsails. Soaked and shivering men were heading below.

"Thank you, Boats, Grubb," said Kinkaid appreciatively. "Now you'd both better get into some dry clothes."

"Aye, Captain," came the weary replies.

An equally soaked Mr. Weatherby approached him now with his report from his vigilance in the shrouds. "I can just make out the lights of St. Nazaire, Captain," he said through chattering teeth, and shivering uncontrollably. "Which puts us about five miles from the mouth of the Loire, dead ahead."

"Thank you, Mr. Weatherby, that is good to know, and get yourself below, too. Oh, and have Lieutenant McDowd place a guard at Mr. Palfrey's door, to inform me if he leaves his cabin for any reason."

"Aye, Captain."

The ship was pitching and tossing once again over the scrambled waves of the Bay of Biscay, but Kinkaid could take little comfort in the fact, even though they were so close to their landfall now. A nervous Mr. Simpson had thankfully kept himself unobtrusively out of the way as Kinkaid and his crew attended to their duties and timely repairs, and even now he refrained from asking what their chances were as he stood next to Kinkaid on the wet and windblown quarterdeck, both with their collars turned up against the blow, both gazing toward the west. Even on this dark and rainy night, they could easily see the frigate less than a half mile off the starboard quarter, both knowing, indeed the entire ship knowing, that if the winds did not mitigate, they would soon be within range of her heavy cannons, at least twelve to eighteen-pounders.

Never had Kinkaid felt so gloomy, so out of control, as he realized the full meaning of their situation. They soon might be caught and the news of Saratoga would never reach Franklin in Paris. Never mind that his career would likely be over, but the dreaded memories and horror of the prison ship *Jersey* penetrated his mind as he searched in vain for some solution. He was not yet fully recovered from the weakness of his recent illness and at times feelings of dread and desperation overtook him that he had to shake off with the sheer force of will as he took deep breaths against the constriction in his chest. He appreciated Mr. Simpson's silence, but he avoided the looks from his officers and crew.

He felt them looking his way; of course they looked to him now for some way out. But how? So absorbed was he in his private hell that he did not notice when Mr. Phillips approached.

"Sir?"

"Uh, yes, what is it, Mr. Phillips?"

"It's Mr. P-Palfrey, sir. He says he would like to s-speak with you, sir…uh, in his stateroom, if you would. Says it's extremely im-portant."

"Extremely important? Very well, Mr. Phillips. I shall see him directly." The last man he wanted to waste his time at the moment was Mr. Palfrey, with an enemy ship giving chase less than a half mile behind them, yet there was little he could do to change the fact and it was at least a temporary distraction, was his thought.

Kinkaid vaguely remembered as he made his way below that Mr. Palfrey had been at the bow when the jib boom had snapped. And that Palfrey had said something about mischief being done. It was with these thoughts that Kinkaid knocked on the masters' mate's door.

Mr. Palfrey opened the door, saying, "Ah, Captain, thank you for taking the time to see me." He wore a robe of beige wool. His hair was still wet but neatly combed back. A book of Shakespeare's plays lay on the cot. Palfrey picked up the book and said, "Please sit down, Captain."

"I haven't time for a long conversation, Mr. Palfrey."

"Of course not. I am well aware of the situation," answered Palfrey, "but I believe you will be interested in what I have to say concerning the matter at hand."

"Which would be?"

"Well, that I found your seaman Sterling straddled over the bowsprit just before it broke."

"And for what reason were you there?"

"Why, to relieve myself."

"So you believe Sterling did something to cause the…accident?"

"Of course I am no expert in such matters, Captain, but it does seem somewhat suspicious, don't you think?"

"Somewhat," allowed Kinkaid. "Is there anything more you wish to tell me?"

"I confronted him…Sterling, before you arrived on the scene," continued Palfrey. "Asked him what he was doing out there on the spar in such horrible weather."

"You don't say?"

"Yes. He told me to mind my own business. That's when the boom gave way. Gave me a terrible fright."

"But then we mustn't take counsel of our fears, must we, Mr. Palfrey?" said Kinkaid, the offhand comment surprising even himself.

Mr. Palfrey huffed and said, "It is not an unfounded fear that concerns me, Captain, but the treachery of a scoundrel and a traitor. In fact, I would suggest you place that man in irons for the duration of our passage, for the sake of our mission."

Kinkaid hesitated before answering. "I will take your suggestion into consideration, Mr. Palfrey. Until then, I thank you, sir, for your most interesting information."

"I hope you will find it useful, Captain."

When Kinkaid reached his tiny cabin, there was Cato, already handing him his heavy weather coat. "Thank you, Cato. And I'll have my pistols, as well."

"Very good, sir."

The rain had changed to sleet when Kinkaid returned to the deck, the pistols stuffed into his belt under the bulky coat, where he found all of his officers on the quarterdeck and even some of the off watch crew, all eyes squinting through the foul weather toward the frigate that had halved the distance since he last looked at her. Boatswain O'Toole was now bundled up in a dry set of clothes and a heavy coat. Only Mr. Simpson, still huddled behind his turned up collar, oblivious even to the icy sleet stinging his face, did not seem to notice Kinkaid's return to the quarterdeck, his gaze concentrated solely upon the following warship, a potent reminder that she would not be ignored as Kinkaid had enjoyed ignoring the small British packet.

Kinkaid looked at her through his telescope. He noticed the dirty fore course, and there, under her bowsprit was a gold-painted figurehead. Now he saw a flash and a puff of smoke issuing from her bow, followed by a dull boom. He took his eye from the telescope in time to see the shot splash well short. Only now did Mr. Simpson turn his head with a consternated look.

"Testing the range," Mr. Sykes informed him. "Give her half an hour."

"And then?"

Sykes opened his mouth to answer Mr. Simpson, but the stern look from Kinkaid silenced him.

The frigate had drawn to a thousand yards before her forward cannon spoke again. This time the shot fell some fifty yards off the port bow. She had the range now, and Mr. Sykes knew better than to state the fact.

"Clear for action," said Kinkaid.

"Aye, Captain," came Mr. Sykes's response, and the call to quarters that brought the few remaining crew out on deck, including Mr. Briggs. Nicky Sterling took over at the ship's wheel, replacing Seaman Cole who made for his station as foretopman.

"Load with shot, Mr. Hill, but don't run them out yet."

"Aye, Sir!"

"Mr. McDowd, I'll have your marines on deck."

Kinkaid ignored the frantic but well-executed activity on the deck as officers and men took to their action stations, his mind groping for a way to save them. Soon reports began coming to the quarterdeck, that the decks had been sanded, all guns were loaded, and each division of men and marines were standing by.

Mr. Sykes summed it up. "The ship is ready, Captain."

"Very well."

The frigate continued her slow progress, closing foot by foot as the sleet began to give way to snow flurries, tiny flakes driven almost horizontally by the wind. At a thousand yards she began a slow turn to starboard. Her captain had decided to chance a broadside. There was nothing to do but watch and wait as her first guns forward were brought to bear.

The anticipation of receiving cannon fire was too much for Mr. Rosetti, who began to ask, "Well, is she going to fire at us or…?" But his complaint was answered with three flashes and almost instantaneously came a crash and the deck swept with flying splinters as the muffled sound of the guns echoed across the driven, storm-tossed gulf. Two shattered bodies lay just in front of the quarterdeck, another writhing in agony, as Venture Smith's crew rushed to the man's assistance, Carlisle, the rammer on number three.

"Return to your guns!" he heard Hill shout from the waist. "The dead over the side; Mr. Carver will see to the wounded!"

Carver and the other loblolly boys were on the scene in an instant and carried the moaning Carlisle below. The dead were unceremoniously heaved over the side by Smith and Harris, unrecognized by Kinkaid since he was watching the next ripple of flashes and bursts of smoke that erupted from the black side of the frigate, only to be instantly ripped away by the driving wind. The deck under his feet shuddered with the impact of three balls crashing low alongside the hull and then a loud popping sound as a ball tore through the mainsail over his head. At least no men fell this time. With her port batteries discharged, the frigate was already turning onto her original course and would quickly make up the distance lost in her attempt to cripple *Active*.

"Mr. Sykes, I'll trouble you to get below and assess our damage," ordered Kinkaid. "I will expect your report in five minutes."

"Aye, Captain."

The frigate was seven hundred yards off their starboard beam as the snow flurries began to fall in a heavy curtain of gray, almost hiding the enemy ship. Her black hull blended with the black sky and sea. Only her sails, at least contrasting against the dark sky, gave away her deadly presence, and the occasional flash of her forward stern chasers, throwing balls of lead their way. Kinkaid muttered a curse against his luck and the fickle weather, knowing he could have easily lost the frigate in the snow had it fell only a half hour earlier.

Nicky Sterling, standing at the ship's wheel, overhead Kinkaid's muttered curse and said, "I believe we shall be safe, Captain."

It was a foolish comment and Kinkaid ignored it. As it was, the enemy frigate was surging ever closer and would soon pull alongside and crush them with her next broadside, delivered at point blank range. Off in the distance came an eerie sound, barely heard, a gong; perhaps a church bell pealing, but it was of little concern compared to the enemy ship and so Kinkaid only half took in its significance.

Here came Mr. Sykes now from his inspection. "We've

two holes at the waterline, Captain. We're taking on water, but Grubb is attending to it and says he should have them plugged in no time."

"Can the pumps keep up?"

"Uh, I'm not sure, sir. Depends on how quickly Grubb works, I suppose."

"I suppose is no answer, Mr. Sykes," said Kinkaid, irritated that his First Officer had not inquired of Grubb as to the effectiveness of their pumps in relation to the amount of water they were taking on.

"Of course not, sir."

Kinkaid returned his attention to the frigate as a feeling of helplessness overcame him. But then she did something completely unexpected. She was making a sharp turn to starboard, still over five hundred yards away. She could have closed the gap in half an hour and swept their decks with a point-blank broadside of grape, inflicting irreparable damage to their gun deck and gun crews, but now her guns would not be very accurate or very effective at the longer range with the seas this choppy. Even so, Kinkaid's stomach tightened as the frigate turned broadside to them and she loosed another volley, this time skipping their balls across the gap. But the waves were too high for such a tactic and most balls were stopped short. Only three crashed against their hull, two close to the waterline, and one into the bow, sending splinters flying into the repaired jib, cutting it in a dozen places, yet the sail held.

"That was lucky for us, sir!" said Mr. Sykes.

"Mr. Sykes, I'll thank you to get below once again and check on the damage. And this time let me know if the pumps are keeping up," said Kinkaid, at a loss as to what they could do. Luck, it seemed, had deserted them, for the captain of the enemy frigate would surely rectify his mistake in turning too soon and take the time to gain on them before finishing them off. Kinkaid had a terrible decision to make. He would either have to surrender his ship or fight to the death. The strange sound of a bell reached his ears once again through the curtain of falling snow, a bit louder this time.

Mr. Hill approached him after Mr. Sykes had left the quarterdeck and bravely growled, "We'll give her a dose of her own medicine when she gets close, Captain."

Kinkaid turned and took note of their gunners standing ready behind each and every gun on the open deck, courageous sailors all; loyal, determined to do their duty, no matter what decision their captain made. A glorious sight, yet never before did the weight of command seem so heavy.

But then something even more incredible happened, and it was Mr. Rosetti who first noticed. "She'sa turning, Captain! She'sa keepa turning, Captain!" He had reverted to a strong Italian accent in his excitement and disbelief.

Yes, it was true. The enemy frigate was actually turning away from them. She should have turned toward them, but now she had made a mistake and would have to tack through the wind, a laborious and time-consuming process.

The snow had abated somewhat and they could easily see her through the blowing flurries. The captain of the enemy frigate had certainly made a mistake, but the snow was not heavy enough to give them a chance to hide from her. All they could hope was that she might be caught in irons as she turned into the wind, giving them at least a respite from certain death or capture.

But she did not even attempt to complete her turn. When her stern pointed directly toward *Active*, she kept heading directly away from them, an incredible and unbelievable sight. The name placard across her stern read *Vanguard*.

"I believe she'sa let us go, Captain," said Mr. Rosetti in stunned disbelief.

It was Mr. Simpson who provided the explanation. "The authority of the coastal nation terminates where she can no longer control it with her weaponry. Gentlemen, we are inside the limit of sovereign authority." It was the only explanation that made sense.

Even Kinkaid stood there dumfounded, not completely understanding why the frigate had so suddenly abandoned her quarry. It was Mr. Sykes who, returning to the deck and noticing the frigate turning away, asked, "But what do you mean, Mr. Simpson?"

"Only that the limit of sovereign authority is measured by a swath, the width of which does not exceed the distance of the flight of a cannonball from the shore...an average distance of about three miles. We are less than three miles from shore, are we not, Mr. Weatherby?"

All on the quarterdeck looked toward shore now, for the first time since the chase. All noticed the lights of St. Nazaire through the snowflakes, close off the larboard beam. There, just off the starboard bow, was a buoy with a bell on top, bonging occasionally.

"I make us closer than one mile, Captain," answered Weatherby with a toothy grin. "In fact, we are entering the mouth of the Loire." Which explained the choppy seas. "That dim glow of light on the horizon, dead ahead, is our destination, sir, the port of Nantes."

"A Royal Navy captain has his orders," said Simpson, snow on his hat, "and paramount is not to violate international law, especially one that could precipitate a crisis leading to war with another country. England not at war with France, not as yet, anyway; it seems our reprieve has been precipitated by international law, Captain."

"Your report, Mr. Sykes."

"Grubb has the holes shored up, sir, and he says the pumps are making good progress."

"Very well," said Kinkaid with some relief. "But let's change the men at the pumps right away, shall we?"

Yes, they were safe, and it seemed a miracle. And only now did Nicky Sterling's foolish words come to mind before the enemy frigate turned away and all seemed lost. What had he said? *I believe we shall be safe, Captain.* What did Sterling know that nobody else knew? What made the man say such a thing? Of course, Sterling had been steering the ship. He knew they were close to land, heard and saw the buoys of the Loraine inlet. It was the only explanation that made sense, yet…

Kinkaid's relief was such that his legs began to shake, to the point where he braced himself against the binnacle, and hoped no one would notice. But he had nothing to fear, as all eyes were upon the enemy frigate, *Vanguard,* now only a ghostly shape through the howling snow, beating back into the Bay of Biscay, the red bell of the buoy bonging clearly now as it passed close off the starboard beam as if in welcome.

VIII
Post-Chaise to Hay Wagon

"Why Cato, where did you find the butter to make these croissants?"

"Not only butter, Captain," said Cato, "but I was digging around in my delicacies chest last night and happened to discover this jar of orange marmalade."

"How fortuitous," exclaimed Kinkaid as Cato proudly set the prize down, "my favorite," suspecting all the while that his crafty but thoughtful steward had likely saved the tin of butter as well as the jar of marmalade for just such an occasion when stores were scarce, and so pretending to enjoy the 'discovery' pleased him immensely.

He was just finishing a letter to Elizabeth when Mr. Phillips knocked on the frame of his cubicle.

"Compliments from Mr. Sykes," reported Phillips, "and he asked me to inform you that our p-pilot is about to come aboard, sir."

"Very well, Mr. Phillips. Please tell Mr. Sykes that I shall be up directly."

"Aye, Captain."

Kinkaid found Mr. Simpson on deck; gazing through the misty morning air toward a small sloop that dropped her sails and drifted up against the ship, whereupon a short man with a funny hat climbed up the ladder to the quarterdeck.

The man doffed his hat to Kinkaid and said, "Bienvenue en France!"

"Mr. Simpson, it seems we are in the right place."

"All because of you, Captain."

Their pilot with the funny hat, a Monsieur Guillaume from the port of St. Nazaire, may have worn a dirty black suit and smelled of spoiled cheese, but he navigated the ship with confidence, passing his hometown off the port beam and taking them up the channel of the river Loire. The port of Nantes was still some 15 miles up the river and there was little for Kinkaid to do but watch from the rail as Monsieur Guillaume expertly guided the ship through the mixed traffic of fishing boats, merchant coasters and barges that traveled the well-marked channel while speaking rapid-fire French with Mr. Simpson who plied him with numerous and sundry questions. They passed farms and fields, quaint cottages with their garden plots and fruit trees, and now and again a small village where people stopped to look at the strange foreign warship gliding by. It was almost noon before they reached the colorful and bustling port of Nantes under a pale blue sky. Monsieur Guillaume brought the ship alongside a dock where a ship was being built. The carpenters made a great deal of noise pounding and sawing as they planked her hull, some occasionally looking their way at the ship with the unfamiliar ensign flying.

Once all lines were secured and the ship moored alongside the dock, Kinkaid passed the word for all officers to gather on the quarterdeck. First, he introduced the thin man with the thin mustache that Monsieur Guillaume had brought to the ship that afternoon. "This is Monsieur Clermont. He will be assisting us with our revictualing. Be sure to introduce him to Mr. Wells." Then he told them, "I will be departing for Paris with Mr. Simpson and Mr.

Palfrey in the morning. Mr. Weatherby will accompany me. Mr. Sykes, you will be in charge of the ship until I return. O'Toole, you will remain as well, as master at arms, to ensure that our crew are provided a taste of liberty when they are not employed aboard ship, and to see that infractions are deal with fairly but severely."

Kinkaid noticed the slight wince from his crusty Boatswain's Chief and added, "Just see to it that the men are kept busy and stay out of trouble, Boats."

"Aye aye, Captain."

"Now then, I am not certain how long I shall be gone; probably no longer than a fortnight, but I will expect weekly reports to be carried either by Mr. Briggs or Mr. Phillips, who will also keep the ship informed as to my instructions and whereabouts, so check with the shore about transportation; in the meantime I shall be looking into setting up a permanent liaison between us. Any questions?"

Mr. Sykes asked, "Can you be more specific about liberty, sir?"

"Each watch will enjoy one day of liberty a week, to commence after morning muster and to end at midnight. Officers will be free to come and go at your discretion. And Mr. Sykes, you will remind the men that they are representatives of their country and to conduct themselves accordingly. Any infractions will result in a man losing his liberty privileges permanently. Is that clear?"

"Quite, sir."

It was early the following morning when an eager Mr. Simpson proposed the plan and at seven a.m. O'Toole piped Kinkaid, Mr. Weatherby, Mr. Simpson and Mr. Palfrey ashore, with all their baggage. There was a moment of discomfort when Mr. Palfrey came up on deck and noticed that Nicky Sterling was out on deck, a free man and not in irons as he had suggested, and Mr. Palfrey made it quite clear by his sharp looks that he was perturbed by the fact.

Other than this minor incident, the air was cool and invigorating and it was nice to walk again on solid, albeit cobblestoned, ground again. Mr. Simpson seemed to know where he was going and led them away from the busy docks up a narrow alley where rows of colored fabric hung on lines over the narrow street. Open doorways revealed women stirring huge cauldrons that gave off great clouds of steam.

"Dye manufacturers," said Mr. Simpson. "The city is famous for them."

The narrow alley soon brought them to an open market square.

"Now there is the Chateau des Ducs de Bretagne," said Mr. Simpson, pointing through the crowd of morning shoppers toward the ducal castle with its moat and towers that bordered the square, "where the Edict of Nantes was signed in 1598."

"Granting religious freedom to French Protestants," said Mr. Weatherby, not to be outdone in the French history department.

"Very good, Mr. Weatherby," acknowledged Simpson. "Don't you love it, Kinkaid; the city, the atmosphere, the Frenchness of it all?"

"I feel like a tourist," admitted Kinkaid.

"But you *are* a tourist," Mr. Palfrey insisted on pointing out.

Simpson laughed. "And why not enjoy it, right Mr. Weatherby? Now where did Weatherby go?"

Kinkaid directed Simpson's gaze to the fruit stand where Weatherby was conversing, in equal parts halting French and sign language, with a very pretty fruit vender. He soon returned with four ripe and juicy pears that he passed out to them.

A fat Frenchman stood on a raised platform in the center of the square and was shouting loudly to a group of wealthy businessmen that had gathered before him. Now that he had their attention he pointed dramatically toward the curtains behind him and three naked black men were shoved onto a stage.

"Slaves!" spat Mr. Simpson in disgust.

"Let's get out of here," suggested Kinkaid; it was horses, not humans they were seeking.

Mr. Simpson asked one of the businessmen something and the man pointed toward a park where a line of coaches sat waiting.

"Follow me," said Simpson.

The first coach was a monstrosity, capable of carrying up to thirty passengers. A dozen riders were already aboard, munching bread and cheese, drinking wine and laughing and talking boisterously. Two children were crying because an older child was spitting on them over the seat.

"No, not that," said Mr. Palfrey.

"You're right," said Simpson. "A private post-chaise will suit us much better."

The next coach was open to the weather and contained a sleeping man on the faded black leather seat. Mr. Simpson passed it by. There, seated on the sidewalk next to a lamppost, was a blind and scrawny boy in tattered shirt and trousers, his hair matted and dirty, his mouth hanging wide open. He must have heard Mr. Simpson's approach, for he immediately stretched out his dirty hand and pleaded most forlornly, "Merci, monsieur."

Simpson reached into his pocket and placed a coin in the beggar's hand, which he immediately tested between his teeth and then adroitly slipped into his tiny leather purse.

The second coach was enclosed, and with black with yellow trim that was supposed to pass as gold leaf but was too bright to fool even the most undiscerning traveler. Next to it stood an unshaven and burly man in huge and heavy boots, wearing a soiled and matted sheepskin coat. He doffed his greasy nightcap and greeted Mr. Simpson in a friendly manner. Mr. Simpson returned the friendly manner but their conversation soon turned into a heated argument when Mr. Simpson looked closely at the four horses that stood forlornly in their harness with their heads down.

Finally, the two seemed to come to an agreement, for the burly driver laughed and tossed a coin to the seemingly blind boy who had been sitting so sadly beside the lamppost and now he caught the coin, sprang to his feet and off he ran.

"Why, of all the cheap tricks," said Mr. Palfrey.

Mr. Simpson explained, "Well, it seems we've found our man. Monsieur Garlac's horses look rather tired and his price seems high, but he promises to keep and protect us from highwaymen and bandits that he claims are waiting for us along our route."

"He is going to protect us?" said Palfrey scornfully.

"Perhaps we should take a different route," said Weatherby.

"I suggested as much, but he insists that there is but one road to Paris from here."

"I thought all roads led to Paris," said Kinkaid.

"You're thinking of Rome, Captain," Weatherby corrected him.

"No matter," said Simpson, "for I suspect his tale of bandits is meant to coerce the higher price from us. Unavoidable, it would seem. The boy has gone to fetch a horse for Weatherby. A fast stallion, he's promised. The boy will meet us at the dock with the horse and our driver suggests we go there now."

But before allowing them into the coach, the driver insisted they pay him not only for the stallion, but for the entire trip. Simpson argued with him again and they finally agreed that he would pay for the stallion now but would only pay half the cost of the trip now and half upon their arrival in Paris. The agreed upon sum tendered, they piled into the coach and were driven back to the dock where Cato waited patiently next to their pile of baggage at the bottom of the gangway, and a very large pile it made. With O'Toole's help, Mr. Simpson's huge trunk was placed on the rear luggage rack. Mr. Palfrey's smaller trunk was placed on top of it, along with his boxes of pistols and swords, and Kinkaid's new leather suitcase with his new suits and uniforms as well as the remainder of the luggage was piled onto the roof and tied down with a confusing mixture of knots by the burly postilion.

O'Toole, contemplating the shoddy job of tying down the luggage, shook his head and said, "No sailor ever tied a knot like that, Captain. I'd better check it myself."

But the postilion would have no checking. Instead he began shouting and gesticulating, warning O'Toole to stay away from his coach.

The postilion climbed down when he was finished, clapped his hands in satisfaction, gave Chief O'Toole a shove away from his coach, and said, "We go, no?"

"Tell him he'd better keep his hands off me, sir, or I'll…"

"Easy, Boats," said Kinkaid. "We'll be sure and check those lines while we're under weigh while he's not watching."

"Something tells me we had better check more than that," said Mr. Palfrey as a big black horse came clopping down the road with the scrawny boy on its back.

"Here is your ride, it would seem, Mr. Weatherby," said Mr. Simpson as he took the reins. The boy leaped off and accepted another coin from the postilion before running up the road from whence he had come while Mr. Simpson finished inspecting the stallion's teeth and haunches.

"Not a young horse," proclaimed Simpson, "but serviceable. What do you think, Mr. Weatherby?"

"She'll do," said Weatherby, hopping into the saddle with that indomitable grin. He looked particularly heroic and gallant with one of Kinkaid's pistols tucked into his belt, not to mention the cutlass dangling from his side.

"Well, at least until you reach the first way-station where she can be traded for a fresh mount of equal quality. You know how to recognize the sign, Mr. Weatherby?"

"The sign of the wheel and the horn."

Mr. Simpson took a leather binder out of his valise and handed it to Weatherby. "And you know what to do with this."

"I'll make certain to give this to Dr. Franklin in person and no one else, Mr. Simpson," Weatherby assured him as he tucked the package under his shirt.

"Are you certain you have enough money?" Kinkaid asked him.

"Aye, Captain," he answered, "All that Mr. Simpson gave me."

"More than enough, I'd say," affirmed Simpson. "But are you sure you have the paper with Dr. Franklin's address on it?"

"Not only that, but I've committed it to memory," Weatherby assured him. "And don't worry, Captain, I won't lose the pistol or your cutlass, either."

"Well then, I suppose you're off," said Kinkaid with a

mixture of pride, faith and misgivings. He was sending Mr. Weatherby off on a journey of almost three hundred miles, alone, to bring the news to Benjamin Franklin with all haste, a young boy, yes, a bright and resourceful boy at that, but a boy nonetheless.

O'Toole must have felt the same, for he said, "Mr. Weatherby, you look after yourself, now."

"Don't worry about me, Boats," answered Weatherby as the stallion began prancing with anticipation. "I'll be meeting you along the road before you know it." And with that he spurred the horse to a trot and off he rode.

"I wish I was going with you, sir," said O'Toole as everyone watched Weatherby ride up the street and around the corner with nary a glance behind him.

"We go now," announced the postilion.

As they were settling into the coach, Mr. Rosetti called from the deck, "Enjoy Paris, gentlemen!"

Mr. Phillips stood at the rail and waved while Mr. Sykes merely stood there, waiting to be in sole command of the ship, no doubt.

The road out of the city was paved with stones and since this part had been recently repaired the ride was quite comfortable. Their postilion, Gerlac, sang bawdy French songs in a booming voice as he drove the carriage while Mr. Simpson enjoyed playing tourist guide, pointing out the varied features of the passing landscape, the rows of tall poplars that lined the road, the various crops in the fields, the castles, chateaux and forts along their route. But soon the stone road became quite bumpy, shaking and jostling the passengers until even the exuberance of Mr. Simpson was dampened as he sat some two hours later, slumped on his seat, tired by the rough treatment.

They stopped at a crossroads around noon and bought

long, fresh loaves of bread, Brie and wine which they preferred to eat in the coach, everyone wanting to make good time, to get to Paris as quickly as possible. The only trouble was that their postilion was not so inclined to hurry, and he lingered at the bakery while he leisurely took his meal, and no amount of pleading or begging from Mr. Simpson had the desired effect of hastening him.

"Here, I know how to move him," said Mr. Palfrey as he tossed the coachman a coin.

Gerlac caught it, looked at it in surprise and promptly traded it for a bottle of wine for the road, and pocketing a goodly amount of change in return.

"You'll spoil him, Mr. Palfrey," said an amused Simpson. "That was a ten-franc piece. A bottle of wine only costs a franc."

"If money has no effect on the man, perhaps more forceful measures…"

"Now, now, Mr. Palfrey. Patience is a virtue."

Mr. Palfrey did not answer, but his grinding jaw said it all.

The sun was setting when they came to a tiny village along the river, where Mr. Simpson spotted the sign of the wheel and the horn at the town crossroads, a way-station for the courier route. Mr. Simpson called for the driver to halt and was met with vehement protests.

"He says there's a better place only ten kilometers farther along," explained Simpson.

"Well, my back is about to break and I refuse to go a step farther," insisted Mr. Palfrey.

"My feelings, exactly," said Mr. Simpson before he opened the door of the still moving coach and leaped out. Only then did the vehicle come to a stop with loud and profane protests from Gerlac.

Simpson paid a visit to the way station office, returning

with the confirmation that a young naval officer speaking bad French had indeed stopped there earlier in the day and had exchanged his horse for the continuation of his journey to Paris. They then were told that there was no room at the way station, but the manager soon found them lodging for the night in a cheap but comfortable hotel.

They were on their way again at first light in the morning. It remained cloudy all day with a fine mist falling and the road became rougher yet, for in places whole sections were missing, the squares of stone taken up by local farmers, no doubt, to add a room to their hovels, shore up culverts or mend sheep corrals, leaving rutted mud puddles in their place, causing the driver to cease his loud singing. But now he began to swear indignantly, and the more wine he drank the louder he swore, but everyone was so bone weary, slouched in their seats throughout this second day on the road with their heads lolling on their chests, that the swearing of the driver became part of the rhythm of their bouncing, jouncing ride. It was dark when the coach finally came to a halt in front of a lone farmhouse.

"We make goodnight here," said the postilion, placing his hands against his cheek in the universal gesture of sleep.

The exhausted travelers filed into the farmhouse without muttering a word, ducking under the low doorway of the thatch-roofed hovel and seating themselves on benches at a low table with a stained tablecloth.

What they did not notice was that Mr. Palfrey linger outside. And when Gerlac reached for Mr. Palfrey's valise, he grabbed the stocky postilion by his collar and knocked him to the ground with a stern warning to, "Stay away from that!" His look was murderous and Gerlac slunk away in fright.

Later, Kinkaid thought Mr. Palfrey looked like a dead

man sitting across from him at the table with his eyes closed and his mouth hanging open. A toothless old woman brought carafes of wine which the men sipped until the food was ready.

"What are these?" asked Mr. Palfrey, coming out of his stupor and gazing at the offering; two lumps of cooked meat and some gray vegetable in a thin gray sauce.

"Pigeons," said Mr. Simpson. "They're not bad, actually."

"Pigeons?"

"I've had worse, but these turnips taste funny," complained Kinkaid.

"Kohlrabi, Captain," explained Cato happily. "They're delicious if you give them a chance; although the sauce could be better."

The roast pigeons reminded Kinkaid of eating seagulls on the prison ship, *Jersey*. Actually, the food wasn't that bad with a bit of salt and pepper sprinkled on it, but then everyone was too hungry and too tired to complain much. Their meal over, Gerlac informed Mr. Simpson that he would stay in the barn with the horses and watch over their baggage. Then the old hag took them upstairs to their quarters, a small, low-ceilinged space with a couple of straw beds.

"Isn't there another room?" asked Kinkaid, wondering how four men were going to sleep in two beds.

"I'm afraid not, Captain," said Simpson. "Mr. Palfrey and I will share this one."

"Mr. Africanus…"

But Cato would have none of it, insisting, "No, Captain, I shall sleep on the floor and that is my final offer, sir."

Kinkaid couldn't argue with that, after all Cato was his steward. And so he had a bed to himself, such as it was. Since there were no pillows, they used their coats for the purpose.

"At least the wine was good," said Mr. Palfrey, looking on the positive side as they drifted off to sleep."

"And cheap, too," added Simpson.

All night long Kinkaid tossed and turned, scratched and itched, either from the straw or from the bedbugs, and having only to look forward to more jouncing and bouncing in the coach on the morrow.

It was a chilly morning and they rose with the sun with stiff joints and aching muscles. But the rolls and coffee were good and Kinkaid was enjoying his second cup when Mr. Simpson came back from the barn with the news, "Gerlac is gone."

"Gone?" asked Kinkaid. "Gone where?"

"To parts unknown. It seems he's made off with the coach and absconded with all our baggage."

"The filthy scoundrel!" exclaimed Cato. "With your new suits and uniforms, Captain."

"I knew we shouldn't have trusted him!" roared Mr. Palfrey. "My entire wardrobe, gone! What shall we do now, Mr. Simpson?" Of course he knew that he might have edged the man into thievery by his threat.

"Well, I still have my money pouch and at least we have our coats and we can always replace our clothes," concluded Simpson sensibly. "As for our transportation, I suppose I will have to speak with our hostess about finding us another way to Paris."

Simpson went into the kitchen and had a long talk with the old hag. He returned with a triumphant look on his face and announced, "I'm told that the public coach will be by in two days, but since I am not prepared to wait that long, she has agreed to lend us her cart and ox for twenty francs and one hundred francs collateral, the hundred to be returned when we return her cart within a fortnight."

"The shrewd old hag," observed Mr. Palfrey. "She's probably in cahoots with that damned postilion; why he's probably her son."

"Quite likely," agreed Simpson, "but she will send us off with a packed lunch for each of us."

"How very thoughtful," said Kinkaid.

The cart was certainly large enough, and with enormous wheels. Open and filled with hay, it easily accommodated the five of them with no baggage except their bread and cheese lunches. Cato insisted on taking the reins on the hard bench up front while the others stretched out on the straw in the back. The brown ox was a slow and plodding beast, smeared with mud up to its knees, and the entire rig was anything but dignified or elegant, but with the roads so badly rutted, at least speed was not to be desired.

"At least it's a dry and sunny day," observed Mr. Simpson, stretching his aching back. Hardly dispirited by their misfortune, Simpson went on to comment on the benefits of their newly acquired mode of transport. "You know, it may not be fashionable, but this is actually more comfortable than that terrible post-chaise," he said as he lay back on the straw with his collar turned up against the chilly breeze and his eyes closed, sunning himself.

"Yes," agreed Kinkaid as the ox relieved itself in great patties that splattered on the cobblestones, "and a fine example of French culture."

Mr. Palfrey sat in gloomy silence, while Simpson smiled tolerantly, saying, "Wake me when we get to Paris."

But it was to the shouts from a young man on horseback that woke Mr. Simpson from his nap that afternoon.

"Yippee," yelled Weatherby when he spotted Cato on the wagon.

Kinkaid stood up and watched as Weatherby spurred his tired mount to a gallop and then brought the red sorrel to a halt in a cloud of dust.

"I trust you delivered the dispatch to Dr. Franklin?" asked an aroused Simpson.

"To the man himself," answered Weatherby, beaming proudly. "He was in conference with a Mr. Deane and Mr. Lee, and you should have heard them whooping and hollering when they read General Washington's dispatch."

"What happened then?" asked Mr. Palfrey.

"Mr. Franklin insisted they sit down right away and write a letter to the King of France and the court of Spain, indeed, to let all of Europe know of Britain's humiliation. And he insisted I remain overnight or I would have rejoined you all yesterday."

"You've done magnificently, Billy," exclaimed Simpson.

Weatherby climbed down from the horse, proud and happy, and smiling a big winning smile that only made Kinkaid smile too as he embraced Weatherby and told him, "Good to see you again, Mr. Weatherby."

"Good to see you too, sir," he answered, and then lovingly stroked the muzzle of the horse. "She's a fine mount, Captain. You should see her jump. And you know, sir, Dr. Franklin suggested we buy a few mounts to help you maintain communications with the ship. He said he can arrange a small stable for us at his residence, so that we are independent of foreign intervention or interference."

"Well, I'm not certain our funds would be sufficient…"

"Oh, Dr. Franklin says not to worry about such matters, as it will come under his expense account. Do you think we can keep her, sir?"

"If the mount pleases you and if Dr. Franklin suggested we keep a small stable to maintain communications, then I don't see why not."

"Excellent, Captain," beamed a happy Weatherby.

It was a relief to hear that Dr. Franklin had taken it upon himself to ensure his easy access to the ship. It was also a load off his mind to realize that their important news had successfully been delivered. But even more than this, it was an immense relief to see Weatherby again, all in one piece.

Only now did Weatherby come to the realization that the company he had left behind at the dock was not traveling in the same coach that they had started in. Far from it. Not only that, they seemed to be missing all of their luggage. "What happened?"

IX
Frivolities and Flatteries

Mr. Simpson made them all rise before dawn on that last day, so excited was he in anticipation of returning to Paris, a city he had been raving about since the day they left. His companion, however, continued to brood and remained largely uncommunicative as well as unmoved by the sights, lending a degree of gloom over Mr. Simpson's exuberance. In a private aside, Mr. Simpson took it upon himself to apologize for Mr. Palfrey's inhospitable behavior.

"We must take the good with the bad, I suppose," was the best Kinkaid could say.

"Well, as I see it, the first characteristic of a good traveling companion is to keep a pleasant disposition in the face of all, even the most dire setbacks, and the loss of a few pistols and swords is certainly not a dire setback, and is therefore no excuse for inhospitality."

"Well said," agreed Weatherby, overhearing the conversation.

By and by they could see the line of buildings and spires in the distance in the early light, overlaid with a smoggy haze, and Mr. Simpson, in his excitement, could not help but proclaim, "There she is, Paris!"

It was a mild and sunny morning when their cart finally entered the outskirts under a pale blue sky. But their excitement soon diminished, for they had expected to see broad avenues and boulevards lined with magnificent palaces and gardens. Instead they were met with a maze of narrow streets lined with stinking gutters running with sewage. Instead of palaces there were only row after row of dirty and dilapidated hovels. Instead of impeccably dressed men and women of taste and culture they saw only the haggard faces of poor and ragged people who looked like they were slowly starving to death. It occurred to Kinkaid that the only thing saving them from being mobbed by beggars and assaulted by thieves was that nobody paid them any heed arriving in the back of a rickety hay cart. This was not the city of Paris Mr. Simpson had described, and he could only protest, "But we are not yet in the city."

And he was right, for when they arrived at an intersection in a particularly grungy ghetto, Weatherby pointed to the road heading south, which soon took them to a small and quaint village of elegant homes and formal gardens. A sign along the road indicated they were entering the village of Passy.

They were all thrilled and a bit awed to be greeted by the famous Dr. Benjamin Franklin himself, a big stocky man wearing glasses of his own invention, who exclaimed after introductions had been made, "I am overjoyed to welcome you all to my humble dwelling. And you have brought the best news I have heard in months, news that will surely change the course of history. But as I'm certain you must all be quite fatigued from your journey I will see to it that you are immediately shown to your rooms so that you may rest and rejuvenate. Later I shall look forward to speaking with each and every one of you this evening at dinner."

Each were allowed their own room, all very sumptuous and elegant, and though they all were indeed quite fatigued from their journey it was difficult to rest, so excited were they all, even a bit shocked by the sudden transformation of their opulent surroundings and even more by the realization that their primary mission of delivering Mr. Simpson and the news of Saratoga had been accomplished.

Mr. Palfrey soon disappeared, claiming important business for the war effort. Mr. Simpson was nowhere to be found, having gone off with Dr. Franklin to discuss matters of state. And Cato had introduced himself to Franklin's kitchen staff, his chief intention to learn all he could about French cooking. The rest met again around the giant dining room table that evening, filled with giant candelabra and giant plates piled high with all sorts of gustatory delights, with diligent waiters rushing in with another course even before the previous course had been fully consumed.

There must have been twenty or more guests around the table that first evening, as many ladies as men, with French and English being spoken all at once, a noisy crowd growing noisier as the wine flowed. Franklin introduced everyone and then seemed to say very little except to whisper once in a while to a matronly yet quite comely and elegant Madame Brillon seated beside. There was his wealthy landlord, Jacques-Donatien Leray de Chaumont. There was the small, dapper and distinguished Charles Gravier, Comte de Vergennes, the Foreign Minister to Louis XVI, as well as many other notable Frenchmen of the royal court. Franklin's colleague commissioners to France, Silas Deane and Arthur Lee, were there, with Mr. Simpson seated between them. There was a Dr. Bancroft, Franklin's personal secretary. And there, seated across from Kinkaid, was a happy and animated Lieutenant William Weatherby, who seemed to have found an old friend, the very lovely Marie de la Renier, who he first met in the Caribbean, and with whom he had kept up a correspondence. Her father, the Marquis de la

Renier, wealthy shipping merchant of dubious character, made a brief appearance in the company of Mr. Palfrey, but then both excused themselves fairly early because of business matters.

It was, at first, a bit disconcerting to see the women wearing so much make up, with little effort to hide the fact. They powdered their entire faces without restraint, painted perfectly round red rouge circles on their cheeks, added false eyelashes and pasted black so-called beauty marks in conspicuous places, looking for all the world like clowns, not to mention the pink and green and yellow wigs they piled high on their heads, trailing snakes of ringlets. If this was not enough, the men did the same, albeit with a modicum of restraint. And the clothes; such finery Kinkaid had never seen. Even their conversation revolved around frivolity, bragging to one another about the hounds, horses, or furniture they recently purchased, their new carriage, servants, or the food they recently consumed. Worse, by their language these French of the nobility openly held their unfortunate countrymen, whom they referred to as the Third Estate, in utter contempt. Of course, as an ambassador of one's country, Kinkaid and his compatriots had little choice but to hold their tongues and pretend they were not disgusted by their society. There was no escape, and the only thing to do was to join in the frivolity.

Dr. Franklin made good on his word about making a small stable of mounts available to Kinkaid, and soon Mr. Briggs and Mr. Phillips were taking turns making regular runs from the chateau to the ship, thereby giving each of the young men brief tastes of Parisian life.

It was three weeks later when Mr. Weatherby and Marie invited Kinkaid to the theatre in the city. They had also invited Mr. Simpson and Mr. Briggs, but Mr. Simpson had taken Mr. Briggs into the city earlier in the day to do some shopping. After all, Mr. Simpson would not let an officer who might be seen in his company to wear shoddy uniforms, and anything not new was considered shoddy to Mr. Simpson. And since Kinkaid hated shopping, especially for clothes because of those sharp clothiers who were always fawning over one and telling you how smart you looked in their latest fashion, weather it was true or not, it was agreed that Kinkaid would meet them at the theater, which is why he was riding in the coach alone, in his best uniform.

It had rained earlier in the evening and the wet streets reflected the lights of the city; the streetlights and the lights of the theatre district, with all their posh shops and expensive restaurants, all doing a brisk business. No poverty here; only fashionably dressed men and women out to enjoy an evening's entertainment.

There was the theater now; a large crowd was gathered outside. As the coach drew near Kinkaid noticed the large puddle of water at the curbside, but before he could warn the driver the coach ran through it, splashing the legs of a tall fashionably-dressed man.

The man turned with an oath. "Damn you!"

Why, if it wasn't Mr. Palfrey, his normally cold gray eyes burning with unmitigated fury.

"I'm terribly sorry, Mr. Palfrey, but you see there was no time to warn the driver," said Kinkaid in apology, yet even as he said it he knew he should have said something else, for it sounded like he had known the puddle was there and had splashed him intentionally.

"How dare you! I'll have you know I paid handsomely for this suit just this morning!" he complained loudly, looking down his imperious nose. But then he just as quickly collected himself. "Actually, I am somewhat surprised to see you here, Captain. I was not aware that you were an aficionado of refined culture." An insult if there ever was one.

A few people turned in reaction to the loud and harsh words, and now they noticed the American Naval Officer who had just stepped down from the coach. Someone shouted, "Capitaine Jones!" which caused a furor in the crowd, whereupon they jostled Mr. Palfrey aside to catch a glimpse of who they thought was Captain John Paul Jones, already famous in Paris for his daring exploits aboard the *Providence* and now the *Ranger*. But as quickly as they realized it was not the famous American Captain they soon lost interest.

"Captain! Captain Kinkaid! Over here!"

"Mr. Weatherby, am I glad to see you."

"Well, I'm glad you could make it, Captain," said an excited Weatherby in all sincerity. He had not noticed Mr. Palfrey and said, "Follow me, sir. The others are already inside. We've saved you a seat."

The theater lobby was as crowded as the entrance and they had to push their way through. The usual crowds of French nobility were there; more to be seen than to see a play, to be sure. Finally they arrived at the seventh row of seats where Marie de la Renier sat in a golden gown between Mr. Simpson and Mr. Briggs and there was much hand shaking as if they hadn't seen one another for months.

Finally he turned to the lovely Marie, bowed, and said, "I am honored and delighted to once more gaze upon your lovely countenance, Mademoiselle de la Renier." Unaccustomed to outlays of flattery, Kinkaid feared he may be laying it on too thick.

But Marie never batted an eyelash, returning, "I am so happy to see you, Captain Kinkaid. And you know, they say the play is superb. I hope you will enjoy it."

"How could I not in such company?"

The play was not about to begin as yet, and so the socializing continued with everyone standing and gesticulating over the seats. Mr. Simpson was in his element, of course, and Weatherby's French was more than passable, having been schooled in the subject and then helped in his education by his bewitching companion. But since Kinkaid's French did not improve with practice, and overwhelmed with their fast jabbering about topics that held little interest for him, Kinkaid contented himself to stand there and pretend to understand, only occasionally throwing in a "Oui" or a "Merveilleux" here and there to show his attendance.

At one point, Weatherby pointed to a distant row of seats and said, "Look Marie, there is your father."

"So what do I care?" answered Marie with some disdain. "I don't wish to see or hear of him."

And so it was with some relief when the heavy maroon curtains finally drew aside and the play began. Even so, it took some time before the restless audience took their respective seats and settled down.

The set was certainly "merveilleus," as was anything artistic at which the French excelled with flair. The backdrop was particularly well done; a scene of a bay, with sailboats and ships flying gay flags and banners, painted with atmosphere, and with happy clouds floating above, the whole bestowing an appealing expansiveness. And in spite of the fact that the play took place during one of the many wars between France and England, the story was full of gaiety and romance.

Therefore it was difficult not to enjoy the song and dance entertainment, and Kinkaid almost forgot himself for a time, lost in the fanciful, carefree world of music and romance, yet his innate sense of duty could not completely forget that other men were carrying on the war, some dying, while he sat here, watching nonsense. The actors and actresses were handsome and beautiful. The actresses especially, were very beautiful, especially the lead actress. Her voice, her grace and fluid movements only added to the effect, and Kinkaid could not take his eyes off her. The costumes were perfect, he noticed, especially the uniforms; the red madder of the English, the royal blue of the French. Perhaps they were the real thing. Perhaps…

Weatherby had noticed Kinkaid's discomfort before the play began and now he leaned over and asked, "I trust you are enjoying yourself, Captain?"

"Immensely, Mr. Weatherby. So much so that I wonder if we might be invited backstage when the play is over?"

"I don't see why not, Captain," answered Weatherby with a knowing smirk. "Marie knows the principle actress, Mademoiselle Bertrand, and I'm sure she can arrange something."

And arrange something she did, for after the play was over they were conducted to the backstage area where a party was being held over bouquets of flowers that the patrons had tossed upon the stage during the encores at the end.

Mademoiselle Bertrand was been fawned over by a coterie of admirer's, but when Marie approached her she broke away from them and came over, gave an exaggerated curtsy, which brought the men to bowing, and then she began to speak, very fast, and perhaps it was her fast way of talking, not her overwhelming beauty, which kept Kinkaid from catching even the gist of what she was saying.

Weatherby made the introductions and then translated,

"Mademoiselle Bertrand wishes to tell you that she is honored and flattered that such a handsome American Navy officer, such as yourself, would want to meet her."

"Well, I...I mean, I..."

Weatherby could see that his captain was overwhelmed by the moment, indeed, coming closer to incapacitated, and decided to answer for him, telling Mademoiselle Bertrand that his captain was enamored of her beauty, but even more by her dazzling stage performance, and that he only wished to express his admiration, but that his French had escaped him in his swooning excitement.

All of this flew over Kinkaid's head in his embarrassment, and all he could do was stand there with a foolish smile on his face, until he remembered his chief reason for coming backstage, and now he blurted out, "The uniforms, Mr. Weatherby. Ask her about the uniforms. Are they genuine, or at least authentic? And if so, are any of them for sale?"

Weatherby could not hide the wince of disappointment on his face, but he collected himself and asked the young beauty what Kinkaid wanted to be asked, and now the look of disappointment on Mademoiselle Bertrand's face could not be plainer. She spat a short answer and walked away in a huff, rejoining her swooning companions with a coquettish gaiety that only a consummate actress could assume.

Marie rolled her eyes in astonishment, but Mr. Simpson merely laughed and said, "It seems your backstage deportment could use some refining, Captain."

If Kinkaid was embarrassed, he did not show it, but kept to his original purpose, asking, "But the uniforms. Did she say if the uniforms were for sale?"

"I believe we might speak to the backstage manager for such information, sir," offered a somewhat disconcerted Weatherby.

They soon did this upon Kinkaid's insistence. The gist was that the uniforms could be purchased from the same costumers that supplied the theater. They were not cheap, but Mr. Simpson agreed to pay for them out of his expense account, and Kinkaid was promised two dozen uniforms of various sizes, twelve British and twelve French, all authentic recreations of the real thing; more than passable, immaculate, to be delivered in a week.

Kinkaid would have been happy to return to the estate after that, but Marie said that the evening had only just begun, insisting, "Oh, but we really must take dinner at the *Chez Leon*. All the actors and actresses go there after the play; why everyone will be there."

Indeed, everyone did seem to be there, the crowd outside the very ritzy restaurant milling about just like at the theater. But as fortune would have it, the maitre'd soon spotted Marie and brought them all inside. The trouble was, the only table available was right in the middle of the crowded room and they were all constantly jostled by the restless patrons as they ate and drank and conversed loudly in the noisy and smoke-filled establishment.

It was well past midnight and Kinkaid had had enough, but not wishing to appear the rube, he forced himself to tolerate the tiresome business. He was sitting there, sipping his wine, and doing his best to appear as gay as everyone else when he heard a woman scream behind him, and then a familiar voice, slurred almost beyond recognition.

"Oh, don't give me that. An actress you say? Ha, why you're no better than a common wench."

It was a staggering Mr. Palfrey, and he had clutched in his hand the wrist of the actress that Kinkaid had embarrassed himself over the military uniforms, Mademoiselle Bertrand.

The young girl was being forcibly dragged from the

establishment while clearly and vociferously voicing her protest.

Kinkaid stood up and demanded, "I say, unhand this lady at once."

"I suggest you mind your own business, Kinkaid, and I've had about enough of you for one evening." Whereupon he slapped Kinkaid across the face with his glove.

By now Marie was at Mademoiselle Bertrand's side and was holding her other hand in hers, shouting her outrage, which brought a chorus of encores from the boisterous and inebriated crowd of patrons.

Kinkaid returned Mr. Palfrey's slap with a slap of his own, albeit with the back of his hand.

"Captain Kinkaid, I shall demand satisfaction for this outrage!"

By now Mr. Weatherby and Mr. Briggs were on the scene and both insisted upon demanding satisfaction from Mr. Palfrey as well, whereupon Mr. Simpson forced his way between them all, and speaking in no uncertain terms, demanded, "Enough of this nonsense. And Mr. Palfrey, while it is no excuse, you, sir, are drunk!"

And so the fight was broken up. Mr. Palfrey stumbled outside. Kinkaid's group lingered only long enough for them to gather up their coats and hats before leaving.

Mr. Simpson then took it upon himself to apologize for his obviously drunk colleague. "I'm terribly sorry about this rather uncouth scene, Captain. I assure you that I shall have a very serious talk with…"

"Mr. Palfrey is a grown man, Mr. Simpson," said Kinkaid, "and I shouldn't unduly worry myself about it."

"Nonsense, Captain. There is no excuse for such behavior. After all, he is representing the interests of the Colonies, and I shall have to speak with Mr. Franklin about this. Frankly, I am shocked. Why, such behavior from a gentleman is unconscionable. I can't imagine what got into him."

The uniforms arrived as promised, and it was some weeks later, weeks spent at many a noisy dinner party with many elegantly dressed, made-up and coiffured ladies and gentlemen, that Kinkaid found himself becoming more than a little agitated. Part of this was that he was finding himself increasingly left to his own devices, and there was more to it than simply having no ship to command. Mr. Simpson had sent a French tailor to each of their rooms in order to fit them with fine new suits and uniforms, their own and those they had purchased from the costumers, and after that Mr. Simpson was rarely to be found, off hobnobbing with French royalty. Mr. Weatherby was spending most of his time with his lovely friend Marie, who was slowly but surely becoming more than just a friend, and who could blame him for that? There was at least one person who he was not disappointed to rarely see, and that was Mr. Palfrey, who seemed to keep himself quite busy with his procurements at the port of Le Havre.

But more than this, Kinkaid found himself having qualms about his own female acquaintances, especially one Mademoiselle Jeanette Bertrand, the beautiful actress who he had initially insulted, but who now seemed to show up at almost every social event that Kinkaid attended, a very pretty and very talkative young lady who he found increasingly attentive and he increasingly attracted to. He was even making more of an effort to speak proper French. An unsolicited friendship to be sure, but the temptation to encourage her attentions and fantasize about her was only adding to his guilt and uneasiness, especially when he wrote letters to Elizabeth, which was happening with less frequency.

There was only one thing to do, and he must do it with resolution; stop all this frivolous nonsense and get back to navy business. He had submitted in good grace to the social niceties for long enough and now his patience and endurance were wearing thin, to the point that he would prefer to be shut below decks in a cold and damp cubicle aboard a bounding ship on an unruly sea than be submitted to another elegant dinner party where he would have to spout his bad French and laugh at bad jokes and take foolish personal opinions seriously, not to mention allow himself to be tempted by the dazzling and seductive Mademoiselle Bertrand, more dangerous than an enemy broadside.

Not that these weeks were all a complete waste of time, for he had also learned much, just as Mr. Simpson said he would, except perhaps not what Mr. Simpson said he would learn. Oh, he had certainly seen how the French lived, at least the French of wealth and standing, a mostly self-indulgent, scandalous-yet-carefree existence for the most part, earning vast sums through rents and the sweat of others, yet paying little in taxes, while the common people barely eked out a living, yet paid the most in taxes, the bloody and disastrous results of this unfair system yet to be realized.

Kinkaid also learned that Franklin's associates were not so enamored of Franklin as the French seemed to be, especially the sour Arthur Lee, who made no secret of his suspicions of all he met, even accusing Franklin's secretary of being a spy, and holding no awe of Franklin, believing him lazy, vain, and as self-indulgent as the French. Kinkaid observed as well how Franklin enjoyed his opulent surroundings, his spacious and elegant house, his indulgent excesses which gave him terrible attacks of painful gout, and his romantic flirtations which were the talk of Europe. He had even upon occasion seen the Madame Brillon sitting in Franklin's lap, the two laughing and pretending as if they were playing chess, and although the great man's romantic escapades were legendary, Kinkaid suspected that much of this was fabricated, even fed by Franklin himself, perhaps in part to feed his ego and romantic fantasies, but even more to ingratiate himself to French tastes.

But more than this, Kinkaid could also see that Franklin was no fool and was playing a tricky diplomatic business with an unsophisticated artfulness that passed for naiveté. He could see that Franklin also tired of constantly having so many guests for dinner, but realized that this was another means by which Franklin added to the ardent support for all that he was working toward, an alliance with France. Franklin even pooh-poohed Lee's fear of spies, insisting that he never did or said anything that he would not do or say in public, and that spies often make more trouble for those they worked for than those they worked against, even suggesting that he used suspected spies to pass on false and misleading information.

The reality was that spies outnumbered diplomats in France by ten to one, not only around the French court, but in any of the various ports used by American or French ships that were moving military supplies to the colonies, which was why Franklin did take it upon himself to warn Kinkaid and his coterie about them, especially warning them to be careful in their correspondence, which was certain to be read by the other side, letters both coming and going.

When Kinkaid asked Franklin if he was not concerned by all this spying activity, he responded, "I would not be surprised if half of the secretaries in our own delegation were not working for the other side. But first, what can we do about it? Second, I find that it confuses the other side to employ them as not, for I hear that Whitehall is tearing their hair out over their constantly contradictory reports. Why every captain and seaman from Calais to Cherbourg are plied with money and drink for information regarding sailing schedules, but even this is used against them by dropping false information and taking alternate routes. No, Captain, it is nothing to lose sleep over, and my advice to you is to simply observe reasonable precautions and don't worry about the rest."

As for Franklin himself; Kinkaid was awed by the man. He read in his face a man of intelligence, integrity, tolerance, and sincerity. More than this, Kinkaid saw in Franklin a remarkably complicated, energetic and very busy man. Busy with his printing press and writing articles; poems and stories for the French and European press in order to gain support for the American cause, not to mention that his "Poor Richard's Almanac" was all the rage in France; busy with his scientific experiments, and almost as often entertaining Madame Brillon with their friendly games of chess and harmless romance.

Then there was that supercilious American naval officer, Captain John Paul Jones, who regularly showed up at Franklin's many soirees, begging him for a ship, and finally being promised one, the L'Indien, a 40-gun frigate being built in the shipyards of Amsterdam. The overbearing Jones even had the temerity to try to persuade Kinkaid to serve as his third officer if and when the ship sailed, as if Kinkaid were without a command, and so it was with some relief that Jones, having gotten what he wanted, was now preoccupied with one of his many dalliances.

In spite of his various and sundry activities, Franklin was also frequently off on meetings with the comte de Vergennes at Versailles to discuss negotiations for a treaty of amity and commerce with the French, a treaty he had been working to secure for two years and that was finally about to be consummated, based on the miraculous victory at Saratoga. And a tricky business it was, Kinkaid soon learned, for the French desperately wanted to see Britain fall, yet they were reluctant to openly oppose England or openly support the American cause. So while they secretly sent military supplies to American shores and lent vast sums of money for such supplies, they were at the same time afraid that America would make a premature reconciliation with Britain...and Franklin used this knowledge adroitly in order to move things along, at one point accepting a not-so-secret meeting with a British agent named Wentworth, which only played on French fears and brought the note from Vergennes, asking for a secret meeting with the French court to discuss treaty negotiations, which would include a French declaration of war with England.

It was only after such back and forth political and diplomatic shenanigans that Franklin was finally assured of an alliance that would eventually win the war, and that gave the great man the time to meet with Kinkaid over matters of mutual concern, to Kinkaid's immense relief.

"I am especially aggrieved to learn of how our sailors, seamen and officers alike, are treated by the British in their so-called centers of detention," complained Franklin. "They are fed scantily on bad provisions; they are without warm lodging, clothes, blankets, or even fire. They are not allowed letters or visitations from friends or relatives, not even from those agencies in England who would ease their suffering. I have tried in many ways to appeal to their sense of decency and honor. I have offered prisoner exchanges; I have asked to simply visit their prisons to ascertain the true state of affairs; I have even offered to pay for packages of clothing, blankets and food to be distributed to our men. Yet I have consistently been rejected on every front. And this in spite of the accusations of barbarity levied against them in the European press as they learn of these abominations. And now that the restrictions on American shipping have been lifted by the French court, I see nothing stopping us from making some bold attempt to resolve in some way these terrible transgressions against the laws of civilized societies."

"Of course I am entirely in agreement, sir," answered Kinkaid. "Having been subjected to such indignities aboard the British prison vessel *Jersey*, I am ready to undertake any mission that will benefit our American friends held by our enemies."

"I like your spirit, Kinkaid. But such an undertaking would be fraught with great risk. What would you propose?"

It was exactly what Kinkaid hoped Franklin would ask. "A bold and daring plan, sir, to free by whatever means necessary, as many American prisoners as possible."

"A direct attack upon one of their prisons, then?"

"Well, let us say an indirect attack, using subterfuge and surprise as much as possible. Freeing a large population would be one thing; getting away with a large group would be another matter and the greatest difficulty of such an endeavor."

Franklin stroked his chin and said, "Yes, of course; surprise, quickness and daring must be the key ingredients, then."

"Precisely," said Kinkaid.

"Of course I will approve of any endeavor you are resolved to undertake, and leave it entirely up to you to devise an appropriate plan, Captain. And if there is anything

I can do to assist, please do not hesitate to ask, anything at all."

"I am grateful, sir," said Kinkaid in all sincerity. "There is perhaps something that you may do. You must certainly have friends in many places. Perhaps you could help us ascertain which facility in Britain holds the greatest number of American prisoners."

"An easy enough task," said Franklin with a laugh, "for I know exactly our target already. And I also have someone you will like to speak with; a fellow in my employ that spent some time there recently and can tell you all about the place."

Finally, a chance at action again, and an action that could help many fellow sailors. All that was required was a good plan, and for that he would need to meet with his officers and ready his ship. As was his nature, Kinkaid was of a mind to instigate action at the first opportunity. The trouble was, Mr. Weatherby was, as usual, not in his quarters and he would have to either go out and find him or wait until he returned. Finding Weatherby would have been easy enough, but realizing it would necessitate taking him away from Marie, his guilty conscience made him adopt the later course.

X
Three Birds with One Stone

It was not until later that evening that the clopping sound of Weatherby's horse could be heard in the courtyard of the chateau.

Kinkaid waited patiently in the parlor of the residence while Weatherby turned his mount over to the stable boys. When he entered he was slapping his gloves in the palm of his hand, and his face seemed troubled.

"Why what is it, Mr. Weatherby? Is all well between you and Marie?"

"Between Marie and I all is well," answered Weatherby, "but not so well between her and her father. She's thinking of moving out."

"I'm sorry to hear that."

As eager as Kinkaid was to tell Weatherby of the new development, an agitated yet excited Weatherby was even more eager to share some news of his own.

"Sir, I believe I may have stumbled upon something which might interest you."

"Such as?"

"Well, you asked me to keep an eye on our protégé, Mr. Palfrey, and so I've been doing exactly that, sir."

"And?"

"Well, I have just learned that Marie's father, the Marquis, has a meeting with our esteemed Congressional Agent tomorrow night, after dinner."

"I wouldn't place much suspicion on such an occurrence," Kinkaid had to caution him. "As I'm sure you're aware, Mr. Palfrey's duties require him to obtain shipping in order to convey his purchases to our shores, and one would expect the Marque to enter his bid along with all the other shipping merchants for such contracts."

"I realize that, sir," gave Weatherby, "but this midnight meeting is to take place at a not-so-respectable bistro in a not-so-respectable part of the city."

Kinkaid gave a noncommittal, "Hmmm, I see."

Weatherby dug into his pocket and pulled out two neatly folded sheets of paper. He handed one of them to Kinkaid, explaining, "And I found this in his apartment."

"You broke into his apartment?" Kinkaid was shocked.

"You told me to find out what I could of the man, sir."

"But taking something from his apartment…"

"Actually, it's a copy. He yet retains the original, tucked between the pages of The Bible, of all places, so he will suspect nothing."

Kinkaid gave Weatherby a sideways glance, grinned, and said, "You would think of everything."

"Have a look at it, sir, and tell me what you think."

The English alphabet was written in three neat rows, and alongside each letter were other letters and a series of numbers. At the bottom of the page was a formula of sorts. Kinkaid's puzzled look made it obvious that he had no idea what he was looking at.

"It's a code, sir," explained Weatherby. "You see, each letter of the alphabet is represented by a number from one to twenty-six, those numbers changing daily according to this formula that relies on the day of the month. It's really quite ingenious, yet simple at the same time."

"I see, Weatherby," said Kinkaid uncertainly. "Well, I

would guess that dealing with arms merchants, especially these days..."

"I also found this, sir," said Weatherby, handing over the other paper.

"Why, it's a letter addressed to me. It's from Elizabeth." Now this was something that struck close to home.

"Read it, sir."

Kinkaid read through the letter. It was not a long letter, just average for Elizabeth, saying the usual things, about the family, including a few embarrassing lines that lovers share. But at the bottom was a most unusual sentence. "Beware Mr. Palfrey." It was a disturbing revelation.

"My God, Weatherby, what can this mean?"

"I'm not sure, sir, but it seems that your wife must possess some information leading her to believe that our Mr. Palfrey is a very dangerous man. Put together with everything else, you have to admit that Mr. Palfrey comes across as a very mysterious fellow."

"Yes," Kinkaid had to agree, "very mysterious, and very dangerous, as well. But being mysterious and dangerous is in itself no crime, and we have no proof of anything. Yet...Weatherby, could you decode any message sent by this method?"

"Why, certainly, Captain, as long as these instructions remain unchanged. But there is more, Captain. I have also learned from Marie, quite by accident, I assure you, that the Marquis has recently hired a certain captain...by the name of McDougal."

"McDougal? What of it?"

"Well, sir, Marie has seen the man...at a distance I should admit, so the identity cannot be absolutely verified, but she seems to believe the man bears a striking resemblance to an old pirate acquaintance of ours from the Caribbean."

"Blackstone?" The very idea seemed implausible. Yet wasn't the pirate Blackstone's real name Justin McGregor? It could very well be more than coincident, especially if Marie had actually seen the man.

"I have not been able to confirm the suspicion, Captain, but I believe we might have an opportunity to ascertain the truth of the matter tomorrow evening, if you are of a mind for a bit of subterfuge."

The idea was more than intriguing. "Exactly what did you have in mind, Lieutenant?"

It was a cold and cloudy night, and there was no moon to light the way of the two ragged vagabonds as they wandered between the narrow alleyways, each more narrow and disgusting than the last, the piles of garbage and filth in which they poked in hopes of finding palatable sustenance were so malodorous, so revolting, that the taller of the two kept holding his scarf over his nose to keep from retching.

They stopped for a moment under a swaying banner depicting a pig, a red pig, the faded and blistered paint on the sign reading Le Cochon Rouge. They were about to enter when the door burst open and out flew a skinny wretch being thrown bodily into the foul-running gutter with the shout, "Ne bougez pas!"

As they hesitated, one vagabond turned to the other and whispered in perfect English, "Better let me do the talking, Captain."

They entered with some trepidation through the squeaky door, all eyes upon them from a half-dozen grimy men sitting at the scattered and scarred tables. A fireplace cast their eerie shadows on the drab and soot-covered walls as they made for an empty table in a dark corner of the room, a room already very dark. Only one candle burned on one table next to the fire where two men played cards. No sooner had they sat down when an ugly old woman with rotten teeth approached them, whereupon Weatherby ordered two mugs of beer, which required they be paid for in advance. Their beer brought, they were just as quickly ignored.

It was the perfect place for a secret rendezvous, as no respectable businessman would ever have entered such a dilapidated hovel in such a squalid part of the city. And the cloak and dagger might have even been fun if not for the terrible stench that permeated everything and was inescapable.

The two dared not speak, not even in whispers, all the better to maintain their anonymity, nor did they remove their bulky coats or unwrap their scarves that partially hid their faces. Yet they need not have worried. The two men sitting closest to the fire playing cards had begun arguing and were becoming increasingly loud, which attracted the attention of the others, who poked one another in the ribs and waited in eager anticipation for a sudden outburst of violence. But it was not to be, for a short and stocky man soon afterwards entered the bar, followed by a broad-shouldered man who carried himself as one who was not to be trifled with.

The two were obviously not to be mistaken for mendicants, or even rough and tumble working-class types, for although neither was particularly well-dressed, their drab coats and hats were at least clean and presentable.

The card players immediately snatched up their game, rose and made room for the two strangers, who seemed not to be such a strangers after all, but well, almost expected…and esteemed enough to give up their best table, although no one greeted them or said a word as the card players found another table to continue their game.

The two newcomers made immediately for the vacated

table where the candle burned, the short and stocky one taking the bench with his back to the fire. He took off his coat, scarf, and hat, and placed them on the bench beside him, before looking about the room. It was only as his face caught the light of the fireplace that Kinkaid recognized him. Sure enough, it was the Marquis de la Renier. His companion kept his coat and hat on and with his back to them could not be ascertained. The two were immediately brought bowls of soup, bread, and drinks by the old toothless hag who fawned over them with happy and gratuitous banter, the Marquis laughing and returning her remarks which made her snicker and show her rotten teeth which she tried to cover with her gnarled hands. The larger man remained silent, only grabbing a baguette and greedily slurping up his soup with a large wooden spoon.

Only occasionally did the Marquis glance in their direction and each time Kinkaid was careful not to make eye contact, but look down or pretend he was speaking to his companion. Kinkaid was beginning to feel some agitation by the time the Marquis and his burly companion finished their meal, but then the door squeaked open once again, and this time there was no mistaking the tall man with the salt and pepper, bristle-like hair that stood straight up from his head when he removed his hat; Mr. William Palfrey, newly-appointed Congressional Agent for the United Colonies, who immediately took a chair and placed it between the two at the table by the fireplace, shaking hands with each in turn before sitting down. The three men immediately began to converse, and although Kinkaid could determine that they spoke English, he could not hear much of what they were saying over the increasingly loud banter of the querulous card players.

"Should we should move closer?" asked Weatherby,

gesturing toward an open table.

"Not without drawing attention."

Perhaps there was a perfectly good reason why these men were holding a clandestine meeting at midnight in this dubious, out-of-the-way bar. Perhaps dealing in arms and war materials required such shady undertakings, especially since no actual treaty had been signed by the French that would make such pursuits openly legitimate. But then there might be something altogether crooked going on, something that could profoundly affect and hurt the American cause, therefore it was quite maddening, being so close to such a suspicious gathering and not being able to hear what they were discussing.

The card players were now shouting French obscenities and the Marquis had to appeal to the old hag to quiet them so they could continue their discussions, in his good-natured way, of course.

But the men only shouted louder when the hag approached them with her appeal for quiet. Now one stood up and threw the deck of cards into the other's face, whereupon they were instantly at one another's throats. They knocked their own table over, and then proceeded to knock other tables over as they grappled and swung their heavy fists, hitting mostly air, to the delight of the other patrons, all except the three businessmen seated at the table in front of the fireplace who now all turned in the direction of the fighting card players.

The Marquis began to shout now, appealing for order, and then ordering the "imbeciles" to "Boucher!" All to no avail.

Now the burly man with their backs to them stood up and turned on the oblivious antagonists, instantly recognized by Kinkaid and Weatherby as the former pirate known as Jack Blackstone, aka Justin McGregor, now Captain McDougal.

He strode toward the pair, grabbed each by the neck in his massive hands and bashed their heads together, knocking both senseless. One landed at Kinkaid's feet and was not stunned enough or else lacked the sense to stay down, requiring the big Scot to smash his fist into the man's face, the crack reverberating like the sound of an ax on hardwood, dropping the man senseless and bringing total silence to the once noisy bar. Now Blackstone stood there, not three feet from Kinkaid, looking directly into his eyes, eyes that registered a surprised recognition.

The gig was up, and Kinkaid's mind raced to form an explanation when Blackstone merely gave him a wink and said, "I guess they won't be bothering us for the remainder of the evening." Then he turned and strode back to the table and resumed his seat with his companions who laughed and made much of the incident as the others in the bar helped the former card players to their feet and out the door.

Kinkaid could only look at Weatherby in consternation. They had been recognized for certain, yet Blackstone had ignored the fact. Very strange, very strange indeed, and all Kinkaid and Weatherby could do was sit there in their duel bewilderment.

Their meeting now broke up, with Mr. Palfrey leaving first. Then the Marque rose and put on his coat and hat. But Blackstone remained seated, saying in a voice all could hear, "It's early for me, sir. I believe I'll stick around…enjoy a quiet nightcap."

Blackstone waited for at least three minutes after the Marquis had left before he rose and came over to the table where Kinkaid and Weatherby sat in alarmed trepidation.

"I knew you were in Paris, Kinkaid," said Blackstone, "but I didn't expect to see you again, much less speak to you."

"Should I call you Blackstone or McGregor…or is it Captain McDougal now?"

The big pirate laughed out loud. "I've not the luxury of a permanent moniker, unlike those who owe allegiance to cause or country," said the big man, "so Captain McDougal will do for now. But all that aside, I may have some things to tell you that may be of interest. May I join you?"

"Pull up a chair, Captain," said Kinkaid.

"With pleasure," said Captain McDougal. Then he turned to Kinkaid's companion, offered his massive hand and said, "Mr. Weatherby is it not?"

Weatherby had to grin in spite of himself at the man's unrestrained and impetuous manner. "Right you are, Captain." The handshake was as hard as the man's cold blue eyes that nonetheless twinkled with a merry recognition of the sudden oddity of the situation. Kinkaid and Weatherby had gone to a lot of trouble to come disguised in order to ascertain the ramifications of a suspicious meeting, only to have been found out by none other than their former nemesis from the Caribbean, Jack Blackstone, who openly confronted them and was now seated at their table as if nothing unwarranted were occurring, a most unsettling turn of events.

The two were soon made aware of all that the pirate was now engaged in, a scheme to defraud an insurance company of a luxury ship and an expensive cargo, bound for America, to be diverted to the Caribbean.

"So you see, I'm to act the scoundrel once again, to make off with the Marquis' ship and Mr. Palfrey's cargo, all to be sold so they can collect on their insurance, all profits to be split three ways, of course, at least that is what I am led to believe; the same sort of scheme that set me on my road to perfidy and damnation in the first place some years ago."

"As if you have no choice in the matter," observed Kinkaid skeptically.

"Ah, but escaping one's past is not an easy thing. After all, a man needs employment, and a man with my reputation has little to choose from, not to mention that there are always those who would benefit from my connections."

"But what is to keep you from simply keeping the profits of the ship and the cargo, certainly more than what the insurance will pay?"

"The question that concerns me more is: what is to keep them from turning me in when I come to collect my share? I wouldn't trust that scoundrel Palfrey with his own mother's purse. Why, that man would cut your throat for a farthing. But to answer your question, Captain; the crew is loyal to the Marquis, and believes they will keep me to my word," laughed the pirate. Then he reflected and said, "Perhaps they might keep me honest, at that, but that is not what galls me; it's that I am the one risking a rope around my neck. I know my word means nothing to you, Kinkaid, and it's my own doing to be blamed for that, but I mean to tell you, Captain, that I'm sick of the business, tired of having no place to hang my hat." Then with a laugh he added, "In case you hadn't noticed, I'm getting on in years and have my future to consider."

It surprised Kinkaid to hear the rough and reckless man speak in such terms, and there was a nagging suspicion that he was being played again. Yet there lurked a certain sincerity, almost a heartbreak, in the man's voice. And what did Blackstone have to gain by approaching them and so much as admitting the scheme? There was only one logical conclusion; Blackstone wished to go straight, wanted to live a normal life again, had come to the realization that the path of a pirate lead to only one certain destination, the end of a rope.

"Perhaps we might come to a mutual agreement after all. If you can assure that your cargo gets into the right hands and you've a mind to assist us with a certain endeavor, I'm certain it will do you a great service in the eyes of Dr. Franklin, who, as you must know, holds great influence in our government, in granting pardons, endowing citizenship, things of that sort."

"Now you're talking, Captain; just name your price, I am once again at your service."

Kinkaid could only laugh and admit, "That is what I'm afraid of," causing nervous laughter all around, the three recalling their former collaboration in the Caribbean that ended up becoming a bloody sea and land-based duel to the death, all because of this pirate's duplicity, and as far as Kinkaid was concerned, Blackstone had a lot to prove in the area of trustworthiness.

"The first item you might assist us with concerns our American friend, Mr. Palfrey."

"He is the one I worry about the most. A very dangerous fellow, that one. Why, he is a professional duelist; killed at least four men already who have crossed him. I wouldn't want to take him on, I'll tell you that."

It was disconcerting to hear of a tough scoundrel like Blackstone admit to fearing a man, yet Blackstone certainly feared Mr. Palfrey.

"Yes, Mr. Weatherby here has been taking lessons in arms from him while on our passage."

"If you had to face him, what weapon would you choose, Weatherby?" asked Blackstone.

"Hard to say. I think pistols," answered Weatherby. "He is a master swordsman, with a long reach and is devilishly quick for a tall man. With a pistol, I'd at least have a chance.

I'm a fair shot. And besides, if I had to die, I'd rather it be by a quick bullet than cut to pieces."

"Yes, Mr. Palfrey described to me a duel he had with a swordsman of some renown," said Blackstone. "Said he had to disable the man before he could go in for the kill. Which means slicing into vital arteries, joints, organs; rather bloody business all around."

"That is all very interesting," said Kinkaid, "but I don't believe any of us will have to face him. We'll simply arrest him when we have enough evidence."

"What kind of evidence?" asked Blackstone.

"Well, can you tell us anything about this?" asked Kinkaid, presenting Blackstone with the copy of the code obtained by Weatherby.

"I see you are farther ahead of the game than I thought. But this in itself will not result in a conviction as a traitor in a court of law."

It was encouraging to find that Blackstone admitted to recognizing the strange lettering right away. It was even better when he told them that not only was Palfrey in the shady business of dealing arms and running insurance scams, but was also in the employ of the English, regularly sending coded messages to London about American activities in France via a certain fast sloop with a particularly long red pennant flying from its mainmast, now ported at Le Havre, the same port where Blackstone had his ship, the one loaded with Mr. Palfrey's very expensive and much needed war supplies for Washington's army, which would end up in British hands if not for Blackstone. Kinkaid felt he had no choice but to place his trust in the man once again. And once again, he had to accept that it would be up to Blackstone to honor or abuse that trust.

"Perhaps we might come up with a plan whereby Mr.

Palfrey will reveal himself," ventured Kinkaid.

"That should be easy enough," gave Blackstone. "Palfrey makes his drops every Thursday at midnight in the cemetery of Le Havre, his coded message is picked up an hour later by a courier who delivers his message to the ship, giving both time enough to be clear and unknown to the other. A reasonable precaution, so as to maintain their mutual security, at least in theory."

"Yet one which affords us our chance to intercept his message, decode it, and replace the original."

"Exactly."

"Do you know who this courier is?"

"No, only what he looks like. A dark man with a black mustache that might be the real thing or it might not. To include him in our scheme would be too risky."

"Hmm. Yes, I suppose, but he could be our Achilles heel if our timing is off or if anything else goes wrong. Aside from that, the trick will be for us to give Palfrey some secret information, the importance of which he will be certain to pass on."

"Who will you leave behind to intercept his message?" asked Weatherby.

Of course it would have to be someone having Kinkaid's complete trust. Yet, almost anyone on the ship had his trust, so that was easy enough. And they would not have to possess any special skills. Just go to the cemetery and watch where Palfrey leaves his message, pick it up, make a quick copy with the additional false information, and replace it at the drop for the courier to pick up.

"You won't have to leave anyone," said Blackstone. "I can attend to that business easy enough."

Kinkaid hesitated. Could he trust Blackstone, especially with the man's own proposal? It sounded too much like a setup.

Blackstone suspected as much and offered, "You could leave one of your men with me to make sure. Besides, like you said, something could go wrong; I might need some assistance."

"Perhaps," said Kinkaid. "You describe the courier as having a dark complexion and a long black mustache that may or may not be genuine. Who does that remind you of, Weatherby?"

"You must be referring to Mr. Briggs, Captain."

"And a very fine actor, if my memory serves."

Weatherby could not help but chuckle at the reminder of Mr. Briggs once pretending to be an English ship's officer in the Caribbean, a very drunken performance as it turned out, but played to perfection by the brave but rather high-strung young midshipman. "Mr. Briggs will be perfect in the role, Captain."

The three talked into the wee hours of the morning and it wasn't until after three that Kinkaid and Weatherby left Blackstone at the tavern. What they didn't notice as they walked up the dark street were five scowling men lurking in a nearby alley, waiting only for a burly man to emerge from the bar in order to exact a brutal revenge.

It was a great relief to find the coach waiting for them some five blocks from the tavern, the one they had hired to wait for them, and it was not until they were well on their way back before Kinkaid could get over his nervousness enough to allow his excitement to get the better of him.

"I can't believe it, Weatherby. "

"I know, sir. Meeting Blackstone again…and under these circumstances. Why, it seems too good to be true."

The words came as a blow and Kinkaid felt as quickly deflated. "Yes, I know what they say about what seems too good to be true. Oh well, there's little to be done now except hope he comes through. If not, at least he knows nothing of our mission."

"True, sir. The worst that can happen is that Palfrey, Blackstone and the Marquis get away with their insurance fraud at the expense of Congress."

"Yes, but wouldn't it be grand to disrupt that scheme?"

"Perhaps we might ensure just that. Sir, I was thinking," said Weatherby, his quick mind working overtime. "Why give Palfrey any information at all? Why not just add some on our own when Briggs intercepts his message, pass on some false information without Palfrey's or Blackstone's knowledge? Of the kind which will kill two birds with one stone."

"Do go on, Weatherby."

"Well, sir, having access to Palfrey's messages provides us with at least some evidence against him, and perhaps we might be able to add to that over time if he does not find us out. But more *au courant*, there is certain to be a force sent against us after our mission is successful, a force large enough to blockade whatever port we return to…"

Kinkaid immediately understood the implications of Weatherby's line of reasoning, even when he slipped in a French phrase here and there, a line of reasoning that Kinkaid had not considered, to his embarrassment, simply because it was far in the future, yet it was of paramount importance. "Of course you are right, as usual, Mr. Weatherby. The Royal Navy will insist upon exacting a heavy price for their humiliation when this is over. If they can't catch us, they will likely wait for us to come out. If we are to leave France safely, we must send them off on a wild goose chase, preferably to the east."

"The Port of Calais," suggested Weatherby.

"Which makes it three birds with one stone, Weatherby," exclaimed Kinkaid, pointing out, "Mr. Palfrey provides us evidence of his treachery, the Royal Navy are made to believe we are where we are not, and Blackstone proves his loyalty, all in the same stroke. And only Mr. Briggs will know of it. But our timing must be right. Let's see, Christmas is on a Thursday, the same day as the drop."

"We should be returning just as the message goes out,"

"The whole thing is nothing less than brilliant, Weatherby," said Kinkaid with some smugness.

"Captain, you and I are in the wrong business; this is by far too much fun" returned Weatherby, grinning.

"It is grand fun, Weatherby. But let us not be too hasty in our self-congratulations. Let us not forget that we have fellow seamen to rescue first."

XI
Only With Audacity, Pure and Simple

Kinkaid's French had improved enough so that he could actually follow the story the pilot, Jacques, told him, of his service in the French Navy. It seems he had lost his left arm at the elbow to an English cannon on the Island of Martinique in 1762, but he knew his business and conducted *Active* with a calm professionalism out of the port of Nantes, down the river Loire, and out into the Bay of Biscay, whereupon Kinkaid not only paid the man his fee, thanking him profusely in bad French when he was picked up by a small lighter out of St. Nazaire, but he even gave him an excellent bottle of Bordeaux, to Cato's evident displeasure.

Perhaps Cato was right to begrudge the pilot one of their best and most expensive wines, after all the man was only doing his job. But Kinkaid was feeling generous, and it could only be attributed to his profound pleasure in being at sea again. It was good to breath the salt air, to feel the stiff breeze on one's face, to stand on the deck of a rolling ship, a ship he knew and trusted, with men he knew and trusted, even if the weather was foul, with sporadic showers and scarcely a glimpse of the sun for the last three days as they tacked laboriously up the coast until arriving at the Ile d'Ouessant, where they finally made their turn into the gray-green waters of the English Channel, and favorable winds out of the northwest.

And it was not until now, out here where the elements could be felt, that Kinkaid could more objectively regard Paris, her masses of people starving while royalty lived off the fat of the land, a place seething with injustice, a place awaiting her own revolution when heads would role from the bloody blades of the guillotine. His view of Franklin, however, could not be diminished, and the great man, with friends in many places, had been of immense help in finding comfortable and trustworthy transportation back to the ship and then in procuring ample supplies for the voyage. What was more; Franklin kept his suspicions to himself as to the reason why Kinkaid preferred to omit Mr. Palfrey from such tasks, Kinkaid only telling him, "Oh, I'm sure Mr. Palfrey has his hands quite full as it is without troubling him over our skimpy requirements." His only wish would have been for Franklin to let them depart without the uncomfortable going-away party he had thrown, in which the lovely Jeanette Bertrand attended. A most awkward affair.

Mr. Hill's broken face was broken even more by his inability to keep from smiling upon Kinkaid's return to the ship. Kinkaid knew that Hill had most likely been bored to tears by the extended time in port, rarely leaving the ship because he knew no French, and having little or nothing to do to relieve the boredom, and all the while not knowing if or when Kinkaid would return, it must have been an intolerable wait. Having rarely seen Mr. Hill smile, even before his terrible injuries, it seemed somewhat silly, even embarrassing, to see him suddenly in such a jovial mood, a mood that had remained with him even now.

Unlike the staid and steady Mr. Hill, the exuberant Mr. Rosetti probably enjoyed his time ashore more than most, as he spoke the best French and made himself right at home, even finding a loyal paramour in the town, and so it was with mixed feelings that he bid her farewell as the ship left the dock, to the good-natured ribbing of his fellow officers, but even so he could be found muttering happily in Italian as he went about his duties with his customary flair.

And of course Chief Boatswain O'Toole had been more than happy and relieved to pipe Kinkaid aboard, happy to once again have a boatswain's purpose, and relieved to relinquish the role of disciplining sailors who found no end of ways of getting into trouble ashore, especially one Nicky Sterling, who found no end of ways to get himself to one situation in or another while ashore, finally requiring that O'Toole confine him to the ship for the last three weeks. And, according to O'Toole, Harris remained aboard as well, proving his loyalty to his friend, Sterling.

Then there was Cato; although he enjoy immensely being in France, his home country, he was once more in his element aboard ship, in charge of his small domain, turning out delicious fare, all with a French twist, having stocked his larder with salt, sugar, coffee, barrels of flour, crocks of butter, an array of cheeses, all of which added their aromas to the officer's quarters, fresh meats, fruits and vegetables, chocolates and bon-bons, and all sorts of delicacies, and not to mention an assortment of wines to please the most discerning connoisseur, minus one very fine bottle of Bordeaux, and he was soon turning out fresh croissants and baguettes from his tiny oven.

Even Mr. Sykes was once more in fine form as his grumpy self, having given up the fast-growing beagle puppy to a family on shore with three romping children and a large yard.

Mr. Briggs and Mr. Phillips were also happy to see them again, even though they had tasted of Paris life for a few days every two weeks, mostly hanging out with Weatherby and Marie. He then had apprised Mr. Briggs of his assignment, and Weatherby had instructed him in the use of the code, but it was with more than a little trepidation that Kinkaid sent him off to Le Havre, where Blackstone would put him up and plan their little escapade. But then Briggs was a grown man and could take care of himself.

Yes, all was quite as it should be, a happy ship with a happy crew, happily going about its normal duties, and, as far as the officers and crew were concerned, off on some unknown destination, all things quite normal and as it should be. Even Mr. Weatherby spoke philosophically about leaving Marie, for he was at least comforted to know that he could look forward to seeing her again once their mission had been accomplished.

Yes, it was good to be at sea again. Yet, if there was one man aboard ship who was not so smug and happy as all the others seemed to be, it was Kinkaid, pacing up and down in his relative solitude on the windward side of the ship, after a break from the many drills he had initiated, worried about the efficiency of his ship after so much time spent idle in port. Of course there was the mission to consider, but this was something he could plan and then carry out through a logical progression of thinking and actions. Then there was the vaguer problem of dealing with Mr. Palfrey when he returned, a problem that nagged at the back of his brain and seemed to offer no clear conclusion or logical progression, other than having to arrest the man if and when he could find enough evidence against him. But foremost on his mind was the latest letter he had received from Elizabeth, handed to him as they were departing from Franklin's residence, a hastily written note telling him she was about to take passage aboard one of her father's ships, the *Malvern,* so as to come and be with him in Paris. On the face of it, good news, for he dearly missed her. Yet there was about this unexpected news that made him uneasy. Of course, there was the dangerous prospect of crossing the Atlantic in winter that made him uneasy. Storms were frequent and severe, trying to even hardened seamen. Then he had to ask; what could have possessed her to undertake such a journey? Had she learned of the shenanigans of the French court? Did she suspect him of an illicit alliance? Or was there something even more complicated, possibly sinister, behind the seemingly impetuous decision. After all, she had vaguely warned him about Mr. Palfrey in a letter that Weatherby had found in the very man's possession, which meant that he certainly knew that she was on her way to join him in Paris. It was a disturbing thought and his wrought nerves were coalescing into a hard and dark fist that took root in his stomach.

He soothed himself by reasoning that the core of his anxiety was that the surprising news of her decision to join him served as an unwelcome distraction, keeping him from concentrating on the task at hand, for he had not fully formulated his rescue plan as yet, having found that the best solutions were usually arrived at by allowing them to cook, as it were, in his subconscious. Of course he would not have explained it in that way, having gone about the exercise purely by instinct, but that is how he had learned to resolved such things, which did not obviate a great deal of nervous agitation and contrariness, part and parcel of the loneliness of command, hence his uncommunicativeness since leaving port, and when the crew noted that they were not traveling west, back to American shores as they had anticipated, but north and then east, into the channel, Kinkaid, detecting a grumbling among some members of the crew, may have overreacted when he loudly berated Mr. Sykes for not keeping the men busy enough as they passed the Cap de la Hague.

The English Channel was a busy place, where ships from any number of countries might be found, taking or receiving goods from northern European ports. Of course it was called the English Channel and not the French or Dutch Channel for good reason; England ruled it with her overwhelming sea power. And these days, French ships were particularly nervous, as their country might declare war against Britain at any moment, without their captain's hearing the news until it was too late, their ships and cargos claimed by an English warship or privateer, and so French ships naturally hugged their country's shoreline. For this reason, so did the *Active*, keeping well clear of British patrol vessels well offshore.

They were in the Baie de la Seine now, and the sandy beaches and low hills of Normandy could just be seen through the late morning haze, with a church steeple appearing here and there, indicating scattered inland villages.

"Sail ho, almost dead north, Captain!" came the call from the lookout.

It was the third time that morning that such a hail came from the masthead, and it required roughly determining the course of the sighted ship by the lookout and then steering away from her, while losing the least headway toward their immediate destination, the French port of Le Havre, at the outlet of the Seine, some fifty nautical miles to the east.

"She's heading west by south, Captain! Danish for certain!"

"Come two points to starboard, helm." If the sighted ship maintained her course and distance, there was no need to take more than the minimal evasive action. And by maintaining a five to ten mile distance from French shores and flying the French standard, they were able to sail in comparative anonymity. If they could indeed keep to their same course, they should be off the coast of Le Havre by morning.

It was twenty minutes later that the sails of the ship could be seen from the quarterdeck, a pale gray triangle barely visible against the pale gray sky, her red national ensign with the white cross easily identified and the only note of color on the bleak horizon. She was passing off their stern now and was soon lost from sight.

Here came the Marine Commander, Lieutenant McDowd.

"I'm pleased to report that we have sorted out those uniforms to my satisfaction Captain. Which means you shall have a dozen fully-armed and equipped Redcoats at your disposal as needed, sir, and volunteers all."

It was just like the young marine Lieutenant to do immediately what another man might put off until later, and it gave Kinkaid something less to worry about, although the likelihood that all those men who found uniforms that adequately fit them might have volunteered could only be taken with a grain of salt, especially since none of them, including the intrepid Lieutenant McDowd, had the slightest idea what they were about to attempt, and the realization caused Kinkaid a pang of guilt.

More than this, the report interrupted Kinkaid's cogitations, at least for the moment, and he forced a smile and said, "I am glad to hear it, Mr. McDowd, and I believe it is time we talked some things over in my stateroom. This evening at supper, then?"

"At your service, Captain."

Mr. Hill had the watch and Kinkaid approached him and

said, "I'd like you to join me for supper this evening, Mr. Hill."

"Why, thank you, Captain."

Kinkaid pondered a moment longer before summoning the officer of the deck.

"Mr. Phillips!"

"Aye aye, sir," said Phillips, running up and saluting his captain.

"My regards to Mr. Rosetti, Mr. Weatherby, Mr. Sykes, and Boatswain O'Toole, and I wish you would pass along my invitation to join me for supper tonight in my cabin."

"I'll inform them right away, sir," answered Phillips and off he ran.

Only now did it occur to Kinkaid that there was one person he should have informed about the dinner before he invited all the others. Worse, there was no officer of the deck to tell Cato. He would simply have to do it himself.

"Mr. Hill, I believe I shall retire below. Please send for me if the weather changes or a ship approaches."

"Very good, sir."

Kinkaid wanted very much to return to the deck after he informed Cato of his decision to invite half a dozen of his ship's officers to supper, but he had already told Mr. Hill that he would retire and as silly as the situation was he did not want to appear indecisive, so he stubbornly made himself lie down on his cot and try to relax. Yet he had not considered that he would have to listen to Cato fuss about in his tiny kitchen as he prepared a veritable feast, what with all the fresh stores at his disposal, and it was all very annoying. Of course Cato loved cooking, but what added to Kinkaid's annoyance was that Cato had the habit of whistling French tunes when engaged in his cooking marathons, one gay ditty after the other, until Kinkaid thought he take no more and vociferously object. But he contained his exasperation and held his tongue and tried to remember to count his many blessings instead.

Supper time finally arrived, but only after an interminable period, and it was with sincere relief that he invited each and every man and officer into his cramped wardroom, and now they all sat elbow to elbow as Cato brought in the first course; thin, lightly-basted, mushroom-covered lamb chops, with a side of perfectly steamed and buttered asparagus.

Kinkaid allowed the men to enjoy their sumptuous repast and grow relaxed from the wine before he told them the primary reason for the invitation. He laid out his plan in broad terms and after sincere and hearty endorsements all around, considered various suggestions, before concluding, "Very well, then. I thank you all and am satisfied that we are in agreement as to our general course. We shall continue to carry out drills to improve our state of readiness, and I look forward to meeting again with all of you to finalize our plans before the action."

Weatherby then led them to a hearty hip-hip-hurrah for what they were all eagerly about to achieve, while Cato received accolades from all.

After dinner, Kinkaid could not help but notice Mr. Phillips standing beside the mainmast shrouds. At first he gave the young man little notice, for any off-watch officer might come out on deck to breath the fresh air or have a smoke. But it soon occurred to Kinkaid exactly what the boy was up to as he worried a length of small stuff that he kept knotting and unknotting in his trembling hands. Phillips had been left out of the dinner meeting because Kinkaid had decided that the young midshipman should remain aboard ship with Mr. Sykes, the only reason being that at least one officer should remain aboard with Mr. Sykes, the one with the least experience with missions involving the possibility of having to fight their way out of danger.

Yet, Kinkaid considered, how was a young midshipman to gain any experience unless he were offered the opportunity? Was he unconsciously trying to keep the boy out of harm's way? Yet he had to consider how this would play with the midshipman's pride, not to mention his standing with his colleagues.

Kinkaid waited as Mr. Phillips continued to play with his string. Finally the young man gave a long sigh, stuffed the string into his pocket and strode solemnly to where Kinkaid stood. He began, "Captain, if I m-may. There is a m-matter which I hope you would consider."

"I've already considered it, Mr. Phillips..."

"B-but sir..."

"...and I have determined that you shall accompany the shore party, as a prisoner."

Phillips stood there with his mouth open as he repeated in his mind Kinkaid's words. "Why thank you, Captain. Thank you very much."

It was later, after Phillips had gone below that Kinkaid approached his venerable gunnery officer who had just come up on deck to relieve the quarterdeck watch.

"Mr. Hill, it comes to my attention that I may have erred somewhat in my plans for our shore mission; that I may be leaving the ship with an inadequate range of experience...that is, should anything go wrong..."

But Mr. Hill was already aware of Kinkaid's business. "I understand that Mr. Phillips has been chosen to take my place, Captain, a decision I heartily endorse. After all, I would not wish the captain to be worried about the readiness of the ship, what with three-quarters of our crew ashore." And with that crooked smile, Hill added, "You can count on me, sir."

Kinkaid returned a sly smile of his own and said, "As always, Mr. Hill, and for that I am much relieved and much obliged."

There was one bit of information that Kinkaid had not shared with his men and officers at the dinner meeting, which was the reason why they had anchored within sight of Le Havre the next morning, even ordering the placement of signal lanterns, one at the top of each mast.

"Breakfast has been secured, the decks have been scrubbed, all bright work attended to, and my inspection of the ship is concluded to my satisfaction," reported Mr. Sykes. Of course he was burning to ask his Captain why they were anchored in such an unprotected seaway at so early in the morning when there was a fresh breeze that would have carried them closer to their destination, but, like all the other officers, he dared not ask. Only Mr. Weatherby knew the reason, yet he prudently acted as perplexed as the others.

Kinkaid never left the deck, only watching the harbor as they waited there, being tossed about by the wind and waves for almost six hours, as one ship after another passed, either entering the mouth of the Seine or leaving it, a few coming quite close, close enough to ascertain that *Active* was a warship, a small warship, but a warship nonetheless. Of course all of the captains of those ships were curious as to why a ship would anchor in such an unprotected part of the harbor, bouncing up and down as the waves rolled under her, but of course none mustered the temerity to ask, only because they would not welcome another foolish captain questioning why they would anchor in such an uncomfortable spot.

It was late afternoon and the crew were at dinner. Kinkaid had Cato bring him a bowl of onion soup with bread and butter as he kept his watch on the harbor, and by now he was growing impatient and perplexed as the incoming breakers kept pounding them at the bow, sending spray flying over the forward transom and even reaching the quarterdeck. Had Blackstone already forgotten his part of the bargain? Had something gone wrong with his deal with the Marquis and Mr. Palfrey? Even worse, Mr. Briggs was over there somewhere. Had something happened to him, as well? Should he risk going ashore and ascertaining why? The sun was low in the sky now under a cloud cover that was breaking up, casting a warm glow on the painted buildings along the bay, but Kinkaid could scarcely appreciate the romantic view, for he was by now thoroughly irritated.

Weatherby could see that his captain was clearly perturbed and, being the only man aboard who knew why, wanted to say or do something to ease his nerves, but could think of nothing except, "Perhaps there is a good reason, Captain."

"There had better be," hissed Kinkaid.

"I wouldn't worry too much about Briggs, sir," continued Weatherby. "Blackstone has no reason to harm him."

"That's right, Captain," said Nicky Sterling, out of the blue. "Don't worry about Mr. Briggs. He has the light of the Star over him."

Another strange comment from a very strange man, but Kinkaid knew they were both right. Worry would not help Mr. Briggs, nor would it help him with the job at hand, that of rescuing American prisoners. He would deal with Blackstone later.

"Raise anchor; take us out of here!" he ordered loudly, causing Mr. Sykes to flinch since he had been standing next to Kinkaid at the rail.

"Aye, Captain," came the ready reply. "Set anchor detail! All hands turn to! Prepare to wear ship!

To hell with Captain Blackstone, or McGregor, or McDougal, or whatever the bastard's name was; he didn't need that scoundrel. And he could not very well concern himself about one man when so many more were at stake, even if that one man was Mr. Briggs. Kinkaid could only stew about the missed rendezvous as the anchor windlass clanked interminably. Finally Mr. Sykes reported, "Anchor secured, Captain. We're under jib and mains'l."

"I can see that," answered Kinkaid harshly, miffed at the unnecessary reminder.

"Helmsman, head us West-norwest," said Kinkaid to Nicky Sterling at the wheel as they came about into the faltering evening breeze. At least the breakers were smoothing out and would no longer be pounding them as they drove against the incoming tide.

"Aye aye, Captain, West-by-norwest it is," answered Sterling, noting the underlying wrath in Kinkaid's words and eyes.

"Mr. Rosetti, you have the deck," said Kinkaid. "Keep us under easy sail. I'm going below for a bit."

Normally Kinkaid would have elucidated his orders, such as telling Rosetti to send for him if British shipping were detected, or if the wind or weather changed, but he was so angry, no, more than angry, closer to enraged, by the seeming perfidy of the pirate who had promised that he would meet him outside the harbor of Le Havre that very morning, to accompany him with his fine ship full of military supplies for the American cause, to help with the rescue mission by taking half of the freed prisoners, even to lend a few guns in case they had to fight their way clear. He was so enraged that he could scarcely speak without revealing his emotions in his voice. Of course he knew that Rosetti needed no reminders, that he was the consummate professional officer that needed no elucidation of orders; if he needed calling the captain, he would be called.

He did not even light his candle, but plopped back on his cot, meaning to get an hour or so of sleep, knowing that he would not dare to sleep until their return after they were well clear of any danger. Cato poked his head through the curtain, but Kinkaid merely waved him away, whereupon Cato removed himself, knowing the moods of his Captain by now. Normally Cato would have lighted his candle for him, brought him a clean dressing gown, hung his uniform in the closet, asked if he wished a nightcap, but tonight was not a normal night, and if he slept at all he would do so in his uniform. Kinkaid was disgusted, more with himself than with the perfidy of a pirate, disgusted for most likely being taken for a fool, again, and it was some time before he came to the realization that there were many other reasons that caused him to lose his temper, to let his nerves get the better of him…that knot in his stomach over Elizabeth's last letter, the fact that his plans had not been finalized, not to mention changed. Last, but certainly not least, was the fact that he may have jeopardized the life of a fine young midshipman. He lay there on his cot for some time before he could relax, before a fitful sleep overtook him, and when he was awoken two hours later, they were well into the English Channel.

"She was right about there, Captain," said Weatherby, standing at the rail and pointing three points off the starboard beam. There was a light fog and scarcely a breeze, a typical lull between blows in the Channel, a damp and unwelcome place in winter, whether blowing or not. "Possibly a frigate, if my eyes didn't deceive me. About a cable distant, on a reciprocal course."

"Since when have your eyes deceived you, Lieutenant?" asked Kinkaid as he looked through the telescope, bracing it in the mizzen shrouds.

The question took Weatherby by surprise, but was welcome proof that his captain had come out of his bad mood.

"Can't see anything but gray, but if there is a frigate out there, I hope she keeps on her course. Most likely a patrol vessel, keeping an eye on the French coast. Of course if she's a leading element…we'd better come to starboard; head directly north."

"Make it so, helm," said Weatherby, officer of the watch.

"Aye aye, sir."

It was just after nine and the wind had died considerably, the sails almost lax, the rhythmic sound of surging waves alongside replaced by a soft and steady gurgling sound.

The prevailing winds in the Channel were from the northwest, which meant that they would have to tack back and forth as they crossed the one hundred mile distance from Le Havre to Portsmouth, meaning the ship would actually cover twice that distance in a twenty-four hour period, making the passage across the middle of the English Channel during the night and planning their arrival near the Isle of Wight sometime in the afternoon of the next day.

It was easy enough to avoid shipping, especially since few ships traveled the middle of the channel in these uncertain times, preferring to remain within sight of friendly shores. Even so it was nerve-wracking to be out here in mid-Channel, even at night, flying the Union Jack in case a ship came close enough to identify them. At least there was something they could do that would occupy Kinkaid and those who would go into harm's way with him for an hour or so this evening, those loyal and steady men and officers who he depended upon, and who depended upon him.

"It's time we finalized our plans, Mr. Sykes."

"I'll pass the word, Captain."

After all the wrangling in his mind, after considering all of the known and unknown factors, after all the permutations, Kinkaid finally determined that there was only one certain way in which to go about this mission, and that was with audacity, pure and simple.

XII
Newfound Men and Lost Keys

If there was one thing that brought the full realization of their mission, it was the tense but quiet transformation of the ship and crew as they neared the English coast, now visible as a hazy blue line on the northern horizon, the yellow light of the sun shining through a misty noon haze.

Kinkaid had the ship linger some ten miles out for another two hours; they had made the passage in less time than he had anticipated and he did not want to enter Portsmouth harbor until sunset, ensuring that they made their escape during the night of the new moon.

"Royal Navy frigate off the Starboard beam!" came a shout from the lookout late that afternoon. "Heading right for us!"

Kinkaid looked at her through his telescope, and determined that she was about six miles distant. She had just come out of Portsmouth harbor and was pointing in their direction. Of course any ship would point directly toward them as it cleared the mouth of the harbor. If she passed nearby they would have to render honors. This they could do, but there remained the question of posing as a British warship, and there might be hard questions to answer.

"O'Toole, get some sea anchors out!" Kinkaid wanted to slow the ship without reducing sails, for to do so might raise suspicions. It would at least give them more time to ascertain what course the enemy frigate would take when she cleared the roadstead.

Kinkaid continued to watch the progress of the British frigate as O'Toole had four sea anchors tossed over the side and the ship soon slowed noticeably under the considerable drag. Twenty minutes passed like an eternity before Kinkaid watched her turn sharply to starboard. She would pass through the straight behind the Isle of Wight. It was a relief that they would not meet her, but it was too early to relax. It was an hour before sunset.

"Retrieve sea anchors. Take us in."

Out on deck were Mr. Sykes and Mr. Hill, both wearing ill-fitting British officer's uniforms. Mr. Syke's was too tight, with the buttons on his coat ready to burst, while Mr. Hill's coat hung loose from his lanky body. In sharp contrast were Lieutenant McDowd and his marines, standing amidships, all smartly dressed in the madder red uniforms of British soldiers, with white cross belts and breeches, and black cocked hats. Each carried a musket complete with bayonet. Kinkaid was similarly dressed in red, albeit as an officer, with a sword at his side.

Only a minimum crew ran the deck, as most were below, out of sight. Mr. Weatherby and Mr. Rosetti in their oldest Continental Navy uniforms, along with a grinning Mr. Phillips, who could scarcely contain his delight at finding himself included in the shore party. A foolish instinct, to be sure, to find joy in placing one's life on the line, but a patriotic instinct, reinforced by peer pressure, which all war demanded, indeed depended upon, from the young and naïve, seeking some nebulous glory.

The Isle of Wight passed off the port beam as the sun began to dip behind the island, casting its shadow on the low clouds above. They were at the mouth of Portsmouth harbor just as it began to grow dark.

Portsmouth was an island city, connected to the mainland by a series of bridges, and now all appeared peaceful and quiet as they made their approach to the docks, where some dozen or more ships were moored. Most were coasters and merchant brigs, but at least four were Royal Navy warships with their black and yellow paint schemes; one small sloop, two frigates, and a huge first rate of 100 guns. The sloop was moored opposite the two frigates at one pier. The sloop would be fast; at least an equal to *Active,* in both speed and armament. The frigates, however, with their 32 to 44 guns, could blow *Active* out of the water with a single broadside, that is, if they could catch her. One, especially, caught the attention by all on the quarterdeck as her stern pointed their way; *Vanguard*, the very ship that had chased them into Le Havre a month before. The first rate, however, was in the famous dry dock, already in use for over two hundred years, having her hull careened and her fittings replaced. Even her masts had been removed for replacement…no threat at all.

But there was more to think about than the *Vanguard* or a possible ship-to-ship fight, and Kinkaid took a deep breath and tried to calm his mind as they made their approach to an open berth with a large number three painted on a round board nailed to a piling. To his great relief, no one seemed to pay much heed to the arrival of a small warship.

Except on the other side of the pier sat a shabby-looking merchant brig, where a half dozen idle sailors stood at her rail beside the light of a single lantern, watching *Active's* approach.

"Let's not be shy, Mr. Sykes," prompted Kinkaid.

"Ahoy there!" called Sykes to the men on the brig. "Off your duffs and lend a hand here!"

The idle sailors ran quickly to the pier to catch lines

thrown to them from the deck of the *Active*, and as the ship was singled up a fat man in a huge black coat and black hat came out onto her deck and stood watching as he puffed on his pipe. He waited until all lines were secured before calling out, "What ship you be?"

Sykes did not hesitate, but answered, "*Active*, out of Falmouth!"

"Never heard of her!" came the reply.

"Newly assigned!" answered Sykes.

"I know the *Nonsuch* out of Falmouth; are you with her?"

"Yes!" lied Sykes.

"Why are you berthing here? Navy ships berth down the quay there!"

"Didn't know there was a law against berthing where I pleased!"

"Well, why don't you know? You should know! The Harbor Master will let you know, and in no uncertain terms! Piers 1 through 5 are for merchant ships only!"

"I'll keep that in mind next time!"

"Well, when the Harbor Master comes around he'll kick you out of here, no question of that."

"Thank you, good captain, for that information! Now if you'll let me get on with my business, I'd be much obliged."

"Don't say I didn't warn you. By the way, how's Captain Forsythe?"

"Who?"

"Captain Forsythe, of the *Nonsuch*! How is he?"

"Better!" ventured Sykes, pulling nervously at his collar.

"End this," whispered Kinkaid to Sykes.

"That's good to hear!" said the nosy captain of the brig. "Didn't think he'd make it; terrible sick last I knew! Back on duty, then, is he?"

"Aye, coast watch!"

"Again? Ah, no rest for the weary, I suppose!"

"End this now," whispered Kinkaid, this time more urgently.

But the garrulous captain of the shabby brig would not stop. "Haven't been to Falmouth for some time! But say, what be your business?"

"No business of yours, but if you must know we've a hold full of American prisoners to be remanded!"

"No room in Portsmouth jail for them! Didn't you hear? They're filled up! Putting the overflow in prison hulks farther down the quay. Surprised you didn't know that!"

Sykes hesitated now, his brain scrambled by the meddling merchant captain. Finally he answered, "I've orders to deliver these prisoners to Portsmouth jail, and I aim to follow those orders if it's all the same to you, and I'll thank you to leave me be!"

"No need for sharp words!" answered the curious captain, removing his hat. "I'll be Captain Morris of the brig *Daffodil*, the sweetest and prettiest little brig out of our fair port, and I take my hat off to you, sir, for keeping our shores safe from marauding rebels…and damn them all, I say! What name have you, good Captain?"

"Captain Brown!"

"May I invite you over for a nightcap, Captain Brown?"

"Not tonight, thank you, sir! Had a busy time of it out there, chasing a rascal of a privateer, and now we need to get her crew off the ship before I can sleep tonight! I'll share breakfast with you, though, if you're still here in the morning!"

"We're not going anywhere; waiting for the navy to organize a convoy. The two tons of tea in my hold should be well steeped by the time it gets to New York. So I'll keep a fresh pot on for you then! And a good night's sleep to you,

Captain!"

Sykes merely doffed his hat in return, hoping the conversation was truly at an end.

Kinkaid glanced toward the deck of the brig and hoped to see her inquisitive and garrulous captain return to his cabin, but he remained standing stubbornly at the rail, watching their every move. At least he was silent, for the moment. "Good job, Mr. Sykes."

"God, I thought he'd never shut up, Captain," said Sykes under his breath.

"Did you hear him refer that scow as the sweetest and prettiest little brig?" asked Weatherby. "God, such hyperbole."

"Hyper...what?" asked O'Toole, never having heard the word before.

"It means exaggeration," said Weatherby, elucidating, "hy-per-bole."

"Hyperbole," repeated the Chief.

"To our business, now," Kinkaid reminded them.

O'Toole and a dozen seaman had been carrying bales of oil-soaked rags up onto the deck while Sykes had been making conversation with the captain of the *Daffodil*.

"Mr. Rosetti, take five men in the gig and as much of those rags as you can load into it and cross the harbor, over to those warehouses where our informant tells me they keep their naval stores; the perfect target for our diversion. But wait until you see us returning with the prisoners before you light your fires."

"Just like we planned, Captain."

"All right, Mr. Sykes, here we go."

"Open the main hatch!" ordered Sykes to the deck crew. "Turn out all prisoners!"

Up they came, all forty-three of them, almost half the

crew, while all remaining cooks and stewards, carpenters and coopers, would fill in as deck hands while the rest went ashore, posing as prisoners.

With the meddlesome captain and his idle seamen on the deck of the merchant brig looking on, Lieutenant McDowd was first off the ship, followed by his marines, and an impressive sight they made in their arms and uniforms as they lined up in two rows of six on either side of the gangway. Then came Weatherby, Briggs, Phillips, O'Toole and the rest of the prisoners, forming a triple line between the red coats.

As McDowd readied the formation, Kinkaid said to Mr. Sykes, "If by some chance I do not return by first light…"

"I know, Captain," said Sykes, "but I'm sure there will be no need for that."

"I hope you're right, Mr. Sykes. Until later then, and wish us luck."

"Of course, sir."

"Good luck, Captain," said Mr. Hill.

Kinkaid took his place alongside the line of men, then McDowd gave the command, "Prisoners, forward, march!" and off they went, heading toward Portsmouth Prison, some five city blocks to the northeast.

They were soon on High Street, passing the Greyhound Pub, where a warm candlelight could be seen behind steamed windows. Kinkaid heard O'Toole say something to Mr. Phillips about how nice it would be to "get a pint to go before we're thrown into a cold dungeon."

"Silence, there," came the harsh retort from Lieutenant McDowd, "or I'll have ye flogged right here in the street."

"Did you hear that 'hyperbole'," O'Toole said to Mr. Phillips, finding his chance to use his new word. At least he displayed the proper look of a man fearful of retribution, but

Mr. Phillips had to hold his hand over his mouth to hide a sheepish grin.

"Easy, Mr. Phillips," said Kinkaid in warning.

It was ten o'clock on a Thursday night and the bustle of the city had subsided; only a few revelers, mostly sailors on liberty, passing to or from one pub or another were out on the streets, and they mostly stood silently aside as the line of marching men passed, except for one drunk British tar who jeered at them, shouting, "I hope yea all rot in our jail, yea damned rebels!"

"I'd be minding my own business!" gave McDowd, overacting the part, thought Kinkaid.

Sure enough the commotion brought three men out of the Blue Oyster Tavern. One, a short fat man, wore a bulky uniform coat of sorts. He stood in his heavy boots, looking on at the men marching by with a scowl on his face and his hands on his hips. A large and ornately-carved ivory pipe hung from his mouth and he starting puffing on it in agitation, sending up a huge cloud of white smoke. Then he demanded, "Where are these prisoners going?"

Kinkaid stepped forward and replied, "To the prison."

"By whose order?" asked the fat man, taking his pipe from his mouth.

"And who are you, sir?" asked Kinkaid.

"I am the Portsmouth Harbor Master, and I'll have an answer to my question."

"These prisoners are to be remanded to the jail by order of Captain Brown, of the *Active*."

"The *Active*? Never heard of her."

"Out of Falmouth, newly assigned," said Kinkaid, repeating Syke's lie.

"The jail is full," said the fat man, close enough now so that Kinkaid could smell the alcohol on his breath, even over the smell of tobacco. "Didn't anybody tell your Captain that prisoners are to go to the hulk farther down the quay?" His two henchmen stood behind the fat man, outwardly smirking.

"Just following orders, good sir, and if you don't mind, I'll let the warden tell me if the jail is full or not," said Kinkaid, hoping a forceful approach would work.

"Well, it's your time to waste, I suppose," growled the fat man, taking a large puff on his pipe. "Now where is this *Active* berthed?"

"Uh, pier three," Kinkaid had to tell him.

"Three? Well, we'll see about that." And off the man strode, toward pier three, with his two cronies trailing in his cloud of smoke.

McDowd came over and asked, "Trouble, sir?"

"Could be," he said. "Just hope Sykes can handle it."

"Mr. Hill is with him, Captain," came the reminder.

"So he is. Let's get on with it, shall we?"

"By all means, sir."

It was not a good start, docking at the wrong pier and gaining the attention of the Harbor Master, no less. Yet how were they to know? There was nothing to do now but carry on, and with all haste.

The prison was a large stone building, taking up a city block, looming over them as they approached it some three stories high. The entrance was a huge wooden door, reinforced with iron, some twelve feet square, with a smaller door cut into it. All was closed tight and no guards could be seen. A tower stood attached to the left of the huge door and now someone called out from above, "What be your business, sir?"

Kinkaid looked up and could see the shadow of a man standing at a narrow slit, high up the tower. "Well, can't you see? I've prisoners to be remanded!"

"I can see that, sir, but we're full! Prisoners are to be remanded to the hulks from now on. I'm surprised you weren't told!

"I've my orders and I'll see the warden if you don't mind."

No answer came forth. Kinkaid's mind raced, searching for something to say, something that would mean opening the huge gate to them.

Then, "I'll call the Sergeant of the Guard."

"I said the warden!," demanded Kinkaid. "And be quick about it!"

"Aye, sir, I'll let the Sergeant know!"

It was a tense eight minutes, waiting below in front of the locked gate, before keys could be heard jangling on the other side and the small door opened. A well-built and rather handsome man in the uniform of a British Major greeted them, rubbing his sleepy eyes. He wore his sword belt over the right shoulder, held with an ornamental belt plate, the latest fashion among officers.

"Good evening, Captain," said the man, stoking his large handlebar mustache with a handkerchief. "I am Major Hornsby, warden of this prison. Whom do I have the honor of addressing?" The man's nose was running and his voice sounded nasally. He was obviously suffering from a bad cold.

A rotten odor drifted out from behind the Major, a worse stench than any shipboard odor that Kinkaid had experienced. It reminded him of the *Jersey*, where he had been imprisoned not long ago, and he had to wince as he answered, "Captain Middleton, at your service, Major." A burly sergeant and two sentries stood dutifully behind the Major.

"My Sergeant tells me you have orders to deliver your prisoners to me." He took out a handkerchief and wiped his runny nose.

"I sincerely regret having to awaken you at such an hour, Major, but I am under the strictest of orders to bring these prisoner here."

"I was not told that more prisoners would be sent here, Captain. We are overfilled as it is."

Kinkaid felt the urge to push his way through the door, to force their way in. He was about to do this when the Major sighed and said, "However, I suppose we could house them in the courtyard for tonight. But only because it is so late. In the morning you will have to take them to the hulk out in the harbor, the one next to the *Somerset*, the large frigate."

"I am in your debt, Major."

"Open the gate," said the Major. "Bring them in, but you must give me your word as a gentleman that you will collect them at first light."

"Upon my honor, Major."

The heavy gate creaked open, revealing a large open area lined with a dozen cells where the dim shapes of human beings were haphazardly sprawled behind the bars in the flickering candlelight.

"Come now, get a move on, prisoners!" ordered Lieutenant McDowd. "Get inside, quickly now!"

It took no more than five minutes for the men to shuffle inside and group themselves along the line of cells, containing men that were stirring to life inside the barred cells. The smell was an overpowering mixture of sweat, shit, piss, vomit, sickness, disease and death, and it was difficult to breath. An office on the left proclaimed "Guardhouse." A dirty sign over an open door on the right read, "Garrison." A spiral staircase led up the tower.

"Who be you?" asked one of the awakened prisoners behind the bars as the Sergeant of the Guard locked the gate behind them. "Are you American?"

The Sergeant of the Guard spun around and shouted, "Shut up, rebel, or I'll…"

Another prisoner, a skinny man with a long scraggly beard called out, "Holy Mother of God, is that you O'Toole?"

O'Toole gave Kinkaid a nervous look, but Kinkaid took it as his queue and said to Major Hornsby, "I am Captain Kinkaid of the *Active*, and am pleased to inform you that your prison in now in American hands."

"What? Why, why, of all the dirty tricks," stammered a surprised Major Hornsby as Kinkaid relieved him of his sword and fancy belt. "You won't get away with this, you know." But the men in the cells behind him were already cheering and waking their comrades.

"By God, I knew it was you, O'Toole," said the skinny man behind the bars.

"Of course it's me, Quinn. Now hang on a minute and we'll get you out of there."

"To arms!" shouted Kinkaid as McDowd's marines relieved the guards of their weapons. "To arms, men. We bring you freedom!"

Mr. Weatherby and Mr. Phillips ran upstairs with their respective groups as had been planned. Two large rooms were upstairs where upwards of a hundred prisoners were reportedly housed. They took the lethargic guards by complete surprise and roused the prisoners, while McDowd and his marines quickly fanned out and took charge of the garrison where they easily overpowered the sleeping off-duty soldiers. They found a small sickbay attached at the back of the garrison, where three men lay on cots, one in obvious delirium. O'Toole and five seamen climbed the stairs of the tower, but found no one there. All that was left was to free the men in the cells behind them.

"The keys, if you please," ordered Kinkaid. "And be quick about it."

The Sergeant of the Guard stiffened and said, "I can't imagine where they might be." All of the guards stood mute and smug.

Kinkaid asked, "Quinn, where do they keep the keys?"

"They're usually on that peg over there." But there were no keys on the peg now.

"Search these men," said Kinkaid. "Search the entire place; the guardhouse, garrison, sickbay, that storage shed over there."

Mr. Phillips came down the stairs now, informing Kinkaid, "All is secured upstairs, Captain. Shall we bring them down?"

"How many?" Kinkaid wanted to know.

"Seventy or eighty, sir."

"Tell Mr. Weatherby that we shall be departing forthwith but to stay put at present."

"Aye, Captain."

Meanwhile, McDowd's men ransacked the place, first searching each of the guards, roughly at that. Then looking into all the drawers in the guardhouse office, finding a loaded pistol, which McDowd tossed to O'Toole. Every shelf was searched in the large storage shed, every drawer torn out and dumped onto the floor, scattering corn, barley and flour, but no keys.

"We've searched everywhere, Captain," McDowd had to report.

"Keep searching," was all Kinkaid could say. "They have to be around here somewhere."

A large brass spittoon sat next to the wall behind the guardhouse desk. Kinkaid walked over to it and gave it a good kick, sending it clattering against the stone wall, spilling it's brown liquid contents as it landed upside down. Kinkaid kicked it once again and there, amongst the disgusting spittle, was a long brass key.

"Your handkerchief, if I may, Major," demanded Kinkaid.

Kinkaid took the white cloth and picked up the key with it, gave it a proper wipe, handed the soiled hanky back to the Major, who let it drop to the floor, then handed the key to O'Toole, saying, "See if this fits, Chief."

It was the key they sought, and O'Toole took great pleasure in opening each and every cell in turn along the wall, all twelve of them, releasing four to six cheering and happy men from each, bringing a total of 57 men. The Major and his guards and sentries were herded into those cells as quickly as they were emptied, to the delight of all.

Quinn came out and hugged O'Toole like a long lost brother, "Jesus, Mary and Joseph, am I glad to see you, Michael O'Toole."

"Likewise," said O'Toole, "but the last time I saw you there was more of you."

A balding man with a scruffy beard approached Kinkaid with a bad limp and said, "Thank God, and thank you, Captain Kinkaid. Thank you from all of us."

The newly freed prisoners heard the speech and gave Kinkaid a rousing hip-hip-hurray, to which Kinkaid raised his hands in protest.

"Remember me?" asked the bearded man.

Kinkaid eyed the man closely but could not place him.

"Captain Hammond, of the *Columbus*."

"Good God, it is you!" exclaimed Kinkaid, recalling the foolish captain who had allowed himself and his ship to be taken by British frigates in the North Atlantic. "Good to see you, Captain." But he was shocked by what he saw. Once a plump and healthy man, now his coat hung loose from his emaciated body; his cheeks were sunken and he had lost most of his teeth. At least he was alive.

"Inform Mr. Weatherby that we are leaving here." Then he turned to the prisoners and said, "I can only imagine how happy you all must be to be released from your confinement, but I must ask you to keep a sad face as we bid farewell to this place. So act like prisoners; I'm sure you know how by now."

"Why, call me Shakespeare," said the skinny Quinn with a gap-toothed grin.

Men laughed and sniggered, then, "Aye, Captain," came the resounding answer. "You can count on us, sir!"

"McDowd, make sure the sick and wounded are brought along," Kinkaid thought to remind him.

"I saw some stretchers at the back of the sickbay, Captain."

"Good. And some of you strong men can help with that."

"That we will, Captain," came the eager reply.

They were soon out of the prison, marching in a long and bedraggled line back toward pier three, the lame and sick on stretchers bringing up the rear. At first Weatherby and Phillips helped Captain Hammond by holding him up between them as they hurried along, but so elated was Hammond that he soon shook them off and ran with a hopping limp, grinning like a toothless ape.

"Stow that grin, Hammond, or you'll give us away," said Kinkaid, chancing a joke, yet not knowing if they would find the *Active* ready to carry them to sea or if the gig was up, putting them all back in Portsmouth prison or on one of those horrid prison hulks out in the harbor.

But he was relieved to see that the ship was still there, lying peacefully alongside pier three, just as he'd left her. And there, across the harbor, he could see two, no three separate fires along the walls of the warehouses. Even as he watched a black smoke began to rise from them; Mr. Rosetti's timing was perfect.

Yet, something was amiss. Only two sailors stood on the quarterdeck of the *Active*. Where was Mr. Sykes or Mr. Hill?

Both sailors' had their attention was on the shabby merchant across the pier, and there, on her quarterdeck, stood Mr. Sykes and Mr. Hill, both. Kinkaid ran across her gangway to her quarterdeck where they stood and noticed that a man was floundering in the water some ten yards out. He obviously could not swim and was shouting for help. Nicky Sterling had a musket and was pointing it at the man, asking "Shall I shoot him, sir?"

Hill grabbed the barrel of the gun, saying, "No, you fool."

"What is happening here?" asked Kinkaid.

Hill answered, saying, "We had to hold the Harbor Master and his men, Captain. But then that damned Captain Morris started asking questions so we had to come over and take charge of his brig, too. They're all safe and sound in our hold sir, but one of their seaman eluded us, and now he's out there swimming to warn the British Navy; trying to swim, anyway."

The man was thrashing desperately in the water while shouting for help, but he was a poor swimmer and kept sinking under, and his gurgling cries could not be easily understood.

"Should I shoot him, sir?" asked Sterling once again. I think I could hit him fairly easily from here. If he gets any farther…"

"No, don't shoot," said Kinkaid. The poor man was

coughing more than he was shouting now, and becoming exhausted by his efforts.

Kinkaid could see that Rosetti and his five men were already returning in the gig as the fires they had started were blooming into bonfires all along the warehouses. Now bells could be heard on various ships in the harbor, merchant brigs and warships alike, which meant the fires had been noticed. Hopefully most of their crews would be dispatched to put those fires out.

Hill pointed across the harbor where a gig was putting out from the side of the *Vanguard*, filled with nine men. "Looks like we're going to have company soon, Captain."

"Let's get the hell out of here," said Kinkaid.

They scrambled back to the ship where crew, marines, and prisoners were all scrambling aboard, quickly filling every space on her open deck, with more still crowding aboard. Kinkaid could only hope they had room for all of them when the idea hit him.

"Captain Hammond, are you ready for command of a ship?"

"I certainly am, Captain, and when I get another I want to come right back here and…"

"I meant now, not later! I want you to take twenty men and follow us out of here in that brig!"

Hammond stood there with his mouth open, unable at first to grasp the idea, and it wasn't until some members of Hammond's own crew from the *Columbus* started cheering that it penetrated. "Men, you heard what Captain Kinkaid said. Let's act lively now, we've a ship to sail! You haven't forgotten how to sail a ship, have you?"

"No sir!" came the rousing reply.

"Hammond, follow us as we clear the Isle of Wight, then take a course of south by west for a couple of hours before making for Le Havre!" Kinkaid was of a mind to split them up; make it more difficult for their pursuers.

"Mr. Sykes, get as many below as you can!" shouted Kinkaid as Hammond and his men ran across the pier to the deck of the *Daffodil*. "Quickly now, O'Toole! Cast us off! And I want Sterling at the wheel!"

O'Toole was the last man to leap aboard as the ship drifted free and Nicky Sterling took over at the ship's wheel. They soon had the main and jib up, catching a slight breeze off the land and the ship had headway.

Rummy Quinn had kept close to Chief O'Toole throughout the rescue and now he asked him, "Say Chief, can you spare some tobacco for an old sea dog?"

O'Toole, always generous, pulled out a hefty wad from the back pocket of his tars and gave it to Quinn, an old hand he had served with for many years.

Quinn took it and said, "Haven't had a good smoke for six months. Wish I still had my pipe."

"Here, you can use mine," offered O'Toole, something the crusty chief would never do, but this was a special occasion.

Quinn knew as much so he said, "Ah, a chaw of tobacco is one thing, but I would never impose on another man's pipe, Chief. I'll just suck on this till I can procure another somewhere."

"As you wish, Rummy."

The light air from the land was behind them and would push them out toward the open ocean, but very slowly. Hopefully, stronger winds could be counted upon offshore. Kinkaid looked back down the harbor and could see that the gig from the *Vanguard* had turned back toward the frigate from which it had embarked. They would be chased, and that was a certainty.

"At least it'll be a dark and cloudy night," said

Weatherby.

"With at least four hours before first light," mentioned Rosetti

Mr. Hill added to the hopeful chorus. "If we could find better winds out in the channel, Captain, perhaps find a fog bank, we might have a chance."

Hopeful words from desperate men, and men who had until recently been confined in a veritable hell-hole, with little to look forward to but further torture, starvation, abuse, sickness, and eventually death. But for the moment they were happy men, free men, laughing and joking, slapping one another on the back, some renewing old acquaintances from past ships they had served together on, swapping stories, and it brought a feeling of accomplishment. But only the easy part had been accomplished. The hard part was before them and all but uncertain, and their speed would be reduced due to the weight of so many bodies.

"How many are confined below?" Kinkaid asked Mr. Sykes.

"The Harbor Master, his two friends, and seven from the brig."

"Dead weight. Toss them over the side."

"Right away, sir."

The ten men were soon hauled up on deck and bodily and unceremoniously heaved over the side, with only the irksome Harbor Master fighting his way clear, at least for a moment, while voicing formidable curses and bitter threats, to the delight of all. But he was soon surrounded by a dozen strong and determined men who promptly closed in on the fat man and raised him up. They had him at the rail when O'Toole stopped them.

"Just a moment, boys," said O'Toole, reaching into the Harbor Master's bulky pockets. Finding the elaborately-carved ivory pipe, O'Toole took it and said, "Proceed," whereupon they heaved the heavy Harbor Master's body over the side.

Mr. Sykes ran to the rail as the fat man hit the water with a resounding wallop, and shouted, "Pier three is over there, Mr. Harbor Master!" At least they could all swim, although the Harbor Master had to shed his bulky coat to keep it from taking him down.

O'Toole handed the newly-claimed pipe to his amused friend, Quinn. "For your pleasure, Rummy; may you smoke it in good health."

Rummy Quinn gave an exaggerated bow, then admiring the finely carved pipe, said, "Thank you, Chief, you are a generous spirit and a true gentleman."

O'Toole could not resist saying, "Did you hear that hyperbole, Mr. Weatherby?"

This brought laughter all around, but the mirth soon dissipated as all on deck could see that one fast sloop and two frigates had turned out their crews and would soon be after them. At least the breeze was meeting some gusty winds out in the bay and the distance from the enemy ships was increasing. But the current state of affairs would not last, for British crews were fast. Fast at getting a ship to sea, fast at sail handling, fast at gunnery. Kinkaid bit his lip and felt a growing knot in his stomach as he realized how vulnerable they would be, two ships on the British lake, chased by angry British ships out to take their revenge with iron and steel on flesh and blood men…rebels to them, and deserving of no mercy. He was glad to see that Hammond's men on the *Daffodil* had cleared the pier in good time and were closely following with most of her sails raised already.

"Make all sail," said Kinkaid.

"Already done, Captain," answered Mr. Sykes.

Kinkaid looked up and saw that Mr. Sykes was right. All the canvas they could possible hang was up and billowing with the increasing gusts as they left the harbor.

"Keep us at fully-manned action stations. All others will find some place below."

"As you wish, Captain."

Their deck was jammed with men, all looking aft, beyond the *Daffodil*, at the mad scrambling of British frigate crews hastily casting off the lines of their ships. The former prisoners allowed themselves to be herded below, but Rummy Quinn seemed to be stuck like glue to the side of his old shipmate, O'Toole, but Kinkaid ignored the man as he stood respectfully off to one side of the quarterdeck, calming smoking his newly-acquired, elaborately-carved ivory pipe.

XIII
Liberty or Death

It was almost midnight and the lights of the harbor were receding into the black of the night, and an exceedingly black night it was with no moon and a canopy of low-lying clouds that hid even the meager light of the stars. Even so, at least three Royal Navy ships were after them and it was certain that they would make every attempt to sink or capture the vessel that had made fools of them by so brazenly entering their harbor, setting fire to their warehouses, and making off with so many prisoners, Americans all, and even a merchant brig.

They quickly lost sight of Hammond's *Daffodil* when their courses diverged after they cleared craggy shore of the Isle of Wight, and it gave Kinkaid some satisfaction to know that it would be easy for Hammond to pose as a English merchant brig and follow more closely the enemy shore, for that was what she was, and pursuing vessels would expect them to head directly for the French coast, not toward Ireland.

For the first hour they rode with the wind, south by east, with studding sails catching every errand gust, and averaging all of six knots.

"Look, Captain," said Weatherby, pointing behind them.

Kinkaid peered into the blackness, but could see nothing. "What do you see, Mr. Weatherby?" he had to ask.

"A ship, sir. Between us and Portsmouth."

It was true. The hazy glow from the lights of Portsmouth could just be made out to the northwest, and if one was patient a dark smudge could be made out where the shadow of sails blocked the light now and again. Only a very sharp eye could have noticed.

"Yes, I think I see it. It follows directly in our wake."

"I hope it's not Hammond," said Kinkaid. "I gave him explicit instructions…" Kinkaid knew Hammond to be a fool, yet it was unlikely to be the *Daffodil*, since they had watched Hammond's ship move off to the west, in the direction Kinkaid had told him to go, but to hope it was anything other than Hammond was worse.

A bubble of froth formed a ship's wake and a savvy captain could follow it to its source if they were close enough, for at some distance the foam would eventually dissipate. The pursuing ship must be following their trail of foamy wake, and if they are gaining…

Mr. Sykes overheard the conversation and asked, "What can we do, Captain?"

It always irritated Kinkaid when Mr. Sykes asked one of his foolish questions, and now was no exception. Kinkaid answered simply and confidently, "We'll do what we must, Mr. Sykes." But even as he said it, Kinkaid knew it was no answer at all, and only proved that he had no answer.

The bold statement hung over the quarterdeck for a moment before Mr. Weatherby answered, "That's it exactly, Captain."

"That and more, Sir," reiterated Mr. Rosetti, catching the spirit.

"Hear, hear, Captain," said Rummy Quinn, finally speaking up. "Don't worry about us, Sir. By God, we'll fight any damned ship that dares follow us, to the death if necessary. I'll be damned if we'll go back to that hellhole you saved us from!"

A group of former prisoners huddled at the amidships hatch, held below by Kinkaid's orders, but watching and listening to all that took place on deck. Not only that, but passing all they saw and heard to all those confined below, over one hundred able-bodied men, and now one of them shouted, "Quinn speaks for us all, Captain, you can be certain of that! We'll fight her to the death if need be!"

All heard the brave speech, and Mr. Sykes could only blink in consternation at Quinn's and then his fellow seamen's vociferous oath, but it compelled him to say, not without some misgiving, "Very good, sir. We shall do what we must."

Nicky Sterling was grinning from ear to ear at the voices of courage and determination. Of course the support was gratifying, yet even now Kinkaid had little idea of what he hoped to accomplish. They could slow the ship and create less of a wake, less foam, but then the following ship would draw closer even more quickly.

"Let's change course, helm," ordered Kinkaid. "Take us due south."

"Due south it is, sir," answered Sterling, giving the wheel two turns.

Perhaps the wake would be dissipated faster if it were lying at an angle to the wind and waves. It was at least something to hope for.

The ship seemed to pick up speed after the turn, which was illusory, for it only seemed as if they were moving faster as they took the wind off the starboard stern quarter instead of directly aft. Instead of smoothly following in the direction of the waves the bow was now cutting across them at an angle, causing the ship to heel and pivot as it rose and plunged in a corkscrew motion, the sails shifted to catch the new direction of the wind, the seas moderate.

The glow from the English coast could still be seen, but barely, yet on their new course the following ship could not be detected against the background, and so Kinkaid had to assume they were still being followed by at least one ship. He had not slept for twenty-four hours and though his eyelids were drooping, he dared not relax his vigilance, but kept a sharp eye on the blackness beyond their stern quarter, with Mr. Weatherby stubbornly beside him.

The midnight watch passed without incident and the morning watch commenced. Venture Smith took Nicky Sterling's place at the wheel, Lieutenant Rosetti replaced Mr. Sykes as Watch Officer, and all lookouts were relieved by their watch mates. But Kinkaid remained on deck, as did Mr. Weatherby and Mr. Phillips, all standing silent vigil, straining tired eyes aft, into the pitch black night. The small group of men at the amidships hatch also remained where they were, some intently watching and listening, but most slumped in drowsiness.

Another hour passed before Mr. Weatherby pointed and said, "There, sir."

Kinkaid tried to see what Weatherby was pointing to, but saw nothing but an occasional gray smudge where a wave made a whitecap not far behind them. "I can't see a thing, Weatherby."

"She's there, sir," came Weatherby's certain reply.

"Call out all hands, Mr. Rosetti...and tell them to keep it quiet, if you will," Kinkaid ordered.

"Aye, Captain. All hands to action stations."

No bells or drums summoned sailors out of their hammocks and onto the decks, but they came up nonetheless, some bleary-eyed but many with stern and determined looks on their faces, the men at the hatch moving aside and letting them pass. Soon many of the prisoners stowed below decks began to come up as well, forcing Kinkaid to remind them that only those assigned to action stations were allowed topside, keeping their battle efficiency above all else. The men did as they were told; the same small group taking their place watchfully at the hatch.

Nicky Sterling again took his station at the ship's wheel, their best helmsman, having slept for all of forty minutes, but looking alert nonetheless.

There came Mr. Hill, a look of determination on his scarred face.

"Mr. Hill, I'll have all guns loaded with double shot."

"Double shot it is, Captain," came Mr. Hill's ready reply.

"There, Captain," said Weatherby, pointing again as the ship's crew took their action stations.

Sure enough, there it was, the bow wave unmistakable. They had been followed and found, but by what ship? How big; how strong? "What is it, Mr. Weatherby?" asked Kinkaid, yet fearing the answer.

"A frigate for certain, sir, half a cable off," came Weatherby's bald reply.

"There she is, Captain," said Phillips, pointing.

Kinkaid's heart sank and only now did he see for himself the cut and line of her stem, the shine from her wet bowsprit and jib boom reaching out of the dark. Soon he could make out the dirty fore course, the gold-painted figurehead. She was the Vanguard for certain, the very same speedy frigate that had chased them into the Loire. There, a group of dark figures, peering back from her bow, one pointing toward them. An instant later came a flash of flame, a puff of dirty white smoke and the boom of a cannon, a bow chaser, a cannon mounted on her bow designed to damage a pursued ship's rigging and effect performance. The shot tore through the mizzen main with a loud pop. She would use grape when she came closer, and closer she would come, that was a certainty.

"All guns loaded, Captain!" came Mr. Hills shout from amidships.

"Very well, don't run them out yet!" ordered Kinkaid. "Mr. McDowd!"

"Sir!"

"Have your marines stand by, but not in the tops just yet."

"Very good, Captain."

Mr. Sykes took one look aft as he returned to the quarterdeck and said, "We don't have a chance, Captain."

"Thank you, Mr. Sykes, for your words of encouragement," answered Kinkaid angrily.

Sterling kept silently to his post at the wheel, steering the ship with a peculiar grin on his face. It occurred to Kinkaid to ask the man if they would be safe this time, but he promptly dismissed the notion for the foolishness that it was.

Venture Smith stood beside his gun and crew, heard the exchange and offered, "Just let her come close, Cap'm, and Bertha will make her sorry, sho 'nough!"

Even the normally taciturn Harris could not help but shout, "That's right, Captain, just let her come close!"

The same man at the hatch could not contain himself and he shouted, "We'll fight them, Captain Kinkaid!"

"That's right, sir," said Quinn at the mizzen mast. "Just give us the chance!"

"Easy there, Rummy," said O'Toole to his friend. "Captain Kinkaid knows what he's about."

It was always the same, before imminent action. The brave, almost cheerful words of men who were about to face death square in the face. What else could they do? What other choice had they? They could not run from their station, and to show fear was out of the question, would shame them in the eyes of their fellows as well as entertain certain defeat. The choice to fight or strike was only with the captain, but in this case, as far as Kinkaid was concerned, he had no choice.

"Boats, lay out a dozen grappling lines amidships, if you please. Help him, Quinn."

"Coming right up, Captain. C'mon Rummy," answered O'Toole before scrambling below with his friend.

Another report from the bow chaser and this time the ball went whizzing through the mizzen topsail.

"What are we going to do, sir?" asked Mr. Sykes in his maddening way.

"We will do what we must, Mr. Sykes," growled Kinkaid.

"Aye, Captain," said Mr. Sykes, put in his place but none the wiser for how Kinkaid expected to save them from a fate which seemed all too certain; death or captivity.

Kinkaid had had no time to think of a plan. His mind was numb from exhaustion, his eyes red from lack of sleep. Yet, in spite of this and against all reason, he felt a certain clarity of purpose that he could not have explained, then or later. Much of it was based upon one simple fact; the rescued prisoners preferred anything except a return to a British prison...even death. Kinkaid had experienced the horrors of the Jersey himself, and knew the bitter reality, the terrible fate such men faced.

Their weakness had been their slow speed, the ship slowed considerably by the weight of hundreds of men aboard, rescued prisoners but dead weight...until now. And now it became obvious that this very weakness was their strength, and their only hope. If only he could maneuver the ship. If only he could bring her into an advantageous position, away from those guns that lined the decks of the frigate, away from those black ports that showed the mouths of nine or twelve-pound cannons. If he could just get close enough, they might have a chance.

Once again the bow chaser boomed, sending a ball crashing into the stern, smashing through Kinkaid's cabin below.

Up came O'Toole and Quinn, along with two others, carrying on their shoulders rolls of medium-sized rope with grappling hooks at their ends. O'Toole immediately had them placed neatly upon the deck at regular intervals so that they would not become entangled.

The savvy captain of the frigate had stationed men at the bow and had been lucky enough to come upon their wake, which they had diligently followed. The crowd of men there must have felt like smug conquerors, their victim only minutes away from capture or destruction. There looked to be only a half dozen marines in her rigging; perhaps she was undermanned, many of her crew on holiday leave, others off fighting the warehouse fires. Yet, so confident was her captain that he had not even bothered to erect boarding nets.

Kinkaid took in the angle of the wind pennants on the main shrouds. "O'Toole, Quinn, pass out arms to every man down below, but tell them to remain there until I give the word."

"Aye, sir," said O'Toole with a grin, "We'll pass out every musket, pistol, saber and blade. And any man left out will get a marlinspike, belaying pin, hammer or rigging knife. We'll make sure they're all armed to the teeth, Captain."

Seaman Quinn said, "And I'll make certain they remain below until your command, Captain."

Nicky Sterling, at the ship's wheel, now spoke up. "Sir,

I'd like your permission to join with the boarding party when the time comes."

Kinkaid hesitated. Sterling was their best helmsman, having a feel for the ship and her handling characteristics that few men possessed. But once they were alongside, there would be no need for a skilled helmsman, and he answered, "Permission granted. But only after you've brought us alongside her stern, and it's one chance we have. Do you understand?"

"If the sails are rightly handled, sir, I'll put her exactly where you want her."

"Mr. Sykes, send for Rogers. He will relieve Sterling here upon my command."

"As you wish, sir."

Another flash erupted from the bow of the enemy ship, another puff of dirty gray smoke, another ball winging their way. Kinkaid saw the dark shape, saw it come right at him, time seeming to slow, and he instinctively flinched. The ball passed right over his head and he heard it nick the mizzen mast just behind him. Then he heard a groan.

He turned to a horrible sight. The ball had ricocheted off the mast and hit Harris, cutting him in half, the ball passing through his stomach. Harris lay in the scupper, next to a blood and gut covered 'Bertha," a shocked look on his face. His legs, still attached at the hip, had been carried further down the deck.

"Dead over the side!' came the shout from Mr. Sykes, and already some men were heaving Harris's legs over the rail, so accustomed were they to following orders without question or hesitation.

"Good God," said Sterling, "the man's not dead!"

Venture Smith had the trunk of Harris propped in his arms, his gun crew bent over him.

"Dead over the side!" shouted Sykes once more.

Harris looked up, took a deep breath and said, "Over I go, lads. I'm no use to you now." And with that he fainted away, dead, whereupon he was heaved over the side.

A stunned and shocked Venture Smith picked up a rag and began to clean his gun, wiping away at the blood and guts of a man no longer with them.

Sterling stood grimly at the wheel and Kinkaid heard him say, "God, take Reginald Harris; he was a good man and an even better friend."

"Seaman Sterling," said Kinkaid, concerned about his helmsman's attention to duty.

"I'm all right, sir."

The enemy ship had closed so that her bow cannon could not be pointed down far enough to hit them with any effect. Besides, it was obvious and inevitable that they would have to strike or be blown to bits by a broadside. Yet, with the wind filling her sails from behind, it would be impossible for her to slow quickly. Kinkaid waited. Let her come closer. Ever closer.

O'Toole returned to the deck and reported, "They're an eager lot, Captain, and armed to the teeth. And they promise to stay put until you give the word, sir." O'Toole had an ear to ear grin, but Kinkaid just stared at him and O'Toole did not understand why.

"It was Harris, Boats," said Mr. Weatherby. "He was hit; killed."

O'Toole turned to where Harris usually stood and saw Venture Smith continue to wipe away at the blood and guts with his now thoroughly soaked rag.

Seaman Rogers stood nervously on the quarterdeck, as ordered, uncertain why he had been summoned. But Mr. Sykes was grimly staring at the enemy frigate bearing down on them, less than a hundred yards away now, and said, "God, what have you got us into, Captain?"

"Whatever it is, it's now or never, Mr. Sykes. Mr. Phillips, have your men stand by at the sheets!" shouted Kinkaid over the wind. "Prepare to loose all sails!"

"Prepared, sir!" came the instant reply.

The frigate had closed within forty yards. There stood an officer at the bowsprit with a speaking trumpet in his hand. He raised the device and Kinkaid heard him say, "You shall strike at once, or we will sink you!"

"Ready on the grappling lines!"

"Ready, Captain!"

The frigate was making her turn to port, to deliver a broadside.

"Mr. Weatherby, haul down our ensign!"

"You're going to strike, sir?" asked Sykes, incredulous.

Weatherby was already lowering the flag, knowing his captain's intention. Kinkaid hoped it would keep the frigate from firing into them, from loosing her broadside. Her black gun ports were open and she was in the perfect position to do so now, but so far his ruse had worked. The captain of the enemy frigate held back his order to fire upon them, not knowing if they had intentionally hauled down their ensign as they had demanded, the universal signal of surrender, or if a ball had cut its halyard. But he would also expect *Active* to heave to if they were striking. Kinkaid would oblige.

"Loose sheets! Back the tops! Starboard your helm!"

O'Toole, with three pistols jammed in his belt and a cutlass in his hand, was dancing a jig beside the mainmast as Nicky Sterling spun the wheel sharply to starboard. Now O'Toole exclaimed, "We gave her a salute, now we'll give her a what for, by jingy!"

All the lines that held the sails taut against the wind were suddenly sprung free. The canvas shook and rumbled overhead, sounding like thunder. Sheets whipped free until brought under control, all to the shouts of Rosetti, Phillips, and the deck officers, working the ship as a team while Sterling managed the wheel, their combined efforts bringing the ship broadside to the wind and she came to a dead stop.

"Rudder amidships!" ordered Kinkaid, but Sterling had already adroitly flung the wheel back, bringing the rudder in line with the keel. "Mr. Weatherby, raise the ensign! Mr. Hill, ready larboard guns!"

While their ship came to almost a dead stop the frigate continued her turn and drifted sideways with her forward momentum, pushed from behind by the wind. The captain of the enemy frigate could look down on them now from his quarterdeck. Even her gun deck was too high for them to train their guns against them, so close were they, with her stern coming around and drifting ever closer, and now her lines of guns pointed toward nothing but empty sea.

"Lieutenant McDowd, man your stations aloft!"

The deck and rigging was a bustle of activity as men climbed the ratlines to the topsails while others stood by with grappling lines that would be thrown onto the quarterdeck of the frigate. At the same time, Lt. McDowd's marines scrambled to station themselves, half in the shrouds, half in the waist, their muskets at the ready and two at the mounted swivel gun high above, loaded with canister.

"Mr. Hill, hold your fire until I give the order!"

"Aye, Captain!" answered Hill. Then he turned to his gun crews to encourage them. "We'll soon give them a hot howdy-do. Keep your powder and slowmatch dry! Watch that linstock, sailor!"

By the time her captain realized what Kinkaid was attempting, it was too late; her speed, weight, and momentum were too great, and her stern drifted right up alongside *Active*'s port beam, the words *Vanguard* emblazoned in golden letters over Kinkaid's head. Sterling had guided them in as precisely as any helmsman ever steered a ship.

"Grapple her!" he shouted to the sailors waiting with their hooks and lines. "Open fire, Mr. McDowd! Mr. Hill, run out your guns!"

Lines with triple hooks went sailing across the gulf, entwining themselves in the ratlines and rigging of the enemy frigate as sailors on the deck eagerly grabbed the lines and hauled with all their might while Hill's gunners hauled their double-shotted cannons toward the open ports.

"Mr. Rosetti, Mr. Phillips, form your divisions for a boarding party!"

"Aye Captain," came a chorus of replies as the staccato sounds of a dozen muskets fired upon the quarterdeck of the enemy ship, downing most of the officers and men standing there. The sharp crack of the swivel gun soon followed, sending sixteen steel balls ripping through the flesh and bone of men attempting to remove the grappling hooks.

"Would you care to join us, Mr. Weatherby?" asked Kinkaid, handing Weatherby one of his pistols.

"By all means, Captain."

"Rogers, relieve Sterling at the wheel!"

"Aye aye, Captain!"

"Thank you, sir!" said Sterling. Then, turning to O'Toole, he asked, "Can you spare one of your pistols, Boats?"

"By all means," answered O'Toole, handing one over.

Kinkaid waited until the ships touched, then gave Mr. Hill the eagerly anticipated order.

"Fire at will!"

Six cannons roared as one, sending a dozen twelve-pound

balls of iron crashing through the body of the frigate, shattering the stern windows of the captain's cabin and wreaking havoc from stem to stern across her gun deck. As the smoke cleared, a few heads could be seen peering down at them from the quarterdeck, only to be greeted with another shower of musket balls by McDowd's marines, followed by another murderous hail of pellets from the swivel gun.

"Up from below! Turn them loose, Quinn!"

"Prepare to board!" bellowed Kinkaid over the din of musket fire and shouting men. Up from out of the hold burst the former prisoners, each carrying a deadly weapon, each seeking a personal vengeance. "Mr. Sykes, you have the deck!"

"Fire!" The deafening roar of the twelve-pounders rocked the ship again, tearing a gaping hole in the stern of the frigate, and ripping through gun crews that were helpless to shoot back. Hill scurried from gun to gun, encouraging his gun captains to, "Keep up a hot fire!"

Kinkaid climbed upon their bulwark at the mainsail ratlines, steadied himself, then turned and exhorted the men waiting with pistols and blades in the waist to, "Follow me!"

Taking hold of a grappling line, Kinkaid swung himself feet first against the shattered stern of the frigate, grabbed hold of a battered stern lantern and pulled himself up as forty men scrambled up beside him, elbows and knees jarring him as he raised himself above the stern rail of the enemy ship. Only Nicky Sterling was faster and was the first man to have his feet touch the quarterdeck of the enemy ship. He helped Kinkaid climb over the rail.

The open quarterdeck revealed a dreadful sight, with dead and dying officers scattered about the deck, men lying in pools of their own blood. The captain lay against the wheel, one hand clutching his wounded thigh, the other held a pistol, which he slowly raised. Kinkaid kicked it aside, whereupon the captain promptly fainted from loss of blood and the shock of his wounds.

Men continued to climb over the stern and went swarming over the decks, dealing death and injury to any who contested them, with Sterling out front. Discharging his pistol into a British marine, he grabbed the man's musket as he fell, aimed it at another marine in the tops and brought the man crashing down onto the deck amidships. Now he grabbed up the saber of a fallen officer, fighting like a man possessed, and driving back half a dozen English tars with his wild flailing.

Hill continued to blast away at the gun deck from stem to stern with his twelve-pounders as a fierce fight developed at the quarterdeck ladder where Mr. Rosetti and Lt. McDowd were beating off sporadic attacks from disorganized groups of sailors who had taken it upon themselves to repel the invaders. It was apparent that the enemy frigate was indeed shorthanded; missing at least half her crew, and another stroke of luck.

One intrepid British officer in a red coat was attempting to rally a dozen marines in the waist, forming a skirmish line. Kinkaid saw the swivel gun at the rail, noted it was loaded and searched for a match. There, in a bucket beside the ship's bell.

Mr. Phillips ran up, picked up the smoking match, blew it to a glow, aimed the gun, and touched it off. A blast and the marine line was shattered as they raised their weapons. Half lay still, the other half moaning and struggling to regain their feet as Phillips rushed them with a group of vengeful demons to demand their surrender, which they did, stunned and demoralized.

Weatherby ran to the main hatch where smoke was pouring forth, slid shut the cover and bolted it. He was standing there on the cover, waving to Kinkaid when a keg of powder ignited on the gun deck below, blowing off the cover and tossing Weatherby against the starboard deck rail. Yet he rose immediately on unsteady legs and gave Kinkaid a jaunty salute to show he was unharmed.

Those few enemy sailors on the main deck had little choice now but to throw their hands up in surrender at the overwhelming force of aggressive men that confronted them. Fires and explosions still raged below.

"Pass the word for Mr. Hill to cease firing!" ordered Kinkaid. "Mr. Phillips, her ensign is yours!"

One look into her hold told the terrible and sickening story. Hill's broadsides had devastated her gun deck, blood-soaked from stem to stern. Bodies and parts of bodies were everywhere. Men were screaming in agony. Fires were burning out of control and untended bags of powder were exploding as a thick smoke poured from her gun ports and deck hatches.

"Quick! Everyone off the ship!" shouted Kinkaid. A magazine could explode at any moment, sending them all to perdition. He checked on the crumpled figure on the quarterdeck but found the captain dead, sitting in a pool of his own blood. It took some time to get everyone back aboard the *Active*, and as the sailors on the frigate came to the realization that their captors were abandoning them, they scrambled to organize themselves to try and save their burning vessel.

Kinkaid was the last man off the enemy quarterdeck, caught by O'Toole and Mr. Rosetti as he leaped aboard.

"Cut us free!"

The men slashed and hacked at the grappling lines that

had held them fast and now they drifted away as flames danced above the deck rails of the *Vanguard* and began to catch her sails on fire, a hellish sight that lit up the black night and cast a red glow on the faces of the men around him, making their leering faces look indeed like demons, laughing demons.

"Three cheers for Captain Kinkaid!" came the shout from an excited Nicky Sterling as a joyous Mr. Rosetti and Mr. Weatherby congratulated him and slapped him on the back.

"Hear, hear!" he heard Mr. Phillips shout.

"You did it, sir," said Mr. Sykes, only too relieved and grinning from ear to ear.

The men, relieved and exalted in victory, cheered exuberantly. They had conquered the stronger ship and naturally attributed it to the tactical genius of their captain. But Kinkaid's first thought was that sheer luck and survival instinct had won the day. Of course seamanship had made it possible, but he had employed a dirty trick, though he need not justify himself on that account; survival and the importance of his mission was justification enough, and so he allowed himself a moment to appreciate their unlikely triumph. They had conquered when all had seemed lost and now he felt an overwhelming sense of relief and gave a silent prayer of thanks, even as he felt sorry for those men he had overcome, those poor sailors on the enemy ship, only following orders like any seaman would, fulfilling their duty to their country. And then there had been the horrible death of Sterling's only friend, Harris.

"Make sail; get us away from here," said Kinkaid as he watched the frigate burn.

Sails were raised and all eyes were on the burning *Vanguard* as they left her to her fate. Twisting sheets of flame roared up her mizzen and mainmasts, catching her sails afire. Loaded cannons began to discharge from the heat and flames and men could be seen leaping overboard as they realized their ship was doomed. An instant later a horrific explosion tore her in half, the heat and concussion felt aboard the *Active*, causing everyone to flinch from the fiery blast as flaming timbers, spars, and shredded sails rose high into the black sky, the blinding flash reflecting off the low clouds, turning night into day for one brief second.

"Jesus, Mary, and Joseph!" exclaimed O'Toole.

Her mainmast toppled and little remained but her quarterdeck jutting out of the sea, her crooked mizzenmast still ablaze, a great torch lighting up the stormy night, reflecting off the black tossing waves. Then bits of timber and flaming debris began to rain down all around them.

"Watch for sparks!" came the warning from Mr. Sykes

"O'Toole, get both boats in the water," said Kinkaid. "Pick up survivors. And quickly, before her friends show up."

"Aye, Captain."

Mr. Hill stood beside Kinkaid at the rail and said, "The old Randy must have looked like that when she went up, Captain."

Kinkaid could see the anguish in Mr. Hill's eyes as his gunnery officer remembered the fires and catastrophe aboard the frigate *Randolph* that had disfigured his face and body, an inescapable and painful reminder that he would carry for the rest of his life.

A thin line of yellow light traced the eastern horizon as the last of the survivors were hauled aboard and secured below, fourteen men in all. Some were badly injured, others terribly burned, keeping Mr. Carver busy and challenging his burgeoning medical knowledge to the utmost.

Kinkaid kept the ship on high alert as they crossed the

Channel, making due south, toward the relative safety of the coast of France. But as often happens in the Channel, they ran into a heavy bank of fog halfway across, which caused him to reduce sails to the minimum. They proceeded at only a couple of knots, but at least they were sailing in the right direction, and, he hoped, away from danger.

He was about to leave the deck for some much needed sleep, when they heard the dull boom of what could only have been cannons.

"Hard to tell the exact direction, Captain, in this fog," said Mr. Sykes.

"Somewhere out there, sir, I'd say, at least a mile from us," guessed Weatherby, pointing off the starboard bow quarter, always an astute judge of sea conditions.

"Helm, bring us two points to larboard," said Kinkaid, wishing to keep clear of the sound of those cannons. He could only hope it wasn't Hammond in the *Daffodil* that was the target of those guns. Yet it was highly unlikely, practically impossible, really, that such a slow brig could have reached French shores ahead of them.

Fifteen minutes went by as all listened intently, and then there, another report; four, five muffled booms, this time seemingly farther away.

Then silence for a half hour, an hour, then two hours, before the rays of the rising sun began to break through the fog, burning it off by the morning watch bell at eight, and they made more sail. The coast of France was still some forty miles distance, hidden just over the horizon, but the gray waters for as far as they could see to the south was clear of shipping, other than the occasional fishing yawl. Kinkaid was so tired he found himself slumping with his eyes closed against the binnacle.

"You'd better get some sleep, Captain," said Weatherby

quietly by his side.

"Yes, I think I will," mumbled Kinkaid, then rousing himself, said, "Keep us on this same course; it should take us to the mouth of the Loire. Be sure to wake me if a ship is spotted. And definitely when the coast can be seen."

"To bed, Captain," insisted Weatherby, already knowing what his captain would expect from his watch officer.

"If you insist, Mr. Weatherby," said Kinkaid with a grin. "Oh, and a double allotment of grog to the men."

The shattered windows of his cabin let in a cold breeze, but Kinkaid scarcely noticed as he fell heavily onto his cot. Cato had been waiting and piled on four woolen blankets, whereupon Kinkaid slept the sleep of the dead as the ship made its best time south.

XIV
Triumph and Tribulation

It was late afternoon when the sunny shores of France could be seen off the bow and Mr. Rosetti sent the messenger to wake him. Grubb and his carpenters waited until after he had washed and shaved before going to work repairing the damage to his cabin. There were no extra windows to replace the shattered glass, so they were neatly boarded over, but two remained intact, still providing at least some natural light into the small space.

The first thing Kinkaid did was to pay a visit to the cockpit where the sick and injured, American and English sailors alike, were being tended by Mr. Carver and his loblolly boys. It was a hellish scene, the deck still slippery with traces of blood and vomit. Two men had recent amputations, others were badly burned and were moaning in agony. But most showed a brave face when they saw Kinkaid and made comments about "very warm work tonight, sir," while others returned kind replies as he mumbled the same trite words he always used in the attempt to ease their suffering, as if words could do such things.

They were only five miles off the coast when a dingy brig was sighted off the starboard beam. Sure enough, she was the *Daffodil*, and they waited for her to slowly work her way toward them. When she was close enough Kinkaid could see that she was intact and that Hammond had sailed her safely back. He hailed Hammond when they drew alongside and told him to follow them toward the mouth of the Loire.

Now he sat in the wardroom while the carpenters finished their work, reading the battle report over one last time, noting with satisfaction the factual turn of events, first the number of American prisoners they had rescued, 129 in all, although three had died from previous injuries and sickness. He then mentioned all of his officers, first "Mr. Rosetti's burning of the warehouses that also provided their diversion and made their escape possible," then recognizing Mr. Phillip's and Mr. Weatherby's leadership as they "led their boarding parties with unmitigated bravery in overcoming the enemy," and then Lt. McDowd's "foresight and alacrity in directing his marine contingent which was responsible for the ruinous loss of enemy officers resulting in the lack of organization that made possible their success in boarding the enemy frigate." He also made a special note of "Seaman Sterling's vigorous attack against the defenders of the enemy ship in complete disregard for his personal safety." It crossed Kinkaid's mind as he wrote this that men such as Seaman Sterling, though troublesome in times of peace are often heroes when war turns their excitable natures loose. He then mentioned the devastating explosion and resultant sinking, and the fourteen British prisoners rescued; thirteen seamen and an officer, plucked from the Channel, two seamen dying of their burns. He signed it and then closed the logbook as Cato set a platter of sliced ham before him and then filled his favorite wine glass with one of their best Chardonnays.

"It's starting to snow, Captain," Cato informed him.

But Kinkaid was too hungry to answer, shoving a forkful of ham into his mouth.

"Just a moment, sir, and I'll bring you your German

sweet-and-sour red cabbage and turnip to go with that. Even made some cranberry sauce."

Kinkaid managed to down the ham before asking, "What is the occasion, Cato?"

"Why it's Christmas day, Captain, and it looks to be a white Christmas, at that."

He had been too tired, too busy, and too distracted to consider the date, not even when he had written the date on his report. Christmas day…and there was so much to be thankful for. It seemed a shame to eat by himself on such a day, especially after the successful conclusion of their mission.

"Where are the off-watch officers?"

"Topside, mostly, sir. Thought they'd give you a bit of peace and quiet. Shall I have the Officer of the Watch provide a report, Captain?"

"Do we have enough for a full table?"

"I made our biggest ham," said Cato proudly, hoping for a party. "Do you think I'd forget the others? Plenty for all, sir."

"Then by all means invite them; a celebration seems in order."

"I should say so, Captain."

"In fact, I believe I shall have us heave to long enough to allow Captain Hammond join us. We'll make a party of it, in the wardroom."

The crew seemed to be enjoying themselves to the hilt, judging by the laughter and frivolity coming up from below decks, and this was only confirmed when Captain Hammond came aboard and forced Kinkaid to pay a visit to those mass of jubilant and carousing men crammed into the hold from stem to stern. Of course this was more than simply a holiday celebration, especially to the newly-freed prisoners, who were now feasting on fresh food from the ship's stores, not to mention the double allotment of grog that Kinkaid had ordered be dispensed, but it was embarrassing to withstand the rousing cheers they gave him, led by a very inebriated "Rummy" Quinn, even referring to Kinkaid as "our savior," before making his escape to the wardroom, where all of his off-duty officers had assembled.

"Three cheers for Captain Kinkaid!" gave Mr. Rosetti as Kinkaid entered his cabin.

"Thank you, but three cheers for all of us," said Kinkaid, raising his hands in supplication as the cheers went on.

"Why, you'll be acclaimed a national hero for certain, once the press gets wind of this," boomed Captain Hammond loudly.

"Captain Hammond is right, sir," said Mr. Hill, raising his wine glass in tribute.

"That's right, Captain, you're going to have to overcome your innate humility," confirmed Mr. Weatherby, "for as an international hero…"

"Enough of that, now," pleaded Kinkaid. "Cato, bring on the feast!"

"Coming right up, Captain," answered Cato, standing patiently by for just such an order, his platters and bowls all hot and ready for the table, now bedecked with fine linen, candelabra, and a new and ornate set of silver, all graciously provided by Mr. Simpson before their departure. And as the food came out and each and every dish was favorable received, Kinkaid could not help but consider the truth of what his officers were saying. The French press would hear of their daring rescue mission first, since they would soon be taking all of the sick and injured into Le Havre, but then the English press would pick up the story, to the anger and consternation of an angry English King and his minions who adamantly supported the war against America.

The feast began in joyous thanksgiving and frivolity. And the boisterous Captain Hammond did his best to keep the merriment alive after telling Kinkaid that his little dilapidated brig, *Daffodil*, turned out to be a very lucrative prize, her hold filled to capacity with two tons of tea, as well as various manufactured goods such as farming tools, fittings and harnesses for wagons and coaches, lanterns, rolls of textiles, and even some fancy furniture ordered by rich New Yorkers. Hammond even seemed to have developed a fire in his belly from his prison ordeal, a belly now much smaller than when he commanded the *Columbus*, due to his many privations, and he went on about how he intended to take his revenge on the British by outfitting a privateer when he returned home.

"Yes sir, I've had a lot of time to think about it," he related, "and I think one of those fast New England sloops should do the trick. And none of those Quakers either…the real thing, at least nine-pounders, a row of six on each side."

Yet it occurred to Kinkaid, as Hammond went on, that the loud former Captain of the *Columbus* might have considered, as he sat rotting in a British prison, his heavy drinking habit as well as his inattention, negligence and inept seamanship that had led to his capture in the first place.

But as the wine took effect, and with the reminder of home, the guests became downright melancholy. After all, his officers and crew had been away from home for many months now and it was only natural that they should look forward to their return.

Mr. Weatherby missed his Marie, back in Paris. Mr. Rosetti missed at least two women in Nantes. Mr. Sykes missed his gun-shy puppy. And even the normally taciturn

Mr. Hill confessed to missing Mrs. Waverly, the woman in Boston who had nursed him back from the dead and whom he hoped to marry. And if this wasn't enough Hill even related how his new gun captain, Venture Smith, missed his girlfriend, Bertha, who he had named his cannon after, telling everyone, "cause her legs look like dat der cannon," which at least brought laughter from around the table.

And as the strains of Christmas carols wafted in from the crew's quarters, Kinkaid could not help but find himself thinking of a slightly crooked nose and lovely green eyes framed by locks of auburn hair, and for the first time he relaxed enough to consider the news that she would soon be joining him in Paris as a wonderful idea, and something very much to look forward to.

There came Mr. Phillips, Officer of the Watch, peeking his boyish face through the wardroom door. "There's a sh-ship off the larboard bow, Captain. French flag, and s-seems to be hailing us."

"I'll be right up, Mr. Phillips."

"I'll accompany you, Captain," said Mr. Sykes.

"Very well, Mr. Sykes. Please excuse me, gentlemen, but duty calls. However, please feel free to carry on with the merriment."

"Aye, Captain, if you insist! We do need to lighten our load, after all!" boomed Hammond, now thoroughly inebriated. "Cato, my glass is empty again. Now, how did that happen?"

It was good to breath the cold fresh air of the open deck after eating and drinking too much in the confines of the wardroom. The snow was falling in large flakes, but the ship approaching them was close enough to make out the French colors flying from her halyards, the lights of Le Havre in the distance behind her. Someone with a lantern was standing at the bow, waving it, apparently signaling for a parley.

"Heave us to, Mr. Sykes."

It was a fancy French ship, at least twice the size of *Active*, a large merchant brig, capable of carrying cargo as well as rich, well-paying passengers. And she looked familiar; green and gold, with painted saints lining her stern terrace. She was the *L'aigle Altier*, the Proud Eagle, and the Marquee de la Renier's flagship. And there, on the quarterdeck, were two familiar figures.

"Ahoy, Captain Kinkaid!" came the baritone shout through a speaking trumpet.

"Ahoy, Captain McGregor!" Kinkaid waved in recognition, but could scarcely wait to find out what excuse the shifty pirate might offer for standing him up the day before. Even so, he had brought his ship out to meet him, and there was Mr. Briggs standing next to him on the quarterdeck, all in one piece and waving a greeting.

He didn't have to wait long, for as soon as both ships hove to, McGregor quickly put out in a fancy gig that made straight for *Active,* Mr. Briggs right beside him.

Kinkaid watched as the gig drew near, and by now all of his officers, including Captain Hammond, had also come out on deck, their celebratory feast over, it seemed. Briggs was in uniform, but McGregor was dressed in an expensive dark green suit and wore a fancy black hat with an ostrich plume sticking jauntily from its peak, looking the rich merchant. But as the gig drew ever closer, it was the face of McGregor that looked different. Dark; black-and-blue, actually, and lots of cuts and bruises around the eyes and cheeks, and with a fat lip. And his left arm was in a sling. The man had been severely injured. But he grinned mischievously as he rose and struggled up the ladder, assisted by Mr. Briggs.

"Greetings, Captain Kinkaid, and a very Merry Christmas

to you," boomed the stout Scotsman.

"Good to see you again, McGregor." Answered Kinkaid affably enough. "And am I glad to see you, Mr. Briggs."

"The feeling is mutual, Captain," gave Briggs, saluting.

"What happened?"

"Those ruffians I bested in the bar waited for me with some of their friends. Busted me up pretty good; laid me low for almost a week. Sorry 'bout that. I would have come with you but the Marque put me in a hospital. Didn't even know where I was when I come to. And poor Mr. Briggs here was left to fend for himself, I'm sorry to say."

"It was no bother, Captain McGregor," said Briggs. "And don't worry, Captain, our business was concluded satisfactorily. The sloop left this morning with our message aboard. I'll tell you all about it later."

"That's right, a magnificent job if I say so myself, Mr. Briggs. Didn't need my help, after all. And judging from this cheerful looking lot, and that fat brig that follows you, I see you didn't need my help, either, Captain," said McGregor, nodding to Kinkaid's officers and taking note of the ragged-looking men crowding the deck, albeit a cheerful-looking lot of ragged men. "Sort of makes an old pirate feel rather useless, what?"

Kinkaid had to laugh in spite of himself.

McGregor laughed too and said, "Kinkaid, as always, you are a lucky bastard to have such men under your command. But then you already know that. But say, are we too late for Christmas dinner?"

"As always, your timing is impeccable. Come below, both of you. Cato will be happy to fix you a meal."

His officer's dinner having broken up, the three repaired to Kinkaid's small table in his recently-repaired cabin.

"It warms my heart to see you safe and sound, Mr.

Briggs," said Cato, bringing in a hearty red Burgundy. "And I have some nice dishes warming for you."

"Why thank you, Mr. Africanus."

"Cato, good to see you again," said McGregor in sincere greeting.

But Cato, ever suspicious of the known pirate, merely raised his eyebrows, answering, "And you, Captain."

McGregor insisted that Kinkaid tell him all about the daring rescue, which he was forced to provide, in broad strokes.

"So Kinkaid, not only did you make good your escape and make off with a rich prize, but a British frigate was unlucky enough to catch up with you."

"That about sums it up," admitted Kinkaid, shaking his head at the improbability of their triumph.

"Well, overconfidence can be a dangerous foe."

"And the fact that she was underhanded."

"And you over-handed."

"Yes, we were lucky."

"Well, a good captain makes his luck, and I take my hat off to you, sir." gave McGregor with some sincerity.

"Thank you," answered Kinkaid, "but Mr. Briggs, I am anxious to hear of your adventure ashore."

"Well, Captain," began Briggs somewhat nervously. "Finding Blackstone, uh, Captain McGregor here, incapacitated, as it were, I had little choice but to check into a local boarding house. I knew where and when Mr. Palfrey would make his drop, so I simply hid myself near the cemetery and watched where he put his message, in a small metal box under a small gravestone that slid to the side…very ingenious, actually. The trouble was, the courier became curious as to the identity of Mr. Palfrey."

"Bound to happen, sooner or later, human nature being

what it is," intoned Blackstone. "But of course his timing couldn't have been worse, that is, for Mr. Briggs here."

"That's right, Captain," continued Briggs. "I had just picked up the message and only saw the man's shadow on the stone as I was placing it back in its original position when I knew I had to do something."

"Tell him what you did," said Blackstone.

"Well, sir, of course I had to waylay the man."

Blackstone laughed loudly and slapped his knee. "Did you hear what he said, Kinkaid? 'Of course I had to waylay the man.' That's exactly what he told me. Made me laugh out loud then, too!"

Blackstone could be annoying, but Kinkaid had to laugh as well. "What do you mean, Briggs, you waylaid the man?"

"Well, sir. I hit him over the head with the gravestone. Knocked him out cold. Then I carried him to my room at the boarding house, took his clothes, tied him up and gagged him, then put him to bed."

"Hahahahahahah," laughed Blackstone, practically falling on the floor with hilarity. "Did you hear the man? 'Put 'im to bed,' he says."

Briggs was smiling, but could not fathom what Blackstone found so funny. "Well, I had to, sir. Then I translated the message, added the information about our being ported in Calais, then put on his clothes and delivered the message with no problem at all. The quarterdeck officer even gave me a pound sterling for my trouble, which paid for my lodgings and expenses. Why, I still have half of it."

"Hahahahahahaha," laughed Blackstone again, thoroughly amused by the tale told by Mr. Briggs. "Why, the man has found his calling, and a lucrative one at that!"

"That is a good story, Mr. Briggs, a very good story, indeed," Kinkaid had to admit, amused himself by the way

Briggs modestly told his story, but more than this, feeling a deep admiration for the young midshipman's poise, cool courage and ability to think on his feet.

"The sloop left just yesterday," said Briggs, reaching into his pocket.

"Should be making it's delivery about now," observed Blackstone, wiping the tears from his eyes.

"Here is Mr. Palfrey's original coded message," added Briggs, handing the paper to Kinkaid.

"Good work, Mr. Briggs. Very good work, indeed."

"And an easy piece of work it was, Captain."

Kinkaid could not have been more grateful, and relieved. And it seemed Blackstone was actually making good on his bid to follow the straight and narrow path.

"Oh, there is one other thing that might interest you, Captain," said Blackstone. "We heard some cannon fire in the middle of the night."

"Yes, we heard that too, but it was so foggy…"

"Well, my first thought was that it might be you, so we went to investigate. Found nothing but a boat floating in the fog, a dozen men in her. Having no compass they didn't know which direction to row; all they could do was wait for the light of day and the fog to lift. From an American ship, called the *Malvern*. Anyway, we took those men aboard. I'll turn them over to you and they'll be glad to see you, a fellow American."

"What ship did you say?"

"The *Malvern*, out of Boston they said."

Kinkaid sat stunned.

McGregor noticed Kinkaid's suddenly white face, the distracted look. "What is it, Captain?"

"My wife…she was on that ship."

"Oh my God, sir," said Briggs.

"Your wife was coming here?"

"So she said in her last letter. Tell me, what happened?"

"It seems a couple of British warships found her and gave chase in the fog, most likely looking for you. Seems her captain, name of Wilson, not knowing the coast hereabouts, headed toward shore…ended up on the rocks, busting a hole in her bottom. The men I picked up said she was going down fast, so…"

"And her passengers? What of them?"

"I don't rightly know. They couldn't tell me much, but…"

"I want to talk to them, right away," said Kinkaid, already rising from the table.

"So you shall, Captain."

His mind was racing, and the tightness in his chest felt suffocating as he rode in the gig with McGregor, who thankfully kept silent for once. The dream he had had when he was with fever had never really left him, of staring into dark waters where locks of auburn hair swirled and a boney hand reached out to him. God, had it been prophetic? Had Elizabeth drowned? Was she dead?

No sooner had he made the deck of the fancy French ship when he insisted on visiting with the rescued American sailors, eleven men in all, who he found at the table in the crew's mess, sipping tea. So distracted was he that he scarcely noticed the rows of very large brass cannons on her main deck, recently added to make her into a formidable privateer.

A rough young man with a tattered wool cap and a corncob pipe explained, "She went down fast, Captain, everybody scrambling about. Captain Wilson was the kind of man who would be the last to leave her, sir, and he made every effort to get both our boats off. The ladies should have been first to go, but they insisted on getting their baggage first, so Captain Wilson told us to shove off and he would follow with the others. But it was so foggy we lost sight of her as soon as we pushed off. We floated out there for over an hour, not knowing which direction to row…when Captain McGregor came along."

There was nothing else to say, so the men sat there, somewhat nervously, watching for Kinkaid's reaction. Any seamen would be concerned about being accused of abandoning their ship before making certain that their passengers, especially women, would be saved. But Kinkaid would not question them about that. After all, it was her captain's responsibility and he was not here to answer any questions.

"That's the way it was, sir," affirmed another seaman, an older man with kindly eyes. "Perhaps they made it off."

"That's right, Captain," said the young man hopefully. "Perhaps they made it to shore…or were picked up by a fishing boat." Even as the man expressed these hopes he remembered the wild waves as they crashed against the rocks that had sank their ship, an unkind place to launch a small boat with any hope of reaching shore safely. And any fishing boat captain would not be foolish enough to fish so close to such a dangerous shore.

"Yes," said Kinkaid numbly. "Yes, perhaps so. Well, thank you men for your information. Of course I will be happy to take you aboard, add you to my ship's roster. We will be taking our injured to shore first, and then it's concluding our business in France before heading back to Boston."

"Thank you, Captain," answered the kind older man, "We are much indebted to you, sir."

"Yes, well…"

"And we hope you find your wife, sir."

"May God look after her."

McGregor noted the forlorn look on Kinkaid's face when he returned to the deck. "Bad news, Captain?"

"I...I don't know. Perhaps. Can you show me a chart of the shore where you found the boat?"

"Of course, Captain."

XV
Wise Choices

Kinkaid took the ship to the area that McGregor had pointed out on his chart, the area where the *Malvern* went down, with McGregor in the *L'aigle Altier* following at some distance behind, the larger ship having trouble keeping up. Nicky Sterling was at the helm. He had not been informed as to the reason for their coming to this area along the French coast, but he knew something serious was taking place by Kinkaid's demeanor and the way the officers left him alone.

Even far out Kinkaid could see that it was a rough shore and no place to take a ship. Moving as close as he dared to a line of froth that revealed where sunken rocks lurked, he soon made out the bare pole and hanging spars of a mast, sticking forlornly out of a place of crashing waves.

"A bad place, for certain," gave Mr. Sykes, never knowing when to hold his tongue.

"Perhaps she made it to shore, Captain," said Mr. Weatherby.

"Perhaps," gave Kinkaid, trying to find some hope in the words.

"Turn us around," he ordered. "Back to the Loire. We have sick and injured men to take ashore."

"And perhaps some word, sir," said Mr. Rosetti.

They made a rendezvous with the *L'aigle Altier* and transferred almost a hundred men to her, men that would return with her to American shores, some of whom might return in prize vessels that the two captains hoped to take along the way as per their agreement, rich cargo and merchant ships carrying freight and war materials to British forces in the Colonies. McGregor noted the grim expression on Kinkaid's face and mentioned not a word about the loss of the *Malvern*, only doffing his hat as Kinkaid left them anchored in the mouth of the Loire, and assuring him, "You can be certain that I shall be waiting right here for you until you're ready to leave."

The sick and injured were taken ashore at Le Havre, and it wasn't long before word spread, telling of the daring rescue of American prisoners from a British jail, the story proclaimed in the newspapers the very next day and spreading like wildfire throughout France, certain to make Kinkaid a household word.

And by now Nicky Sterling had learned from O'Toole the reason for their useless trip along the rough Normandy coast and began consulting his deck of cards.

But all of these things were of little concern to Kinkaid, for there was no word about Elizabeth, or the fate of possible survivors of the unfortunate *Malvern*, now just another broken hulk, mingling her ribs and planks among other broken hulks along the craggy Normandy coastline, perhaps Elizabeth's bones as well. What was worse was the nagging thought that those Royal Navy ships that had chased the *Malvern* onto the rocks had been most likely drawn to this side of the channel by him, mistaking her for the *Daffodil*.

He wanted to set out and scour the countryside, but he had a ship to command. Instead he did the next best thing. Mr. Briggs and three men would visit the villages and make inquiries along the coast where any boat might have come ashore, while Mr. Weatherby would ride to Paris to find if she had shown up there. Until they returned, Kinkaid stewed, distracted and irritable. The fact that it had been raining almost every day since making port only added to his gloom.

On the third day a messenger clattered up to the ship. It brought a congratulatory note from Franklin. Included was an assurance from Franklin that a treaty with France was imminent, that a declaration of war between France and England would soon follow, as well as words of regret over the fate of the *Malvern,* and assuring him that all efforts were being made to assist Mr. Weatherby in determining Elizabeth's whereabouts. A welcome note, to be sure, but not the kind of message Kinkaid was hoping and waiting for.

It was later that same day, just as the sky grew dark that Mr. Rosetti knocked on his door with some urgency.

"What is it, Mr. Rosetti?"

"A man came to the gangway and gave me this, Captain." It was a rolled sheet of paper, tied with a red string. "He insisted I give this directly to you, sir, then left rather quickly."

"What did this man look like?"

"Well, sir, he had a hood over his head; couldn't say for certain. He looked dark…wore a mustache."

"Thank you, Mr. Rosetti."

Kinkaid waited only until Rosetti closed the door behind him before breaking the string and reading the note. It read:

Kinkaid,

You are greatly mistaken if you believe possessing a copy of a code is enough to convict. I knew Elizabeth was coming. I informed those who would be interested; therefore it is I and I alone who is to blame for the fate of the Malvern and those aboard her. If you are the man of courage I know you to be you will welcome a chance at satisfaction, therefore I will expect you to meet me on a field of honor. Le Havre cemetery at dawn. Come alone. No seconds are required. The choice of weapons shall be yours and will be provided unless you insist upon your own.

W. P.

Kinkaid's blood was boiling, so enraged was he. Somehow he knew it would come to this, a duel between them. What he could never have anticipated was that he would welcome such an opportunity, in spite of the man's self-professed abilities. If Elizabeth was dead, Palfrey was the cause of it, notwithstanding the guilt he harbored against himself. She had only taken passage aboard a ship in winter to bring him something, to protect him, perhaps to provide the kind of evidence he needed. Yet, even as he contemplated this fact, he realized that Palfrey was goading him. But if a court of law could not deal with the man, here was his chance and he would take it, and with pleasure.

Mr. Phillips had the morning watch as Kinkaid made the deck.

"I'm going ashore for a couple of hours, Mr. Phillips."

"Uh, it's very early, Captain," said Phillips. "Why, n-nothing is open yet."

"I am quite aware of that, Mr. Midshipman," said Kinkaid testily. "Have you never heard of a morning constitution?"

"Of c-c-course, sir," answered Phillips, thoroughly rattled by Kinkaid's abrupt manner and sharp words. "M-my father takes one every morning. Do enjoy yourself, Captain."

"Yes, well, thank you, Mr. Phillips. I shall do that."

It was still quite dark, and the morning fog made it even darker, matching Kinkaid's mood. Though by the time he had left the dock area, his footsteps on the cobblestones seemed to resound off the buildings with a disturbing tone, and he found himself hoping he wasn't waking any sleepers. A curious concern for a man possibly going off to die, was the strange thought, and it gave him a chill, and almost a feeling of regret for accepted Mr. Palfrey's challenge. What if Elizabeth yet lived? What if she were somewhere here in France, delayed for some reason or another? What if she were even now trying to find him, only to find that he had foolishly died in a duel with a man he could not possibly defeat? It was maddening to think such things, and he hated himself for it, and so he walked even more quickly toward his fate, an uncertain one at best.

There was the sign at the next intersection reading *Rue de Cimetiere*. A little farther and there, through the fog, was the entrance to the cemetery. The gate was open as if in invitation. He stood there between the wrought iron doors for a moment, looking up the path between the gravestones and saw no one. He began walking up the path and soon noticed two men standing in the path, one short, the other quite tall.

The short one called out to him. "Capitaine Kinkaid?"

While the taller of the two remained aloof at some distance the short man came forward. It was the Marquis de la Renier, immaculately dressed in a dark purple coat and black hat. Next to him were a row of boxes. "I regret that we meet under such circumstances, mon Capitaine."

"Let's get on with it, shall we?"

"But of course, sir. What weapons do you choose?"

"Pistols."

"Good choice, sir. Pistols at twenty paces, it shall be. Please excuse me while I prepare them, sir."

The Marquis picked up a heavy rectangular box and placed it carefully on the broad top of a low tombstone, opened the box and took out one of the pistols.

Kinkaid read the name on the stone, Bernard Lambert, and suddenly all his French lessons came to him in bright clarity. Bernard meant brave bear and Lambert, let's see, land and bright. Brave bear in the land of the light? Was he about to die? Was he thinking straight, or had Nicky Sterling corrupted his mind? Here he was, about to face a very dangerous foe in a duel to the death and what was he doing? Seeking esoteric knowledge in the name on a tombstone. He had to focus, or he would certainly soon be joining Bernard Lambert in the land of the dead.

The tall shadowy figure now approached them.

"You have not disappointed me, Kinkaid," came the familiar voice, a steady and confident voice, a voice that, every time he heard it seemed to steal something from his inner core. "And I must admit that pistols are your best choice."

Kinkaid could think of nothing to say, so he simply stood there, feeling a tightness in his chest, watching the Marquis as he finished loading both pistols, the first of which he offered to Mr. Palfrey.

But Palfrey demurred, saying, "Ah, but let us not forget our manners Monsieur de la Renier. Captain, would you care to inspect the first weapon, to see if it meets with your approval? You may choose either weapon."

What else could he do? Kinkaid took the proffered weapon in his right hand. It had the feel and heft of the ones that Elizabeth's father had given him, although these had the stamp of an English maker on the stock. "I am satisfied with this one."

"Then I shall be satisfied with this one."

"Very good choice, Captain," said the Marquis.

The foolish remark by the Marquis almost brought Kinkaid to laughter, surely a sign that his nerves had reached a breaking point. It was maddening, the false courtesy, the refined rules of dueling, as if a game made of killing could possibly be refined.

With their respective weapons in hand the Marquis now instructed them. "Please stand back to back."

Kinkaid now faced the iron gates where only a few moments before he had had a choice about whether to risk his life against impossible odds. Now he had no choice, at least if he valued his honor. But what of life itself? Was it worth trading for honor? Damn, why did his brain work like this? He held the pistol up in front of him, the way he had seen duelists hold their pistols in magazine engravings. The barrel was at the level of his nose. He noticed it was shaking. He must pull himself together. Steady wins the game, came the crazy thought. But at the moment all his thoughts seemed crazy, worthless to anyone, especially to himself.

But then came the craziest thought of all. That he was about to die an ignominious death this very morning in this depressing cemetery in France, at the hands of a criminal, a traitor, perhaps even a madman. He would never witness another sunrise. So be it. So this is what it felt like to die. The moment he accepted the idea all fear left him. The barrel of his pistol no longer shook. He took a deep breath and felt a soothing calm envelop his mind and body like a warm blanket.

"I shall count to ten," came the words of the Marquis. "At each count you will take one step. At the count of ten you shall each turn and fire your weapon. May God have mercy."

All thoughts left him as the Marquis counted. He visualized taking aim, holding steady and pulling the trigger smoothly, as he had learned in practice sessions with his own pistols. The only difference was that his target would be a man, a man who likely caused the death of his beloved wife. He would take that man's life or was prepared to die trying; resolved to his fate.

"...seven, eight, nine, ten."

Kinkaid turned and raised his pistol at the shadowy figure that stood twenty paces from him. He took careful aim at the center of the man's chest, saw the fire and cloud of smoke spew from Mr. Palfrey's weapon and expected to die as he calmly squeezed the trigger.

The sound of both pistols bounced eerily off the tombstones, muffled by the fog. And there, through the smoke, he heard a groan and saw Mr. Palfrey fall.

Kinkaid stood there in shocked disbelief, relieved, even surprised to be alive. The Marquis ran to where Mr. Palfrey lay, knelt over him and placed his ear against the man's chest. A still smoking pistol lay in the wet grass beside him.

Kinkaid, pistol still in hand, asked, "Is he..?"

"I'm afraid so, Captain; it seems you have prevailed," answered the Marquis, without lamentation or exultation, simply a neutral statement of fact.

A carriage clattered up the street and stopped at the iron gate. Kinkaid heard shouting, then saw a number of figures hastening toward them through the fog.

It was Mr. Weatherby and Mr. Briggs. Then Marie behind them. And behind her...

"My God! Elizabeth!"

"Jonathan!"

She ran into his arms, almost violently, and only now did he drop the pistol.

"Thank God you're live."

"Where have you been?" he asked.

"Oh, first in a boat, then a farmhouse, then a carriage

stuck in the mud, then some kind lady's chateau, then…Oh, Jonathan, what does it matter? I've found you!"

Weatherby and Briggs were already carrying the body of Mr. Palfrey to the coach. "We'll take care of this, Captain, if you don't mind walking back to the ship."

"We don't mind, do we darling?"

"Of course not. Not at all."

Marie remained at her father's side, standing at the tombstone of Bernard Lambert, replacing the pistols in their box. Then he closed the lid and handed something to his daughter, a small object that he held in his pudgy hand.

"What is this, Papa?"

"That, my dear, is the bullet that should have killed Captain Kinkaid."

"Oh Papa, I love you!" she said, hugging and kissing her father.

"Never make mention of this to anyone. Do you promise?"

"I promise," said Marie as she dropped the ball into the wet grass.

SNEAK PEAK: The following is the first chapter from Michael Winston's latest novel, "Baptism of Fire," volume one of the Sgt.

Smith WWII Trilogy, about a squad of soldiers in the 1st Infantry Division, fighting Rommel's Africa Corps in the hills and desert country of Tunisia in 1942. A true story, based upon documented history as well as stories my father told me.

Chapter I
Aboard the H.M.S Glengyle, off the coast of Algeria
1842 Hours, November 7, 1942

It was nice to have a moment alone, away from the sounds and smells of the bunk bay, to reflect out here on the fantail of the H.M.S. *Glengyle*, as the sun was setting behind the task force of over two hundred ships, an impressive sight, with three rows of a hundred transports in the middle, escorted by another hundred warships, including the impressive Royal Navy Battleship, H.M.S. Rodney, armed with her six sixteen-inch guns. But most of the warships were slim, fast destroyers that scurried around the edge of the convoy seeking elusive German U-boats. In fact it was only earlier that morning that one of the few American transports, the U.S.S. *Thomas Stone*, carrying 1,400 soldiers of the 9th Infantry Division, had been torpedoed and had to be left behind, her fate uncertain.

In spite of this, it felt more like a pleasure cruise than an invasion force. Regimental bands played music for the entertainment of all, and men tossed medicine balls and held boxing matches on the fantail. Officers had stewards that brought them their tea in bed every morning, they wore their dress uniforms to formal dinners, and Indian cabin boys filled their tubs for them and asked them in the evenings, "Bath, sahib?" Monotony was the real enemy; only to be defeated by the boundless imagination of bored young soldiers. Even the lights along the Vichy-controlled North African shore were burning bright, evidence that nobody over there was much concerned about an invasion.

The day before yesterday they had watched as the Rock of Gibraltar passed off the port beam. Now Smith was gazing toward the opposite shore, at the lights of what Lieutenant Driscoll had mentioned around noon was the shore of Algeria. Driscoll also told him that they were only a small part of the force; that two more convoys were with them, one with General Patton and another with General Ryder. But what interested Smith more was when the Lieutenant told him that he knew where they were going, and that there would probably be a sergeants' call sometime that evening. Even so, it was easy enough to guess that they were going to help the British in their fight with Rommel, the German general the papers were calling the Desert Fox, a military genius who had ignominiously chased the Brits back into Egypt. But the latest news from the desert was that the British had not only held at El Alamein, but were driving Rommel back out of Egypt, back into Libya. Perhaps that was their destination; Libya.

His name was Dana Charles Smith. He was twenty-two years old, a good-looking kid with light brown hair from Saranac Lake, New York, and it felt a little strange to be on a British troop transport heading east through the Mediterranean Sea. It felt like a long way from home, a very long way indeed, and because they were going to war it was only natural that a young man might wonder if he'd ever see home again.

For as an even younger man, Smith had hunted the spruce forests of the Adirondacks for deer, fished her dark waters for native trout, bass, and northern pike. He had played football for Saranac Lake High School as fullback, and even became captain of the team. He had also played hockey, skied, and once even took a thrilling ride down Mr. Hoevenberg's Olympic Bobsled Run. While in high school he had held a part-time job at the local golf club as a caddy, then joined the CCC and helped blaze the trails and build the log lean-tos in the mountain park when the depression hit. Then he had joined the army and then there was Sarah, the girl he had left behind.

But now the mountains and the forests and the sports and the girls were just a pleasant memory, almost unreal, his new life taken up with training and more training; wearing, living and breathing olive drab, and learning the tools of the soldier's trade, at first with little more than brooms for rifles and beat up trucks to pose as tanks; from Indiantown Gap then onto the Queen Mary to England and now here, somewhere off the coast of a strange land called Algeria.

He wore a small American flag on one shoulder, a patch with a red number one on the other, signifying that he was in the First Infantry Division, also known as the "Fighting First" or the "Big Red One," American's oldest Division, having distinguished itself in the First World War. Smith had just been made sergeant by an accident of seniority and was in charge of a squad of twelve men, men who he had come to know through a summer of training and hell-raising at Tidworth Barracks near Salisbury, England, about 50 miles southwest of London.

Smith stood there, smoking a Lucky Strike, and watched as the sky grew ever darker and stars began to twinkle in the clear night sky. A half hour later he had thoughts of turning in when he noticed the signal lights flashing from the lead ship again, the position that the sailor's called "Dead Man's Corner," followed by answering signals from the following ships, a common enough sight. He could only wonder what it meant, but a few minutes later the lead ship made a sudden turn to the south, toward the shore; in interesting development. The *Glengyle* was the third ship in line and had just completed her turn when Private Kevin Donlevy, from Philadelphia, stepped up beside him.

"Captain Reese wants all sergeants to report to his office right away, Sarge." Private Donlevy was a scrawny, mild-mannered kid with glasses and the squad's most unlikely hero. A member of Baker Team, his M1 Garand seemed bigger and heavier than his skinny arms could handle, yet he had handled it and proved a better than average marksman.

"Thanks Donnie."

Captain Reese was a damned good CO, in Smith's opinion. Firm but fair, and he led from the front, setting by example what a soldier should be and the men respected him. He looked like a soldier, too, with his square jaw and solid shoulders. First Sergeant Grabowski was there, too, a short, burly man with hairy arms and an aggressive manner. He walked with a slight limp, but if anyone knew soldiering it was Ski. He was also known as one of the best boxers in the Division, and although Smith had done his share of fighting in the ring, he wasn't stupid enough to take on Ski. Lieutenant Driscoll was also there, as were a dozen other sergeants of the 3rd Battalion of the 26th Infantry Regiment, some buttoning up their shirts, a few still in t-shirts, all hovering around a table in the center of the crowded cabin. On the table was spread a map showing a shoreline and a port.

"All sergeants present, Sir," said Lt. Driscoll. Yeah, Driscoll was a baby-faced shavetail, but at least he wasn't a 90-day wonder, but hailed from West Point, and a pretty smart and decent kid. His grandfather had been a brigadier in the Civil War and he had a lot to prove, which in Smith's mind could be an asset or a liability, only time would tell. But Smith had been impressed by Driscoll's willingness to learn. After royally screwing up a training exercise because he didn't follow the advice of First Sergeant Grabowski, Ski had firmly taken the young officer aside and had a little conversation with him. After that Driscoll was more than willing to listen to Ski's advice, even seeking him out at times.

"I know you've all been anxious to learn where the hell we're going," said Cpt. Reese, without fanfare, "and now I can tell you. Colonel Stark only informed us Company Commanders three days ago as we were entering this big pond and that's why you haven't seen much of us. The place is called Oran, and we've got to take it away from the Vichy French who control it, and we've got to do it fast, before they can send for reinforcements. We're going to land forces on either side of the city. The 16th and 18th Regiments will land on these beaches to the east. General Allen with be with them. And we will land right here, to the west, with General Roosevelt."

Smith knew that both Generals had fought in World War I and that both were tough, fighting sons-of-bitches who said things like, "Work hard and drink much, for somewhere they're dreaming' up a battle for the First," and "Nothing in hell must delay or stop the First Division," and "March to the sound of the guns." They seemed fearless and embodied all the pride and the myth that the First Division possessed.

"Of course we hope this is a surprise operation," Captain Reese went on. "We also hope the French will welcome us as liberators and we can go in and have a party instead of get shot at, but those are a lot of hopes and we can't count on hopes…"

Captain Reese went on for almost an hour, explaining that loudspeakers would announce who we were and why we were there as they were landing. He suggested they check their notebooks they had been given earlier, that translated such ideas as "Don't shoot, we come as friends," and "Down with the Boches. Down with the Macaronis. Viva la France." Smith had one phrase down pat: "Ne tirez pas!" Don't shoot!

Captain Reese then went on to explain every objective and who was to do what and when. It seemed awfully complicated, but Smith had learned that every effort was a team undertaking and to concentrate mainly on the part his team would fulfill, in this case to land his squad with the first wave shortly after midnight, skirt the town of Bou Sfer that Second Platoon was supposed to secure, and then go straight up a long hill not too far inland.

First Squad's assignment, unless serious opposition prevented it, was to immediately make their way as far up the 2000-foot slope of Djebel Murdjadjo as they could, as one of four forward Regimental reconnaissance elements, in preparation for taking the heights overlooking the city of Oran. Of course Lt. Driscoll had volunteered for the assignment, and then had chosen Smith's First Squad to go with him. They'd have a mortar team for support. The rest of the 3rd Battalion would follow, securing the town of Bou Sfer before pushing up the hill behind First Squad.

Smith had a habit of grinding his teeth when he was nervous or concentrating on something and ever since Lt. Driscoll had pointed out the fact to him one day he had since tried to make a conscious effort to let his jaw go slack when he realized he was doing it again. Somebody else mentioned he did it in his sleep too. I guess that's why his jaw hurt sometimes.

Smith noticed that there were other places on the map that began with the word Djebel. They were all placed at the top of hills, so he guessed that the word must mean "mountain." It was hard enough pronouncing the strange names, but what concerned him more was that their landing was not going to be as much of a surprise as Captain Reese said it would, since they were going to announce their presence over loudspeakers and with an aerial display of the American flag as they were hitting the beach, which took away the element of surprise, and wasn't surprise the first tenant in the book of victory? But the Captain had explained that it would give the French a chance to give up to their American liberators and in that case it would be an easy victory and nobody would get shot or killed.

Only one man had a question when Captain Reese had finished his briefing. Sergeant Grabowski wanted to know if they were going to have any tank support, whereupon Captain Reese told him, "No, not where we're landing. It's all in our hands, and a strictly infantry operation. A battalion of light tanks will be landing about fifteen miles to the west, but they will be pushing inland and then coming up on Oran from the rear, so we can't expect any help from them, at least not until later."

Smith returned to the bunk bay and informed his squad of the sudden development and told them to get their gear ready, which cause a lot of murmuring and even a subdued cheer here and there, then an intense check of equipment and careful packing. Not that the men had much of anything else to do except check and recheck their equipment since they'd been on this tub; clean their gun one more time, and sharpen that knife once again until it cut like a razor. Some of the men put their time to better use writing letters home, hoping it wouldn't be the last time their family, friends or sweethearts would hear from them.

In the middle of all this preparation came an announcement over the ship's intercom that Colonel Alexander N. Stark, Jr., their regimental commander, had a few words for them, and so the men listened to what he had to say. He started with a few words of encouragement and said he had faith in them and then went on to tell them how most of the people living in Oran and the surrounding area were Europeans and that the beach area they were landing in was a popular resort area, then he ended with, "Let's give them every chance to surrender peacefully with honor, instead of forcing them to fight. This could be a terrible mess if bungled, so let's think clearly."

Then a voice came over the intercom telling them they couldn't smoke until they hit the beach. The ship was blacked out and they would approach the shore undetected if possible. And then Captain Reese got on the horn and urged everybody to get some sleep until they were called out on deck.

Of course Smith couldn't sleep. Who could, knowing they were going into combat in a few hours. So he laid there on his bunk, like all the other men, trying to fathom the unfathomable, imagine the unimaginable, and ponder the possibilities, and feeling a bit confused about invading the shore but being warned by the CO not to bungle things, but mostly hoping he would give a good account of himself, his first opportunity to prove to Captain Reese that he had chosen the right man to lead 1st Squad. The worst part was not being able to smoke, and he found himself grinding his teeth.

"Sarge?" It was the rough voice of Private Samuel Novak, of Charlie Team, a big kid with a low forehead from Nebraska who would carry and operate their Browning Automatic Rifle, or BAR.

"Gemmel says they're gonna give us a rough time, the Frenchies, just because their officers are scared of the Krauts."

"Well, I guess we'll find out soon enough. Whatever happens, I know that you and Gemmel are gonna give *them* a rough time if they start any funny business; ain't that right, Roscoe?"

"Is the Pope Catholic?" said Private Roscoe Wells. A simple man who tended to speak in maxims, Wells was from Sioux City, Iowa.

Smith's tough talk was part of being a sergeant, but at the moment it seemed more contrived than ever. Gemmel, from the woods of Pennsylvania, carried the bulk of the ammunition for the BAR and would help feed the gun.

Novak laughed a deep, nervous laugh, but it was good to hear it. "Yeah, Sarge, you can bet on that."

"I just can't wait to get off this rocking tub," said Private Zdanowitz, known as Zd, the company maniac. Zd had suffered from seasickness almost all the way from England. The good thing was that he had kept mostly to his bunk and out of trouble.

But mostly it was eerily quiet in the bunk bay that night as the ships made their approach. Even the twenty-four-hour-a-day crap game had come to a close.

Smith had almost fallen into a deep sleep when Gemmel asked, "Say Sarge, do you think Andy knows how to use that stovepipe the Captain gave him?" Gemmel meant the bazooka, a new weapon only given to the squad as they were boarding the ship, so nobody had been given much in the way of training with it, although Private Andrew Cushman said he'd been reading up on it.

"I hope so, Gemmel. Now try to get some sleep, ok? I imagine we'll have a busy day tomorrow."

"Yeah, sure Sarge. Sorry."

It was a good team Smith had, and he took some confidence from the fact. They had also gone through a hell of a lot of training. Every man had had thirteen weeks of basic training, followed by some more weeks of advanced infantry training where they were taught how to take care of and use the M1 Garand rifle, and some of the boys got pretty good at consistently hitting the bull's eyes on their targets. But shooting at a target and shooting at another human being was a different matter, and they were taught to kill in other ways as well, with grenades, with bayonets, and even in hand-to-hand combat. They learned how to set up defensive perimeters, and judging terrain and digging foxholes were important elements of that. And not only did they have to learn about their own job and weapons, but about everybody else's jobs and weapons too, in case somebody got hit, and it was impressed upon them that they were part of a team, which meant that they learned to rely on one another, to trust their buddies. They also learned that no matter what happens during combat each and every one of them had to do everything in their power to accomplish the mission, even die if that's what it took. And they learned all of these things until they didn't have to think about it, until it all became second nature.

But mostly they got tough and callous to things like heat and cold, and rain and hunger and thirst and fatigue and even injuries. And what they lacked in experience they made up for with an overabundance of energy and determination. Hell, they were

American kids, off on some grand adventure. And what was it he had heard Lt. Driscoll say about them when he handed out their dog tags? That they "were like dogs in that all they wanted to do was please." The recollection made Smith smile. But Driscoll was right. Other than a few crazy pranks and harmless misadventures back in England these were a bunch of naïve but good kids who tried in every way to become good soldiers. Zdanewitz, or Zd, was their worst goof-off, followed by that big-mouthed Italian kid, Scarletti, but even they knew when to draw the line, and Zd turned out to be a good scout for Able Team. Hell, these kids might even teach the Germans a few things. But first they had the French to worry about.

It was almost one in the morning when Smith and the squad came out on deck, all fully loaded down with from 70 to 100 pounds of equipment, and some could hardly walk. The sea was glassy smooth, the deck a dark and silent place, with stars shining bright in the sky. Men were whispering if they spoke at all, and somebody said something about President Roosevelt just making an address to the French people in French, telling them we were coming to restore their liberty. The shore seemed very near, however, and the lights of Oran were brighter than ever as men began to lower themselves into the landing craft alongside.

Here came Lt. Driscoll, his baby face smiling and looking nervous at the same time like a kid going to his first prom, except he carried a carbine instead of a corsage.

"Your men ready, Sergeant Smith?"

"Yes, Lieutenant."

"You synchronize your watches?"

The question made Smith look at his Bulova that his father had given him last Christmas. "Yes, Lieutenant, everything has been done that can be done."

"Jeez, Lieutenant," said Roscoe Wells, "You ought to know by now that First Squad is a smooth, well-oiled machine."

"I knew you'd say that, Wells. Ok, First Squad, over the side."

They'd practiced climbing down those damned clumsy rope ladders before, but it was always a tricky business, fully laden with all their combat gear. Some men carried mortars or a heavy machine gun, others rounds for the mortars or bazookas. So you couldn't really do it in a hurry; you had to make sure your feet were placed just right, the rope snug against your heel, or you took a chance of slipping down and falling on top of the man below you. Big Sam Novak was always the first man down; nobody wanted him falling on top of them, especially with that big BAR. But it turned out to be a good idea because he was good at steadying the others as they came down the ladder.

The landing craft filled with thirty-two men, two squads and two mortar teams, and it no sooner puttered away from the ship when a white flare went off over their heads.

"What's that flare mean?" asked a nervous Private Kevin Donlevy as the sailor at the .30 caliber machine gun behind them yanked back on the bolt to load it.

"I think it means that the first landing party is ashore unopposed," answered Lt. Driscoll, still smiling like a Cheshire Cat.

"Where are they, Lieutenant, that first landing party?" asked Private Wells in his thin, reedy voice, the heavy radio on his back making his shoulders sag.

"Way over on the other side of town, at a place called Arzeu."

"Why do they have such funny names?" asked Corporal Hanson, Smith's assistant squad leader. The scar on his cheek looker whiter than usual.

"Now where are you from, Corporal?" asked Scarletti.

"Why you know that, Mario; Cincinnati."

"Yeah I know that, but did you ever think that Cincinnati might be a funny name to them?"

"Whatyamean, everybody's heard of Cincinnati," insisted Hanson.

"Yeah, right."

It was nervous banter, but as long as the men were quiet Lt. Driscoll tolerated it. He was still smiling.

Smith looked over the side and could just barely make out a series of frothy, incandescent wakes made by the long line of landing craft on either side of them, all heading in the same direction, toward a dark line indicating where the surf ended and the beach began, where a few lights shone.

"You really like this sort of thing, don't you, Lieutenant?" Smith teased Driscoll.

"Yeah, I do sorta like this, Sarge. I was made for this stuff, you know."

"Your grandfather will be proud of you, Sir. Hey, we were all made for this stuff, weren't we, guys?" A little pep talk couldn't hurt.

"That's right, Sarge. The first of the first is we!" came the familiar refrain.

Scarletti, the wise-guy, said, "I was made to eat pizza."

"All right, hold the noise down; this is a surprise attack," Driscoll reminded them as he rose up on his toes and looked over the transom, toward the shore.

"Sir, with all due respect, if this is a surprise attack, what's with all the loudspeakers?" asked Zd, from Bangor, Maine.

"The surprise is that we're not surprising 'em," said Zak Porter, an Onondaga Iroquois Indian from Syracuse, New York. Some private had called Zak "Chief" early in their training and Zak had said in that low, calm voice of his, "Every Indian in the American Army is called Chief, but I ain't no Chief." Nobody ever called Zak Porter "Chief" again.

"Yeah, that'll make 'em really nervous and confused," added Zd. "They won't know what to do." Zd and Zak were Able Team, both good scouts, and they made an efficient and reliable team. The other men in the squad started calling them "Z" team until Lt. Driscoll found out and he quickly put a stop to that; no need for more confusion.

"Shut up," said Driscoll. "We're getting close."

It was silent in the boat after that, only the low rumble of the motor and the water sloshing alongside.

"Get ready!"

The flat-bottomed boat skidded to a halt in low breakers and Driscoll yelled, "Ramp down! Go, go, go!"

Driscoll was the first man out, actually running up the ramp as it fell splashing into the surf, followed by all the others, scrambling to keep from knocking each other down. Smith was right behind him and Novak right behind him, the barrel of the BAR jabbing Smith in the shoulder as they both jumped off the ramp into the surf up to their knees. Some water splashed up into his face and he could taste the salt, his first taste of North Africa.

Then all he heard was the sound of their boots sloshing through the water, and then chugging up the sandy beach. He was only dimly aware that other men from other landing craft were also running through the surf and onto the beach, in some places cluttered with beach chairs and tables with canopies, and further up the beach were rows of cabanas with gay flags hanging from their roofs.

They reached a shingle of loose rock and shells that made a crunching sound under their boots, and Smith felt some relief that his eyes had adjusted to the dark somewhat. He was even more relieved to find that nobody was shooting at them. Even so it was a very dark night and men slipped and stumbled over unseen rocks and slippery surfaces, and Smith was surprised to see so many trees and bushes, even wide stretches of grassy areas. There were only a few houses, but some of them seemed quite lavish and extravagant, like homes he'd seen of Malibu Beach in California where movie stars lived, with palm trees and walls around them to keep out the riffraff.

"Spread out," Smith instructed them. "Form a line abreast, left to right; Able, Baker, Charlie."

Driscoll waited until the men had formed a line, and then he pointed inland and yelled, "Follow me!" Just as he had imagined he would, thought Smith, the brash young Lieutenant reveling in the glory of it all.

They jogged up a low rise, crossed a narrow dirt road and took cover in a shallow ditch on the other side that provided the extra cover of a row of low vegetation interspersed with various densely canopied trees and a few palm trees. More houses could be seen maybe two hundred yards farther inland, a dense cluster of them; a small town of sorts, probably Bou Sfer.

"Able Team out on the right," said Driscoll. "Follow that cut; see if it goes up the hill. Charlie Team on the left; check out that building with the shiny roof. Double time!"

"You heard the Lieutenant!" shouted Smith, pumping his fist. "Move it out!"

The men in their respective units scurried off in opposite directions, all except for Baker Team; Corporal Aedan Hanson, Kevin Donlevy, Andy Cushman with that bazooka tube on his back, Charlie McCain, and Roscoe Wells, all crouched silently behind them.

Smith watched as "Big Sam" Novak of Charlie Team ran like a bow-legged bull, carrying the BAR in a ready position, with the bipod attached, ready to throw it down at the first sign of opposition. Gemmel scurried after him, carrying over his shoulders rolls of 30-06 Springfield ammunition for the light machine gun. Three other riflemen followed them; Harold Holmes from Mineral Springs, Texas, Mario Scarletti from Brooklyn, and Saul "Lefty" Lefkowitz, from Philly, their medic. Everybody was weaving slightly, too, not only by the heavy equipment they carried, but their gait was thrown off by being on a ship for so long, making it feel like the land was heaving up and down.

Lt. Driscoll pulled the map from his pocket, spread it out on the bottom of the ditch and shined his red-filtered flashlight on it. By now the mortar team had made it into the ditch as well and Driscoll said to the corporal of the mortar team who carried a carbine, "Uh, what's your name again, Corporal?"

"Whitlock, Sir."

"Ok, Corporal Whitlock. Just stand by for now."

"Yes, Sir."

Driscoll looked at the map again.

"I think we're right where we should be, Sarge; here, at Les Andalouses."

"What's that mean, Lieutenant?" Smith knew that most of the Arabic names meant something. He also knew that Lt. Driscoll loved to show off his knowledge of just about anything and everything.

"Les Andalouses? I think it means a wet place."

"I thought this was supposed to be desert country."

"Not here along the coast. See that hillside? It's covered in grape vines."

"Must be wine nearby."

"Get your mind on the war, Sarge."

"Kinda quiet for a war."

"Yeah, too quiet. I don't like it."

"No glory in quiet, right Sir?"

"That's it, Sarge. Ok, that little town over there is Bou Sfer. Second platoon is supposed to secure it. We need to sweep around it, to the right, if there's no opposition, and I don't see any opposition, so let's get moving."

The whole battalion was landing right behind them and men began to cross the beach and then spread out in a ragged line along the dirt road, forming up for the push inland. A few scouts were already exploring into some gardens and buildings along the road, others climbing over fences and stumbling through rows of low brush and broad-leafed bushes interspersed with large aloe plants, making toward the little village.

The staccato sound of a machine gun opened up slightly to their left, yellow tracers streaming down from above, moving as if in slow motion in a gentle arc over the town of Bou Sfer and down to the beach where men were still coming off landing craft.

"Well, there goes the quiet; at least now we know where we stand," said Driscoll with some satisfaction.

"Looks like it's coming from that outcrop, Sir. What do you want to do?"

"Didn't I just send Zd and Zak up along that gully, there?"

"Yes, you did, Sir."

"Well, let's see if it goes up to those grape fields. If so, we can skirt the village and get up that hill with at least some cover."

"What about that machine gun up there, Sir?" asked Corporal Hanson.

"That's Second Platoon's problem. They're gonna have to put some fire on it and try to flank it, I would guess. Our job is to get on up that hill, and pronto."

The sound of a BAR opened up on the left, a dull, muffled rat-tat-tat, its tracers arcing up toward the enemy position.

"Who is firing that BAR?" asked Driscoll.

"It's coming from that stone building over there, Sir, where you sent Charlie Team," Smith reminded him.

"Novak's got the right idea, but we need him with us. Corporal Hanson, go tell Novak to stop wasting ammo and get his team over here."

"Yes, Sir."

"Ok, I want the whole squad with me, Sergeant."

At that moment a tall thin man in a white robe ran up to them, gesticulating wildly and jabbering in Arabic.

"Now, what the hell does he want?" asked Driscoll with some irritation.

"Don't know, Sir. Maybe that's his house Novak was using," guessed Smith.

"Yeah, well, we don't have time for this. Where the hell is Able Team?"

"Zd and Zak are already moving up the gully, like you ordered, Sir. If we just follow them…"

"A Driscoll doesn't follow anybody. Godammit, where the hell is Novak?"

"Everything ok here, Lieutenant?" asked a familiar voice behind them. It was Captain Reese, with Sgt. Grabowski and a couple of riflemen.

"Yes Sir, I'm just collecting my squad to take them up the hill."

"Very well. I see there's a fanatic up there on the left, but other than that…"

Another machine gun started firing down onto the beach from their right now, positioned way up on the ridge.

"Well, maybe two fanatics." Only now did Captain Reese notice the tall Arab man standing there, mumbling to himself. "Who the hell is this?"

"Don't know, Sir. I think he lives in that house over there. I think Novak woke them up."

"Well, we don't have time to chat with civilians. Carry on, Lieutenant."

"Very well, Sir."

A jeep drove up behind them, with four men in it. The driver shouted the call sign, "High ho, Silver!"

Lt. Driscoll gave the answer, "Awaaay!"

The jeep stopped and an old man wearing a knit cap with a carbine in his hand shouted, "Captain Reese. Get 2nd Platoon into that town right away!" The name "Rough Rider" was painted under the windshield.

"Already happening, Sir!"

"And is that you, Sgt. Grabowski?" exclaimed the old man. "Jesus Christ, if you aren't uglier today than you were the last time I saw you!"

"Well, you're not exactly the handsomest man on this beach, Sir!" returned Grabowski as he ran to catch up with Captain Reese.

The old man laughed and slapped his leg. Now he looked down the beach and noticed a half dozen men on horseback riding toward their right flank. "Let's see what they want," said the old man to the driver, and off they went, tires skidding on the gravel road.

A moment later a shot could be heard, and when Smith turned to look he saw a rider fall off his horse. The old man emptied his carbine at the group of riders and the others hightailed it back from whence they had come.

"Who the hell was that?" asked an incredulous Donlevy, new to the outfit.

"Why that is our Fightin' First assistant commander, General Teddy Roosevelt, Jr.," said Lt. Driscoll in admiration.

"Jeez, he looked like a hobo from Brooklyn," observed Scarletti.

Novak and Gemmel came running back from the house, followed by Corporal Hanson.

"All right, everybody with me. Let's move it out!"

They left the tall thin Arab man in the white robe standing there in the ditch, and they all headed for the gully where Lt. Driscoll had already sent their scouts of Able Team, to reconnoiter up the hillside.

They could see Zd and Zak about a hundred yards ahead where the gully entered an orchard of sorts, maybe nut trees, now bereft of fruit. The two machine guns up on the hill were still firing sporadically on the beach area, shifting from target to target as men from various platoons moved farther up the hill. But American mortars were taking them under fire now. And there, coming up from the beach, a bunch of soldiers were hauling a light howitzer across the rough shingle.

"That will make them pull their socks up," said Lt. Driscoll to no one in particular as they caught up to Able Team.

Zd turned around and noticed the rest of the squad following them, whereupon he waited until the Lieutenant came up before he and Zak moved off again, staying about fifty yards ahead of the squad. They followed the gully for a few hundred yards until they came to the bottom of the hill. So far they had not seen a soul, not to mention any sign of belligerent French, except for the cavalry that General Roosevelt had shot at, although they could occasionally hear the dull sound of artillery off to the east, and even some loud explosions now and again, whether land or ship-based they could not tell.

They came to where a vineyard started, the rows of vines heading straight up the hill, where they found Zd and Zak waiting for them, both kneeling on a little terrace of the vineyard where a low stone wall offered at least some cover. Zak was crouched beside the wall looking up toward the next terrace, some hundred yards farther up the hill where a small one-room stone building with a corrugated metal roof sat. It was getting toward three in the morning now and there came a hint of daylight, the landscape turning from a dull gray to a dull green. The machine gun on the right was still yammering occasionally.

"We gonna flank that gun, Sir?" asked Zd.

"No, we have bigger fish to fry. And right now time's a wastin', so let's get a move on, Private. But not too fast, let's keep an eye out."

"Away we go, Sir," said Zd and off he went, right up the hill between a row of grape vines, staying low while peering intently forward and to each side, Zak about five rows over, with Smith, the Lt. and the five men of Baker Team spread out behind them, their equipment flopping from side to side as the hill grew steeper and the going more strenuous. Novak with Charlie Team followed off to the left; Corporal Whitlock, with his mortar team, brought up the rear. Smith noticed only now that he still had water in his boots that was squishing with every step he took. He started to worry about getting blisters when suddenly Zak dropped to the ground in front of them and yelled, "Grenade!"

Nobody heard the grenade hit the ground; they were all too busy hitting the ground themselves and covering their heads when it went off with a flash and a loud bang some ten yards in front of Zd, who was holding his helmet on his head to keep it from falling off and to ward off any shrapnel.

"Ow! I'm hit; I'm hit, Godammit!" yelled Zd, half hidden in a cloud of dust, his body in a fetal position.

"Shit!" exclaimed Lt. Driscoll. "Lefkowitz!"

"Yeah, yeah, I'm comin'"

"Lefty" Lefkowitz was their medic, a nice Jewish kid who wanted to become a doctor when the war ended. He ran by Smith and Lt. Driscoll, slid up alongside the wounded Zd like a baseball player sliding into second base, then dragged Zd back behind the Lieutenant. Everybody was looking up the hill, trying to see where the grenade had come from and hoping no more would follow, then feeling a little surprised that no more came, nor was anybody shooting at them.

"Where'd you get it, Zd?" Lefty wanted to know.

Zd just held his hand out; maybe he was in shock.

"Jeez, it's nothin'," said Lefty. "The grenade must of kicked up a stone; you got a scratch. I'll put a Band-Aid on it if you want, Zd, but you ain't getting no Purple Heart from that one."

Roscoe Wells, relieved, said, "Time heals all wounds."

Novak grimaced and said, "How about time wounds all heels, Roscoe."

Zd looked at his hand and said, "It hurts like hell."

"Yeah, well, it aughta hurt; it hit your knuckle. You want a bandage?"

"Nah, don't bother."

"Hey look, you got a nice little scar on your helmet," observed Lefty.

"Yeah," said Scarletti. "Good thing that didn't hit your hand or you *would* have gotten a purple heart."

"Yeah, and then you'd be lonely in the sack," joked McCain.

"All right, spread out," said Lt. Driscoll. "Zak, flank right. See if you can tell what's in front of us."

"It came from that little shack up there, Sir," came Zak's low dry voice. He always sounded slightly bored, and it was comforting to know that even combat would not change that.

"Smith, take Hanson and McCain with you to the left. Scarletti, you and Holmes follow Zak up on the right. The rest of us will stay put; give you covering fire if you need it."

Whitlock had crawled up beside the Lt. and asked, "You want me to drop a few rounds on it, Sir?"

"Uh, not yet, Corporal, but you can set up just down the hill there."

Smith crawled on his belly over the hard, dry compacted soil, then squirmed his way through five rows of grapevines before crawling up the hill, toward the next terrace, with Handley and McCain crawling behind him, and he found himself thinking that it was going to be a long day, a very long day.

He made it to the terrace and looked through the dried grape leaves toward the little stone building on his right where Zak had said the grenade came from. He could see a little open window on the side of the hut but he couldn't see very well inside the hut. In the front, facing the terrace path, was a closed wooden door and another little open window. He saw Zak run across the terrace, over the low stone wall and into the next row of grapes farther up the hill. They were on three sides of the hut now.

Smith rose up and scurried across the open terrace too, hopping over the wall while hoping nobody would shoot at him as he did so. Hanson scurried over right behind him, quickly followed by McCain.

"Hanson, you and McCain go up a little farther; come down from behind it." Smith could see drops of sweat on McCain's upper lip as he looked nervously around through the grapevines. McCain was always a little high strung. Even so, Smith knew he was grinding his teeth and he didn't even try to stop doing it. "Zak and the others are on the other side, so don't get jumpy. I'll try to get closer, to toss a grenade through that window, then we'll rush it."

"Good plan, Sarge," said Hanson before he crawled up the hill with McCain right behind him.

Smith squirmed his way through three more rows of grapevines before he got nervous and stopped. He could see the window through the brittle leaves and there, some movement. Somebody or something was definitely in that little shack. But if they'd thrown a grenade at them they'd have to pay the piper, that was for certain. Smith pulled a grenade out of his fatigue pocket and pulled the pin. It wouldn't go off until four seconds after he released the metal spoon. He sidled toward the edge of the building, and then tossed the grenade through the opening.

He heard the spring sound of the handle go flying off, arming the explosive device as he pressed himself to the ground.

At that moment the wooden door of the stone shack flew open and out rushed two men in uniform. Both hit the ground as the grenade went off inside the shack, and the sound made Smith's ears ring. Now the two just as quickly stood up with their hands in the air, and the older one was shouting, "Ne tirez pas! Ne tirez pas!"

Smith knew exactly what that meant. He stood up and cautiously approached them, pointing his M1 at the nearest one, a young boy with a downy mustache. The poor kid's eyes were big as saucers and he was shaking like a leaf as Lt. Driscoll and the others came scampering up the hill. The other was an older man with gray at the temples and some insignia of rank on his shoulder. Zak came up behind him and pulled his pistol out of his holster and admired it.

"Beretta. Nice souvenir," said Zak as he stuck the pistol in his belt.

Hanson and McCain were already searching inside the hut and came out as the Lt. and the others reached the terrace.

"Nothing inside but a couple of ammo boxes, Sir, and some empty food tins," said Hanson, carrying an old bolt-action rifle that had seen better days. "Oh, and this."

"What the hell is that?" asked Lt. Driscoll derisively.

"Why, this is a Model 1886 Lebel," said Hanson. "Has twice the range of an M1. I'd like to hang onto it, if you don't mind, Sir. Found half a dozen boxes of ammo for it, too."

"If you don't mind lugging an extra rifle along, I guess that's your business."

"Thank you, Sir."

"Hey, I think we got us an officer," said Scarletti.

"Smith, Hanson, check them out," said Lt. Driscoll. "Zd, you and Zak scout ahead, make sure we don't get company. And one team on each side of us; spread out and take cover behind that wall." Driscoll looked down the hill and was satisfied to see that Whitlock had his mortar set up and he gave the Corporal a wave.

Hanson frisked the young boy and found nothing but a slim wallet that he handed back to the kid. But Smith found a map tucked into the officer's tunic, which he took out and handed to Lt. Driscoll.

Driscoll spoke for some minutes in broken French to the officer, a Lt. in the French Militia and his aide, it turned out, sent down the hill as forward observers.

"Said he didn't expect us to be up here so soon. He also said that there's at least a reinforced company up there in pillboxes and slit trenches, supported by mortars, if you can believe that. Anyway, this map seems to show their positions and could be of use, and G-2 is gonna want to talk to them. Hanson…"

"Sir, could you make somebody else take the prisoners down?" said Hanson, before the Lt. could finish.

"Holmes, take these two and the map down to Capt. Reese or anybody who knows where G-2 is. As for the rest of us, let's have some water; take a short break."

"Can we smoke, Sir?" asked McCain, a skinny, nervous kid from Jacksonville, Florida who always had a cigarette dangling from his lips.

"Uh, not yet. I don't want to draw undue attention on us, just in case."

Only now did Smith notice the long shadows they were throwing on the hard surface of the terrace path, the beginning of a bright and sunny day, it looked. They were almost a third of the way up the hill and it seemed they could see halfway across the Mediterranean, now crowded with anchored ships way out into the hazy morning light.

Somebody was tossing some garbage over the side, from the stern of one of the transports, maybe even the H.M.S. *Glengyle*, and a large flock of seagulls were dipping for morsels, their cries heard even over the sound of distant machine gun and mortar fire, the only reminder that they were in a battle, except for the scene at the beach, where men were swarming. Piles of supplies were already on the beach and various types of small craft were plowing back and forth from the ships to the beach and back again. And pack howitzers were already throwing shells up the hill onto obvious enemy positions.

Smith's pants were dry by now and he thought it would be nice to sit down on the stone wall and take his boots off and put on a dry pair of socks, but suddenly a machine gun opened up on their right, farther up the hill, followed by another, then some sporadic small arms fire, now two blasts from a mortar or light artillery.

"Jesus Christ!" said Lt. Driscoll as everybody hit the ground. Driscoll hesitated for only a moment before he said, "Ok, let's move out; we've got a war to win." And up the hill he went, leading the way like any good soldier with the name of Driscoll, toward the sound of battle.

They hadn't gone far when there came Zak, down through the vineyard, carrying Zd over his shoulder.

"What the hell happened?" Driscoll asked him.

Zak put a groaning Zd on the ground. Zd's pants were split and bloody and he had a painful grimace on his face. Lefty ran up and quickly checked the wound, saying, "What the hell have you gone and done now, you crazy bastard?"

"Godammit, what happened?" Driscoll wanted to know.

Zak sighed and said, "I told him they were up there, Sir, but you know Zd. Two machine gun nests, one on each side and troops in slit trenches scattered between. Said he wanted to get their attention, so he stood up, and..." Zak started chuckling. "And he got their attention all right. We're not gonna go much farther, Sir."

"Fragments in his leg, Sir," said Lefty. "Not too bad. I'll give him some sulfa and a shot of morphine."

"Zd, can you walk?"

"I think I can hobble, Sir," said Zd bravely through gritted teeth.

"What should we do with him, Lefty?" asked Driscoll as Lefty began wrapping the leg with a Carlisle bandage.

"Well, he's not gonna bleed to death, Sir, but those fragments are gonna have to come out. Then I'm sure he'll be all right. As for now, I'd say we put him in the shack, out of the sun, and wait 'til we can get a stretcher to carry him back down."

They had just carried Zd into the stone hut and Lt. Driscoll was contemplating whether or not he should send a man back down to bring a stretcher team up for Zd. He wanted to do right by the man, yet he was already short-handed if it came to a fight. That's when they heard someone shouting behind them, coming from down the hill. "Hey, what unit are you?"

"First Squad, I Company, First Platoon of the Twenty-sixth? Why?" hollered Driscoll.

"Got a message for you!"

It was Sergeant Ehlers, of Second Platoon, with two riflemen. They came up and the first thing Ehlers said was, "We ran into one of your men taking your prisoners down the hill. Good work, Lieutenant."

"Thanks, Sarge."

Then Ehlers explained the situation to Driscoll and Smith. "We've got the beach and Bou Sfer secured, but are encountering some stiff opposition all along this ridge and are having trouble maintaining communications up the hill to forward units. What have you seen so far?"

"Just those two we sent down, but they're up there all right, and they wounded one of my men. He's in the shack there. If you could have a stretcher team sent up to take him back down."

"I will surely do that. And Capt. Reese wants you to know that he wants you guys to stay put and make a show of strength, keep them pinned down while he gets the company up here."

"How goes it with General Allen?"

"The Rangers took the dock area at Arzeu rather quickly, and the 16th and 18th Infantry Regiments were able to move five or six miles inland, but not before some shore batteries gave some ships a hell of a pounding before they could be put out of action. The good news is that all troops are ashore and are moving on Oran. The bad news is that St. Cloud and this hill are holding things up and Allen is furious because his invasion timetable is falling behind."

"Well, I've got ten men and a mortar. We'll do what we can."

"I know you will and I'll tell the Captain that, but don't start anything you can't finish. Oh, and we'll be sending some food and water up, too. How are you for ammo?"

"Haven't fired a shot yet, but anything extra would be fine."

"I'll see to that right away, as well as that stretcher team. And good luck to you."

And with that, Sergeant Ehlers and his two riflemen went back down the hill.

"Sgt. Smith, you heard the man. Let's set up a defensive perimeter with this stone shack as our strong point. Fan the men out and get them dug in. Then I'd say it's time for breakfast."

"Can we smoke now, Sir?" asked McCain again.

"Yeah, ok," said Lt. Driscoll, looking at his watch. "Jesus Christ, its 0640 already. How time flies when you're having fun. We are having fun, aren't we?"

Zd had heard the Lt. outside and, feeling the effects of the morphine, answered, "Rollicking, Sir! A real laugh-riot! Hey, anybody got a cigarette?"

Made in the USA
San Bernardino, CA
14 November 2012